He turned suddenly and cupped her jaw with one hand. "I don't want any harm to come to you, Randi. You've been through enough."

Her heart raced at his warm caress, and she turned her head to press her lips against his rough palm. Murmuring against his hand, she said, "I'll do whatever I can to help you."

He pinched her earlobe and returned his hand to the steering wheel. "We'll help each other."

She studied his profile and confusion stirred in her belly. Was that his plan? Help the poor, vulnerable amnesiac so she'd do anything he asked? Tell him anything he wanted to know?

Was he playing her? She'd become so dependent on him that she'd do anything to stay by his side. What if telling Gage Booker everything jeopardized other people? What if spilling her guts to him meant betraying people she loved? People she didn't even know about yet?

ABOUT THE AUTHOR

Carol Ericson lives with her husband and two sons in Southern California, home of state-of-the-art cosmetic surgery, wild freeway chases, palm trees bending in the Santa Ana winds and a million amazing stories. These stories, along with hordes of virile men and feisty women, clamor for release from Carol's head. It makes for some interesting headaches until she sets them free to fulfill their destinies and her readers' fantasies. To find out more about Carol, her books and her strange headaches, please visit her website, www.carolericson.com, "where romance flirts with danger."

Books by Carol Ericson

*Brothers in Arms
‡Guardians of Coral Cove
**Brothers in Arms: Fully Engaged

TRAP, SECURE
&
NAVY SEAL SECURITY

—

Carol Ericson

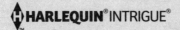
HARLEQUIN® INTRIGUE®

ISBN-13: 978-0-373-69717-5

TRAP, SECURE
Copyright © 2013 by Harlequin Books S.A.

The publisher acknowledges the copyright holder of the individual works as follows:

TRAP, SECURE
Copyright © 2013 by Carol Ericson

NAVY SEAL SECURITY
Copyright © 2011 by Carol Ericson

Recycling programs for this product may not exist in your area.

Printed in U.S.A.

www.Harlequin.com

CONTENTS

TRAP, SECURE

CAST OF CHARACTERS

Gage Booker—Prospero Team Three agent who's hot on the heels of an international arms dealer and discovers a beautiful woman with amnesia instead. If the woman turns out to be the arms dealer's mistress, it might be Gage's lucky day...or his worst nightmare.

Randi Lewis—She has no memory, no life, no identity and she's supposed to trust the sexy spy who rescues her. Does she have a choice?

Nicholas and Angelina Zendaris—Randi's charges, her love for them is the only reason she stays in the Zendaris household, and the children repay her by saving her life.

Jessica Lehman—A friend of Randi's from Texas who can tell Randi who she is—if she lives long enough to do so.

Lawrence Jessup—A CIA officer in Panama who offers to assist Randi, but his assistance takes a sinister turn.

Dr. Helen Murdoch—This CIA psychiatrist is more than willing to help Randi recover her memories—just as long as they're the right memories.

Dr. Elle Fonesca—Gage's twin sister hypnotizes Randi to help her regain her memory, but worries that her brother's attraction for the amnesiac will only complicate matters.

Dr. Helen Murdoch—An international arms dealer who was burned by Prospero Team Three; now he wants revenge, and nothing's going to get in his way this time

For Neil and the boys, always.

Chapter One

Randi Lewis clutched the book of fairy tales to her chest as a second thump shook the room.

The children laughed, and Nicky poked his finger at the book. "Did the witch scare you, *mademoiselle?*"

Randi eked out a smile. Nicky didn't seem to notice the strange bumps in the nights and the comings and goings of an assortment of odd characters to his father's palatial home in the middle of the jungle.

But Randi had grown more and more aware—and leery—of them.

Her grandmother had warned her about taking a job in this luxurious but strange household. "*Drogas,*" Abuelita used to say. Drugs.

But the locals had assured her Nico Zendaris was no drug lord, and Randi had needed the job to help her ailing grandmother. Now with Abuelita dead, nothing was keeping Randi in Colombia.

Nicky's younger sister, Angelina, tapped her knee. "More story, please, *mademoiselle.*"

Nothing except these motherless children.

Tugging on one of Angelina's dark curls, Randi met the girl's big, dark eyes and said, "But this is the scary part, Angelina. You always cover your ears during this part."

Angelina dropped her lashes, and her gaze slid to the door. "More story, please."

Tears choked Randi's throat. The activities and people in her father's house *did* scare Angelina. The girl preferred the make-believe fears of witches and giants to the very real fears of shadowy men, her father's outbursts and being uprooted and shipped off to other countries at a moment's notice.

Randi peeled the book from her chest and cleared her throat. "The witch fed the children more and more food—roasted duck and mashed potatoes and thick slabs of bread and cheese and ice cream sundaes."

Nicky howled. "You're making that part up. They didn't have ice cream sundaes in those days."

"Shh, Nicky. Don't yell." Angelina stuck her fingers in her ears.

Patting his sister on the head, Nicky rose to his knees. "I want to see the picture, *mademoiselle*. I want to see the picture of ice cream sundaes."

Randi turned the book around to face the kids. Something crashed right beneath them, and she dropped the book.

Angelina scooted closer to Randi and wrapped her arms around her legs.

Randi dropped her hand to Angelina's shoulder and squeezed. "Don't worry. I'm here."

The crash even caught Nicky's attention, and he looked up from the fallen book with a pair of round eyes. "What was that?"

"I'm not sure." Her gaze darted to the intercom on the wall. Mr. Zendaris often used it to communicate with her when she had the children in this room—what he called the nursery—even though Nicky was seven and Angelina had just turned five.

Her tongue swept across her dry lips. She rose from the chair and almost crept across the room to the intercom. On the way, she locked the door of the nursery.

She pressed the intercom button. "Hello? Is everything okay downstairs?"

Mr. Zendaris's security had set up the intercom so that the people on the other end could hear her, but she couldn't hear them unless they pressed the button on their intercom. Not that she needed an intercom to hear the noises, shouts and upheaval from downstairs.

Both children whimpered and crowded against her. She pressed them close with one hand and spoke into the intercom again. "Hello? This is Mademoiselle Lewis. I'm with the children. Is there a problem?"

A male voice growled back at her. "Stay where you are."

On shaky legs, Randi led Nicky and Angelina back to the carpet where they'd been reading. With her fingertips, she pushed them down. "Stay on the floor."

She sidled against the wall until she reached the large window that overlooked the rolling back lawn of the property. The spotlights that usually glared brightly enough to pick out every blade of grass had been snuffed out. The crescent moon playing peekaboo with the clouds didn't offer any illumination.

The stillness of the scene outside contrasted with the frantic activity below them. This sounded like more than one of Mr. Zendaris's rampages.

Someone pounded on the nursery door. "Open up."

Randi's heart galloped in her chest, but she recognized the voice of one of Zendaris's security guards, Costa. She didn't like Costa, or his overpowering cologne, but at least he treated the children with care.

She crossed the room with Nicky and Angelina hang-

ing on her arms. She unlocked the door and threw it
open. "Costa, what is going on down there? It's fright-
ening the children."

Sweat gleamed on Costa's bald pate as he swooped
down and swept up the kids, one in each massive arm.
"You don't worry about the kids anymore."

"What do you mean?" Randi's blood ran hot and
pounded against her temples. "Nicky and Angelina are
my responsibility."

Nicky let loose with a long wail and Angelina looked
like a wax figure clamped against Costa's side, her
gauzy pink scarf trailing on the floor.

Randi reached out to smooth Angelina's soft curls
from her face and drape the scarf over her head, but
Costa jerked back toward the door. "Not anymore, *mademoiselle*."

Nicky began to squirm and shriek. Adjusting his grip
on the kids, Costa backed out of the room and kicked
the door shut.

Randi lunged for the door and grabbed the handle.
It turned, but the door wouldn't budge. She banged on
it with her fists. "Open this door. Let me out of here."

Someone grunted on the other side of the door, and
Randi knew she was a captive. But why? If Mr. Zendaris
were just uprooting the kids again and taking them to
one of his other homes, why imprison her in the nursery?

On other occasions he'd calmly informed her of his
plans for the children and she'd taken the opportunity
of their absence to stay with Abuelita for a while. She
even accompanied Mr. Zendaris once or twice to Paris,
Athens and Budapest.

What changed? Why the commotion downstairs?
Why had she been sequestered in the nursery?

She pummeled the door, but only managed to hurt

her hands. She scooped up Angelina's scarf from the floor and wound it around her neck. Taking a turn around the room, she folded her arms across her chest, her fingers digging into her biceps.

A thwacking noise penetrated the room, and she ran to the window. A large, black helicopter descended from the darkened sky. Its lights illuminated the lawn and beyond the manicured grass to the dense foliage that ran to the high walls surrounding the property.

Randi's breath hitched in her chest, and a chill snaked up her spine. Here and there, members of Zendaris's security force were scattered along the wall, weapons clutched in their hands.

Was the compound under some kind of siege? And did Zendaris plan to leave her behind to face his enemies on her own?

The air in the room stifled her. She opened the French doors to the balcony that jutted over a flagstone path below. She needed fresh air and freedom, but this route offered no escape, two stories high and with no visible means of reaching the ground.

She wedged her hands on the flimsy railing that encircled the balcony. She'd prohibited the children from coming out here since very little stood between them and a long drop to the unforgiving flagstones.

The moist, heavy air caressed her skin, and she dragged in a breath. The sweet, milky smell of the carnations bordering the lawn tickled her nose just like on any other night.

But this was not any other night.

The helicopter had landed on the lawn, its blades whirring and stirring up debris that danced in the air. If her grandmother were still alive, Randi would go to her, but she'd died over a year ago and still Randi had stayed for the sake of the children. Now Nicky and Angelina had been ripped from her arms.

She heard voices and shuffling outside the nursery door, and she spun around to face the room. The door handle turned slowly, transfixing Randi's gaze. She held her breath.

Montaña, one of Zendaris's henchmen, poked his head into the room. In the three years she'd been in Mr. Zendaris's employ, she hadn't figured out if Montaña was this man's real name or a moniker given to him for his size—as big as a mountain. His eyes widened as they scanned the room. Then he caught sight of her on the balcony.

The look he sent her sucked the air from her lungs. She took an involuntary step back.

"W-what do you want? What's going on?"

Montaña grinned, his gap-toothed smile sending a wave of fear crashing through her body. Montaña never smiled.

He took one lumbering step into the room. The knots in Randi's stomach tightened, putting pressure on her lungs and nearly cutting off her breath. She felt for the railing behind her and glanced over her shoulder at the drop into darkness.

Clenching her fists, she swung her hands in front of her. "Where is Mr. Zendaris? I demand to see Mr. Zendaris."

The mountain pointed beyond Randi's shoulder into the night, toward the whining helicopter.

She swallowed. "Where are the children? I need to see Nicky and Angelina before they leave. I always help them pack."

Again, like the grim reaper, Montaña silently raised his arm and pointed out the window.

Could she bluster through this? The man was an idiot, a big lump of clay. At least she could outrun him. Dash around him and find someone, anyone with a bit of reason.

Why would Mr. Zendaris want to harm her? The children loved her and she loved them back. He'd commented on it many times in the past. He'd believed the hand of fate had intervened when Randi had shown up in Colombia with her grandmother on the one-year anniversary of his wife's death.

She clamped her hands on her hips and stamped her bare foot. "I'm going to find the children. I'm going to say goodbye to them. Then I'm going to report you to Mr. Zendaris. This is an outrage."

Shrugging, the man lifted his hands and wandered into the room. He bent over from his great height to scoop up the book of fairy tales, in which he could easily star as an ogre. He flipped the pages once, twice, and then tossed the book onto the chair where Randi had been sitting, reading to Nicky and Angelina.

Were they really already on the chopper? Was Angelina afraid?

Randi's heart ached. Then she gritted her teeth. "I'm leaving. You have no right to keep me a prisoner here."

She marched from the balcony into the room, heading for the chair where she'd kicked off her shoes. She unwound the scarf from around her neck and draped it over the back of the chair, reaching for her shoes.

Montaña grunted and slipped a gun from his pocket.

Randi straightened to her full height and pulled back her shoulders. "I'm telling Mr. Zendaris about this right now."

Could Montaña hear the quaver in her voice? Did he

even care? He must be here on Zendaris's orders. The man did nothing without Zendaris's approval.

Montaña advanced on her, holding the gun in front of him.

Randi backpedaled to the balcony, scuffing her heels. A bead of sweat ran down her face. Now the sweet, cloying scent of the flowers smelled like death.

Her feet hit the rough tile of the balcony and still she backed up toward the railing.

Small footsteps galloped up the stairs amid yells and screams. Nicky and Angelina burst into the room, sobbing and screaming. "*Mademoiselle!* Mademoiselle Randi!"

"Get back! Leave!" Randi thrust out her hands, even though the kids seemed miles away from her.

Montaña growled and charged toward Randi, pointing his gun in the general direction of her head. Both of the children attacked his legs, and Nicky lunged forward to grab his arm just as he was squeezing off a shot.

Red-hot pain seared Randi's left arm and she toppled backward. The railing cracked beneath her. The children screamed. Randi threw out her arms. They whirred like the blades of a helicopter as she fought to keep her balance.

She lost.

Chapter Two

Gage Booker rappelled down the high wall that surrounded the compound deep in the jungle of Colombia. Ahead of him, members of the Army Special Forces team hit the ground and fanned out onto the property. They'd already taken out the guards stationed at the outer wall, but the international arms dealer, Nico Zendaris, would have additional security guarding the lush grounds and ostentatious mansion.

Gage's boots met the ground, sinking into the verdant growth that extended to the manicured lawn ringing the house. Before making his way through the underbrush toward the house in the wake of his support team, Gage stopped and sniffed the air. Jet fuel. In the middle of the jungle? His pulse quickened, and he crouched, peering through the bushes at the white mansion gleaming across the rolling lawn. His muscles tensed. His jaw ached.

Lights dotted the windows here and there, but no lights illuminated the outside of the house. A place like this would have security floodlights, sensors… The special team of Green Berets had to be circling the house by now. Where was the gunfire?

It had been too much to hope for that Zendaris would be on this property at the time of their raid, but Pros-

pero had heard murmurings that he might be here.
Although Gage would've liked a crack at Zendaris, especially after the hell he'd put his Prospero team members through, this particular mission didn't depend on
Zendaris's presence.

It was enough that they'd finally located one of the
elusive arms dealer's residences. They didn't even have
a picture of him, at least not one without him in a dis-
guise. Nobody knew what the real Nico Zendaris looked
like. If Gage could gather photos from the house, they'd
be one step closer to identifying him.

He hoped to gather more than just photos. He
planned to search and infiltrate Zendaris's computers,
emails, safes, bank accounts. Their source had indicated
Zendaris spent a lot of time at this residence. Surely he
kept personal effects here. Even a phantom had to put
down roots somewhere.

A shout rose from the lawn. Adrenaline pumped
through Gage's veins. He clutched his M4 carbine and
crashed through the bushes.

Gripping his weapon in front of him, Gage charged
onto the grass, its soggy blades squelching beneath his
boots. The Green Berets had secured the perimeter of
the house. Shadows moved across the windows, but the
silence prevailed.

Captain Denny, the man in charge of the mission,
strode from a set of double doors that opened onto a
patio at the edge of the yard. "Booker?"

Gage lowered his weapon and puffed out a breath.
The shout he'd heard before had been an all-clear signal.

He called back to the captain. "Over here."

Captain Denny swore a blue streak as he marched
across the patio. They met at the edge of the lawn, and
Denny barked, "Put some light on this situation!"

From somewhere in the darkness, two powerful flashlights crossed beams, lighting up the patio. The light gleamed on the black stripes beneath the captain's eyes, lighting his eyes on fire.

"They beat us to the punch, Booker. Except for those few pushovers on the outer wall, the place is deserted."

Denny's words landed with a sickening thud against Gage's temples. They'd been double-crossed. He clenched his jaw against a flickering muscle. "How bad is it?"

"Bad." The captain jerked a thumb over his shoulder. "Computers yanked out of walls, drawers dumped, closets ransacked and wall safes emptied."

Gage swore and kicked at a lawn chair on the patio. It teetered on one leg for a second and then fell over. "Personal items?"

"Not much. Looks like this slimy SOB has eluded you again."

Gage slung his weapon across his back. "I'm going in."

The captain stepped aside and began shouting orders to his men. Not that he had many orders left to give. The Green Berets had successfully completed their mission—gain access to and secure the grounds and house. They'd done that.

It was Gage's mission that had failed.

He entered the house through the double doors, his boots scuffing on the ceramic floor tiles. A sweeping staircase curved to the second floor and a tinkling chandelier hung from the cathedral ceiling. Paintings adorned the walls, objets d'art lined the shelves.

The weapons business must be good.

Trailing his hand along the built-in shelves, Gage scanned the items—no personal photos. He stepped over shards of glass on the floor—all that was left of the doors belonging to a mahogany case that had been cleared of most of its contents. Had pictures of Zendaris sans disguises once graced this cabinet?

He took a right turn into a cavernous dining room. The dining table reflected the image of a candelabrum centered on its gleaming surface. A vase of flowers nearby, the blooms fresh and buoyant, perfumed the air. Gage crossed the room and pushed through swinging doors to a kitchen, outfitted with enough accoutrements to please the most discerning chef. A kitchen table, tucked in a nook, overlooked the sprawling backyard.

The smell of grilled meat and garlic lingered in the air, and a half-empty wine bottle rested on the counter-top. Someone had eaten a hearty meal tonight before abandoning ship.

He yanked open the Sub-Zero refrigerator—its shelves were stocked with enough food to feed a small army. Zendaris had probably employed a small army at this opulent abode.

Cursing, Gage slammed the door, rattling the contents of the fridge. By the look of things, Zendaris himself could've been in residence only hours before the raid.

He'd have to question the locals, but he knew he would hit a dead end there. The local inhabitants generally knew to keep their mouths shut when dealing with powerful neighbors like Zendaris. The man probably had a few of them in his employ—his eyes and ears in his absence.

And Zendaris's absence from this location would be permanent now that it had been compromised.

Tomlinson, one of the Green Berets still occupying

the house, called to him from the stairs. "Booker, you down there?"

Gage hit one of the swinging doors with the heel of his hand. "In the kitchen."

"You need to see what's on the second floor."

Gage's heart jumped. Had Zendaris left something behind? He sped through the dining room and took the stairs two at a time, his heavy boots pounding against the tiles, creating an echo in the empty house.

Tomlinson stood by a doorway and beckoned to him. Gage stumbled into the room and almost tripped over a low table scattered with picture books. "Son of a..."

Gage circled the room, the bright, cheery colors and patterned wallpaper of cartoon characters making him dizzy. "Zendaris had kids, and they stayed here, lived here."

A sour lump rose from his gut. At least the kids hadn't been in the line of fire. If the Green Berets had met resistance entering the house, they would've shot first and asked questions later.

No matter what their father had done, kids were innocents. He knew that better than anyone. He and his sister couldn't be held accountable for the stunts their father the politician had pulled over the years.

Tomlinson gestured to the gaping French doors leading to a dark balcony. "The only doors in the house left open."

"Maybe Zendaris spirited the kids away through the window."

"Maybe he had to grab something from that balcony."

On his way to the French doors, Gage trod on a book. He bent over to pick it up. He ran his index finger along the well-worn, gold-leaf cover. "Fairy tales. Yeah, those kids aren't going to be living any fairy-tale life with that maniac."

He tossed the book onto a deep-cushioned chair and spotted a gauzy pink scarf hanging over the back of it. He plucked up the scarf with two fingers. The gold threads woven into the material caught the light, and the scarf shimmered in his hands. Some instinct drove him to raise the scarf to his face. An exotic, musky scent tickled his nostrils and he inhaled deeply.

Definitely not a perfume for a young girl. Maybe Zendaris had a twentysomething-year-old daughter. Gage didn't even know if Zendaris was old enough to have a daughter in her twenties. He crumpled the scarf in his fist and shoved it into the pocket of his fatigues.

A radio crackled and Tomlinson jumped to attention. Captain Denny's voice boomed into the room. "Out of the house, Tomlinson. Now. We're meeting at the front of the house."

"Yes, sir!" He backed up to the door leading to the hallway. "I'll leave it to you, Booker."

"Thanks, Tomlinson. Good job tonight."

Gage clumped onto the dark balcony. The border around the balcony was low enough to sit on—not the safest setup for kids. But then having an arms-dealing father wasn't the safest setup for kids, either.

In an attempt to add a measure of safety to the low wall, someone had tacked up a wooden border.

Gage's nostrils flared. A portion of the border had broken away. He crept toward the edge of the balcony and fingered one of the pieces of wood. This was a recent break.

He leaned over the balcony and his heart slammed against his rib cage. A figure, crumpled on the ground, was inching toward the grass from the flagstones.

"You there—halt!"

The blackness of the night obscured his vision, and he strained to make out whether the person had a weapon. "Stop!"

The figure continued to crawl forward, and Gage patted his pockets for a flashlight. He'd left it out on the patio and had parked his radio in the kitchen. He scanned the yard, but the Green Berets had congregated in the front of the house.

He swung his weapon in front of his body. "Stop or I'll shoot!"

Still the form eased forward like a snake on its belly.

Gage blew out a breath. At the rate the guy was moving, he'd never make it to the wall before Gage got down there. And once at the wall, he wouldn't be able to do anything, anyway.

Unless he had a weapon.

Hoisting his own gun, Gage scrambled back through the room and jogged down the staircase. Captain Denny's voice bellowed from the front of the house. The mysterious, crawling figure would never be able to circle to the front of the house, but the crawling could be an act.

Gage made a quick detour to the kitchen where he swept his radio from the counter. He strode across the hallway, crunching through the broken glass.

He burst through the doors leading to the back patio and ran onto the lawn, veering toward the left where he'd seen the figure from the balcony. He squinted into the gloom. The clouds had moved over the small slice of moon again, throwing this side of the compound into total darkness. The other side of the house boasted all the light and activity.

The humidity sucked the air from his lungs. He

pulled in another breath and wiped his sleeve across his sweating brow, his gaze crisscrossing the lawn in front of the balcony with the broken railing.

A moan filtered through the air, and the hair on the back of Gage's neck stood at attention. His feet followed the sound, closer to the flagstones than he'd expected. The guy must've stopped crawling.

Gage slogged through the damp grass and froze. Seems the man had found the strength to stand, after all. A white oval lifted and dark pools peered at him.

He aimed his gun at the person's head. "Hold it. Do you have any weapons?"

The small-statured man extended his arm toward Gage, and Gage's finger tightened on the trigger of his carbine. "Don't make any sudden moves. I've got a weapon pointed at you."

The figure took a few jerky steps, dropping his arm to his side.

Gage pushed the button on the radio. "Captain Denny, I need light at the back of the house. There's someone out here."

Denny answered. "Ten-four."

Motioning toward the man with his weapon, Gage said, "I have reinforcements. Put your hands behind your head and drop to your knees."

The man wavered and his arms dangled at his sides. Seconds later, several soldiers charged around the corner from the front of the house, coming up behind Gage. They drew up beside him and aimed their powerful spotlights at the figure swaying on the lawn.

Gage's jaw dropped as the beams of light illuminated a…woman.

The woman blinked. She raised an arm to her face,

resting the back of her wrist on her forehead, covering her eyes.

The soldier on one side of Gage cursed, and the soldier on the other side muttered unnecessarily, "It's a chick."

Gage stole forward, leading with his M4. "Don't reach for any weapons, or I'll shoot."

Hell, for all he knew, the woman could be a trained assassin. If she lived in this compound, her loyalty lay with Zendaris. He could even be face-to-face with Zendaris's mistress. Their intelligence had indicated Zendaris kept multiple lovers.

His nerve endings buzzed. If they could capture one of Zendaris's girlfriends and grill her, there's no telling how much information she could give them.

His step lightened as he drew closer and verified the woman didn't have anything in her hands and no indication of a weapon—at least none that he could see. Her slim, black slacks hugged her hips and legs and her dark-colored blouse stirred in the gentle breeze. How could he have ever thought she was a man?

"Put your hands in the air where I can see them." He moved within steps of her, so close he could smell the perfume he'd noticed on the scarf—exotic, hypnotic.

She tilted her head and a dark ponytail slid over her shoulder. Still, she didn't speak. She lifted the hand from her forehead and raised it, palm out.

Gage drew in a quick breath as he noticed the blood streaked across her face. "You're injured."

She nodded once and pitched forward.

Gage dropped his weapon where it hung over his shoulder and swooped in before she hit the ground, catching her beneath the arms. Her head bobbed against his belly, and her knees buckled, swaying inches above the wet grass.

He hitched her into his arms, cradling her head. His fingers met a sticky patch of blood matting her hair on one side. He shouted to the soldiers standing in a semicircle, gaping. "Medical. Who has the medical supplies?"

"We'll set up something on the back patio, sir."

The men sprang into action and by the time Gage arrived at the patio with the woman clutched to his chest, the soldiers had already set up a stretcher, water and the contents of a first-aid kit, all illuminated by two spotlights.

He laid the woman on the stretcher, and she pinned him with her wide, dark eyes. "W-who are you?"

Did she mean in general or him specifically? She had to know they were U.S. Military come calling for her…lover.

"I'm Gage Booker and these men are from the U.S. Army Special Forces, but then you probably already know that. Why did they leave you behind?"

Her eyes clouded over and her lashes fluttered. "I don't know."

One of the soldiers nudged him aside. "I'm the medic on this assignment, Booker, but stay close to assist me."

Gage moved aside, a jumble of emotions churning in his gut as he watched Perkins clean and dress the woman's head wound. How had a pretty, young woman like this wound up in Zendaris's clutches? Then he scoffed at himself. That's just it: pretty and young. What else did Zendaris need? And she'd probably grown accustomed to the lifestyle he'd offered—until he ditched her.

"Hello." Perkins ripped the sleeve from the woman's

blouse and pointed to her arm. "This is a flesh wound from a bullet. Just creased the skin."

The woman turned her head and glanced at the ripped flesh on her arm like she was examining a cut of beef at the market.

"How'd you get that?" As far as Gage knew, no shots had been fired other than the initial volley when they'd taken the men at the outer wall.

Captain Denny loomed over the scene. "Has she given you any information yet?"

Perkins shook his head. "She's in shock, sir."

After Perkins tended to the bullet wound and bandaged the gash on her head, he turned away to pack up the supplies.

Gage held a bottle of water to the woman's lips and she drank deeply. "Do you have any other injuries?"

"No."

Gage helped her to a sitting position and ran his hands along the smooth skin of her arms, back and legs. She sported a few nasty abrasions, but she didn't wince at his touch and he didn't see any more blood. She'd obviously fallen from that balcony and hit her head, but how'd she get the gunshot wound?

If he hoped to get any information from her, she'd have to start talking.

"Booker, we're heading out. Our mission's complete."

Gage stood up and saluted Captain Denny. "Thank you for your assistance, sir."

The captain eyed the woman sitting on the stretcher. "You'll take it from here?"

"I've got it."

"We're exiting through the front gates. It's a straight shot to the choppers from there."

Perkins snapped the first-aid kit shut and placed it on a table. "I'll leave this with you. Don't let her fall asleep. She probably suffered a concussion, and she's still in shock. Make sure she stays warm, even in this climate."

"I'll be taking her to a hospital just to get her checked out."

"That's a good idea." Perkins pressed a bottle of pills into Gage's hand. "Have her take one of these twice a day—antibiotics, so her wounds don't get infected, and make sure she gets a tetanus shot when you get her to the hospital."

Gage shook the bottle of pills. "Thanks, Perkins."

The Green Berets left Zendaris's compound with a lot less fanfare than when they arrived, turning the mission over to him.

At least the raid hadn't been a complete failure. He'd be leaving Colombia with a prized witness—one of Zendaris's mistresses.

He crouched next to the stretcher, and the woman took another swig of water. Her cheeks sported new color and her dark eyes had lost their glassiness.

He shook a pill into his hand. "Take this."

She plucked the pill from his palm and downed it with her next gulp of water.

"I'm going to take you to a doctor. Perkins is okay in a pinch, but we'll see if you need further medical treatment." He tilted his chin toward her battered body. "Who did this to you?"

Her long, dark lashes swept her cheeks. "I don't know."

Zendaris had picked himself a real beauty. Why wouldn't he just take her with him? Maybe he'd never been in residence here, and his henchmen left her behind.

"I know you're not feeling great, but I need to ask you some questions…before we leave." Gage swallowed. He'd always found it difficult interrogating women. Made him feel like a bully. But he hoped he'd made it clear that he wasn't taking her anywhere until she answered his questions about Zendaris.

"Do you want to sit in this chair?" He slid his hand beneath her arm and helped her to her feet.

She took the two steps to the chair without wavering and perched on the end.

He pointed to a blanket one of the soldiers had stripped off a bed upstairs. "Are you cold?"

She raised a pair of sculpted, dark eyebrows. "It's about eighty degrees out here."

Gage grinned, feeling some tension seep from his shoulders. That was the most words she'd strung together all night—and she'd even made a small joke.

"I guess it's the shock. Perkins said you might get the chills."

"I'm fine."

Dragging another chair close to hers, he said, "Okay, let's get started. I'm Gage Booker. What's your name?"

"I don't know."

Prickles of anger needled his flesh. So she was going to play it like that, huh?

"This can be easy, or this can be hard, Miss Idont-know."

She blinked and a small sigh escaped her luscious lips.

Gage bit the inside of his cheek. If he focused on her attractiveness, he'd never get through this. She'd probably used her looks to get out of all kinds of scrapes. But not this time. He pinned his shoulders to the back of his chair.

"You think that's going to save you? If you've been out here…consorting with Zendaris, we can bring you down, too. Make no mistake about it. Where is he? Where is Zendaris? What does he look like? I'm sure you've seen the real Zendaris—in the flesh."

His lips twisted into a sneer because the woman's eyes had grown bigger and bigger with each question until they took up half her face.

"I—I don't know what you're talking about."

"Yeah, right. You've been with him…how long? How do you think he financed this lavish lifestyle? Did he lay some jewels on you? Some designer duds? Give it up, sweetheart, just like you gave it up to Zendaris. Where is he?"

Her full bottom lip trembled, and a big tear splashed onto her cheek.

Gage swept off his black beanie and raked a hand through his hair. Great. He'd made a woman cry—the last thing he ever wanted to do. But the woman in front of him was no damsel in distress. She had to know Zendaris's business and that made her complicit in all the death and destruction that business engendered.

"Look, this will go easier on you if you just cooperate."

She licked her lips, catching the tear on her tongue. "I'd like to help you. I really would, but I can't."

Hunching forward, he braced his hands on his knees. "If you're afraid for your life, we can protect you. We'll give you a new identity."

She smiled then, a tremulous smile that didn't reach her eyes. "That would be nice because I don't even have an old identity."

He narrowed his eyes. What kind of trick was she playing now? "What are you talking about?"

She spread her hands. "I don't know who I am. I don't know why I'm here. I don't know this Zendaris person. In fact, I have no memory at all."

Chapter Three

The man's eyes were slits now—aquamarine slits. How could someone's eyes be so blue? But they were hard and cold. He didn't believe her. She didn't blame him.

He threw his head back and laughed. She shivered. His laugh was as cold as his eyes.

"You want me to believe you have no memory? You don't know your name or who you are or what you're doing on Nico Zendaris's compound?"

She put a hand to her head and traced the bandage there. "I don't want you to believe anything. That's the truth, whether you choose to believe it or not."

The man, Gage, jumped up from the lawn chair, knocking it to the ground. Then he swung around and jabbed a finger in her face. "This could go very badly for you."

"Too late." She covered her face with her hands.

She heard him shuffling on the patio, and as she peered at him through her fingers, he righted the chair. He took a seat across from her again, his knees touching hers.

"What do you remember?"

"Does this mean you believe me?"

"Thought you said that didn't matter to you?"

She'd lied. If he believed her he'd help her, and God

knows she needed help. If he didn't believe her, he'd still help her, at least physically, but his eyes would remain cold every time he looked at her.

"The first thing I remember is coming to on those flagstones. My head hurt, my arm hurt. A strong impulse to get away overwhelmed me, so I started crawling."

"Was anyone around you? Did you see anything or anyone?"

"No. I heard shouting from somewhere, but I now know those were your marines."

"Green Berets, and they're not mine."

She shrugged and pain shot through her upper left arm. The man who'd treated her said she'd been grazed by a bullet. Why would anyone be shooting at her?

"Are you okay?" Gage half rose from his chair.

So he did care—a little bit. "It's my arm. My head's throbbing, too, so if that Green Beret left any ibuprofen in that case, I'll take some."

He slid the first-aid kit from the table and popped it open. He sorted through some small envelopes and pulled one free. "You're in luck."

He ripped the pack open for her and she downed two gel capsules.

"You don't know Zendaris or what you're doing here?"

"I don't even know my own name. That other name means nothing to me. I don't even know where I am."

The impact of her statement sent a rush of nausea to the pit of her stomach, and she doubled over.

"You're not well."

"Would you be well if you woke up with no memory and a gunshot wound? Where am I? Who's Zendaris?"

Her hands had been fluttering in front of her, and he

captured them between his. "You're in Colombia, not far from Barranquilla—at least that's the nearest big city."

Barranquilla. "*Yo conozco Barranquilla.* I know Barranquilla. I—I speak Spanish."

He studied her with those blue eyes. Were they melting a little around the edges?

"Nico Zendaris is…a bad person."

"What were you and your friends doing here? Were you going to arrest him?"

"Was he here to arrest?"

She closed her eyes. He still didn't believe her. "How would I know that?"

He cocked his head, and a lock of brown hair fell over one eye. "Aren't you curious to know what you were doing in the home of a man like Zendaris? A man who could inspire a raid by the U.S. Army Special Forces?"

"I'm curious about everything. Like why didn't you leave with the others? Why did they defer to you when that other man, that captain, was obviously in charge of the military guys?"

The line of Gage's jaw tightened. He didn't like her questions. He liked her tears better, her sighs, her weakness. *Tough.* She couldn't afford to be weak. She had to figure out who she was, what she was doing here and what Gage Booker wanted with her.

"That's my business, and I'm not about to tell a potential criminal."

"Can you help me figure out who I am?"

"Oh, I'll help you. And once you get your memory back, if in fact you ever lost it, I'm going to proceed to pick your brain."

"That's something to look forward to." She put on a sweet smile, even though it hurt her head to do so.

He snatched a full bottle of water from the table and downed half of it. "You're Nico Zendaris's lover."

If he'd intended to shock her with his words, he'd be disappointed. She had no memory of being anyone's lover and until she did, she'd take no responsibility for what that entailed.

"If you're so certain I'm Zendaris's girlfriend, why don't you know my name?"

"Because we know very little about the man. We don't even know what he looks like." Reaching over, he dragged the black backpack toward his feet. He rummaged through the pack, pulled out a file folder and slipped a photograph from the folder. He dropped the picture on the table.

"This," he tapped the picture with his finger, "is you."

She hunched forward, squinting at the grainy color image of a man with a bushy mustache, sunglasses and a blue baseball cap, his arm around a tall, slim brunette.

She pulled back with a start, knocking over her bottle of water. Gage snatched the picture away from the spill.

"What's wrong? That is you, isn't it?"

"How the hell do I know?" She pinched the bridge of her nose. "I don't even know what I look like."

He searched her face, his blue gaze tracking across each of her features. "Against my better judgment, I'm beginning to believe you."

He shoved back from his chair—this time it stayed upright—and extended his hand to her. "Come with me."

What choice did she have at this point? She placed her hand in his, and when he curled his fingers around hers, a warm current flowed through her body. His touch felt like the only lifeline she had.

He snatched up his folder and led her into the house. The tiles felt cool against the soles of her bare feet. As she gazed at the crystal chandelier dripping from the high ceiling, Gage pulled her toward an ornate mirror gracing the hallway.

Turning her toward the mirror and standing behind her, he placed his hands on her shoulders. Her gaze scanned the woman in the reflection. Large, dark eyes stared back at her from a mocha-tinted face framed by wisps of brown hair coming loose from a ponytail. She knew Spanish because she obviously had some Latin blood.

Her eyes met his in the mirror. His gaze still held suspicions, doubts.

He held up the photo to the mirror. "Could be you, right?"

"He has his arm around the woman. Does that make her his girlfriend?"

He fumbled in the file folder he'd placed on a side table and withdrew another photo, same quality. In this photo, the man had the woman in a tight embrace, laying a passionate kiss on her lips.

She exhaled. "I see what you mean, but I'm sure there are lots of tall brunettes in the world."

"Wearing this?" He dug into the pocket of his camos and pulled out a scarf with silver spangles threaded through it. He waved it next to the picture, and she noticed the woman in the picture sporting something similar around her neck.

"Where did you get that? I wasn't wearing it when you found me." She folded her arms across her chest and turned away from the mirror. She didn't want to be some bad guy's girlfriend. She didn't feel like a bad guy's girlfriend. Was he a drug dealer?

He jabbed his finger in the air. "I found this upstairs, right before I spotted you from the balcony. You must've been in that room, and left your scarf before trying to escape."

"Who said I was trying to escape? Maybe someone pushed me. Someone obviously shot me." Despite the warm night, a rash of goose bumps pebbled across her skin, and she hugged herself tighter. "I want to see this room."

"Follow me." He placed a booted foot on the first step of the curved staircase and reached out his hand to her. "Are you feeling okay? You look pale."

"The ibuprofen helped the pain. Now I just want to know who I am." She placed her hand in his. He must still be worried that she'd make a run for it, but the idea of running made her head spin even more.

They continued up the stairs, and she left her hand in his. She didn't feel physically wobbly, but emotionally she was about to crack.

She gasped as she followed Gage into the room. Turning in a circle, she drank in the bright colors and cheery furniture. "This is a children's playroom."

"Yep."

Picking up a book of fairy tales, she traced the edge with her finger. "Does this Zendaris have children?"

"We don't know, but it sure looks like it."

"Unless this room is for the children of his staff. This is a big place. He must support a lot of people living here."

Gage gestured around the well-appointed room. "Seems kind of lavish for the staff, doesn't it?"

She swallowed a painful lump. "Do you think Zendaris could have children with his…girlfriend?"

Gage's eyebrows snapped together as if it had

never occurred to him that she might be the mother of Zendaris's children.

Her knees felt shaky and she sank into the armchair. Something about this room stirred emotions deep within her, plucked at her heartstrings. Could she be a mother?

She flipped open the cover of the book still clutched in her hand. Her fingers traced over some words in Spanish. "Look."

Gage took two steps and hovered over her shoulder. "What is it?"

"It's a note in Spanish. It says, *To Randi, May you have a fairy-tale life, Love, Abuelita,* little grand-mother."

Gage rubbed his chin, sprinkled with dark stubble. "Who's Randi?"

"You're asking the wrong person." She followed the letters with her fingertip. "Could Randi be one of Zendaris's children?"

"Then who's Abuelita? Zendaris, as you can probably tell by his name, is not Latino."

"The child's maternal grandmother? Maybe they're half-Colombian. Maybe that's why they stay here."

His hands dropped to her shoulders and the touch felt like a caress. "Are you up for a little more exploration before I get you out of here? I think you need to see a doctor."

"A head doctor."

"Maybe that, too."

She rose from the chair and tucked the book under her arm. As she did so, she noticed a pair of sandals halfway under the chair. She put her hand on Gage's corded forearm. "Wait."

She slipped her feet into the sandals and grimaced. "Just like Cinderella."

They poked their heads into one adjoining room. Little-girl decor—princesses, ballerinas and mermaids—overlooked a disheveled mess. Someone had tossed drawers and emptied closets. All personal effects had been stripped from the room.

They crossed the playroom to the other adjoining bedroom, and the same scene had been played out in the boy's room.

Gage crossed the hall and she followed, her sandaled feet almost dragging. She didn't want to see what awaited them in those rooms.

Gage pushed open a door, and a powerful, masculine aroma washed over her. The scent of musk made her head pound even more. The closet doors gaped open and empty hangers swayed back and forth. A neatly made-up king-size bed had a commanding position in the corner of the room, facing a flat-screen TV.

Had she slept in this bed with her children across the hall?

The room led to a large master bath and beyond the bathroom, another door beckoned. She stepped into the adjoining room and gripped the book so hard the edges dug into her palms.

This room had a distinctly feminine touch. It, too, had been ransacked, but clothes still hung in the closet. She crept toward the items and yanked a dress on its hanger from the rack. She held it up to her body and spun around to the full-length mirror.

"It's a fit." Gage came into the room with a scowl etched across his face.

Her cheeks warmed. Had she lived here in this house as man and wife with a drug dealer?

She tossed the dress onto the bed. "I still don't remember anything."

"Don't you…Randi?" He pulled a small envelope from the dressing-table mirror and turned to wave it in her face. "They missed something when they ransacked the room."

Her heart jumped as he pulled a slip of paper from the envelope.

He squinted at the note. "It says, *Randi, almost made the trip south to see you when I was in Costa Rica, but remembered visitors aren't welcome. Come home soon. Love, Jessica.*"

"Is there a name and address on the envelope?" Randi must be her name. This was her room, her note. Now that she knew her first name, she'd like to know her last.

He flipped over the envelope. "Just has your first name in care of the Costa residence. Does that name mean anything to you?"

"No, but maybe this is the Costa residence. Maybe you got your signals crossed."

"Not a chance."

"What about the return address?"

"The envelope is ripped." He fingered the corner of the envelope. "I can just make out the name—Jessica Lehman—and the postmark is from Houston, Texas."

Randi's throat thickened and she couldn't swallow. She must have a grandmother somewhere and a friend in Houston. People who cared about her.

Where were they now? Would they be able to help her out of this mess?

She jumped when Gage placed his hand on the small of her back. "I'm sorry, Randi. This must be tough for you."

She pulled back her shoulders and shrugged off his touch. She'd better not get too dependent on him. He wanted her to regain her memory so that he could pump her for information about Zendaris. Once he got what he wanted, he'd abandon her to whatever fate awaited cast-off lovers of drug dealers.

"Does this mean you believe me?"

"If you're lying about having amnesia, you're one hell of an actress, but—" he steepled his fingers and tapped them at the tips "—you could be an Academy Award winner."

She brushed past him and scooped up an armful of clothing from the closet. "I'm not going out in the world without clothes."

"Travel lightly. It's a two-mile hike back to the chopper."

She dumped the clothes on the bed and dove back into the closet for a bag or backpack. She dragged out a red duffel and flicked the tags on the strap. "Too bad there's no full name and address. I might've been able to reclaim my life sooner rather than later."

Gage spread his arms. "I think your life was here, Randi—and it left you."

She dropped onto the edge of the bed, clutching the bag to her chest. "What if those kids across the hall are mine?"

"Then we'll help you get them back." He ducked into the closet and grabbed a pair of sneakers. "I think these will work better out in the jungle than those sandals."

A half an hour later, they stood at the open gates to the compound. Gage had his backpack on his back and his large, black duffel strapped across his body. He'd broken down the scary-looking weapon and stashed it in the duffel.

He'd given her a small pack with a few bottles of water and medical supplies. He'd talked her into leav-

ing the red bag and just stuffing a few items of clothing into his duffel.

"Are you sure you can do this? You just suffered a
concussion."

"I have no memory. What could possibly be worse?"

"Aggravating your injuries with physical exhaus-
tion. We can stay here for a few days, and I can call in
for help."

She shifted the pack on her back. "I'm not staying
here another minute."

"Let me know if you get tired, and follow my footsteps. We're still a long way from morning, and it's still
dark out here."

She peered up through the canopy of trees. Even if
the sun were rising, it would take a while for its light to
reach them beneath the umbrella of branches and leaves.

Gage tromped through the foliage, his boots snap-
ping twigs and crushing leaves along the way.

Randi followed, her mind, or what was left of it,
whirring. If everything Gage had said about her was
true, maybe she didn't want to discover her real identity. But maybe her boyfriend had kept his illegal activities hidden from her. Maybe she didn't know anything
about his business.

That wouldn't make Gage very happy. He'd be counting on her help once she regained her memory. If she
claimed no knowledge of Zendaris's drug empire, Gage
wouldn't believe her, anyway.

She wasn't sure he believed her now.

Despite her injuries, the hike through the jungle
hadn't sapped her strength. Gage had stopped a few
times for water, and it was enough to carry her through.
She seemed to regain strength with each step away from
the compound.

"We're here." He parted some branches for her, and she peered into a clearing. A helicopter beckoned, promising freedom and maybe an identity.

"You know how to fly this thing?"

"I do."

"But you're not U.S. Military."

"I used to be."

If he planned to grill her, she planned to give as good as she got. She'd drop it for now and let him concentrate on flying. "Where are we going?"

"First stop is a CIA compound in Panama. There's a hospital there."

He was CIA? "Then what?"

He hoisted the bags into the helicopter. "We'll see."

She shrugged out of the backpack, and Gage stored that next to the other two bags. Then he helped her into the helicopter and secured her seat belt, his hands lingering near her shoulders.

Had he wanted to touch her? Reassure her? She needed it but she'd ask nothing of him. Getting too close to this man would put her on dangerous ground.

He punched some buttons from the array in front of him and even on the ceiling of the chopper. When the blades started thwacking, she clenched the edge of the seat with clammy hands. The sound caused her insides to twist.

Gage pointed to the headphones hanging in front of her, and she slipped them onto her head. His voice purred intimately into her ears. "Are you okay?"

She nodded and gritted her teeth.

He fiddled with more dials and gadgets, and then flashed her a thumbs-up signal.

Just as the chopper lifted from the ground, a new barrage of noises assailed her. This time Gage swore into her ear, and she jerked her head toward him.

"What's wrong?"

The helicopter shuddered and lunged into the air as the smell of fuel saturated the cabin. With his jaw clenched, Gage slammed a lever forward and the chopper jumped.

She tried again. "Gage, what's wrong? What's happening?"

"Someone's shooting at us."

Chapter Four

The thwacking helicopter blades stuttered, and Randi's heart stuttered along with them. The chopper lurched toward the treetops, which slapped its runners with their branches for daring to invade their territory.

Randi held her breath, mesmerized by Gage's long fingers flicking switches and spinning dials on the console of the helicopter.

"A-are we going down?"

"Not yet."

The smell of gasoline invaded her nostrils, and her fingernails curled into the vinyl seat. Was the helicopter going to blow up?

Her gaze flicked to Gage's face, lined with tension and concentration. She wanted to ask him more questions. She wanted him to reassure her. But she didn't want to distract him. It looked like he had a life-and-death struggle going on with the jerking and dipping chopper.

He lifted the bird above the treetops and the jerking stopped.

Closing her eyes, Randi let out a long breath. "Are we okay now?"

"Not exactly." He dropped his head to peer at the ground below, or what he saw of it shrouded in darkness. "We're safe from the people who were shooting at us, but we're not okay. Do you smell that gasoline?"

"Yes." Her nostrils flared. Maybe they *were* going to blow up.

"It's leaking out of the chopper. We have—" he flicked a gauge on the console with his finger "—maybe ten minutes of flight time before I have to put this bird down."

Randi swallowed as she looked at the blackness out the window. "We're in the middle of the jungle. How are you going to find a place to land when we can't even see anything?"

"Good question. I have about ten minutes to figure out the answer."

"Can I help?"

He jerked a thumb over his shoulder. "There's a pair of night-vision binoculars in my backpack."

Twisting in her seat, Randi reached for the black backpack and unzipped it. She rummaged through the contents with one hand, stumbling over hard edges and metal and dangerous things. Her fingers traced the edges of a lens and she pulled out the binoculars.

"Flick the switch on the top, and then see if you can focus on anything out the window."

She followed his instructions, aiming the heavy scope at the ground as they chugged above it. At first she saw nothing but dark shapes and flashes of light.

"The focus is on the bottom."

Her thumb rolled across the serrated dial, and the shadows below her began to take shape. But she didn't like the shape they took.

"Trees. Nothing but trees."

"Look for any gap, no matter how small."

Her eyes ached as she squinted through the lenses,

tracking the binoculars back and forth across the tree-tops. Her heart did a somersault when she spotted a break in the leafy blanket.

"We're coming up to a gap in the trees. I can't tell how big it is, but it's there."

"Straight ahead?"

"To the right."

The chopper sputtered and seemed to stall, a wing-less bird floating through the air.

Randi's grip tightened on the binoculars, which were in danger of slipping from her clammy grasp. "Keep veering to the right. We're almost above the patch."

Light flooded the ground, and Randi dropped the binoculars to her lap as the trees swayed beneath them. "Why didn't you put those lights on before?"

"Didn't want to advertise our direction to what were probably cohorts of Zendaris. You did a great job."

"I-is that a big enough space to land?" She sucked her bottom lip between her teeth and eyed the rapidly approaching square of ground that looked more like a postage stamp than a landing pad.

"It's going to have to be."

The helicopter coughed and jerked, dropping several more feet.

Randi squeezed her eyes shut and braced her feet against the floor of the chopper. Her stomach dropped along with the helicopter, and she clenched her teeth, trapping a scream in her throat.

The man beside her needed all of his concentration. She didn't want to spook him by screaming in his ear.

When the chopper hit the ground, it jolted her and she bounced once in her seat. Her eyes flew open amid a storm of leaves outside the window, which fluttered and swirled around them in a thick cloud.

"What happened?"

"I squeezed onto the landing pad, but I took out a few branches on my way in." He chuckled and the sound loosened the knots in just about every muscle of her body.

She patted her face and her shoulders. "I can't believe I'm in one piece."

"How's your head feeling?"

"I almost forgot about that in all the excitement." She traced the bandage with her fingertips. She didn't need to forget anything else.

"I still want to get you to a doctor." Gage flipped a few switches and dials on the control panel as the blades wound down and the shower of leaves subsided.

She peered at the small clearing, surrounded on all sides by the verdant vegetation. "I don't think we're going to find a doctor in the immediate vicinity. In fact, where are we? How far did we get from the compound?"

"Far enough away from those friendly folks with guns."

"Now what?"

Gage stabbed at the buttons on his cell phone a few times, and then shoved it in his pocket. "We hike out of here until I can get some cell reception. I still plan to take you to Panama to get you checked out by a medic."

"And to interrogate me."

He raised one eyebrow in her direction. "We'd like to help you, Randi. We're your only lifeline right now."

"That's what worries me."

The blades had stopped spinning, so she pushed open the door of the chopper and slid to the ground, her feet squelching the thick carpet of tumultuous vegetation. The ripe odor of the moist earth clung to her skin. It smelled like life and she planned to get hers back.

Gage scrambled in the back of the helicopter and emerged with his duffel bag. He dropped it to the ground and pointed at the thickest clump of trees. "We're going to head in that direction."

"Do you know where you're going?"

"Taking the fastest route out of this jungle. I saw a road from the air."

"Do you think we can get some gasoline and get that helicopter back up in the air—at least until it leaks again?"

"Not an option. To walk out of here and then walk back in again is a waste of effort." He peered beneath the body of the helicopter. "And judging by the size of that hole in the tank, more gas is not going to buy us much time in the air."

"Are we going to hitch a ride to Panama?" She wedged her hands on her hips and tapped her toe. She didn't trust anyone in this country—except Gage.

"As long as I can get cell reception, we should be able to order another mode of transportation. Besides—" he smacked the side of the chopper "—I think I may have damaged the blades on my way in, so even if it didn't have a hole in the gas tank, this bird is done."

"Then let's get moving." She marched a few steps in the direction he'd indicated before and stopped when she didn't hear his footsteps behind her. She spun around.

He looked up from digging through his bag. "What's your hurry?"

"My hurry?" She drew her brows together as he pulled what looked like a blanket out of his bag. "I want to get to civilization."

He tucked the blanket under his arm. "But the path to that civilization is not all that civilized—especially at this time of night...or morning."

"We're staying here?" She blinked and wrapped her arms around her body.

"You need to rest, especially if we're going to be hiking through the jungle, and it's not safe out there in the dark."

Her gaze slid to the line of trees bordering unknown surprises, and a shiver rolled through her body despite the warmth of the damp air pressing against her. She hugged herself tighter.

"We're going to sleep here?"

"That's the plan." He gestured toward the disabled chopper, listing to one side. "That should be enough to shield you from whatever is squirming on the jungle floor."

"If you're trying to make me feel better about spending the night here, you just failed miserably."

He pulled a bottle from his bag and waved it in the air. "This bug repellant will add another layer of protection."

And who's going to protect me from you?

The thought crept out of nowhere. Not for a minute did she believe she had anything to fear from Gage Booker. Hadn't she just admitted he was the only one she did trust right now? And yet danger hung about him like a loose cape.

Maybe her genetic makeup dictated her visceral response to this man with his weapons, survival skills and take-charge attitude. After all, hadn't she been living with some international drug dealer as his mistress?

She couldn't wrap her fractured mind around that. She couldn't wrap her fractured mind around anything right now, except that a creeping lethargy had stolen over her body and she wanted nothing more than to climb back into the helicopter and sleep for a million years.

Maybe some prince would happen by, plant a kiss on her bruised head, awaken her and restore her memory.

"You look ready to drop." Gage held out his hand. "Come on over here and make yourself comfortable inside the chopper. I want to check your vitals, anyway."

Would he notice her racing heart?

Her feet shuffled through the leaves as she walked toward him.

He took her arm and helped her back into the passenger seat of the helicopter. Her legs hung over the side of the seat and out the door. Gage positioned himself in front of her, and her knees brushed his stomach.

Leaning in, he unwrapped the bandage from around her head. "Doesn't look too bad, although you have a lot of sticky hair covering the wound."

He pulled a water bottle and the first-aid kit from his bag, which he'd dropped to the ground. He dampened a cloth and dabbed the side of her head. "Does that hurt?"

"Not too much."

"I don't think you'll need stitches, but I'll feel a lot better once you see a doctor."

"I'll feel a lot better once I know who I am."

His hands stopped moving and his body tensed. "I hope so."

Even being a drug dealer's mistress would be better than having this black hole of a mind. At least that gave her a starting point.

Gage finished wrapping her head in fresh gauze, and then scooped up his bag. "How's the pain? Do you need another ibuprofen?"

"I'll take another."

He flicked open the envelope and shook one into her palm. "I can give you something to help you sleep, too."

"I'm woozy enough. I'm trying to clear my mind, not fog it up."

"Okay, sit back and relax and I'll join you. Too bad it doesn't have reclining seats." He shut the door, and she tilted her head back against the seat.

The chopper jostled as he climbed in next to her. The blanket dropped in her lap on top of her folded hands.

"Do you want to wrap up in the blanket?"

"It's still warm."

"You can sit on it, tuck it around your body or bunch it up for a pillow."

"What about you?"

He wedged his gun between his seat and the instrument panel and folded his arms across his black T-shirt. "I'm good."

"You're not going to sleep, are you?"

"Sure I am—with one eye open."

"That sounds relaxing." She smooshed the blanket against the door and shifted in her seat, leaning her head against her makeshift pillow. "Maybe I'll wake up with my memory intact."

"Maybe you will."

He almost whispered, which lent an uncertain quality to his words. She gritted her teeth and punched the blanket into shape.

Gage Booker would like nothing more than for her to regain her memory so he could grill her about Nico Zendaris. In the end, where would her loyalty lie?

GAGE NARROWED HIS EYES, his gaze skewering the fluttering leaves—probably a bird stirring in the morning light. He'd kept vigil through the night. The rising sun combed through the trees, but wasn't high enough to reach their little patch of land yet.

He shifted in his seat and stretched, careful not to jostle the chopper and disturb Randi. She'd slept soundly most of the night, no dreams causing her to talk in her sleep, letting slip any clues to her identity.

Who was he kidding? Randi was Zendaris's woman.

Could amnesia lead to a personality change? Would she stand by her man once she regained her memory?

Zendaris must've thought she was dead to leave her at the compound. No way would he leave a living witness—even one who had shared his bed.

That thought tasted sour in his mouth, and he ran his tongue along his teeth as he reached for his water.

Randi stirred and rolled her head to the side. She grabbed the back of her neck, murmuring a few slurred words.

Gage took a gulp of water. When he lowered the bottle, he met a pair of dark eyes, half-shuttered by thick lashes.

"Are you awake?"

"Yeah." She scooted forward, twisting her head from side to side. "We're still in one piece?"

"As far as I can tell." He held out a bottle of water to her. "How do you feel?"

"Sore." She twisted the cap from the bottle and chugged half the water without taking a breath.

"Your head?"

"My entire body." She rolled her shoulders backward. "I guess that dive off the balcony is taking its full toll."

"Your memory?"

She rubbed her eyes. "Still a black hole."

"Let's take care of the pain first." He dumped a couple of ibuprofen gel caps onto his palm and bounced them around in front of her nose before dropping them into her hand.

"For a minute there, I thought you meant a massage." She downed the pills, and then pinched her shoulders with her fingertips. "My body might be bruised, but my neck is stiff from the sleeping accommodations."

"Turn around." He held out his hands and flexed his fingers. "It's the least I can do before we start our jungle trek."

Her eyes widened before she turned around, presenting her back to him. "Do you think we'll reach the road before nightfall again?"

"Definitely. It's not that far." He nudged her hair over her shoulder, its silky strands catching on his calloused fingertips. Then he drove his thumbs into the base of her neck.

She sucked in a breath.

"Does that hurt?"

"It hurts in a good way."

"I'll take your word for it." He circled his thumbs against her smooth skin as her hair tickled the backs of his hands. "Once we get clear of this jungle, I should get some cell reception and someone can pick us up."

"I'll take your word for it."

As he kneaded the knots in her neck, a soft sigh escaped her lips. At least he could bring her some relief before the interrogation started. Not that Prospero would be shining a bright light in her eyes. Randi would sit down with a psychiatrist first and maybe undergo hypnosis.

If he played his cards right, he could get her on their side. If he treated her more like a victim than a suspect, she might give them valuable information on Zendaris.

"That's better." Randi rolled her shoulders. "Should we get going?"

"I think we have enough light now." He dragged his bag out of the back of the chopper and dug through it. "More water?"

She accepted the bottle and chugged half of it before replacing the cap. "Do you have anything to eat in there?"

"No, but we might get lucky and find some fruit on our hike through the jungle—mangoes, bananas, papayas."

"Sounds good to me."

She licked her lips, and he had to drag his gaze away from the sight of the tip of her pink tongue darting from her mouth.

The sooner he delivered her to the CIA facility in Panama, the better. He didn't need the complication of an insane attraction to one of Zendaris's mistresses. Especially since he realized his interest in Randi stemmed in large part from the fact that she didn't know him or his family. How could she? She had no memory at all.

While he stashed the water bottles in his backpack, she slipped from the helicopter without his help. That's another thing he liked about this woman—despite her vulnerability, she seemed to do a lot without his help. Every other woman he'd dated seemed to want something from him, his family name and money.

"Give me the backpack." She held out her hand, cupping her fingers. "I'll leave the big, black duffel with all its spy equipment to you, but I can handle the backpack."

"Turn around."

She presented her back to him for the second time

that morning, and he slipped the straps of the pack over her shoulders. "Let me know if it gets too heavy for you."

Adjusting the straps, she tilted her chin toward the tangle of branches ahead of them. "How far?"

"Maybe six or seven miles. You need to let me know if you feel dizzy or nauseous, and you need to keep taking those antibiotics."

She saluted. "After you."

They slogged through the lush growth of tropical plants and snagged a couple of mangoes and papayas on their way without breaking stride. Gage wanted to put some distance between them and the helicopter in case someone discovered it.

After thirty minutes of hiking, Gage pointed to the carpeted floor of the jungle. "Let's take a break and eat."

Randi slid off the backpack and wedged a shoulder against a tree.

"Are you feeling okay?"

"I'm fine, but I've been dreaming about that fruit ever since we picked it."

"It'll taste better if we sit down and eat it instead of eating it on the move." Gage shook out a tarp and laid it out on the ground. "Sit."

Randi sank to her knees and folded her legs beneath her. She pulled one papaya and one mango from the backpack. "Breakfast is served."

He pulled the knife from its holster on his belt and sliced through the skin of the papaya. He offered Randi a slice on the edge of the knife.

She picked it up with her fingertips and sucked the orange fruit into her mouth. Closing her eyes, she murmured, "Mmm."

"Sweet?"

She swallowed and dabbed at a droplet of juice at the corner of her mouth. "Yummy."

Was she trying to drive him crazy?

He busied himself slicing the rest of the fruit and handing her every other piece from his knife. The tangy sweetness of the papaya and the tartness of the mango mingled in his mouth. The simple breakfast tasted better than any meal he'd eaten at a five-star restaurant.

Or maybe it was the company.

"I must've been starving because that tasted great."

"I was just thinking the same thing." He wiped off his knife with a handkerchief and slid it back in its holster.

Randi tipped a trickle of water in her palm and rinsed off her hands. "What's going to happen when we get to Panama?"

"That depends." Cupping his hands, he held them out to her, and she splashed some water into his palms. "If you still have amnesia, we'll have you sit down with the psychiatrist. Maybe she'll use hypnosis."

"If I still have amnesia?"

He jerked his head up. "Have you remembered anything?"

"No."

"Nothing at all?"

"I remember—" she spread her arms "—this country. Does that make sense? The smells and the feel of the air on my skin—I know this country."

She brought a fist to her chest and thumped once. "I feel it here."

"Makes sense to me." Did Randi come from Colombia? She didn't speak English with an accent, but that didn't mean much. He'd gone to boarding school with a few wealthy South Americans, and by the time they'd graduated from high school and hit the Ivy Leagues, they didn't have a trace of a Spanish accent.

Maybe that's how she'd met Zendaris—her family had dealings with him.

The anger that flared in his gut every time he thought about her and Zendaris had him hopping to his feet and kicking his bag off the tarp.

Randi joined him in an instant and placed her hand on his arm. Her light touch whispered along his flesh.

"Gage, d-do you think those kids could be mine?"

He shrugged, the anger burning more fiercely in the pit of his stomach. "Do you sense you're a mother? Since you feel such an affinity for this country, you'd think you'd feel a similar attachment to those missing children."

She dropped her eyes and brushed nonexistent debris from her pants. "I'm not experiencing some aching sense of loss, but then I've never had amnesia before so I don't know the protocol."

He lifted one eyebrow and shook out the tarp. "How do you know you've never had amnesia before?"

She snorted and the tension that had been building in the air between them dissolved. "If I have those odds, I'd better go to Vegas."

As they continued their trek toward civilization, the trees started thinning.

Randi tapped him on the back. "How long since you tried your phone?"

"About forty minutes." He dropped his bag on the ground and dug his cell phone from his front pocket. He punched a button, holding his phone in the air, his head tilted back. "Nothing yet."

He pointed ahead to where the grasses and underbrush had been flattened into some semblance of a path. "But we're getting close."

Walking was easier on the trail, but Gage still initiated frequent breaks so Randi could rest and drink water. She needed to see a doctor for both her physical and mental ailments.

He wanted to find out what she knew about Zendaris, but he almost dreaded the knowledge. Once she recovered her memories he'd still do everything in his power to protect her from Zendaris. But if she'd aided and abetted him in his crimes, he couldn't do much to save her from the power of the U.S. government.

And he wouldn't want to.

"Look!" Randi waved her hands in front of her. "I didn't think we'd ever get out of this jungle."

A slash of black asphalt sliced through the green foliage that they'd been hacking through for the past few hours.

Gage tried his phone again, but the signal still didn't work. Maybe it never would out here.

"Okay, listen." He tugged on the strap of her backpack to slow down her scramble for the road. "We're tourists. We were staying in Barranquilla. We went hiking and got lost. Got it?"

"Sounds simple enough." She pushed dark hair from her face, and a trickle of sweat rolled to her jawline. "Where are we headed?"

"The nearest town." He resettled his bag across his body. "We'll probably have to do a little more walking along the road before we run into someone. This isn't exactly Grand Central Station." Her shoulders slumped and he instinctively reached out to squeeze them. "Or we can sit by the side of the road and wait."

She straightened her spine. "Let's keep moving."

Randi's never-say-die attitude must've served her well as part of Zendaris's entourage…up until the moment he tried to kill her.

They clambered through the last of the underbrush and hit the road. Gage squinted down the shimmering asphalt and said, "The nearest town is in this direction."

Randi fell into step beside him. "What's going to happen to me if and when I regain my memory?"

"That depends."

"On how much I reveal or how much I was enmeshed with Zendaris?"

"Both."

"Then I'm safe."

"Because you don't intend to reveal as much as you know?"

"Because I'm not in league with Zendaris."

"If you were his mistress…"

"I'm not. I wasn't."

He stopped and grabbed her arm. "Do you remember?"

"No, but I was thinking about it on our hike. I know I wouldn't have been involved with someone like that. I just know it. I feel it."

Gage scooped in a breath of soggy air and dropped her arm. "I don't know if amnesia works that way—on feelings."

"Memories and feelings are linked, aren't they? A memory can make you feel a certain way, and those emotions stay with you. If my lover, the father of my children, had left me for dead, don't you think I'd feel that betrayal on some level of consciousness?"

"Depends again."

They'd started walking again, their wet shoes slapping against the hot asphalt.

"On what?"

"Your true feelings. Maybe you were using Zendaris as much as he was using you. He's a wealthy man and powerful—in some circles. Maybe that's why his betrayal of you doesn't resonate."

He had firsthand knowledge of women who thirsted for wealthy, powerful men. Randi wouldn't be the first.

She whirled on him and jabbed him in the chest with her finger. "You have a low opinion of me, don't you?"

"I don't even know you." He raised his hands, palms out. "I have to make certain assumptions based on your presence at the compound, your appearance, that scarf that matches the one in the photo."

"My appearance?" The finger drilled into his chest.

His gaze raked her long, lean form, the swell of her breasts peeking from the neckline of her blouse, and settled on her face with its high cheekbones, dark cat eyes and patrician nose, nostrils flaring.

She didn't exactly look like Zendaris's housekeeper or *abuela*.

Her flashing eyes narrowed to slits. "What's wrong with my appearance?"

Wrong? There was everything right with her appearance—too damned right. He'd never been attracted to the enemy before, and he didn't like it.

He snorted. "Are you trying to wring a compliment out of me? You saw yourself in the mirror. You could be one of those models on a magazine cover—just Zendaris's type."

Her cheeks flamed, and she turned back toward the road. "Well, he's not my type…and I know it even if you don't."

Blowing out a breath, he fell in beside her. Maybe she'd played him for a fool and just furthered the ruse. Maybe she planned to deny any connection with Zendaris, or maybe she'd just conveniently never regain her memory.

The CIA had ways of dealing with that, and that's what worried him. She did not belong to Prospero, his agency, alone. Others would want a piece of her.

After twenty minutes of walking and not much talking, Gage stopped and tilted his head. "Do you hear that?"

"It's a car."

He turned and took a couple of backward steps, eyeing the road that dipped in waves behind them. A small, blue sedan appeared on one of the rises before disappearing again.

"Looks like we've got company."

"Since I'm apparently such a *femme fatale,* should I roll up my pants and show some leg to get him to pull over?"

"I think we can just wave him down this time— unless he doesn't slow down. Then you can show him some leg."

The car rattled as it came down the hill toward them, a solo driver silhouetted in the windshield.

Gage stepped into the road, waving his arms above his head.

The car slowed on its descent and veered toward the side of the road. It puttered to a stop, emitting a gust of exhaust as the driver killed the engine.

Gage said, "Wait here for a minute."

He jogged to the driver's side of the car where the window was already open. *"Gracias. Necesitamos ayuda."*

The middle-aged man in the car flicked his eyes

from Gage to Randi, waiting by the side of the road. "*Ayuda?* You need help?"

"You speak English?"

"A little. What help?"

"We went on a hike and got lost. We'd appreciate a ride into town." He slid a few bills from his pocket and held them between his fingers.

"Ahh, you went to see the Agualinda Falls?"

Had there been a waterfall on the map? Best not to commit to anything specific. "Just trying to enjoy nature. Stupid, really. Can you give me and my wife a ride?"

"*Sí.* To the next town." The man snatched the bills and stuffed them into his front pocket.

"*Gracias.*" Gage waved to Randi.

She slid the backpack from her shoulder and joined him at the car.

He steered her to the passenger door in the back. "I'll ride up front."

Gage settled in the front seat, one end of his bag on the floor, the other between his legs. He gave up on the seat belt that dangled next to his shoulder.

"Broken." The driver looked in his rearview mirror and touched the side of his head. "Your wife hurt?"

"She tripped over some roots and hit her head on a rock. She's okay."

Except for the small fact that she can't remember a thing about her life.

"The jungle is dangerous. *Muy peligrosa.*"

"We won't try that again without a guide, will we, sweetheart?"

"Uh, no."

Gage stuck out his hand. "I'm Gary and my wife is Renee."

The man ran his tongue along his sweating upper lip. *"Mucho gusto. Soy Marco."*

Was Marco lying just like they were? He seemed more nervous than he should be, picking up a couple of American tourists. Or maybe he didn't believe Gage's story.

The car jostled over the bumps in the road, and it was almost too loud to make conversation. Gage and Marco exchanged comments, but Marco didn't ask any questions and neither did Gage.

After an hour of rattling over the road, Marco pointed to the dusty windshield. *"Gasolina."*

"I'll pay for that. *Yo pago."*

"Gracias."

Marco pulled the car off the road and rolled up to the single pump.

They all crawled out of the car and while Marco began fueling up, Randi sidled next to Gage. "Does your phone work yet?"

"Nope." He twisted his head over his shoulder to take in Marco pumping gas. "Don't you like the transportation?"

"Doesn't Marco seem a little jumpy to you?"

"Maybe he doesn't believe our story."

She puffed at a strand of hair that had floated across her face in the mild breeze. "You'd think he'd be used to us by now. Look at him."

Gage slid another gaze Marco's way. He hopped from one foot to another, his head turned toward the road.

Shrugging, Gage said, "Maybe he's just anxious to be on his way."

Randi matched his shrug. "I'm parched. I don't suppose there's anything to drink in that little shack."

"I saw a soda machine on the other side of the building. I'll see if it's working."

"I'll come with you." She turned to Marco and asked him in perfect Spanish if he wanted a soda from the machine.

Marco nodded and waved.

Gage whispered in her ear. "At least you didn't forget Spanish. What other languages do you know?"

"I have no idea." She covered her mouth with her hand, her eyes wide.

The soda machine turned out not to be a machine at all—just a refrigerated container for some colas in small, glass bottles. They grabbed three bottles and returned to Marco, pulling the hose from the car.

Gage tapped the scratched display of the pump. "I'll pay up for the gas and the drinks. Here's your soda."

Marco took it from him and leaned against the car, crossing one booted foot over his ankle.

Randi followed Gage back to the little shack where the proprietor hovered by the door.

"Gasolina y sodas?"

"Sí. Cuánto cuesta?"

The man told him the price, and Gage peeled off some bills to pay him. They sauntered back to their ride.

He had to get reception once they reached the town or got close. Randi had no passport. The border agents wouldn't allow her to cross into Panama without it. He needed the assistance of the CIA on this one.

Gage slapped at a mosquito and then jerked his head up at the sound of a whining engine.

Marco pushed off the car and took two steps toward the road.

A small, dark car hurtled across the asphalt toward

the gas station. Marco dropped his bottle. It bounced once and cracked, the soda fizzing onto the hot ground.

Adrenaline shot through Gage's body. He dropped his own bottle and crouched over, heading for Marco's car and his duffel bag stuffed in the front seat.

"Randi, get down!"

The approaching car slowed down and Marco swore. Gage yanked his bag from the car.

And the bullets started flying.

Chapter Five

Randi screamed. Something whizzed past her cheek and she dropped to the ground.

The screen door on the little wooden structure behind her banged open. The man they'd just paid stepped onto the porch, a shotgun clutched in his hands. He fired over her head.

Gasping, she clamped her hands to her ears and rolled to the side.

Guns were poking out from the windows of the black car that had been speeding down the roadway. Gage was crouched behind Marco's car, a weapon in his hand.

She couldn't see Marco.

Black smoke from the gunfire wafted through the air, and her nostrils twitched from the smell of the gun powder—so close. So familiar.

She screamed again. This time Gage's name formed from the scream.

"Stay down."

Another barrage of bullets crisscrossed the station. The man on the porch stumbled down the steps and fired off his shotgun again. He grunted and staggered.

From her position on the ground, head down, Randi could see the man's dusty work boots. They shuffled in the dirt and then the rest of him came into view as he dropped to his knees.

"Oh, my God. Gage!"

The man grunted and fell face forward.

Randi rolled out of his way, the dirt sticking to her face and invading her mouth.

She lifted her head in time to see the black car rolling down the road. The gunfire had ceased. Gage still crouched behind the open door of Marco's car, using it as a shield.

The black car rolled off the road and crashed into a tree.

A sob racked her body as she crawled toward Gage on her hands and knees. "Is it over?"

"I don't know, and I'm not approaching that car to find out. How's the guy on the porch?"

"I—I don't know. Marco?"

"Dead."

Her stomach lurched and she gagged.

Gage crawled toward her. "Get in the car, and keep your head down."

She pulled herself into the front passenger seat. From the open door on the driver's side, she could see the bottom half of Marco's legs. She wanted to close her eyes and block out the sight. Instead she trained her gaze on the car that had plowed into the tree.

Gage was still out there, and she'd have to warn him about any movement from that car.

A few minutes passed and he opened the door to the backseat and tossed in his duffel bag. Then he dropped onto the driver's seat and cranked on the car. Once. Twice.

Randi's heart stalled until the engine turned over.

They careened out of the gas station, leaving the

carnage behind them. Gage stepped on the accelerator as they flew past the black car, its passengers immobilized…or dead.

Finally, Randi closed her eyes but it couldn't wipe out the vision of the man on the porch falling into the dirt beside her. She knew his fate, but she asked, anyway.

"The proprietor?"

"Dead."

"What happened back there?" She clasped her clammy hands between her knees. "Was it us? Were the men in the black car after us?"

"I have no idea." He wiped his brow with his forearm. "How would Zendaris's guys know we had gotten into Marco's car?"

"Maybe Zendaris's flunkies sent Marco to pick us up. Maybe they just decided to get rid of Marco along the way."

His brows shot up as he turned toward her. "That's convoluted thinking."

"Why? Because everything else makes perfect sense? Think about it. We had to come out of that jungle somewhere. They sent Marco up and down the road to look for us."

"Why wouldn't they just order Marco to kill us?"

"Maybe Marco's not a killer. He couldn't do the job, so Zendaris sent his assassins to get it done."

Gage shook his head. "You may have lost your memory but not your imagination."

"Really? You think that scenario is so far off the mark?"

His lean jaw tightened. "No."

"Then my luck just keeps getting better and better." She slumped in her seat.

Gage trailed a knuckle across her cheek. "Are you

okay? You didn't get down when I first told you to. I was almost afraid to turn around and look at you."

"Wouldn't want to lose your star witness against Zendaris, would you?"

"Wouldn't want to lose you—Randi—woman of mystery." He flicked her earlobe.

Warmth flooded her limbs, which had been frozen with shock. They were just words—probably lies—but right now she needed those lies.

"I didn't get down at first because I was confused, in shock. I didn't know what was going on."

"I would've tackled you to the ground, but I had to get to my weapon. The first round of shots hit Marco, but I think he got the driver because the car lurched once."

"And the gas station owner happened to be in the wrong place at the wrong time."

"Looks like it. Poor SOB."

"Now what? How can we just take Marco's car? What if someone recognizes it in town? What if we get pulled over by the *polizia?*"

"We have to keep our fingers crossed. We'll ditch the car before we get into town."

"Keep our fingers crossed?" She rolled her eyes. "Do you do that a lot in your line of work?"

"Sometimes it's all we got."

After riding in silence for another twenty minutes, Randi bolted upright in her seat. "Look. It's another car coming."

"Well, it *is* a road."

She held her breath as the car passed them in the other direction. "Someone's going to find the carnage at the gas station."

"Yep."

"You don't seem very concerned." She folded her arms, pressing them against her stomach.

"There's nothing to connect us with what happened back there."

"Except this car with a few bullet holes in it."

"We're ditching the car in another five miles. That leaves a two-mile walk into town. We're still tourists who got lost."

"The police will find the car. Our fingerprints are all over it."

"I'll take care of it, Randi. Which reminds me— we're going to fingerprint you to see if a match comes up."

"Because you're so sure I'm some kind of criminal?"

"You don't have to be a criminal to have finger-prints on file. There are professions that require fin-gerprinting."

"Like teaching." She liked the sound of that.

Gage snorted. "Like some schoolteacher is going to run off with an international arms dealer."

Arms dealer? And here she figured Zendaris was a run-of-the-mill drug dealer.

She braced her feet against the floor of the car so hard she could've punched through the corroded metal. "And what type of woman *would* take up with an in-ternational arms dealer? A stripper? A hooker? Some junkie?"

He threw her a sharp glance. "I'm just saying, be prepared. You have no memory. You don't know what type of woman you were…are."

Tears flooded her eyes and she turned her head to look out the window, the greens and blues of the land-scape blurring together. She didn't feel like a bad per-son. What if everything Gage suspected was true? What if she was some gold-digging stripper who'd decided a man who dealt in death and destruction was a good choice for a lover as long as he could pay?

She didn't want to be that person. She didn't *feel* like that person. Once she regained her memories would it all come tumbling back to her? Would she fall back into the person she was? Would she and Gage truly become enemies?

Gage tapped the glass. "Up there. We're ditching the car there."

Seconds later he aimed the car onto the shoulder of the road where it stirred up dirt and gravel. He continued to drive into the foliage. Branches and sticks slapped the windshield. He nosed the car into a fallen tree trunk and cut the engine.

"Grab the backpack."

She yanked the backpack out of the backseat while Gage threw open the back door and retrieved his duffel. He pulled a T-shirt and a large, square cloth from the bag and tossed the cloth to her.

"Wipe down the dash, door handles, seat belt— whatever you could've touched."

Randi dropped the backpack on the spongy ground and started with the dash in the front seat.

When he finished wiping down his side of the car, Gage crammed the T-shirt back in his bag.

"There's one more thing I want to check before we hightail it out of here."

He shoved the key in the lock of the trunk, and then held up one hand. "Your rag."

She tossed it to him and he lifted the trunk, which squealed on rusty hinges. He poked around and then swore.

"Son of a…"

"What is it, a dead body?" Her shoes squelched against the wet leaves as she joined him on unsteady legs.

He gestured to a bag, not unlike his own, the top gaping open. Neat rows of plastic bags lined the duffel.

Randi's heart flipped and she staggered backward. "Drugs?"

"Coke."

"D-does that mean," she waved an arm behind her back, "all that at the gas station was meant for Marco and not us?"

"Maybe, maybe not. Just because Marco was carrying his own supply doesn't mean he wasn't working for Zendaris. My guess is Zendaris has his finger on the pulse of any drug activity in the area."

"When the police find this car and these drugs, they'll tie them to the mayhem at the gas station, won't they?"

"*If* they find the drugs." He hauled the bag out of the trunk.

"What are you doing?"

He fished a bag from the stack and held it up. "This has enormous value on the street—money to continue to fuel the drug empire down here. There's no guarantee the cops are going to confiscate this. I'm not going to risk this stuff getting on the street, into neighborhoods, fueling even more violence."

He grasped both ends of the duffel bag and hauled it out of the trunk. He lugged it to a small, stagnant pond and dumped it.

The bags of coke tumbled from their neat rows into the muddy water. Gage grabbed a long stick and poked at the bags until they sported holes. Then he skewered them and drove them to the bottom of the pond.

Fine, white powder floated on the water, and Gage stirred the mixture.

Randi spun around, one hand pressed against her stomach. What kind of life did she have? If this was her normal, she didn't care if she ever recovered her memories. She'd create a new life, a new normal.

"Let's get out of here."

"Not so fast. We can cover our tracks even more."

He bunched up the cloth and held a lighter to one corner. The flame flickered, and then gobbled up the material. Gage tossed it into the interior of the car. Black smoke poured from the open windows.

Taking her arm, he said, "Now let's get out of here."

An acrid scent overpowered the fresh air as Gage propelled her back toward the road.

"Is the car going to blow up? Will it set fire to all that vegetation?"

"If it reaches the gas tank it might blow, but I don't think it's going to set off a conflagration or anything. The jungle is wet. The fire's not going to get too far."

"I guess you're right." From the safety of the road, Randi eyed the smoke curling up from the interior.

They walked the rest of the way into town without incident, except for the number of cars they saw. One driver pulled over to offer them a ride, but they declined, having less than a mile to go.

The small town unfolded before them, one main street branching off into others, houses with corrugated tin roofs scattered up the hillside.

The locals gave them a wide berth, although questioning stares followed their progress through the town.

Gage held his phone in front of him. "Service."

"Thank God. Is someone going to get us out of here? Out of this country?"

He stopped and propped up the side of a building with his shoulder while he texted on his phone. "I'm sending out the SOS now."

"Will we have time to eat? I'm starving."

"Me, too." He shoved the phone back into his pocket.

Randi scanned the faces of the buildings lining the street. "I guess this isn't restaurant row or anything."

"Time to use that perfect Spanish you picked up... wherever you picked it up."

A couple with two young children crossed the street and Randi approached them. She asked about restaurants and they recommended a few places around the corner.

"One block up and two over. There are a couple of places still serving lunch."

"I could definitely use some *desayuno*."

"*Desayuno* is breakfast."

"Breakfast, lunch... I can eat anything about now."

They turned onto the street with the restaurants. People still eyed them, but shops and eateries commanded their attention more than two gringo strangers.

Settling on a café with a colorful awning in the front, they stepped inside the small dining area. A waitress balancing two platters of steaming food on one arm waved them to a cluster of empty tables.

They ordered a couple of beers and some fish with rice and red beans. The waitress placed a basket of arepa between them and a small pot of butter.

Gage picked up the bread and broke off a piece. "Do you know what this is?"

"Arepa. It's made from cornmeal."

He added a dab of butter to the piece he held between two fingers. "Now how do you suppose you know that?"

She sighed. "I've obviously lived in Colombia for some time."

"But you speak English without an accent, not even an English accent. You're American."

"Most likely." She broke off her own piece of arepa and slathered it with butter. "But my hair, eyes and skin are dark, so I'm probably Colombian, too."

"You probably are. He must've met you here."

She bit into the bread and the crumbly texture melted in her mouth. Dabbing her lips with a napkin, she said, "Yeah, I guess he found me in a Colombian strip club."

A muscle twitched in Gage's jaw. "That's your narrative, not mine."

"You told me to be prepared." She took a swig of beer from the bottle. "I'm preparing for the worst."

"You haven't—" he poked at some crumbs on the table "—remembered anything yet?"

She narrowed her eyes. "No. Do you think I'm holding out on you? Do you think I will hold out on you once I start remembering?"

"No. I think… I think we've shared too much. These kinds of experiences bring people together, form a bond."

She blinked and stuffed more bread into her mouth. Was he using some kind of psychological ploy on her? Once the U.S. government had her in its clutches, would Gage trade on their relationship to pump information out of her?

Her gaze darted to his face. He had a slight tilt to his head as if waiting for her confirmation about this unbreakable bond they shared because a few bad guys had shot at them—twice.

She shoved another piece of bread in her mouth and folded her hands on the table. She didn't want to confirm or deny anything. She had to look out for herself. She had a lot to lose.

The waitress slid their plates in front of them. The lemony smell of the fish mingled with the sweet aroma of the plantains that bordered the plate.

Gage plucked one of the fried bananas from his platter of food and popped it into his mouth. "Mmm, this I know. I love plantains."

"Since only one of us at this table has a story to tell, tell it." She picked up her knife and fork and sliced off the corner of her fish.

"You know plenty. I'm Gage Booker and I work for the United States government bringing down the bad guys."

"What branch of the government? You talk about the CIA as if it were another agency. Don't you work for the CIA?"

"Let's call it an offshoot."

"Let's call it some covert-ops group that isn't answerable to the normal chains of command." She pointed to the phone in his pocket. "Haven't they answered you yet?"

"Not yet. I received confirmation of my message. They'll come through."

"How'd you end up working for this...offshoot?"

"I started in military intelligence."

"Branch?"

"Army—Green Berets." He scooped up a forkful of red beans. "Who's interrogating whom, here?"

"Your turn will come soon enough. Where are you from? What motivated you to join the military?"

It was his turn to stuff his face. Chewing his food, he raised his eyes to the ceiling. "This is good."

"You're not going to tell me anything about yourself,

are you? Name, rank and serial number? That's it?" She stabbed a piece of fish. "What happened to this special bond we're supposed to share?"

"It's still there. I know nothing about you, and yet the past almost twenty-four hours have cemented our connection." He took a sip of beer, his eyes above the bottle kindling with warmth.

Don't get sucked in.

She shook her head. "A connection that's going to end as soon as you find out I'm Zendaris's stripper mistress."

He choked, and the beer dribbled out of the corner of his mouth. "Have you convinced yourself you're a stripper? Is this something else you have a strong feeling about?"

"Like you said, I'm preparing for the worst."

He wiped his chin with his napkin. "There are worse things than being a stripper."

"Yeah, like being a stripper involved with some scumbag arms dealer."

Gage's phone, which he'd placed on the table between them, vibrated. He swept it into his palm and cupped his hand, reading the display.

"The cavalry is coming to the rescue."

Randi didn't know whether to feel relieved or make a run for it. She settled for something in between. She scooted to the edge of her chair and took a small sip of beer. "Is someone coming to pick us up?"

"They're sending a helicopter tonight, or rather tomorrow morning—early."

"What time?"

"Around two a.m., just outside of town."

The front door of the restaurant burst open, and two men stumbled into the dining room babbling in loud voices. Randi caught every other word from their disjointed discourse.

And it didn't sound good.

"What's going on?" Gage pocketed his phone.

"What do you think?" She pushed her plate away and cupped her mouth with one hand. "The police found the bodies at the gas station."

"And the burned-out car?"

She put a finger to her lips and cocked her head. The men were heading for the kitchen, their voices receding.

"I can't tell." She picked at the soggy label on her beer bottle. "Should we be worried?"

Gage shrugged one broad shoulder. "There's no evidence to tie us to any of it."

"And if there were, would your friends be able to get us out of it—get you out of it?"

"It's not going to be an issue."

A police officer slid through the front door of the restaurant, and Randi held her breath and shot Gage a sideways glance.

"Don't worry about it." He gestured at the waitress for their bill.

"We're strangers. Won't that make them take a second look at us?"

"There's a lot of drug violence in this part of the country. That scene back there is not unusual."

"Then I can't wait to leave."

No matter what awaited her in Panama.

"We're going to get a hotel room, take a bath, get some sleep in a real bed." He tapped his head. "How are your various injuries?"

She blinked, still trying to reel back from the words *bath* and *bed*. "My shoulder is stiff from the bullet and my head throbs without the ibuprofen, and of course,

I still have no idea who I am. Other than that, I can't complain."

"You're a trouper, Randi."

The waitress slid their bill onto the table and leaned in to whisper in English. "Careful. Drug dealers. Violence."

She melted away, calling out to a table of customers.

"Well, at least our waitress doesn't suspect us." Gage snatched the bill from the table and withdrew some bills from his pocket.

"Do you want me to call her back and ask about a decent hotel for the night?"

"I saw one on our way in that should allow us to slip out in the middle of the night undetected."

"Lead the way."

They retraced their steps through the town, which still buzzed with activity. Maybe everyone had heard about the carnage by this time, and the excitement—or the fear—was keeping them on the streets.

Gage pointed to a hotel comprising a couple of buildings with the rooms facing a courtyard. They wouldn't have to sneak through a lobby at two in the morning to meet their ride.

She did the talking at the front desk and Gage paid in cash—for one room with one bed.

Gage jingled the key as they crossed the courtyard. "We can clean up and take a nap. I'll set the alarm on my phone so we don't miss our flight."

He shoved open the door and ushered her in first.

Randi's gaze tracked across the sparsely furnished room, stumbling over the bed with the colorful bedspread. "Are we going to have to walk far to meet up with the helicopter?"

"Not too far." He dropped his bag in the corner of

the room and twitched the curtain aside. "Why don't you take a bath first?"

She placed the backpack next to his bag and pushed open the bathroom door. A neat row of white towels hung next to the tub, which sported a couple of cracks.

"It looks clean enough," she called over her shoulder.

He came up behind her and she jumped.

"Nervous?"

"Oh, not at all."

"I think you can relax now."

"Easy for you to say. You know who you are."

He brushed a lock of hair from her cheek, his finger a whisper on her skin. "I'm beginning to see who you are, too."

She swallowed. "What do you see?"

"Someone brave and resilient."

"Are you still going to see that if you find out I'm in league with Zendaris?"

He dropped his hand and took a step back, the lines in his face forming a grimace.

If it turned out she belonged with Zendaris, Gage would do a one-eighty. He'd despise her then and do anything to break her.

She spun around and slammed the bathroom door in his face.

"Randi?" He smacked the door once.

She couldn't allow him to know how much his approval meant to her. Closing her eyes, she took a deep breath. "I'm going to take that bath now."

"Let me know if you need anything."

Like a new life? A new identity?

"Okay."

She fiddled with the handles until a stream of warm water coursed from the faucet. She shed her clothing, and then clutching the tiny bar of soap in one hand, she stepped into the rising water.

She lowered herself into the tub and lathered up her body. She ran her palm across the flesh wound in her shoulder, now just a scaly crease on her skin. A few inches lower and to the right and she'd be dead.

She reclined, knees bent, her feet braced against the end of the tub. The warm water lapped around her body and her eyelids drooped.

Even if Zendaris had claimed her once, he'd obviously left her for dead. She could make a new start. She'd work with Gage to bring him in.

Brave. Resilient.

A smile curved her lips as she drifted off.

She woke with a start, her heart slamming against her chest. Was that a yell or had she been dreaming?

A split second later, the bathroom door crashed open and two men locked in a deadly embrace fell to the floor.

This was no dream.

Chapter Six

Gage landed on top of the man as they hit the bathroom floor. Water sloshed over the side of the tub. "Stay where you are, Randi."

Driving a knee into the man's chest, Gage drew back his fist. If the guy made a move, Gage would bury his hand into his face.

The man didn't make a move. Blood trickled from the side of the attacker's head where it rested against the base of the toilet at an odd angle.

Gage slapped the man's face. His lids remained still, and his breathing remained steady.

"He's unconscious." He jerked his head up to take in Randi, frozen in the tub, her eyes huge and glassy. "Are you okay? Can you get me the rope out of my bag?"

She nodded and rose from the water while making a grab for the towel hanging on the rack.

He averted his gaze from her lithe, naked body.

She stepped from the tub and hopped over the extended legs of the unconscious man. Seconds later, she dangled the rope over his shoulder.

"Who is he? How'd he get in here?"

"Both really good questions." He rolled the man to his stomach and pinned his arms behind his back. "Can you help me with his legs?"

Randi crouched beside him, water still beading on her arms, the scent of lilacs on her skin.

The towel she'd hastily wrapped around her body slipped as she grabbed the stranger's ankles. Gage dropped his gaze to the rope and concentrated on hog-tying the man's hands and feet.

She yanked at the towel and sat on the edge of the tub, her bare toes curled into the linoleum. She repeated her questions. "Who is he and how'd he get into the room?"

"He walked right in. So either he had a key or he slipped the lock. And I don't have a clue who he is. We didn't have much time to chat, since he came at me with a knife."

"A-are we going to wait until he regains conscious-ness to find out who he is?"

Gage secured the knot and glanced over his shoulder. "I don't think we should hang around here."

"You think there might be more?"

"Maybe." He patted the man's pockets. "Get dressed and pack up the bags if you took anything out. And wedge a chair beneath the door just in case someone else has a key to this room."

Clutching the towel to her chest, she stepped over the intruder's body.

The man had nothing in his pockets, not even a key. How the hell had he gotten into the room? One minute Gage had been checking messages on his phone, the next he'd glanced up at the creak of the door to see a man flying across the room at him, leading with a knife. Their struggle had taken them right into the bathroom. Thank God Randi had been in the tub, out of the way.

Would she ever get a break? A chance to relax and

recuperate from her injuries? Would she get that chance in Panama?

The facility there belonged to the CIA, not Prospero. He would've preferred taking her to a Prospero installation, but they had nothing in the immediate area.

The CIA had been hard after Zendaris, too, so the agents in Panama would be salivating over Randi. That's what worried him.

Gage pushed to his feet and rolled the shoulder he'd driven into the man's chest. He shut the bathroom door behind him after locking it from the inside. Might as well make it harder for someone to get in there to discover him.

Randi had lodged one hard-back chair under the door handle, and Gage grabbed the other chair and wedged it beneath the handle of the bathroom door. Might as well make it harder for him to get out when he regained consciousness.

Randi had zipped up the duffel and the backpack and dropped them in the middle of the room. She pointed to the knife under the table. "I left that for you. Did you find anything on him?"

"Nope." Gage crouched and picked up the knife with a handkerchief. He opened the duffel and dropped it inside. "Might be interesting to see where his prints lead us."

"You're just going to leave him there?"

"Do you expect me to call the police and an ambulance?"

"I expected you to kill him."

"Whoa!" He straightened up, hitching the bag over his shoulder. "I don't need to be on Colombia's Most-Wanted list. He'll be otherwise engaged for a while."

"And us?" She slid the backpack onto her shoulders.

"Where will we be engaged until that chopper comes to pick us up?"

He smoothed the straps of the pack against her back. "I'm sorry. That wasn't much of a rest for you."

"Don't worry about me. Your concern for me almost got us killed."

"What does that mean?"

"If I hadn't been with you, would you really have checked into a motel to clean up and take a nap before the pickup?"

Busted. Heat rose from his chest, and he turned toward the door before it reached his face. "Maybe."

"Liar."

"You *are* with me, and you're injured." He eased open the door and peeked through the crack. Then he drew his gun from his holster. "This time if someone comes at us, it just might result in a dead body. If I start shooting, hit the deck."

"Got it."

He poked his head outside while reaching back and tucking Randi behind him. They slipped from the room into the silent courtyard where wet leaves glistened in the moonlight. They crept along the side of the building and stayed in the shadows.

Randi tugged on his sleeve. "You didn't tell me where we're going."

He put his lips close to her ear, inhaling the lilacs from her interrupted toilette. "You said you wanted me to treat you like any other agent, right?"

She nodded and strands of her hair clung to the scruff on his chin.

"Then let's head back into the wild."

They continued hugging the sides of buildings until

they crossed the road away from the town and back into the rain forest.

The tropical air hung heavy with moisture and the promise of showers. The sodden foliage squelched beneath their feet, and the smell of the ripe earth filled Gage's nostrils, blotting out every last lilac.

"Are we almost there?" Randi's whisper mingled with the faint breeze.

Gage glanced at the GPS on the phone he cupped in his palm. He'd tapped in the coordinates for the pickup location earlier, and the clearing for the chopper shined like a beacon about a hundred yards in front of them.

"Yeah. Almost there. There's a clearing where the chopper will land, but we'll stick to the trees until it's time. We still have a few hours. You should be able to catch a couple of winks before the pickup."

Near the edge of the clearing, Gage pocketed his phone and dropped the duffel bag. He pulled a tarp from the bag and shook it out.

Randi grabbed the opposite corners and they spread it out on the ground. He aimed a can of bug spray around the edge of the tarp.

"Wear this." He tossed a sweatshirt to Randi. "So you don't get eaten alive out here."

She pulled the sweatshirt over her head and sank to the tarp. "I think I prefer the insects out here to the human insects who won't leave us alone."

Gage dropped to the ground and scooted back against a tree trunk, stretching his legs in front of him. "Why don't you lie down?" He patted his thighs. "You can use me as a pillow if you like."

"That's okay." She rolled to her side, bringing her knees to her chest in a fetal position and curling one arm beneath her head.

Was she afraid he'd get distracted again and endanger their lives?

He rested his weapon beside him. "I'll keep watch."

She blinked her long lashes a few times and then closed her eyes. "Wake me up when the chopper gets here."

Sleep stole over her within minutes. Her breathing deepened and the worry smoothed from her face. At least she had faith in his abilities to keep them safe.

She was right. He'd been an idiot holing up in that motel room. He'd just wanted to give her a break. God knows she needed it, deserved it.

Deserved. Sucking in his cheek, he tapped his boots together. What exactly did Zendaris's mistress deserve?

He had to keep his head straight here. He and Randi weren't sharing some wild, exotic adventure together. He'd come to capture her boyfriend and had found her instead. Injured. Vulnerable. But she'd been in league with the bad guys.

He waged war with himself and his feelings for Randi over the next few hours as he kept watch. By the time the chopper's blades cut through the night air, Gage had given up trying to convince himself that Randi was just another witness.

He couldn't resist being drawn to her, and he had to admit that part of that attraction had to do with the fact that he could look into her eyes without wondering if she planned to use him for his money and family connections. But that didn't mean this attraction had to go any further. It would end at the CIA compound in Panama.

And this chopper signaled the beginning of the end.

"Hey." He nudged Randi's shoulder. "Our ride is here."

She mumbled in her sleep and he bent over her to catch the stray words. Would her dreams reveal her identity before her conscious mind?

Her words, slurred and nonsensical, dissipated in the muggy air. He wouldn't learn the truth about Randi from pillow talk.

"Wake up." He squeezed her shoulder again, and her long limbs unfurled.

"Is it time?"

"The helicopter is here. It should be landing in a minute." He held up his hand. "Wait until I give you a sign."

Crouching forward, he ventured into the clearing and spotted the chopper making its descent, its lights dimmed and its blades slowing down.

The CIA had sent one of its high-tech models—not quite a stealth helicopter but not some big, roaring machine, either.

Gage jogged back to Randi. "It's our guy. Help me pack up the tarp."

They rolled up their makeshift bed, and Gage stuffed it into the duffel.

"Are you ready?"

"As ready as I'll ever be."

He led her back to the clearing where the chopper had settled. They both bent forward and ran toward their ticket out of the rain forest.

Gage tossed his bag into the bird, disengaged the backpack from Randi's shoulders and helped her into the backseat. Once he'd climbed into the chopper and pulled the seat belt over his head, he glanced at the pilot.

Dave Cutler—CIA.

Gage had been hoping for one of his own. He'd been hoping for Deb Sinclair—navy pilot turned first female Prospero agent.

He swallowed and grabbed the headphones hanging from the instrument panel in front of him. "You stationed in Panama now?"

"I don't get any thanks for saving your ass, Booker?" He jerked his thumb over his shoulder. "And that very fine ass in the back?"

So that's the treatment the company planned to dish out to Randi. A muscle ticked in Gage's jaw.

"Yeah, thanks. And that *woman* in the back is an injured Prospero witness."

"You Prospero boys don't have exclusive domain over Zendaris." Cutler flipped some switches and the chopper lifted at an angle. "You had your chance. Stark lost those anti-drone plans, J.D. couldn't find them and your tip on Zendaris was a bust."

"Stark is the one who discovered Zendaris had those anti-drone plans in the first place and J.D. got closer to Zendaris than anyone has in years."

"Not as close as Zendaris's girlfriend got."

"You know she has amnesia, right?" Gage twisted his head around and flashed a smile at Randi, grateful she didn't have a pair of headphones and couldn't hear one word he'd exchanged with Cutler since they'd climbed into the helicopter.

"I know she *says* she has amnesia."

"Trust me. Randi doesn't remember who she is or what she was doing at the Zendaris compound."

"We know what she was doing at the Zendaris compound with Zendaris. You're going to believe a woman like that? She's pulling one over on you, Booker." He snorted. "How does she know her name is Randi if she has no memory?"

"We found something addressed to her at the house.

First name only. No passport, no ID." Gage pressed his lips together. He didn't owe Cutler any explanations.

Cutler worked in the black-ops division of the CIA, but more in the capacity of shuttle driver than agent or analyst. He got agents in and out of hot spots. Helluva pilot but a crappy human being.

Folding his arms, Gage closed his eyes.

Cutler's taunting voice floated over the headphones. "Whatever, dude. You might've been taken in by that face and body, and I can't say I blame you, but our guys will get the truth out of her—one way or another."

Gage bunched his fists against his biceps. He'd have no authority over what happened to Randi once they got to Panama. Cutler was right about one thing—the CIA had set its sights on nailing Zendaris just as much as Prospero had. And that compound in Panama would be crawling with company men and women, outnumbering Gage and any objectives he had.

He'd do his best to stand up for Randi. Someone had to.

They skimmed unmolested through Colombian airspace on their way north. The Colombian government had struck a number of deals with the U.S. government and the CIA and FBI in particular, in an attempt to curtail their drug trade. Gage assumed those secret handshakes allowed for air traffic in and out of the country. And he *was* grateful for that.

The tap on his shoulder made him jump. Randi had scooted forward in her seat, leaning toward him.

Slipping his headphones around his neck, he tipped his head toward her.

She cupped a hand around her mouth and her lips almost touched his ear. "Everything okay?"

He nodded.

Her dark eyes shifted to Cutler and then back to his. "Is he taking us to Panama?"

Gage nodded again. She must've sensed the tension between him and Cutler, even if she hadn't heard their conversation.

He pressed a finger against her jaw to turn her head. Then he whispered in her ear, "We're almost there. It's going to be okay."

She gave him a wobbly smile and slumped back into her seat.

Sooner than Gage expected or wanted, Cutler began his descent over a cluster of three or four buildings in the middle of a clearing in the jungle.

"Home, sweet home." Cutler smirked at Gage in a way that gave him a strong desire to punch him in the face.

The chopper settled on a landing pad, and Gage pushed open the door. He jumped out and took Randi's arm. "Careful."

When she was standing beside him, Gage pulled the bags from the back and slung them across his body. Then they both ducked and jogged toward the nearest building.

A man with military bearing and close-cropped silver hair met them at the entrance, barring their way. "You're Booker. I recognize you from our intelligence file. I met your father a few times, too. I'm Lawrence Jessup."

If he expected any recognition from Gage, he'd be disappointed. Gage's father had stopped discussing issues with Gage once he understood his son's contempt for the way he did business.

"Sir." Gage shook his hand and then gestured to Randi. "This is…"

"Zendaris's whore."

Randi stumbled back as if slapped, and Gage instinctively curled an arm around her waist.

"Sir, this is Randi, my witness, and she needs immediate medical attention. I'm not absolutely sure what role she played at Zendaris's compound. I do know they left her for dead, and she wants to do whatever she can to help us."

Jessup's hard eyes raked Randi's form, and she shrank against Gage's side.

"We'll find out what role she played there, but you're right. She needs to see the doctor first."

"I'll take her. Where do we go?"

Pointing to the left, Jessup said, "The doc's in that building."

With his hand on the small of her back, Gage steered Randi toward the two-story building Jessup had indicated.

When they moved out of the man's orbit, Randi gripped his arm. "He has me tried and convicted, doesn't he? What are they going to do to me here?"

"They just want to get to the truth, Randi, but I'll make sure you're not harmed."

"These aren't your people, are they?" She swept an arm behind her. "That guy in the helicopter, that hardass back there... You don't work with them, do you?"

"They're CIA."

"And you're not."

"I told you. We're an offshoot, but the CIA is not our parent organization."

"So they can't tell you what to do?"

"Exactly." Well, not exactly, but he didn't want to spook her. Lawrence Jessup had already done a good job of that.

Gage pushed against the door to the medical building, but it wouldn't budge. Backing up, he tilted his head and waved at the camera. The door clicked and he shoved it open.

Jessup must've already contacted security in this building, notifying them of their arrival.

They stepped into the hallway and the antiseptic smells of a lab assaulted his nose. This facility looked and smelled more suspicious than a simple medical facility. What kind of work were they doing out here?

Randi's feet shuffled on the floor. "Which way do we go?"

A voice from a speaker droned, "Medical office is down the hall. Take your first right."

Gage looked at the ceiling. "Thanks."

Randi huddled against him as their shoes scuffed down the shiny linoleum. "I don't like this place."

He didn't like it, either.

He shrugged. "I don't like hospitals. That's what this reminds me of."

They turned right into a short corridor with restrooms on the right and two windowed doors on the left. Gage twisted the handle of one and nudged it open with his hip.

A couple of chairs functioned as a waiting room with a window into an area with a couple of cots and scales and blood-pressure cuffs.

A female voice called from the back. "Gage and Randi? I'm expecting you. Give me a minute."

In just about a minute, a short woman in a white lab coat bustled into the waiting room, running her hands through her fluffy blond hair—making it fluffier.

"I'm Doctor Murdoch." She squeezed Gage's hand

in a firm grip, and then turned to Randi. "And this is Randi, our patient?"

"Sure, I'll be your patient. Beats being a whore."

Dr. Murdoch smiled and cocked her head, looking like a bird with blond feathers.

"Never mind." Randi stuck out her hand. "Nice to meet you. Are you a medical doctor or a psychiatrist? Because I need both."

"I'm the psychiatrist. Dr. Coolidge will be here shortly to examine your injuries."

"And you're going to examine my head?"

"I'm going to help you regain your memory." Dr. Murdoch patted Randi's arm.

The outer door burst open, and another white coat charged into the room. The man jerked his head up and reached for the glasses perched on his thinning gray hair.

"Is this the patient?"

"That's me." Randi waved.

"I'm Dr. Coolidge." He joined them in the examination room, and didn't seem interested in further introductions. "Do you mind leaving us, Dr. Murdoch?"

The psychiatrist ducked her head. "Not at all. Send Randi over to my area when you're done, and make sure you do a thorough examination. I'll want your report."

She patted Randi's arm again before she left them with the gruff doctor.

"All I got was a summary on this damned thing." He held up a smartphone before stuffing it into the pocket of his lab coat. "So tell me face-to-face what happened and the nature of your injuries. I know you have memory loss. I'm more interested in the head injury that caused it. I'll leave the rest of it to that quack, Dr. Murdoch."

Gage recited the details of Randi's injuries and what the medic at the Zendaris compound had done to treat her before they took off.

Then Randi took over and described how she felt, her level of pain and how often she needed medication.

Dr. Coolidge listened while scribbling. "You have some injuries, too, Mr. Booker?"

"Me? No. Just what you'd expect from a few nights in the rain forest."

"Bug bites?"

"A couple."

"I'll have a look at those and give you some cream." He turned toward the sink and cranked on the water. "Miss…Randi, please undress completely and slip into one of those gowns on the shelf. You can use the restroom and leave your clothes in there. While you're in there, pee in a cup."

"Is that necessary, Dr. Coolidge?" Gage grabbed a gown for Randi and handed it to her.

He tapped his pen against his clipboard. "I have my orders."

"Blood tests, too?"

"Yes." Dr. Coolidge finished washing his hands and yanked a couple of paper towels out of the dispenser to dry them.

"What kinds of tests are you running on her? Pregnancy test?" Gage gritted his teeth.

Dr. Coolidge peered at the clipboard he'd slapped down on the counter. "Yes."

Randi sucked in a breath and almost dropped the gown.

"I have my orders." Dr. Coolidge pushed past Gage to enter another room.

"I'll be right here." Gage took her hand and squeezed her stiff fingers.

Randi's dark eyes took up half the white oval of her face. "I didn't even think... I didn't..."

"I'm sure you're not pregnant. Just get through this part. Coolidge will make sure none of your wounds are infected, and then we can work on your memory."

She gave a half smile and then shuffled into the bathroom.

Dr. Coolidge returned to the examination room with a tube of ointment. "For your bug bites. Not allergic to anything, are you? Nothing festering?"

Just his anger at what Randi had to endure here.

"I'm fine. Are you sure you don't want me to disrobe so you can poke and prod me, too?"

The doctor's shaggy, gray brows shot up. "Only if you want me to."

"I'm going to wait on the other side of this window, if that's okay with you."

"Okay by me."

Randi emerged from the bathroom with the blue gown hanging shapelessly around her body, clutching a clear plastic cup with yellow liquid.

She held up her urine sample. "What do you want me to do with this?"

"You can put it on that plastic tray. No need to label it. You're my only patient today.

"Hop up on the table. Agent Booker is going to be in the waiting room. Do you want me to close off the window between the examination room and the waiting room?"

"No."

Gage tossed his tube of ointment in the air and sauntered to the waiting room. He pulled one of the chairs around to face the window into the examination room.

Dr. Coolidge performed the basics—blood pressure, ear, nose and throat, reflexes. He listened to Randi's heart and lungs through his stethoscope, and then examined her wounds, cleaned and re-dressed them.

He had her recline on the table and checked her ankles and pressed on her abdomen. He seemed satisfied.

"You can sit up now, Randi. I'm going to take some of your blood and then you're free to go, or rather, free to see the shrink."

Gage called from the other room. "Everything look okay, Doc?"

"That army medic did a good job. Her physical injuries are minor, and everything else seems fine."

As Dr. Coolidge withdrew the needle from Randi's arm, the door to the clinic swung open.

Dr. Murdoch poked her head into the room holding a foam cup in one hand. "Almost done in here? I'd like to get started. I didn't get up this early for nothing."

"Hold your horses, Murdoch. I'm done." He had Randi hold a cotton ball against her inner arm while he stuck a Band-Aid over it.

Randi hopped off the table and turned toward the bathroom.

"I got you some coffee." Dr. Murdoch handed the cup to Gage and then bustled into the examination room. "You can come with me, dear."

"My clothes are in the bathroom."

"Those filthy things?" Dr. Murdoch brushed her hands together. "I'd like to get started and then you can have a nice shower, and we'll have some clean clothes waiting for you. Sound good?"

Randi glanced back at the bathroom door and nodded. "I guess so."

Dr. Murdoch ushered Randi through the waiting room with an arm curled through hers, like they were besties.

After the blunt manner of Dr. Coolidge, Randi seemed to relax a little, and Gage expelled a long breath and took a sip of the strong Panamanian coffee.

He opened the door for the women. "I'm coming with you."

"That's fine, but I'd like to get to know Randi one-on-one. You can sit in on some of the later sessions if you like, Agent Booker."

Dr. Murdoch guided Randi down a short hallway and turned into another room with a similar setup to the clinic. They entered a small waiting room, but this one didn't have a window to the back rooms.

Gage hesitated next to one of the chairs as Dr. Murdoch led Randi to the second door. A sudden chill gripped the back of his neck. "Are you good, Randi? Do you want me to come with you?"

"I'm fine. Maybe the next time I see you, I'll know who I am."

The door closed behind them, and Gage dropped into the chair clutching his coffee cup. He fished out his cell phone to send a message to Prospero that they'd landed at the CIA bunker in Panama, but he couldn't get any reception—probably the thick walls.

He pulled a book from the side pocket of his bag and skimmed the pages, glancing up every few minutes at the closed door. He had to start over since he didn't have a clue what he'd just read.

After several more minutes he gave up and dropped the book. He tried his phone again—no luck.

He pushed up from the chair and paced the room, downing the rest of the coffee. He picked up a magazine, thumbed through it and tossed it aside.

He opened the outer door and peered into the deserted hallway. Too early for many people to be up and about.

He sat in his chair and tilted his head back. His eyelids drooped and he gave in to the lethargy stealing over his body like a warm blanket. Maybe the next time he saw Randi, she'd be someone else. Someone free.

His head jerked up. Blinking, he wiped his mouth with the back of his hand. How long had he been sleeping? He rubbed his eyes, and the closed door came into focus. They weren't done yet?

He checked his watch and his stomach lurched. Two hours—Randi had been in there with Dr. Murdoch for over two hours. What could be taking that long? Dr. Murdoch had assured them she just wanted to get started and then Randi could shower, put on some clean clothes, eat and sleep.

Maybe she'd already done those things and they'd left him here conked out in the chair.

He rose and stretched, running his tongue along the inside of his dry mouth. He prowled toward the door to the inner sanctum of the office and pressed his ear against it. He rapped his knuckles against the wood. Silence.

With his pulse racing, he grabbed the handle of the door and tried to twist it. It wouldn't budge. They'd locked him out.

He banged his fist against the door and shouted, "What's going on in there? Randi?"

He took two steps back and barreled into the door,

shoulder first. It shook beneath his weight. He tried again, this time leading with his right boot.

He managed to splinter the wood. Punching his fist against the cracked wood, he widened the hole in the door and reached in to unlock the handle.

He stumbled into the empty room and almost fell across a chair. A small couch faced the chair, and another closed door mocked him.

He charged toward that door and stopped abruptly when it swung open.

"What is going on out here?" Dr. Murdoch's feathers were ruffled.

"What's going on in there? Where's Randi? Why have you had her for so long?"

Dr. Murdoch clicked her tongue and steepled her fingers. "You didn't really think we'd let Prospero take charge of Nico Zendaris's whore, did you, Agent Booker? Randi's ours now."

Chapter Seven

Randi smacked her lips as her head rolled to the side. Had they stuffed her mouth with cotton? She tried to run her tongue along her teeth, but it cleaved to the roof of her mouth instead.

Fog rolled through her brain. She wanted to rub her eyes to clear the fog, but she couldn't lift her hand. It felt like lead. She curled her fingers and jerked her arm.

The restraint dug into her wrist. She couldn't lift her hand because her arm was secured to the table. She wiggled her toes and tried to draw her knee to her body. The restraint dug into her ankle.

She screamed but a choked gurgle was all she heard.

Gage. She needed Gage. But he'd brought her here. He delivered her to these maniacs.

As soon as Dr. Murdoch had gotten her alone, the friendly, fluffy psychiatrist had disappeared. She'd led Randi to a second room off that first one and sat her down at a table, taking the seat across from her.

She'd asked Randi a hundred questions about Nico Zendaris, obviously not believing she had amnesia. After Randi's hundredth assertion that she didn't remember anything about Zendaris or what she'd been doing at the compound, Dr. Murdoch had slapped her hard across the face.

When she'd jumped up from the chair, a man burst into the room pinching a hypodermic needle between his fingers.

Now this.

Randi tilted her chin to her chest and gasped at her nakedness. They'd taken away her hospital robe. What else had they done to her?

The sound of tapping heels drew closer, and Randi strained against her bindings. These people could do anything they wanted to her. What recourse did she have? She didn't even know if she had family to call on. Jessica was in Houston. Who knows where her grandmother was? What good would it do her, anyway? Her own government had turned against her.

And Gage. Had Gage turned against her, too? Had he been playing her from the get-go?

The door swung open and Dr. Murdoch's chattering filled the room. Was the woman even a doctor? More likely a mad scientist.

The man who had greeted them off the helicopter, Lawrence Jessup, came close on Dr. Murdoch's heels.

Randi cringed and tried to sink into the table to hide her nakedness. Jessup didn't even seem to notice. In fact, neither one of them even glanced at her as they walked into the room.

Randi coughed and jerked her limbs to show them she was awake and conscious. Alive. They still ignored her.

Dr. Murdoch presented a clipboard to Jessup, stabbing the paper on top with her finger. "We should go with the truth serum first."

Jessup grunted. "Does that stuff really work? It's just a bunch of babbling. We might not get anything useful out of it."

Randi cleared her throat. "Why are you doing this? I'll help you. I promise I'll help you once I regain my memory."

Dr. Murdoch clicked her tongue. "And what do you propose? We have some leeway here, but the girl is an American citizen."

"Is she? She's a criminal with known associations to an arms dealer, the biggest arms dealer in the world and a scourge on society. We have a lot of leeway here."

Fear sent a rush of adrenaline coursing through her body, which morphed to anger—white-hot rage. She bucked against her restraints and yelled. "Let me go! Get me outta here!"

Dr. Murdoch reached over and almost casually delivered another stinging slap to Randi's cheek. "Shut up or we'll add a gag. Or—" she leaned over Randi until the badge around her neck scraped Randi's breastbone "—you can start talking right now and tell us all about Zendaris."

Tears had sprung to Randi's eyes when Dr. Murdoch's hand had made contact, but she wouldn't give these two the satisfaction of spilling tears. "I told you before. I lost my memory in the fall, but I don't think I'm Zendaris's girlfriend. Ask Gage. Gage believes me."

Did he? If so, where was he? Why was he allowing these people to torment her?

Jessup joined Dr. Murdoch at the table, and his frosty blue eyes drilled into her skull. "You don't belong to Prospero. You're our property now."

She didn't know or care what Prospero was, but she didn't belong to anyone. "I'm not property. I'm a human being and an American citizen, and when I get out of this there's going to be hell to pay."

Jessup loomed above her and spittle formed at the

corners of his mouth. "Are you making terrorist threats against the United States government? Do you think you're going to get your sleazy boyfriend to come after us?"

Terrorist threats? "I'm telling you, I don't have a sleazy boyfriend. If you would just help me regain my memory, I could help you."

She had no intention of helping the CIA anymore, if that's who these people really were. She'd help Gage… or maybe not.

Jessup wiped a hand across his mouth and turned his back on Randi. "I think we can use her to bring him in."

"How are we going to do that? He left her for dead according to Agent Booker. Though I don't know how much we can trust him."

"Use your head, Helen. Isn't Dr. Coolidge running a pregnancy test?"

"He is. You think if she's pregnant, we can use that to lure him out?"

"Exactly."

Randi's stomach rolled. These people were insane.

"But what are the chances of a pregnancy? That would be a stroke of luck, but too much to hope for."

"Who says there actually has to be a pregnancy? Do you have a problem lying to Zendaris?"

Dr. Murdoch shoved her glasses into her fluffy hair and pinched the bridge of her nose. "Zendaris didn't get to his position by being an idiot or naive. He'll require some proof."

"She's here. She's under our control. We can always make sure she's pregnant even if she's not in that happy state right now."

Randi choked and thrashed her head from side to

side. They would actually go that far? They'd use her body as some kind of weapon against Zendaris?

They'd hit her, drugged her and tied her to a table. Why would they have any problem implanting an embryo in her womb?

She screamed again from pure frustration.

Dr. Murdoch snatched a handkerchief from the pocket of her lab coat and stuffed it into Randi's mouth. "Do you want to go under again? Because I'd be happy to oblige, and I have a syringe in my pocket that will do the trick."

Randi gagged on the cloth that smelled of oranges.

"Where is Dr. Coolidge with those lab results? Is he even on board here?" Jessup paced the length of the room and hit the door with his fist.

"He's not on board. He does what he's told but never given any explanations. We can't risk it. That's why I don't want to make a big deal out of getting the results of the pregnancy test. The lab is testing her blood and urine for all sorts of things. If we show particular interest in the HCG results, Dr. Coolidge might get suspicious."

"Who cares if he does? You just said he does what he's told."

"Within reason, Larry. He very well might balk at being ordered to artificially inseminate an unwilling patient."

"Even if it's a matter of national security?"

"Coolidge might be persuaded, but let's just keep this between us for the time being. What are you doing about Booker? The tranquilizer I slipped him in his coffee will be wearing off soon if it already hasn't. He's one fine specimen. I should've given him a larger dose."

Randi's heart skipped a beat. If they'd had to sedate Gage, maybe that meant he was still on her side.

Jessup scratched his clean-shaven chin. "He's another matter. It's one thing to play fast and loose with a terrorist associate but quite another to harm a Prospero agent. The director won't want to sever ties with Jack Coburn. Prospero is too valuable to us."

"Then what are we going to tell him?"

"We'll tell him Dr. Coolidge found something in her lab results that required immediate airlifting to a hospital in the United States. We'll tell him she's no longer here."

"He's not going to believe that. He was hovering over her like she was some jewel in the crown."

"What choice does he have? He'll never find her down here."

"So we wait for the lab results and if she's positive, we get the word out to Zendaris that we have his baby hostage. And if she's negative…?"

Jessup patted the side of Randi's bare hip. "Then we make her positive."

Randi twisted her body to get away from Jessup's touch as her gut knotted.

This was really happening. They were going to force a pregnancy on her by way of some unknown sperm donor.

But Gage didn't know. They'd kept Gage in the dark. And that gave her hope.

Dr. Murdoch pulled the gag from Randi's mouth and got in her face. "Ready to talk yet? Because this is going down. If you're not already carrying Zendaris's spawn, you'll soon be carrying someone's. And we're a patient bunch. We'll keep you here for nine long months and fatten you up until you're nice and ripe, and then we'll lure that scum out of hiding."

"Even if I knew Zendaris's exact location, his birth date, his social security number and his mother's maiden name, I wouldn't give you one piece of information. You're no better than he is." Randi mustered what saliva she had in her dry mouth and spit in the bitch's face.

This earned her another slap, accompanied by a short bark of laughter. "I knew it. You never were going to give him up, even though he left you behind like a piece of trash."

Cocking her head, Dr. Murdoch stepped back and crossed her arms. "You should be thanking me, Randi. I'm more benevolent than Jessup. If he had his way, he'd do more than have you impregnated. As long as I'm here you'll be one very pampered mother-to-be."

Dr. Murdoch picked up her clipboard. "I'll send in an attendant with some food, and you can have bathroom privileges, but no clothing. If you happen to escape, which will be next to impossible, we want you to…uh…stand out."

"No." Jessup barred the door. "Not yet. She stays like this until we get Agent Booker off the compound. If it takes more than a day, because he's a stubborn SOB, she can have water and maybe some liquid food and a bedpan. I want her secured."

Dr. Murdoch bobbed her head and they exited the room, locking the door behind them.

A sob bubbled from Randi's throat, and the tears she'd been holding in check leaked from her eyes and ran into her ears.

Once they sent Gage away, she didn't stand a chance. They'd impregnate her, because she knew damn well she wasn't carrying Zendaris's or anyone else's baby, and imprison her for the duration of her pregnancy.

And then what? What if their plan to lure Zendaris out of hiding didn't work? What if it did work and they took him into custody? What would happen to her? What would happen to the baby?

She'd not only lost her memory, she'd slipped into some alternate universe peopled by Dr. Frankensteins with crazy schemes. How could this happen to a citizen of the United States? She'd done nothing wrong. Even if she was Zendaris's mistress, which she still doubted, they had no right to take control of her body and hold her captive for nine months.

She had one hope and one hope only.

GAGE'S MUSCLES ACHED as he crouched behind the cabinet in the dispensary. Finally, the door to the outer office opened and someone shuffled through the waiting room whistling a tuneless song.

It sure didn't sound like Dr. Murdoch.

Gage held his breath, tensing his body. He peered around the corner of the cabinet as Dr. Coolidge walked into the examination room.

Gage sprang at him and backed him into the bathroom where Randi had folded her dirty clothes in a neat pile. With his arm across the doctor's throat, Gage shoved him against the wall and kicked the door shut.

"Spill. Where did they take her?"

Dr. Coolidge croaked. "Who?"

"The bloody queen. Who do you think?"

"I don't know." The doctor clawed at Gage's arm. "Let up. I'm not the enemy."

Gage hadn't believed the enemy would be at a CIA compound in Panama, either. He'd been wrong.

He let up on the doctor's throat. "What do you know?"

"I got her chart from Dr. Murdoch. She's a quack, that one. The orders were on the chart—physical and blood and urine. That's all I did. You watched me."

"Did you send her samples to the lab yet? What were you ordered to test for?"

"Standard stuff—blood count, anemia, diabetes, HIV."

"Pregnancy."

"Asked and answered. I had instructions to test her blood for HCG, the pregnancy hormone. That's not uncommon, you know. If it turned out I had to prescribe any medication, I'd need to know if she were pregnant."

"And is she?"

Dr. Coolidge hunched his shoulders, his gaze darting over Gage's shoulder toward the closed door. "I don't have the lab results back yet."

"For the pregnancy test? Doesn't that take less than an hour?"

"For any of it. I don't have any results back yet."

Gage narrowed his eyes, and the blood drained from Dr. Coolidge's face.

"But you did get the results back and you found something serious, serious enough to have Randi airlifted to the States."

"Oh." Coolidge's eye twitched. "That was Murdoch. She got the results. I didn't see them. She must've found something."

Gage leaned in, increasing the pressure on the good doctor's windpipe. "You're lying."

"Wait." His eyes bugged out. "Wait. I wasn't lying at first. I didn't get all the results. Nobody said they were in a hurry until…"

"Until what?"

"Until Jessup came by about thirty minutes ago asking for one of the results."

"Which one?" Gage's heart thudded against his rib cage so hard he felt his teeth rattle.

"The pregnancy test."

"And?"

"Negative."

Gage started breathing again. At least Randi would be spared the misery of carrying the child of some man she didn't even remember, some man on every country's most-wanted list.

"What was Jessup's reaction to that?"

"Asked how accurate it was and how early the blood test would detect a pregnancy."

"Well?"

"A blood test is about ninety-seven percent accurate, and HCG can show in the blood about twelve days after conception."

"What did Jessup do with that info?"

"Told me he wanted her tested again in a few weeks."

Gage rubbed the stubble on his chin. "Is Randi still here? Dr. Murdoch lied to me about the test results. She lied to make me think Randi was no longer here. If Jessup wants you to give her another pregnancy test in a few weeks, she must still be here. They want me out of the way."

"That Murdoch woman works closely with Jessup. When suspects come through here, I do the physicals and treat their ailments but after that, who knows?"

"Why'd you call Murdoch a quack? Isn't she a real doctor?"

Dr. Coolidge rubbed the red welts on his neck. "Oh, she's a real doctor, all right. A mad scientist."

"What does that mean?"

"She has her own lab here." Dr. Coolidge looked both ways. "She doesn't think I know about it, but I do. I've seen some reports out of that lab."

"Are you talking about some kind of biological warfare?"

"It's more personal than that—mind-altering drugs, genetic work. She collects DNA samples from everyone—hair, blood, sperm."

"Sperm?"

"I don't even want to know what she has in her freezers and test tubes. The woman scares me."

A cold dread had been sliding across Gage's flesh as Dr. Coolidge talked about Murdoch. This woman had gotten Randi in her clutches. What had she done with her? And why the interest in whether or not she was pregnant?

He could understand the value of having access to Zendaris's unborn child, but Randi wasn't pregnant.

At least not now.

He dug his fingers into Dr. Coolidge's shoulder. "Where is this lab? Where does Dr. Murdoch conduct this research?"

"It's in the third building, the one behind this one. But you'll never get in there. It's guarded."

"Do you have an access card?"

Dr. Coolidge held up his hands. "Not me. She doesn't let me near her so-called work."

"Who gets in there?"

"Lab rats. Attendants. They keep prisoners there sometimes and there are attendants, jailers really, who look after them."

Prisoners like Randi?

"I need to get into that building, Dr. Coolidge, and you're going to help me."

"Aren't they following you around to make sure you make it off the compound?"

"They think I'm sound asleep, courtesy of one of Dr. Murdoch's potions. I figured I fell asleep too quickly and soundly the first time she offered me refreshment. So I pretended to accept the next offering with dinner and spit it out the first chance I got."

"I wouldn't take anything from that woman. You might fall asleep a man and wake up a woman."

"Has one of these attendants or lab rats come in for an appointment lately?"

"Sure, they all do." He pointed to the bathroom door. "May I?"

Gage moved aside and Dr. Coolidge left the bathroom and crossed the hall to a small office. He sat down at the computer and clicked the keyboard.

"Here's one. Dominic Cromwell. Had a bad case of stomach upset—some intestinal parasite."

"Is there any reason for him to come back in here?"

"Sure. I need to give him another dose of medication."

"Do it."

After making other arrangements for their escape, Gage returned to the medical building. He hid in the supply closet as Dr. Coolidge's patient returned for his late-night appointment to pick up his vital medication, but instead of intestinal medication, he got sedated. Gage lifted Cromwell's badge, but Dr. Coolidge wouldn't let him take the man's coveralls.

"If he wakes up stark naked, I'll have a lot of explaining to do."

"You need to get out of this facility, Doc, because by

the time I'm done with the people who run this freak show, there are going to be some indictments coming down."

"I'll take it under advisement. Now go find that poor woman."

Gage did borrow a lab coat from Dr. Coolidge and slipped it on as he exited through the back door of the medical building, Dominic Cromwell's badge hanging around his neck.

He knew the place had to have cameras all over, but if Jessup and Dr. Murdoch hoped to keep their secret lab under wraps, they probably wouldn't want any video record of the so-called patients they took in and out of the lab.

Gage pulled a cap low on his forehead and shoved his hands in the pockets of the coat, clutching his weapon in one hand and a syringe in the other. With his head down he approached the two-story tan stucco building.

A red light on the card reader outside the front door blinked at him. He swiped Cromwell's card and the door clicked. He pushed it open and a security guard greeted him.

"Who are you?" The security guard stepped back and squinted at the badge around Gage's neck.

Since Gage looked nothing like Dominic Cromwell, he did the only thing he could do. He lifted the badge with his right hand toward the guard's face, while bringing the syringe out of his pocket with the left.

While the guard focused on the badge, Gage raised the needle and plunged it into his neck. He caught the guard as he slumped and grabbed him under the arms. He dragged him to the nearest door, which opened into an office, and left him.

He had to work fast. Once someone found the security guard, the alarm bells would go off. Gage poked his head back into the entryway, which remained empty.

He couldn't just waltz down to the basement and start checking rooms. If he could see into the rooms down there first that would be safer and quicker.

On his way to the staircase, he passed one person who barely nodded at him over his coffee cup. Gage jogged down the single flight of stairs and then slipped into the first room on the floor.

When he heard a whir and a click, Gage ducked, but the whirring and clicking continued and he realized lab equipment, computers and refrigerators were generating the noise. He'd like to smash everything to bits in here before he left. Obviously Prospero and probably the rest of the CIA had no idea what was going on out here.

Gage looked up and spotted his chance. He wheeled a cabinet into the corner, climbed on top and pushed up a square of the soundproofed ceiling. He hoisted himself into the crawl space and pulled the ceiling piece back into place.

It wouldn't help if he fell through the ceiling, so he crawled along the supporting frame on the edge of the space. Every ten feet or so, he lifted a portion of the ceiling to peer into the room below.

A couple of times he discovered people in the rooms, but they were lab workers. No Dr. Murdoch. No Jessup. No Randi.

Until he turned the corner.

His blood boiled at the sight below him, and it took every ounce of self-control he possessed not to drop into the room immediately. The creeps had tied Randi to a hospital bed. They'd taken away even the flimsy gown, leaving her naked and exposed.

She had her eyes closed, her head turned to the side.

Gage shifted the ceiling square to the side and put his face up to the opening. "Psst. Randi."

Her head jerked forward, her eyes darting to the door.

"It's Gage. Up here."

Her eyes widened and she pulled against her restraints.

Gage ground his teeth together. "Is anyone outside? Is anyone coming?"

She rolled her head from side to side.

That's all he needed. Gage shoved the panel out of the way and lowered himself into the room. He pulled his knife from the holster tucked into his boot and sliced through the nylon cords that bound her wrists and ankles to the bed.

She immediately rubbed her wrists, and then put her finger to her lips.

Gage whipped off the lab coat and held it open for her as she inched off the bed. When she'd stuffed her arms in the sleeves, he wrapped his arms around her chilled body. Then he pointed upward.

She nodded.

Luckily the bed was close enough to the panel he'd moved to enter the room. Gage climbed onto the bed and held out his hand to help Randi up beside him. When she stood next to him, he crouched before her encircling her just below the hips. He rose, hoisting her up toward the ceiling.

She grabbed the edges of the space and pulled herself through as he propelled her from below.

Once she disappeared through the opening, he stood on the frame of the bed to give him more height. When he was halfway through, Randi grabbed the back of his shirt and tugged him the rest of the way.

He resettled the panel and pointed back the way he'd come. He whispered close to her ear. "Stay to the edges or you'll fall through."

She gestured for him to go first. He didn't want her behind him in case something went wrong, but he could lead the way better. As they made their way through the crawl space, he kept glancing behind him to make sure Randi was still there.

Thank God she'd been conscious and awake.

They arrived at the last room by the stairwell, the lab with the animated machines. Gage punched out the ceiling panel and lowered himself into the room.

Soon Randi's legs were dangling through the opening, and Gage wrapped his arms around her thighs and slid her down his body until her feet found the cabinet.

"How are we going to get out of here?"

"You'll see. I have it all planned." He had most of it planned, but he didn't want to worry her about one minor detail.

They slipped through the front door of the lab building, and Gage hustled her along the edge of the building to Dr. Coolidge's Jeep parked next to the medical building.

He helped Randi into the passenger seat and then hopped in, leaving the headlights dark. When he'd cranked on the engine, it sounded like a jet airplane. The Jeep crawled through the row of other Jeeps in the dark, and then Gage stepped on it and the car hurtled toward the manned guard shack at the front gate.

"How are we going to get through that gate?"

"Not everyone at this compound is involved in the crazy stuff, Randi, and I have a hunch about those guards at the gate."

"You know about the crazy stuff?"

"I know enough. Hold tight."

He turned on the headlights as he approached the guard shack and decreased his speed.

The marine stepped out from his post and Gage blew out a breath.

"Your ID, sir? I have orders not to let anyone off this compound tonight." The marine peered around Gage to have a look at Randi.

Gage glanced at the soldier's name on his fatigues. "Sergeant Peck, I'm a Prospero agent. I work with Jack Coburn. This woman is under our protection. She's a valuable witness, not a criminal, not a terrorist. She hasn't done anything wrong. She's going to be Prospero's responsibility now, not Dr. Murdoch's."

The marine saluted and stepped aside. "Yes, sir."

The gate rolled open and Gage floored the accelerator.

"How'd you do that? How'd you do all of this? Getting into that building? Finding me? Getting this Jeep?"

"Turns out Dr. Coolidge wasn't such a curmudgeon after all. We owe our escape to him."

She grabbed his arm. "They had some diabolical plan to lure Zendaris out by holding his unborn child hostage—my unborn child, too. They were going to impregnate me against my will."

"I figured it was something like that." But hearing Randi voice it made him even angrier and his foot grew heavy on the gas pedal again.

"You did?" Her grip tightened. "Is this some sort of new way of negotiating with terrorists and arms dealers?"

"Obviously Murdoch was using her little lab of horrors for all sorts of unregulated experiments." He gestured to the backseat. "If you're not too sick of them, I bundled up your clothes. They're in the bag."

She clapped her hands together once. "I can't wait to put those dirty clothes on again. You're amazing."

"Don't get too excited. Now I have to get us out of Panama. And you can bet by morning Jessup and Murdoch will make sure we're Panama's most wanted."

Chapter Eight

Randi paused, her hand on Gage's black duffel. She should've known they weren't out of the woods yet, but at least she wasn't strapped to a table like some sort of specimen for dissection.

She dug her clothes out of the bag and dropped them in her lap. She could slip into her underwear beneath the lab coat. Not that modesty wasn't completely futile at this point since Gage had already seen pretty much every inch of her body.

Still, she kept the coat in place as she stepped into her panties and arched off the seat to pull them up. She shifted a quick glance at Gage, but he had his eyes pinned on the road outside the windshield. She yanked on her black pants the same way.

Then she slid her arms from the coat and put on her bra beneath it, and whipped off the whole thing to pull her blouse over her head. Putting on some sweaty, dirty clothes never felt so good.

She bunched the lab coat into a ball and threw it in the backseat. Running her hands through her hair, she let out a long breath.

"Did Murdoch attempt to help you recover you memories at all?"

"She never believed me, Gage, not for one minute.

As soon as she got me into that room alone, she started interrogating me in a hostile manner. She drugged you, didn't she? They talked in front of me like I was some inanimate object."

"Yeah, she did, and she tried it again at dinner so I'd sleep through the night before I shipped out of there in the morning."

"How'd you know I was still there? Did Dr. Coolidge tell you?"

"He didn't know if you were still there or not, but it was clear the only lab results he got back were for the pregnancy test, not any other test that would cause you to be airlifted to the States like Dr. Murdoch told me. Coolidge explained that Jessup was very interested in those pregnancy test results. I started piecing things together from there."

She shivered and hugged herself. How close had she been to being forced to carry some stranger's child? To being forced into some nine-month incubation period?

"How are we going to get out of Panama? Even if we're not on some most-wanted list, I have no passport, no identification, no identity, when you come down to it."

He tapped his phone. "I'm going to send another message to my team, and this time I'm not accepting a CIA escort. It has to be someone from my organization and it has to be someone I know."

"Prospero."

"What? Where did you hear that word?"

"You said it yourself to the guard, but I'd heard it before from Dr. Murdoch and Jessup. What is it? What's Prospero, some deep-cover CIA offshoot?"

"We work with the CIA, but we don't report to that organization."

"Thank God. Will you be in trouble for spiriting me away from there?"

"Not with Prospero, not when I tell my boss what was going on down there. The CIA won't like it, but they're going to have to keep a tighter rein on their covert-ops divisions."

"Dr. Murdoch will deny your accusation. We have no proof and why would anyone believe me?"

"I do." He squeezed her knee.

"Why? Why did you rescue me, Gage? You want Zendaris just as badly as they do. Their crazy plan just might've worked to smoke the guy out."

"You've spent a lot of time in my company. Do you really think I'm the kind of guy who would allow some government entity to falsely imprison an American citizen and manipulate her body?"

She suppressed a tiny sigh. She hadn't gotten the answer she'd been fishing for, but it wasn't half-bad. Gage Booker was one of the good guys and he just proved he'd go to any lengths to protect her—even if he did so from duty rather than from any stronger emotion.

"Well, thank you. I guess I got lucky when you discovered me at the compound."

"We both got lucky." He coughed. "I mean, because I'm certain you'll help us find Zendaris when you start remembering your past."

"Where are we headed now?" Randi scooted to the edge of her seat and peered into the rearview mirror. "And do we have to worry about anyone following us?"

"Not yet. They won't be checking on either one of us until morning, and by then we'll be lost in Panama City."

"Why Panama City?"

"It's big. It's crowded. We can blend in and prepare for the next leg of our trip."

"You're not going to contact Prospero to get us out of the country, are you?"

"I've just thought of a better idea. Let's find out who you are first. I think we can start that search in Texas."

"The note?"

"Exactly. Someone in Houston named Jessica Lehman knows you."

"Houston is a big city, and I'm sure there are lots of Jessicas there. Besides, you don't think I need some professional help?"

"I can get you that, too, but with someone I trust completely."

"Are you telling me you don't trust Prospero?" Randi nibbled on her lower lip. If she couldn't trust the government and Gage couldn't trust his own agency, they were truly on their own.

"I trust Prospero with my life, especially Team Three, but my team is scattered right now and Prospero has a tight relationship with the CIA. The same CIA I just double-crossed."

"You trust Prospero with your life but not necessarily mine. Is that it?"

"Zendaris is a dangerous man, Randi."

"And Prospero will do anything to get him, just like the CIA."

"I don't think anyone over at Prospero is interested in getting you pregnant, but…" He shook his head, color rushing into his cheeks. "Y-you know what I mean."

She snorted. "Yeah, I do know what you mean. But you're saying they might have their own methods of getting me to talk or remember."

"Maybe." He turned suddenly and cupped her jaw

with one hand. "I don't want any harm to come to you, Randi. You've been through enough."

Her heart raced at his warm caress, and she turned her head to press her lips against his rough palm. Murmuring against his hand, she said, "I'll do whatever I can to help you."

He pinched her earlobe and returned his hand to the steering wheel. "We'll help each other."

She studied his profile, and confusion stirred in her belly. Was that his plan? Help the poor, vulnerable amnesiac so she'd do anything he asked? Tell him anything he wanted to know?

Was he playing her? She'd become so dependent on him that she'd do anything to stay by his side. What if telling Gage Booker everything jeopardized other people? What if spilling her guts to him meant betraying people she loved? People she didn't even know about yet?

She had to try to keep some emotional distance between them. She closed her eyes and shifted toward the window, leaning her head against the glass. How was emotional distance from Gage even possible after he'd saved her from a nine-month stint as a human incubator?

After almost an hour on the road, they ditched the Jeep and paid cash for a couple of bus tickets to Panama City.

Randi picked at the white tape on the inside of her elbow that held the cotton ball Dr. Coolidge had placed there after taking her blood. "Ouch."

"You okay?" Gage bumped her shoulder.

She rubbed her arm, squinting at the two pinpricks side by side. Had he jabbed her twice? "My arm's a little sore where Dr. Coolidge took my blood."

"You must have sensitive skin. At least Coolidge saw to your physical ailments."

"Yeah, I'm sure Dr. Murdoch would've taken great care of me, too, as long as I was carrying their little hostage." She wrinkled her nose. "How does someone even hatch a plan like that? I mean, what about the baby at the end of it all? They're dealing with a human being. They're playing God with people's lives, with my life."

Gage ran his knuckles down her arm. "Don't think about it anymore. It's over."

"That part of it's over." She snapped her fingers. "Does the CIA know about the children at the compound? Is that why Murdoch and Jessup came up with this plan? Maybe they figured I was already the mother of Zendaris's children. He got the children out safely before the raid but left me, so he must care about them."

He pulled his hand back and crossed his arms. "Do you think you have kids with Zendaris?"

"No. After, when we first left the compound, I did feel a sense of loss but I don't think I'm a mother. I just don't."

Gage cleared his throat. "Dr. Murdoch didn't do any kind of pelvic exam on you to verify whether or not you'd given birth, did she?"

"Ugh." Randi squeezed her thighs together. "Not when I was conscious, but they had me strapped to that bed while I was out. Who knows what they did to me?"

She traced the needle marks with her fingertips as fear fluttered in her belly. "Y-you don't think they already did the deed, do you?"

"Impregnated you?" His brows shot up. "No. I think there would have to be more preparations.... Right?"

"How would I know?"

Hunching his shoulders, he spread his hands. "I don't think they had time for that."

Randi tapped on the window, eager to change the subject from a possible pregnancy. "We're getting close, another five kilometers."

"First things first. We're going to check into a hotel, get cleaned up and do some shopping. I know you've grown attached to that outfit, but I think it's about time you branched out."

She stretched her arms over her head. "Just don't interrupt my bath like last time."

He grinned, looking so irresistible she didn't know how she was going to adhere to her own rule of emotional detachment. But then all she had to do was mention her possible relationship to Zendaris and he'd cool off faster than a Popsicle in the North Pole.

What would happen to the connection she had with Gage if it all came back to her that she and Zendaris were a couple? It would fizzle. It would explode. It would burn both of them if they continued to stoke this fire between them.

The bus pulled into a busy depot in the center of the bustling city. People crowded the morning streets on their way to work, and shopkeepers swept their sidewalks and opened for business.

Gage found an unassuming hotel in a street lined with them. Requesting two beds, he paid for their room from his seemingly inexhaustible supply of cash from his bottomless duffel bag.

He threw open the hotel-room door and swept a hand inside. "Shower or shopping first?"

"Let's shop first, eat some breakfast and then I think I need a nap."

"Sounds good to me." He dropped the bag and

crouched beside it. "I do have a clean shirt in here, so at least one of us can look presentable."

She aimed a kick at his backside. "Just wait. I clean up really well."

He chuckled and then straightened up, stripping off the khaki-green T-shirt. His muscles bunched and flexed as he tossed the dirty shirt onto a chair and pulled a clean one over his head.

Randi swallowed. How could any woman resist that? Maybe not every woman could. Maybe Gage was married. She riveted her gaze to his left hand as he dragged it through his hair.

No ring, but that didn't mean much. A man on some secret assignment wouldn't run around wearing his wedding ring, especially if he hoped to charm an arms dealer's girlfriend into telling him everything.

Had he been wearing a ring before? She twisted her lips. She couldn't remember her name. How would she remember if some stranger had been wearing a ring on his left hand?

Only Gage wasn't a stranger anymore. He was the only person in her life who *wasn't* a stranger, and now his marital status had become vitally important.

"Why are you smirking? Don't you like this shirt?"

The dark blue color matched his eyes and the soft cotton draped his form, accentuating his broad shoulders and flat belly.

She finally found her tongue to answer him, but by the time she met his eyes with her own, it was too late. His nostrils flared as if sensing her visceral attraction to him. His muscles tensed as if he were ready to pounce.

She spun around, breaking the electric current that buzzed between them. "I'm going to wash my face and hands so I don't look like a complete slouch next to you and your clean shirt."

He expelled a breath behind her and she almost ran to the bathroom, slamming the door behind her. She braced her hands on the vanity and leaned in to take a good look at the dark-haired stranger in the mirror.

Maybe her amnesia had caused this desire in her to cling on to Gage. Who was she kidding? She wanted more than to cling to him. She wanted him. Wanted to meld together with him. Wanted him inside her, all around her, filling her up.

A psychiatrist could have a field day with her—a real psychiatrist, not that crazed Dr. Murdoch. She wanted Gage to fill her up precisely because she was empty.

She had nothing. She had no one—except Gage.

She filled her cheeks with air and then puffed it out. Shopping. Eating. Sleeping. Alone.

She turned on the faucet and unwrapped the little bar of fragrant soap. She washed her face and her hands, scrubbing the last bits of glue from the tape on her arm, and dragged her fingers through her long hair to get the tangles out.

Gage banged on the door. "You're not taking another bath, are you?"

"All done." She pushed open the door, and he stumbled back.

"You look better already."

If he'd stop flirting with her she could get a grip, but maybe that flirting was in his plans, in the Prospero plans. If she concentrated on his possible ulterior motives, it could very well douse the kindling in her belly that she felt every time he touched her.

"Let's go shopping." He took her arm and guided her to the door.

As the kindling crackled into a flame hot enough to warm her blood, she knew she had no control over her feelings for Gage Booker.

She'd just have to trust that he could control his own.

HE LIKED TOUCHING HER.

Gage paced the sidewalk in front of the clothing store where he'd sent Randi with a wad of cash. Jessup didn't know Prospero if he thought hiding Randi in some lab was going to keep Gage out. Rescuing her had almost been child's play compared to some of the situations he'd been in with Team Three.

His phone buzzed and he checked the display.

He stopped pacing and turned down an alley to take the call.

"Jose?"

"My friend. What brings you to this part of the world?"

"Bad guys."

Jose's laugh turned into a hack. "Figures. What do you need?"

"You need to give up those cigarettes, Jose."

"I'm a man of simple pleasures. I'm not going to give up one of them, my friend. Something has to kill us, *verdad*?"

"True, but this job won't. I just need some fake IDs, something to get us out of this country and back into the U.S."

"And you're coming to Jose for that? You bypassing your own people?"

"In this case. You're asking a lot of questions for a man in your line of work, Jose."

Jose coughed for several seconds. "Tell me what you need and I'll tell you when it's ready."

"That's the Jose we all know and love."

Gage rattled off the documents he needed for himself and Randi and sent current pictures of the two of them that he'd taken with his phone. He had his own fake IDs, but the CIA might very well be privy to those IDs and he couldn't chance it—not when he had Randi's well-being in his hands.

He and Jose had finished business before Randi finished shopping.

Gage was parked outside the store by the time she came sauntering out in a new pair of jeans tucked into some half boots, and a blue shirt buttoned over a white, lacy thing.

She didn't look like a woman who'd been strapped to a table less than twenty-four hours ago, but she did look like a woman in need of some TLC. Not that he was the one to administer that, but if not him, who? She had nobody. She had nothing.

Except that brilliant smile.

She spread her arms, a shopping bag hanging from each wrist, and turned around. "Better?"

By the time she did a three-sixty and was facing him again, he'd managed to drag his gaze from her perfectly round derriere and met her eyes with a smile of his own. Not that he hadn't already seen all her assets when she'd been naked on top of that table, but he hadn't looked too closely since that felt like creepy voyeurism.

This didn't feel like creepy voyeurism at all.

"You look great. Still need that food, shower and nap, though."

"Yeah, I guess even new clothes can't hide what I've been through."

"It doesn't show at all, and I have inside knowledge." She pressed some bills into his hand. "Here's the change. I'll pay you back once I discover where I do my banking."

"Let's get some food. I've had plenty of time to case the neighborhood, and there's a café serving breakfast down the street."

When they were seated across from each other over plates of *huevos rancheros,* Randi asked, "What are we doing here that's going to get us out of the country?"

"Already halfway there. We're meeting my contact tonight. He'll have everything we need to make our way to the U.S. undetected."

"You've done that already?"

He sawed across his fried egg with a knife. "It's my job."

"It's your job to rescue people out of situations like mine, too, isn't it? I'd been hoping you'd find me in that lab, but I really didn't believe you would."

"I'm a man of infinite resources."

"How does Jessup know your father?"

Gage's hand froze halfway to his mouth, and his egg fell onto his plate. "What?"

"Jessup said he knew your father. Is your father a spy, too?"

"I guess that might be in his job description. My father's a politician."

"Well, I know he's not the president."

"You know who the president is?"

"I know a lot of things that aren't personal, Gage."

He stabbed his egg again. "That's why we need to get you to a psychiatrist. We need someone to make sense of what's going on in your head."

"How are we going to do that?"

"It just so happens I know a top-notch doctor, but we'll think about that once we get to the States."

They finished their meal and Randi didn't ask about his father again, which was a good thing. Nothing could ruin his appetite faster.

It was midmorning by the time they left the restaurant. As they strolled down the street, Gage pointed to a chemist's shop. "We should pick up some toothpaste and toothbrushes at least."

They perused the narrow aisles and reached over each other to pluck items off the shelves.

Gage's gaze skimmed over the condoms. As tempted as he was, he walked on by. Then he stopped in front of a row of pink boxes. He snatched one from the shelf and held it up to his face as he translated the package. His translation skills didn't need to be expert to figure it out.

He joined Randi in the next aisle and held out the box for her inspection. "Do you want to get it?"

"A home pregnancy kit?"

"Just to ease your mind. I'm sure Dr. Murdoch didn't have time to put her devious plan into action, but if it would make you feel better."

"Okay. I can't use it for a few weeks, anyway. Might as well get some peace of mind and put that whole episode behind me."

They made their purchases and headed back to the hotel.

"You first." Gage pointed to the bathroom. "This time I won't let anyone break into the room."

"That's a relief."

"That's one good thing that came out of our stop at the CIA compound. That man, Marco, who picked us up? I found out that he was a low-level drug courier."

Randi covered her mouth with her hand. "Just our luck. What about the guy in the motel with the knife?"

"He was probably waiting for those drugs. When he

saw two strangers saunter into town, he probably figured we'd had something to do with the disappearance of his delivery. Or Marco informed him earlier that he'd picked us up."

"I must have a black cloud hanging over my head."

"So go get rid of it." He pointed to the bathroom.

She hauled her bags of new clothes with her and shut herself in the bathroom. Gage busied himself with going through his duffel bag to shut out the image of Randi in the shower.

She stepped out of the bathroom on a cloud of sweet-smelling steam with a floral nightgown floating around her body. Its modesty only inflamed his imagination more.

"You're up."

"What?" Heat coursed through his body, leaving his flesh prickling.

"The shower—your turn."

"Did you leave me some hot water?"

"Lots. Do you mind if I take the bed by the window."

"Not at all. The door is locked and chained, but I'd feel better leaving the bathroom door open while I shower. Is that okay?"

"I'd like that. I mean, I'd feel safer with the door open."

Gage ran the shower and peeled off his clothes. He stepped under the warm water, letting it sluice off his body. Through the open door, he could see Randi's long, slim legs on the bed, crossed at the ankles. She was tapping her feet together to some rhythm in her head.

She must be in some strange, dark world. He couldn't even imagine what it must be like to have no memory of who you were. Although there were a few things in his life he'd rather forget.

He groaned and reduced the temperature of the water. If he had to resort to cold showers to get his mind off Randi, he was in trouble. He knew the one thing that would douse his desire—confirmation that she belonged to Zendaris.

But would that do the trick? Wouldn't the fact that he would feel compelled to rescue her from Zendaris make her more desirable to him? His father had pegged that quality in him years ago.

He'd used it to try to entrap Gage in a marriage he believed would've been beneficial to the Booker family and Gage's career in politics. And Gage had almost fallen for it—the woman, not the career in politics.

On orders from his father, the woman, Kacey, had come across like a damsel in distress, pushing all of Gage's buttons. He'd been young and stupid.

He ended the shower and grabbed a towel from the rack. He dried off in the shower behind the plastic curtain, and then wrapped the towel around his waist, tucking a corner in the top.

He poked his head out to check up on Randi. She'd rolled to her side and the floral shift had hiked up, exposing a length of mocha-tinted thigh. Her dark hair, wet from the shower, snaked across one cheek.

Gage crept toward the bed and reached out to sweep the hair from her face.

She jerked and thrashed out with her arms.

Gage jumped back, clutching the towel that had come loose. "Randi?"

Her eyes flew open. "Where am I?"

Gage held his breath. Had she dreamed about her past? Did she remember her identity? "You're in a hotel in Panama. You're safe."

Pressing a palm to her forehead, she scooted up

to a sitting position and wrapped her arms around her bent knees. "I was dreaming."

"And?"

"Not that kind of dream. I was back at the little lab of horrors, and Dr. Murdoch was injecting me with something." She dropped her hand and rubbed the inside of her arm, her gaze skittering across his body.

He felt the heat of her inventory down to his toes. It propelled him toward the bed, toward her. He sat on the edge of the mattress and combed his fingers through her wet hair. "Sounds like a nightmare."

"You were hoping I'd had dreams of Zendaris, weren't you?"

Not exactly. He didn't want her dreaming about that lowlife, but if she did and it led to his capture, wasn't that what he needed?

What he needed was stretched out in front of him. His for the taking. He saw it in her eyes. Felt it in her touch.

She straightened one leg and wiggled her toes against his bare thigh. "Gage?"

He cupped her heel and massaged the sole of her foot. She squirmed but didn't pull away.

Cinching her ankle with his fingers, he pulled her down the bed, until her hip met his. The nightgown had ridden up, and her pink, cotton panties were flush against the white terry cloth of his towel.

Her lower lip quivered and he took it between his teeth. Her sigh warmed his lips. He curled a hand around the back of her neck and drew her closer, deepening the kiss, pressing his chest against the floral nightgown that covered her breasts.

Her nipples hardened beneath the thin material. Her hands, which had been curled into fists at her sides, slipped beneath his towel, her nails digging into his thighs, clawing toward his buttocks.

She rose to her knees and shifted one to the other side of his body to straddle him. She moved against his erection, and he thrust his hips forward in an instinctive response as old as the cavemen.

Cavemen. They took what they wanted without restraint. Without consideration of the consequences.

"Mmm. That feels nice." Randi was trailing her fingernails up his back. Her tongue toyed with his, making him so damned hard he couldn't think straight.

This handful of sweet bottom he was kneading belonged to a government witness. Maybe the only connection to Zendaris Prospero would get in a very long time.

Her hands scrambled for the hem of her nightgown as she bounced in his lap.

If he allowed that nightgown to come off, he'd be done for. There would be no turning back.

He gripped her wrists. "No."

The word came out stronger and louder than he'd intended. He must've known he had to send the command through his thick, lust-addled skull.

Randi pulled back, her face crumpling with confusion. "I—I…"

Gage disentangled her legs from around his waist and staggered from the bed, adjusting the towel around his body—loosely. "This is not a good idea, Randi. We don't even know who you are. I can't take advantage of you like that."

Her eyes narrowed as she yanked down the nightgown to cover her thighs. "Oh, you think you know who I am all right—Zendaris's woman. Do you think you're going to get his cooties by bedding me? Or did the thought of his hands on me turn your stomach so much your hands couldn't follow?"

Gage's jaw dropped. The only feelings of disgust he had were for himself, for his lack of control, his lack of restraint.

"That's not even close."

"Yeah, okay. Whatever." She flipped back the covers and burrowed inside. "Don't worry about it. I'm going back to sleep. Maybe I will dream about Zendaris this time—making love to me. That should put the nail in the coffin of those inappropriate feelings you're having toward me."

She pulled the covers over her head and Gage retreated to the bathroom.

She was right about one thing—his feelings toward her were inappropriate. He'd given his Team Three team member, J.D., a hard time for falling for the woman he'd been assigned to follow and protect. But at least J.D. had known her identity. She'd had her full mental capacity.

Randi had amnesia. He was the only person in the world she knew right now, and he had her life in his hands. How could he exploit that relationship? It was almost like the relationship between a psychiatrist and a patient.

Of course Randi wanted him. He represented everything to her, her very world. Maybe subconsciously she felt she had to put out or he'd abandon her.

That's one thing he wouldn't do. Even if it turned out that Randi had no connection at all to Zendaris, Gage would stay with her until she found her place in this world.

Even if that place wasn't with him.

Chapter Nine

If Gage didn't want her, at least he could put on some clothes.

Randi eyed his sleeping form sprawled on the other bed. His faded jeans sat low on his narrow hips, and one arm crossed his bare chest while the other hung off the too-small bed.

Heat crawled across her flesh as she recalled her assault on him and his firm rejection. What kind of woman attacked a half-naked man without invitation?

Her gaze meandered from his broad shoulders to his six-pack. *Any woman with half a brain and a pulse.*

Sighing, she pulled her damp hair back from her face. And there *had* been an invitation. She'd read it in his eyes, and he'd delivered it with his touch, his kiss.

Then he'd come to his senses. She could very well be his enemy, or at least the friend of his enemy.

Maybe he wanted to entice her just enough to stay with him and bond with him so that when the time came to dish on Zendaris, she'd serve him a heaping plateful. But he could never forget who she was, or who he thought she was.

The sooner she took possession of her past, the sooner they could clear up any issues between them. She'd prove her loyalty to Gage.

Ugh, wasn't that what he wanted? Wasn't that why he wanted to keep her close—both physically and psychologically? He wanted her utter and complete fealty.

Her stomach growled, reminding her why she'd ventured to this side of the room in the first place—and it wasn't to ogle her captor, protector, whatever.

"Gage?"

He remained motionless, like the statue of a Greek god—Adonis, no, someone more heroic and manly. Achilles. How did she remember Greek mythology and not her own name?

She placed a foot against the mattress and pushed. "Gage? Wake up."

Stepping closer, her hand hovered above his shoulder. She didn't want to touch him, didn't want him to think she was coming onto him again.

"Gage!" She waved a hand over his face and his dark lashes stirred, but he rolled to his side, presenting his muscled back to her.

She took a deep breath and poked him with her knuckle. "Gage. We need to eat before we meet Jose."

He mumbled and sat up, rubbing his eyes. "What time is it?"

"It's almost seven o'clock." She pointed to the alarm clock on the nightstand. "We've been sleeping the whole afternoon."

"I don't know about you, but I needed it." He covered his yawn with a fist. "How do you feel? Any more headaches? Soreness in your shoulder?"

Acute embarrassment for jumping his bones? Check.

"I feel fine, but no memories, no dreams." She massaged her forearm. "My arm feels bruised, though."

"Probably some residual injury." He swung his legs

over the bed. "Once we get out of this country, we'll take care of your head."

"If you're not using government shrinks, I don't know how we can march into a psychiatrist's office with this crazy story."

"We're not going to do that. I have connections." He winked and pushed up from the bed. "Where do you want to eat? I suppose room service isn't an option here."

"I noticed a few restaurants back by the chemist. Are we meeting Jose nearby?"

"We'll take a taxi to the meeting, which is in the area of San Felipe. Lots of restaurants there."

"Nice ones?" She glanced down at her newly purchased jeans.

"I'm sure there are some casual places, too." He pulled open the blinds. "You might want to take the rain jacket you bought—looks like a few showers on the way."

Those showers made an appearance by the time they'd left the room. As they stood on the wet sidewalk in front of the hotel, Randi flipped up the hood on her jacket.

Gage stepped in front of her to hail the first available taxi that careened around the corner.

As they clambered inside, Randi asked the driver for a few restaurant recommendations in San Felipe.

He answered in English. "Ah, Casco Viejo. That's what we call it. The restaurants and nightclubs there are very expensive. Something like that?"

"No, something a little cheaper. No nightclubs."

"I will take you to a street near the Palacio de las Garzas. Many choices there."

They sat back as the driver maneuvered through the

rain-slicked streets, which grew narrower as they approached the old part of town.

He squealed to a stop at the curb in front of the French Embassy. "I can't take the car through, but if you turn left up ahead you will find plenty of restaurants."

Colored lights glowed from the restaurants and bars, some in restored colonial buildings, lining the street. They agreed on a place with an ornate balcony dotted with tables.

As Gage pulled out the chair for her, Randi closed her eyes and inhaled the scent of rain and sea. She didn't know if she'd ever been to Panama City before, but she wouldn't mind coming back—to this very spot, with this very man.

"Nice, huh?"

She opened her eyes and met Gage's intense, blue gaze. "I like it. In another time, in another situation…"

She took a sip of water, hiding her face with the glass. She didn't want him to know that she'd been thinking about sharing this scenario with him when they had time to relax, when she knew her identity.

"I think this nightmare will be over for you soon, when you get your memory back."

"Or maybe it will be just the beginning of my nightmare." She flicked her fingers. "We spend too much time talking about who I might be, and no time talking about who you are. How'd you get into the covert-ops business?"

His face closed down and tightened like it always did when the conversation turned to him, as little as that happened.

"I was in the military first. I told you that, didn't I?"

"Yes, but I don't imagine that the majority of men

and women in the service up and decide to join a covert-ops team, do they?"

"I didn't join. I was recruited."

"Ah, and you answered the call of duty."

"Something like that."

"And your father is a politician. What kind? School board member or senator?"

"Senator."

She choked on her water. "I was just kidding."

"I wasn't."

"I-is your father going to hear about your daring escape from the CIA compound in Colombia?"

"Probably." Gage clenched his jaw.

"But he'll be on your side, right?"

Gage shrugged and ran his fingertip down the menu selections. "Seafood should be good."

"He *won't* be on your side?"

"If he is, it would be a first." He snapped the menu shut. "Look, can we stop talking about my father?"

She held up her hands. "If we can stop talking about Zendaris."

"One is pertinent to our predicament. The other is not."

"Your father might be pertinent if he can help us out. If the CIA has put us on the wrong side of international law, maybe your father the senator can bring us back to the right side."

Gage snorted and spun his menu around to face her. "How does this sound? That's garlic, right?"

"It sounds delicious. We'll make it two."

Their conversation continued throughout the meal but with Gage's background off-limits and hers nonexistent, they talked about their impressions of Panama and

Colombia, and Gage compared the countries to others he'd visited, or more likely, worked in.

He'd been all around the world and if Randi had to take a guess, those trips had all been of the covert variety.

Neither of them had alcohol with dinner. Too much was riding on their meeting with Jose. So they shared a dessert over two cups of strong Panamanian coffee.

Randi held the cup to her nose and breathed in. "It smells rich, like moist earth and rain, and the jungle."

Gage took a sip of his brew sans cream and sugar. "It tastes just like that, too."

"Those smells will always trigger memories of this time, no matter what happens in the future."

He clicked his cup into the saucer and covered her hand with his. "Randi, what happened between us back at the hotel…"

She snatched her hand away and hid it in her lap. "Won't happen again. I'm sorry. I don't know what came over me. I think I just got carried away, overwhelmed by the moment and my circumstances. I know all you want from me is my mind, what I can tell you about Zendaris."

"It's not like that." He pushed his cup away and planted his elbows on the table. "I'm attracted to you. Why deny it? But getting involved with you like that— physically—it's not right. It's exploiting you and your vulnerability."

She widened her eyes. He'd pushed her away for her own good? "Don't say anything more. I understand."

"If you think for one minute I didn't want you, didn't want to take you, make you mine." He slouched back in his seat and grabbed his coffee. "That's not helping, is it?"

It *had* been helping. His declaration had made her feel less like a loser—unless it was all part of his plan.

Shaking her head, she said, "Let's just stick to business."

"And we have a business meeting in fifteen minutes." He took one more bite of their *tres leches* cake, and then inched the dessert toward her. "Do you want to finish it?"

"If I take another bite, you'll have to take another picture of me for my ID, since I'll be twenty pounds heavier than this afternoon."

They paid the bill and wandered down to the street. The light rain had turned to a steady downpour, and Randi tugged the hood of her jacket around her head, tucking her hair inside.

"Can we walk to the meeting place?"

"This way." Gage took her arm and they delved deeper into the twisting streets of Casco Viejo.

The later hour had brought out more people, the nightlife and lights of the district attracting them like moths to a flame. But Gage moved her away from the crowds.

They turned a corner and found themselves at the top of some crumbling steps leading to a lower-level street.

Gage threaded his fingers through hers. "Down here."

Knots tightened in Randi's belly as they descended to the uneven street, a single streetlamp throwing a minuscule circle of light on the sidewalk.

"Are you sure you can trust this guy?"

"Absolutely. With my life."

"And mine?"

He squeezed her hand but still tugged her in his wake until they were standing next to the streetlamp.

Seconds later, the scuffing of heels approached from a different direction.

Randi nestled closer to Gage.

A man emerged from the shadows, and Randi's body tensed, her eyes straining to see the figure in the darkness.

He stepped into the light, a large grin splitting his face. "My friend. Long time, no see, *verdad?*"

Gage lunged forward and grabbed Jose's outstretched hand. "Long time, no see, but I know I can always count on you, Jose. This is Randi."

"*Señorita. Que bonita.* As pretty as your picture."

"*Gracias.*" Randi shook Jose's rough hand.

Jose glanced over his shoulder and his gaze tripped up the steps. "A better place. *Vamos.*"

With Randi clinging to his side, Gage followed Jose. They descended another set of stairs, and Randi sniffed the dank air. They had to be below sea level.

Jose ran his hand along a decrepit wall and stopped where it seemed to plow into a stone edifice. "The old tunnels of the city. When invaders came to our shores, we hid beneath the city. They found Panama but not the Panamanians."

He grinned and disappeared into a black hole.

Randi's heart pounded so hard it rattled the zipper on her jacket.

But Gage followed Jose without hesitation, so she did, too.

A sconce on the wall cast weak illumination, but Jose seemed satisfied. He withdrew a large manila envelope from inside his jacket. "It's all here, my friend—passports, Texas driver's licenses, visas, cash."

"I have cash."

Jose's head jerked up. "Shh."

Randi's throat was so dry she couldn't swallow. She put her hand against the wall to brace herself, but it slipped off the slime clinging to the rock.

Thrusting a hand in one pocket, Jose said, "Echoes from the streets above. Take the cash. I get a good—how do you say it?—retainer, from Señor Coburn."

He handed the envelope over to Gage and he also zipped it inside his jacket. "Our business is done...my friend."

Jose's gaze skittered over Gage's shoulder and the whites of his eyes popped in the dark tunnel.

Randi felt a rush of air behind her. Then an arm curled around her neck and ripped her from Gage's side.

Chapter Ten

The arm choked off Randi's scream. The person attached to the arm dragged her back. A click resounded close to her ear.

"Don't move or I'll shoot her."

Gage, who'd been crouching against the wall, sprang forward. He moved in swiftly with a karate-style chop to the hand holding the gun.

Randi's assailant staggered, loosening his grip on her.

Crouching, Gage hooked an arm around her waist and yanked her toward him while driving the heel of his palm into the man's throat.

A gunshot echoed in the tunnel and Randi screamed. She was falling. Falling from the balcony. She thrust her arms out to her sides to keep her balance, but it was no use. She crashed through the wood.

The children.

"Randi? Are you okay?"

Randi's eyelids flew open. She was lying on top of Gage, her nose pressed into his chest. Was the man going to grab her again? Was he going to shoot her again?

Gage cupped her head with his hands and tilted it back. "Did he hurt you?"

"Where is he?" She pumped her legs and rolled from Gage.

Jose was kneeling beside her attacker. He looked over his shoulder. "I think he's dead."

"You think?" Gage dragged himself up from the pavement. "Why the hell did you shoot him, Jose? Now I can't question him."

Jose patted the dead man's cheek. "*Es Americano,* my friend."

Gage swore as he helped Randi to her feet. "You're okay, Randi?"

She nodded and he propped her against the moss-covered wall since her knees were shaking so badly she couldn't stand on her own.

He joined Jose, facing him across the body. "Does he have any ID on him?"

"Not that I can find." Jose rummaged through the man's pockets.

"Do you know him? Have you seen him before?"

"No. I think he was here for you." He jerked his thumb at Randi. "The *señorita.*"

Randi's whole body started trembling and she slid down the wall to her haunches.

Gage left the body to stand beside her, placing his hand on her shoulder. "I think you're right, but how? How did they find us?"

Jose dragged an object from the man's front pants pocket and whistled as he brought it close to his face. "I think this is the answer."

Gage slipped his hand beneath Randi's arm to help her to her feet, but she wasn't sure she wanted to see what Jose cradled in his hand.

He balanced a black, square object on his palm and showed it to them.

Gage plucked it from his hand and turned it over. "Unbelievable. They must've put something in my bag or backpack when I was sedated."

Randi grabbed Gage's arm as he reached for his backpack sitting on the ground. "What is it?"

He straightened up, clutching the backpack, his mouth grim. "It's a GPS tracking device, Randi. Jessup and Dr. Murdoch have been tracking our movements since we left the compound."

She pressed a fist against her mouth, and her stomach rolled.

Gage dug through the pack. "The problem is the devices can be really small. It could be anywhere. I don't understand how they got to my bags, and I'm not even wearing the same clothes I had on there."

"It's not in the backpack." Randi hugged herself, her fingers massaging her inner forearm through the slick material of her jacket. "It's not in your other bag, either, or your clothes."

"What are you talking about?"

She shoved the sleeve of the jacket up her arm and pointed to the inside of her elbow. "It's in me."

GAGE DROPPED THE BACKPACK to the wet cement. Of course. They'd had her spread out on that table at their mercy. Even if they hadn't predicted his rescue of Randi, they'd want to keep tabs on her at all times once they'd gotten her pregnant.

"How do you know this, Randi?"

"My arm. It's been bothering me ever since we fled the compound. Dr. Coolidge took my blood from the same spot, but I've been feeling more than a pinprick and he just stabbed me once. There are two holes in my arm."

Gage took her arm and ran the pad of his finger along her flesh. "It's there, Randi. They implanted a chip in your arm."

She stepped back from him, her dark eyes glassy. "You have to dump me, Gage. They'll find you, too."

He pulled her into his arms. "That's not going to happen. We'll disable it."

"C-can you do that?"

"There's a device that can block the signal."

She melted against his body. "Of course you'd have something. I should've known I could count on you."

He stroked her hair. "There's only one problem—I don't have that device with me. But I can get someone to send it to me."

"You're not going to have time for that." Jose tossed the GPS tracker up in the air and caught it. "They probably have another spy out here. When they can't contact this one—" he aimed a kick at the dead man "—they will send another."

Randi stiffened in his arms. "Jose is right. You should go now, drop me off at the police station or something."

Shaking her gently, Gage said, "Don't be ridiculous. You don't think those people will figure out some story to get you away from the police?"

"There's another way, my friend." Jose held up a knife, its blade gleaming in the low light of the tunnel.

"No." Gage held her tighter. "We can't cut it out of her."

Jose held out the knife, pinching the blade between his fingers. "If you can feel it beneath her skin, it is just below the surface. You can get it."

Randi squirmed from Gage's embrace. "He's right. Get it out of me. I know where it is. I've felt the bump. You felt it. Take it out, Gage."

She took the knife from Jose and presented it to him. "Do it."

"*Uno momento.*" Jose held up a finger and ran from the cave, leaping over the dead man.

"Where's he going?"

"Knowing Jose, he's going to get something or someone to make this a little easier on you. Are you sure you want to do this?"

"What choice do we have? They could track us down again while we're waiting for the blocking device to get here. We wouldn't have one moment of peace."

Had they had one moment of peace yet?

Gage couldn't talk her out of it. He didn't know if he wanted to talk her out of it.

When footsteps squelched against the wet pavement, Gage drew his weapon and tucked Randi behind him.

Jose appeared at the entrance to the tunnel, carrying a bottle. "A few sips of this, and you won't mind the knife."

He twisted off the cap from the bottle of tequila and handed it to Randi.

She wrapped both hands around the bottle and put it to her lips. Her eyes screwed up and her nose wrinkled as she downed the booze.

When she came up for air, a tear rolled down her cheek. "Whew, that's strong."

Gage urged, "Take a few more swigs. Too bad we ate so much for dinner. It would've been more effective on an empty stomach."

She gulped down another shot and wiped her mouth with the back of her hand. "Oh, I don't know. This is pretty effective."

She tipped another quantity of the golden liquid down her throat and coughed and spluttered.

"Whoa." Gage took the bottle from her. "I think you're enjoying this too much."

Jose shrugged and took a sip. "It's good tequila. You should take a shot, too. What you have to do is not pretty, my friend."

Gage wiped the bottle with the hem of his shirt and took a swig.

Then Randi took one more drink.

"Are you ready?"

She nodded once and her chin drooped to her chest as she slurred her answer. "Less do this."

Gage guided her to the ground and removed her jacket. He shrugged out of his own, peeled off his shirt and ripped it into strips.

Then he dumped the tequila over the knife, his hands and Randi's arm.

Jose took another sip and then doused his own hands with the tequila. He crouched beside them and held Randi's arm out straight.

Gage smoothed his finger against her inner elbow and felt the small lump beneath her skin. He pulled the flesh tight and nicked it with the tip of the blade.

A bead of blood dotted Randi's arm.

Gage took a deep breath and plunged into her flesh. He probed and circled until he felt the edge of the chip.

Randi murmured only once. Otherwise, she kept still while he ripped a hole in her skin.

Finally, Gage pulled the knife free, balancing a small chip on its edge. "I got it."

He dropped the knife and tucked the chip into the front pocket of his jeans.

Jose drenched the wound with more alcohol and held the bottle to Randi's lips while Gage wrapped up her arm.

With a piece of his T-shirt tied firmly around her elbow, Gage hooked his arms beneath hers to help her to her feet. She staggered against him.

Jose wiped off his knife and tucked it away. He held out his hand, palm up. "Let me have the chip, and we will have some fun with your friends, *verdad?*"

Gage felt in his pocket and pinched the chip between his fingers. He dropped it into Jose's hand. "Thanks for everything…my friend."

Jose winked and gestured toward Randi, now swaying and hanging on to Gage. "Thank me later when you get lucky."

They split up then, taking different routes away from the tunnel and the dead man inside.

The nightclubs and bars of Viejo Casco discharged several people in the same condition as Randi. A man making his way down the street with a stumbling drunk at his side didn't even cause a raised eyebrow.

"It's out?" Randi repeated the question for about the hundredth time since they'd left the tunnel.

"Yeah, it's out. Don't worry. You're safe now."

"Always safe with Gage. Don't leave. Don't ever leave."

Pulling her close, he kissed her temple beneath her other wound, the one that stole her memory. "I'm not going anywhere, Randi."

He snagged a taxi back to the hotel, where he promptly checked out. Jessup could've already had them tracked to the hotel and just waited until they left before ordering his flunky to make a move on Randi.

They took a taxi to another hotel, this one closer to the airport, and checked in for one night. The hotel clerk gave Gage a knowing look.

Seemed everyone thought he was going to get lucky tonight with Randi.

They got to the room, and Randi crashed diagonally across the bed—the only bed in the room.

A little blood stained her shirt and her clothes reeked of tequila. The moss and slime from the tunnel clung to her damp jeans. She couldn't go to bed like that.

He perched on the edge of the mattress. "Can you sit up, Randi? Let's get these dirty clothes off."

"Take clothes off." She squirmed to a sitting position, her back against the headboard.

She tried to unbutton her shirt, but her clumsy fingers couldn't handle the task.

Gage undid the buttons and slipped the shirt off her shoulders. He left her the white, lacy T-shirt beneath, which outlined her perfect breasts. He pulled off her shoes and unzipped her jeans. He tugged at the pants and she tilted up her pelvis.

Swallowing hard, he yanked the jeans from her hips and pulled them off her legs. He dug in her bag for the nightgown she'd worn earlier this afternoon but gave up trying to pull it over her head.

He rolled her to the side and pulled down the covers on the bed. "Crawl under the covers, Randi. Sleep it off. You'll be okay in the morning."

She scooted toward the exposed sheet, and then Gage wrapped his arms around her and lifted her a few inches from the mattress to tuck her under the covers.

She moaned when her head hit the pillow, and Gage brushed the hair from her face.

"Shh." He kissed her cheek. Then he kissed her tequila lips.

He already lost his shirt tonight, so he pulled off his

jeans and lay beside Randi, on top of the covers, in his underwear.

Then he couldn't help himself. He shifted closer and hung one arm around her waist while he buried his face against her neck. Even snockered and stinking of booze, she drew him to her like no woman ever had before.

He had to get a grip. Zendaris's woman could never belong to him. Never.

Someone had stuffed her mouth with cotton and was beating on the back of her head with a pool cue.

Groaning, Randi rolled to her back and her hand made contact with Gage's bare chest. She opened one eye and immediately shut it against the light that made her head ache.

Her arm throbbed and she plucked at the strip of cloth wrapped around it—Gage's T-shirt. She was a mess, but she'd remembered something last night when Jose shot the attacker.

The sound of the gunfire had brought back those last minutes before she'd been shot on the balcony of Zendaris's palatial home.

She scooted up until her back rested against the headboard. The covers had fallen from her shoulders, and she crossed her arms over her skimpy camisole. At least Gage had left her partially clothed in her underwear. Probably playing the role of the gentleman. It's not like he hadn't seen her naked body before.

She dropped her gaze to his body, clad in a pair of dark blue briefs. He hadn't even gotten under the blanket. Maybe he didn't trust himself with her.

He clasped her calf through the blanket and she jumped. "I didn't mean to scare you. How are you feeling?"

She ran her tongue along the inside of her mouth while yanking the sheet up to her chin. "About how you'd expect someone to feel who'd downed a half bottle of tequila the night before."

"Your arm?"

"Hurts."

"We need to get back to the States today." He slid from the bed and grabbed his jeans from the back of the chair.

"We're flying out today?" She tried to keep her eyes on his face as he buttoned his fly, and did a pretty good job, considering.

"If we can get a flight into Houston."

"Do you think they might be here? Will they stake out the airport?"

"Not if Jose has anything to say about it. Knowing him, the chip that was in your arm is probably on its way to another country or out to sea on a boat."

She peeked beneath the makeshift bandage. "That's going to leave a scar."

"Make sure you clean it well when you're in the shower. I still have some bandages and antibiotic cream in the first-aid kit. I'll dress it when you get out."

She planted her feet on the floor and swayed to the side. "I still feel woozy. And sick."

"We'll get some breakfast and some of that strong Panamanian coffee. Down a couple of ibuprofen while you're at it."

"At the airport?"

"The sooner we get out of here, the better."

Two hours later, they slumped in matching plastic chairs at the Tocumen International Airport. Randi sipped her second cup of coffee of the day and people-watched over the rim.

She hadn't told Gage what she'd remembered last night during the shooting. He'd been distracted all morning with their arrangements. Now they finally had a chance to breathe.

Randi placed her coffee beneath her seat. "Gage, I remembered something last night."

"You did?" He dropped his magazine on his lap and it slipped to the floor.

"It was the gunshot. It brought back the shooting on the balcony of Zendaris's house."

"Why didn't you tell me this before?"

"There didn't seem like any good time this morning."

"What did you remember?" Not one muscle in his face moved even the slightest bit.

"I remember a man, a big man with a gun pointed at me. I backed up onto the balcony. And there were kids. There were kids in the room screaming."

His Adam's apple bobbed as he stroked her arm. "Were they yours?"

"No."

"You sound sure. Is that something you remembered?"

"It's not a feeling or emotion I remembered. It's what they were screaming."

"What were they screaming?"

"*Mademoiselle*. They were screaming *mademoiselle*."

"You're not French…. Are you?"

"I don't think so, but, Gage…"

"What?"

"I speak French."

Squeezing his eyes shut, he pinched the bridge of his nose. "You speak French."

"Yes."

"This is so crazy."

"This is crazy? After all the stuff that has happened to me in the past three days, speaking French is crazy?"

"I know nothing about amnesia, Randi." He passed a hand over his face. "It's so weird that you can remember languages but can't remember your identity."

"If you expect me to explain it to you, you're out of luck."

He swept the magazine from the floor and dropped it onto the small table between their chairs. "Why would the kids be calling you *mademoiselle?*"

"Maybe—" she worried the edge of the bandage on her arm with her fingernail "—I was their nanny or something."

"You forgot about the picture at the airport. If you were a nanny in that household, you were Zendaris's nanny, too."

Heat prickled her skin. "That's not me in the picture. All you have is a tall woman with long, dark hair." She swiveled her head around the airport lounge, trailing her fingers across the crowds of people. "It could be several women right here."

"The scarf. You had the same pink scarf."

"I'm sure we could find a few pink scarves in this airport if we looked. It's a coincidence."

"Helluva coincidence." He blew out a noisy breath and took her hand in his. "I know you don't want to believe you could be associated with a man like Zendaris, but you don't have to be when this is all over. You can make a fresh start, make different decisions."

She left her hand in his, but turned away, her vision blurred by tears. He just didn't want to believe her.

The loudspeaker announced their flight to Houston,

and Randi dashed a hand across her face and slipped the strap of her new handbag over her shoulder. "It's time."

As she stood up, her face still averted from Gage, a familiar face emerged from the crowd swarming toward the departure gates. She rubbed her eyes, but he was still there.

"Gage."

"Yeah?" He was pulling his boarding pass from his backpack.

"It's Jose."

Gage spun around. "Where?"

"Isn't that him?"

Gage tensed beside her. "Something's wrong. Look at his face."

The man's features were twisted and he seemed to be limping.

Gage moved toward him and Randi followed, her heart pounding in time to her footsteps on the linoleum.

As Jose extended his hand, he flashed his customary smile, but it didn't reach his eyes. "My friend. Good to see you."

Gage grabbed his hand and Jose fell against his chest. He rasped, "Get out. Hurry. Get on that plane now. They're coming for you."

Chapter Eleven

Something wet and sticky seeped against Gage's shirt as Jose sagged against him. "Who is it, Jose? Did they track you with the GPS?"

Jose's lips twisted into a grim smile and he coughed. "No, my friend. The people who implanted that chip in Randi are on a—*como se dice?*—wild-goose chase."

"Zendaris? Is it Zendaris's people? What did they do to you?"

Jose shoved off Gage and made a valiant effort to stand on his own two feet. "Get on the plane. They want what belongs to them. They want the *señorita.*"

Randi gasped.

Gage's eyes darted around the airport. Zipping his jacket over the blood stain on his shirt, he strode toward a wheelchair parked outside a shop. He grasped the handles and wheeled it back to Jose, who was now leaning against Randi, who had her arm around his shoulders.

Gage nudged the back of Randi's knees with the chair. "Sit. Let's go."

"B-but Jose."

"He'll be okay. We need to get on that plane."

"He's right." Jose ducked from beneath Randi's arm. "Go. *Rápido.*"

Randi sank into the chair, and Gage gave his friend

a salute as he pushed the wheelchair to the boarding gate. "I'm sorry. We missed the special boarding. My wife is injured."

The line parted for them and Gage thrust their boarding passes at the agent. Then he turned and pointed to Jose. "I think that man needs assistance."

"Thank you, sir." The agent picked up her radio.

Gage paused by the boarding tunnel. Two airport employees approached Jose, who was now propped up against a wall.

He narrowed his eyes. Two men in dark sunglasses were pushing their way through the crowd of people.

Gage turned and hunched over Randi in the wheelchair. The men wouldn't have any problem figuring out which flight he and Randi had taken, but he just hoped those remaining stand-by seats had been snapped up by other travelers by now.

He wheeled Randi along the ramp until they got to the hatch of the airplane.

The stewardess smiled a welcome. "Does your wife need assistance to her seat, sir?"

"No, thank you."

For her part, Randi rose from the chair slowly and leaned heavily against Gage. He kept her in front of him as they maneuvered down the aisle toward their seats.

Should he tell her he'd seen Zendaris's men in the airport, almost at the gate? He watched her drop to her seat and close her eyes and decided against it.

What good would it do? Either those two would make it on the plane or they wouldn't. If they didn't, he didn't want to worry her.

He sat beside her and buckled his seat belt.

Without opening her eyes, she said, "Is Jose going to be okay?"

"I think he had a stab wound."

Randi sucked in a sharp breath.

"He's lost a lot of blood, but if he gets to the hospital right now he should be fine."

"How did they find him? How did they know?"

"It's what Jose does, Randi. He's an informant. He's a wheeler and dealer. Zendaris would make it his business to know the black-market scene in Panama once he tracked us here."

"But how did he track us here?"

Gage lifted one shoulder. "We have our informants. They have theirs. The CIA could've even tipped him off."

"Great." She grabbed a pillow from beneath her seat and scrunched it under her head. "Now we have two sets of bad guys after us. Where are all the good guys?"

Sitting right next to you.

He kept his mouth shut and pulled out his magazine. She obviously didn't think he was a good guy because he doubted her memories about her position in Zendaris's household.

He really wanted to believe she was a nanny instead of a mistress. Or did he? The knowledge that Randi was Zendaris's lover was the only thing holding him back from doing something totally unprofessional.

Making mad, passionate love to a witness…a witness who couldn't remember a thing.

THE PLANE TOUCHED DOWN, and Randi opened her eyes, though she'd been awake for the past hour. She hadn't wanted to get into it with Gage again. She'd just have to regain her memories to prove to him that she and Zendaris weren't an item.

Then what? Did she expect him to open his arms to her?

"Did you sleep?" She stretched her arms over her head.

"Not much. Did you dream?"

"I don't think it's going to work that way, Gage." She pulled her handbag from under the seat in front of her and unzipped it. "I don't think my entire life is going to come back to me in a dream."

"No more children calling you *mademoiselle?*"

"That—" she smeared her lips with Chapstick and then smacked them together "—wasn't a dream. That was a real memory. Jose's gun brought it back."

"Maybe being in Texas will bring back some memories, too. If not, I have someone on the way who will be able to help."

"I hope he's good, this psychiatrist of yours."

"She." Gage unsnapped his seat belt and stood up to retrieve his backpack from the overhead. "The psychiatrist is a woman."

Randi swallowed. His wife? Girlfriend? She must be a very special friend if she planned to fly into Texas from wherever to treat someone on the sly. "Another woman psychiatrist? I don't think I can handle another Dr. Murdoch."

"Elle is as different from Dr. Murdoch as day is from night."

Elle? Oh yeah, this was a special friend.

Randi's knees didn't stop quaking until they'd gotten through customs. Jose was good. Their papers passed with flying colors.

Her stomach flipped at the thought of Jose. Was he in the hospital now? Was he alive?

They landed on the sidewalk with their bags, and Randi turned to Gage. "Where to now?"

"I'm going to rent a car with my new ID. No more hitchhiking, buses and customs agents."

"I didn't mean our mode of transportation. Where are we headed?"

"I'm going to buy a laptop first, and then we'll find a hotel where we can settle in and do a little research."

"Do you think you're going to find me on the internet?"

"We have a few leads."

"And Prospero?"

"I'll contact them…later."

"You're not going to ask for their help?"

"I don't want to risk it, Randi. I trust the guys on my team, but they're not around right now. I trust the head of Prospero, but he has people around him, people with strong ties to the CIA."

"Will you be in trouble for what happened back in Colombia?"

"Until I explain everything that happened. Dr. Murdoch and Lawrence Jessup were out of control. They won't present it that way, but once an investigation is done, they'll be the ones in trouble. But investigations take time. And we don't have time right now."

Randi shivered and hugged herself. "It's cold."

"I guess that means more shopping."

"Having amnesia is expensive."

He slipped an arm through hers. "You're going to get through this."

She wasn't sure she wanted to get through this because once she found her memory, she'd lose Gage.

They bought a laptop and checked into a hotel with

free Wi-Fi. Gage wasted no time setting up on the table by the window.

Randi collapsed across the bed, her feet hanging off the mattress. "What are you searching for? Randi?"

"Don't be a defeatist. We also have a name from your past—Jessica Lehman."

"While you're doing that, I'm going to order some sandwiches from room service."

"Good idea." Gage rubbed his hands together and flexed his fingers. "Where are you, Jessica Lehman?"

Randi trapped the receiver between her shoulder and her chin as she ordered from the menu. Then she hung over Gage's shoulder as he typed in *Jessica Lehman* followed by *Houston.*

A spate of Jessica Lehmans scrolled down the screen, and Gage picked up a pen and grabbed a piece of hotel stationery. "These are mostly social-media sites. I plan to click on every one of them. Pull up a chair."

Randi dragged a chair next to Gage's, and they started going through every link. They dismissed the married women with children, figuring the Jessica who had written to Randi about dropping in on her from Costa Rica was probably single and childless.

After an hour, they'd narrowed their search to three Jessicas living in the Houston area. Two of the three had blocked their content on their pages, but Gage was able to bounce between several different resources to get their addresses.

He pushed away from the laptop and took a bite of his sandwich. "Not a bad day's work. Do you feel up to paying a visit to Jessica one, two and three this afternoon?"

"Absolutely." Her pulse ticked up a few notches.

Would she discover her identity today? Would Jessica know what she'd been doing in Colombia?

Randi finished her sandwich and brushed her teeth. She changed tops and ran a brush through her hair before braiding it. "I'm ready."

"Not so fast." Gage came at her, holding up a gauze bandage. "Let me look at my handiwork on your arm. Maybe we should get you to a clinic today."

She extended her arm to him and he peeled back the old bandage. Angry red encircled puckered flesh.

"Does that look normal to you?"

"It doesn't look bad." He pressed his fingers against the spot. "Doesn't feel warm, either. Elle can have a look at that, too. She's a psychiatrist, so she went to medical school."

What couldn't Elle do? Randi didn't like the way Gage's voice grew warm and almost tender when he mentioned the glorious Elle.

"Let's clean it again and put some more antiseptic cream on it."

"Are you sure there's no tequila in the minibar?"

Gage chuckled as he squeezed a washcloth under the faucet in the bathroom. "Thought you never wanted to see the stuff again."

"It sure dulled the pain."

"This isn't going to hurt a bit." He'd soaped up the cloth and washed the wound on her arm with a slow, circular motion. He rinsed it, dried it and bandaged it all with a gentle touch.

So gentle, Randi didn't want it to end. If this was the only way she could get him to touch her, she'd suffer a million injuries.

Sighing, she rose from the toilet seat. She'd gotten too attached to him. It's like he said before. It was to be expected that she'd glom on to him. Who else did she have?

Maybe she had Jessica Lehman.

Without phone numbers, they had to pay surprise visits on the Jessicas. Because it was Saturday, they got lucky on their first attempt.

When Jessica number one, a redhead, answered the door of an apartment near the downtown area, Randi's stomach dropped.

The woman's face showed no recognition as she slid her gaze from Randi to Gage. "Yes?"

"I know this is going to sound crazy, but do you know her?" Gage tilted his head toward Randi.

By the tone of his voice, Randi knew he'd already figured out this woman wasn't their Jessica.

Her green eyes narrowed. "N-no."

"Are you sure?" Randi tilted up her chin. The woman didn't sound sure.

"I'm sure I don't know you."

"Thanks. Sorry to disturb you." Gage took Randi's arm as he turned from the door.

"But you're not the first to ask me."

They both spun around and Randi tripped against Gage.

"What do you mean? Someone else has come around asking if you know her?"

Hunching forward, Gage braced his hand on the wall beside the door.

The woman flinched, and Randi squeezed Gage's arm. "Someone asked about me?"

"Two men came by the other day. They showed me a picture. When I first answered the door, I didn't make the connection. But after you asked your crazy question, it clicked. You're the woman in the picture."

"What did these men look like?" Gage had backed off and shoved his hands in his pocket.

Jessica folded her arms and hunched her shoulders. "I couldn't really tell you—dark hair, jeans. Normally, I would've never opened my door to two guys, but they caught me in the hallway while I was opening my door. I felt…uncomfortable."

"They had a picture of me?"

"Yeah, asked me if I knew you and where you were. Didn't know the first, so I couldn't help them with the second. I don't think I would've if I could've. They gave me a weird vibe. What's going on? Do I need to be concerned about this?"

"Not at all. My friend just had a little memory loss. We're trying to trace her movements and your name came up."

"And those guys?"

Randi slipped her fingers into Gage's back pocket to steady herself. "I guess they're looking for me, too."

Gage couldn't get much more out of Jessica, so they turned to leave.

Before Jessica slammed the door, she called out, "Be careful. If those guys were looking for me, I'd be worried."

Randi sat ramrod straight in the rental car. "They can't be the CIA. The CIA doesn't know anything about Jessica Lehman. It has to be Zendaris. He hasn't given up on me."

"Which means Zendaris knew about Jessica, knew you might contact her when you got to the States. And he knows you're still alive."

"M-maybe he just wants to find me to make sure I'm okay. He thought I was dead."

"He *left* you for dead, Randi. Why would he care about your well-being now, unless…?"

She clasped her hands between her bouncing knees. "Unless he wants to stop me from talking. He wants to kill me, doesn't he? He wants to finish the job he started at his compound."

Gage clamped a hand on one of her knees to stop its up-and-down motion. "If Zendaris knows you have amnesia, he'd want to stop you before you regained your memory and could tell us anything."

"And by stop, you mean kill."

"I'm not going to sugarcoat it for you, Randi. Zendaris is a dangerous man and you're in a dangerous position."

"Don't worry." She yanked her thin jacket around her body. "You're doing a fine job of not sugarcoating anything."

He raised an eyebrow at her. "Would you want me to? You've always impressed me as the type who would want to hear the truth."

Like the truth about his marital status? The truth about his relationship with the psychiatrist? What gave him that crazy idea?

"Of course I do." She smacked the dashboard. "Now let's go find the other two Jessicas before the real Jessica Lehman reveals anything to Zendaris's men."

They took a short drive from the downtown area to Rice Village where bars and restaurants lined the streets of the college town. Gage parked the car on a residential block, and pointed across the street. "Odd-numbered addresses on that side."

They located the apartment house and pushed a number of buttons at the entrance until someone buzzed them in. It didn't take long. College students were lax about their security.

Little did they know there was a big, cruel world out there.

Gage punched the button for the third floor in the elevator and knocked on the second door down the hallway. No response.

"Should we try later?"

"Yeah, unless we get lucky with the next Jessica."

They did not get lucky. The third Jessica no longer lived at the address that Gage had found, and the current residents of the house were either unable or unwilling to give them a forwarding address.

They returned to the apartment in Rice Village where the bars and restaurants were coming to life for their Saturday-night visitors.

"Maybe we can catch her before she goes out for the night."

Gage knocked on the apartment door again, and still nobody answered.

"I guess this wasn't such a great idea." Randi wedged a shoulder against the door. "Maybe my Jessica doesn't live in Houston anymore."

"Could be."

A door in the hallway creaked open, and a young woman poked her head out and looked both ways. "Are you looking for Jessica?"

Randi shrugged off the door. "Yes. Is she around? I—I'm an old friend."

The woman's eyes widened. "You're a friend of Jessica's?"

"Uh-huh. Haven't seen her in a while and thought I'd drop by while I was in town."

"When's the last time you saw her?" The woman bit her lip and darted a gaze at Gage.

Randi also shot a glance at Gage out of the corner of her eye. Why was this woman giving them the third degree? That was *their* job.

"Umm," Randi raised her eyes to the ceiling, "a year ago, maybe."

The woman puffed out her cheeks and released a long breath, looking as if she'd come to some sort of decision. "I hate to be the one to give you bad news, but Jessica had an accident."

Gage made a quick movement beside her, but it must've been minuscule because Jessica's neighbor never took her eyes off Randi's face.

"An accident?" Randi tilted her head and took another step forward. "What kind of accident? Is she okay?"

The woman narrowed the opening of the door even more, so that she looked like a disembodied head floating in space. "She was hit by a car. She's in a coma."

"Oh, my God." Randi gasped and had to flatten her hand against the wall. "That's terrible. When did it happen?"

"A few days ago."

"It must've been a bad accident."

"That's what the cops are calling it."

Gage cleared his throat and spoke for the first time to the jittery young woman. "What are you calling it?"

"She'd had an argument that day with someone who'd come to her place." She pointed to the worn hallway carpet. "Standing right where you're standing now."

"What were they arguing about?"

"I couldn't hear, but then later that night the car hit

her in a crosswalk. Hit and run. The guy didn't even stop."

"So you think someone hit her on purpose?"

"Seems awfully suspicious, doesn't it?" The woman blinked her eyes at Gage. "Who are you, anyway?"

He jerked his thumb at Randi. "Friend of hers. Is Jessica at the hospital?"

"St. Joseph's."

"Did you get a look at the person she was arguing with?"

"You seem more interested than the cops were." She flipped her hair over her shoulder. "I looked out my peephole, but I couldn't see anyone."

"Did Jessica say anything to you about the argument?" Randi twisted her fingers in front of her. This couldn't be related to her, could it?

"I don't really know her like that. You know, she's a graduate student in the Spanish department, T.A. and everything. I'm just trying to get through my second year."

A graduate student in the Spanish department? Randi swallowed. "Maybe we should see if we can visit her. Has her family been around?"

"Not here, but you know what?"

"What?" Gage's voice had taken on an edge, but the woman had missed it.

"I think that's why the argument didn't register with me—it might've been in Spanish."

Randi's hand braced against the wall, contracted into a fist. "Well, Jessica does speak fluent Spanish, so that would make sense."

"Anyway, sorry about your friend. I gotta go." The neighbor slammed the door, but Randi had the feeling she was peering at them from her peephole.

Grabbing her hand, Gage said, "Let's go."

Instead of leading her back to the elevator, he took a turn toward the stairwell. He let the fire door slam behind them, and then pinned Randi against the wall. "It's her. It has to be her."

"I know." Randi licked her trembling lower lip. "They went after her. "Maybe she refused to tell them anything more about me. Maybe they asked her to contact them if I came to see her, and she refused."

"It's all speculation, but I know one thing."

"What?"

"We need to get into that apartment."

Chapter Twelve

"Break in, you mean?"

Randi's whole frame stiffened beneath his grip. Gage didn't want to keep dragging her along from one misadventure to another. She needed to heal—both body and soul.

But their race to discover Randi's identity just got put on a stopwatch. If Randi didn't recover her memories about Zendaris soon, his thugs would make sure she never did.

He pulled her into his arms, and she molded against his body along every line just like she belonged there. He cupped her face and ran his thumb along her lower lip. He couldn't tell where his pulse ended and hers began.

Brushing his mouth against hers, he whispered against her lips. "Are you up for this?"

"Yesss." Her warm breath feathered the corner of his mouth.

"I can drop you off at the hotel and come back here alone."

"No." She clung to him tighter, grasping his jacket with both hands. "Don't leave me alone."

"Not going to happen." He wedged a finger beneath her chin and kissed her again. "Ever."

She kissed him back, twining her arms around his neck.

He slid one hand into her thick hair and curved the other arm around her waist, dragging her flush against his body. He could take her right now in this stairwell and shut out everything. Shut out the danger. Shut out the voice of reason in his head. Shut out Zendaris.

She pulled away. Breathing heavily, she placed her palms against his chest. "We both know this is a bad idea."

"A bad idea for now." He cinched her wrists and planted a kiss on each palm. "We need to at least wait until Miss Nosey Neighbor leaves before breaking in."

"Let's be grateful for her nosiness."

They jogged down the three flights of stairs. When the cold air hit Gage's face, it brought him back to reality and his responsibility toward Randi. He needed to rein in his lust—or he'd have a lot of explaining to do to Elle.

They climbed back in the car and drove down the street—close enough to monitor Jessica's apartment building, but not right across the street where they might be noticed.

An hour later, the neighbor, wearing a red coat, sailed down the front steps of the apartment building and jumped into a waiting car.

"Let's do this." Gage grabbed his backpack from the backseat, and they headed toward Jessica's building. Someone let them in after the third buzz, and they took the stairs again.

Gage pulled some tools from his pocket and tried the deadbolt first. It wasn't even secured. He picked the lock on the door handle and pushed it open when he heard the click.

A musky, sweet scent washed over him as he stepped into the darkened room. Randi's warm breath teased the back of his neck, and she bumped into him when he stopped.

"Shut the door. I'll turn on the small lamp. We don't want any bright lights shining from this apartment." He sidled to the right and felt the base of a small lamp for a switch, and then turned it.

A soft, yellow glow stole across the living room, and Gage whistled through his teeth as he took in the tossed pillows, upended cushions and rifled drawers.

Randi stamped her foot beside him. "They beat us to this, too."

Gage shrugged. "We had to figure they would. If they went to the trouble of running down the poor girl, they'd definitely search through her stuff. It doesn't matter. They already know who you are. They're just looking for an address or maybe a relative where you'd stay. We're searching for other clues."

He spread his arms. "Does any of this look familiar to you?"

"Nope." She sank to the couch and shuffled through some magazines on the coffee table. "She definitely speaks Spanish."

Gage slipped his flashlight out of his pocket and skimmed the beam across Jessica's bookshelves. "Maybe you were a graduate student at Rice, too. Maybe that's how you two met."

"Oh?" Randi looked up from shuffling a stack of papers. "From graduate student to arms dealer's mistress? That's a leap."

Gage plucked a framed photo from the shelf and held it under his flashlight. "There's a resemblance between the two of you. Family?"

She crept across the room and peered over his shoulder. "Tall, long, dark hair. I told you. There are plenty of women like me in the world."

Gage inhaled the floral scent from Randi's hair as it tickled his cheek, and he closed his eyes. There were no other women in the world like Randi.

His lids flew open as she reached over his shoulder and flicked her fingers at the frame. "It could've been Jessica in that photo from the airport."

"Yeah, if she has a pink, sparkly scarf."

"There are plenty of pink, sparkly scarves in the world, too."

Gage replaced the photo and skirted the TV to reach another bookshelf. Someone had pulled books out helter-skelter and Gage made an attempt to line them up again. Randi's friend didn't need to come home from the hospital to find her apartment trashed. *If* she came home from the hospital.

As he tipped the books back into place, his finger stumbled over the edge of a card sticking out from one of the books. He pinched it between two fingers and pulled it free.

"It's you."

"What?" she called across the room.

"It's a picture of you and Jessica. So if we had any doubt before that she's your friend and sent you that note, it's just been erased."

She joined him and he handed the photo to her. She brought it close to her face and he aimed the flashlight at the picture.

Tracing a finger around the faces of the two smiling young women standing in front of some kind of ruins, Randi said, "It is me."

"Flip it over. There's some writing on the back."

Randi turned the picture over and read aloud, "Me and Randi, Cozumel."

Randi's hand started to tremble and a tear rolled down her cheek.

"What is it? Do you remember anything?"

She shook her head and the tear changed course toward her ear. "That's just it. I don't remember anything, but I had a life. I had friends. I had family. Now I have nothing."

She sank to the floor, clutching the photo to her heart.

Gage crouched beside her and gathered her in his arms. All the danger and excitement had almost made him forget that Randi was a woman with no memory, no past, no life.

Except this life with him.

He kissed the tears from her cheeks. "You have me, Randi. I'm going to be with you all the way."

"Sorry." She rubbed the back of her hand across her nose. "Crying and carrying on doesn't help the situation at all, does it?"

"I don't know. Sometimes it helps."

She struggled to her feet. "The least we can do for my friend is straighten up her place while we're searching so she's not freaked out when she comes back."

"I agree." He shined the light around the room. "Too bad there's no computer."

"Zendaris's guys probably stole it." She took a turn around the room and headed for the bedroom. "Even if I did discover my identity and my home, I wouldn't go there now. They're probably staking it out."

"You're probably right." He came up behind her and squeezed the back of her neck. "If you discover you don't like your current career, you could always become a spy. You're catching on fast."

Clothes tumbled out of Jessica's drawers and closet, and he and Randi searched the pockets and folds for anything the intruders may have missed. More books littered the nightstand, but the drawer of the nightstand contained nothing but a few condoms and sex toys. "Too bad there's no diary or address book."

Randi held up one of the condoms between two fingers. "Maybe Jessica has a boyfriend."

"I think we need to pay her a visit in the hospital. If she does have a boyfriend, maybe we'll run into him there."

They searched the rest of the room and the bathroom, but found no other clues to Randi's identity. If Jessica had kept any information about Randi, it had all been sanitized from this apartment.

Zendaris must know by now that Randi had amnesia and he intended to keep it that way until he could get to her himself.

When they finished their search, Gage turned out the lamp and they slipped into the hallway and down the stairs.

"The neighbor said St. Joseph's, right?"

"She did." Randi pulled out the photo again and studied it as if trying to read her past in the face of the girl she once was. She tapped the picture against her fingers. "At least it looks like we were having fun."

"And you will again."

Had that fun-loving young woman met an intriguing older man and gotten carried away with the excitement? Gage still had a hard time reconciling the Randi he knew with the woman in the picture with Zendaris.

How could someone like Randi get swept up in the jet-setting lifestyle of Zendaris?

If it weren't for that distinctive pink scarf, he could easily believe that Randi had been in Zendaris's household for a different purpose than to warm his bed.

Gage clenched the steering wheel until his knuckles turned white. He didn't know what filled him with more rage, the fact that Randi had belonged to a man like Zendaris or the fact that Zendaris had discarded her like a piece of trash.

He parked in the hospital lot, and they entered the lobby. Even on a Saturday night, a volunteer was manning the information desk.

Randi said, "We're looking for a friend of mine who had an accident a few nights ago. She's in a coma."

The clerk's brow furrowed. "I'm so sorry. Recent coma patients would be in the intensive care unit. That's on the fifth floor. You can check with the nurses' station there."

They thanked her and headed toward the elevator.

"Don't get your hopes up, Randi. You probably can't see her unless you're family."

"You said I could pass for family. I'll give it a try."

When they got to the nurses' station, Randi hunched over the counter to get the attention of a nurse at a computer. "Excuse me. I'm looking for Jessica Lehman's room."

The nurse punched a few more keys and then swiveled her chair to face them. "And you are?"

"I'm Randi Lehman, her cousin."

"Hmm." The nurse screwed up her face and wheeled back to the computer. "You haven't been here before, have you? I'll have to check your name against the list of approved family and friends."

"I'm sure I'm on the list." She crossed the fingers of her right hand. "Jessica and I are like this."

The nurse squinted at the display. "Lehman, Lehman. I have a few Lehmans but not a Randi."

"Who's on there? I have to be on there. Can you read me the names?"

Good idea, Randi.

"Ma'am." The nurse walked her chair back to the counter. "I can't give you those names and I can't let you into the room without authorization."

Randi opened her handbag and pulled out the photo. "Here's proof—a picture of me and Jessica. I'm family. I need to see her."

Randi waved the picture under the nurse's nose, but the nurse didn't even look at it.

"Miranda!"

Gage glanced up at a middle-aged woman coming toward the nurses' station. The woman called out in a loud voice again. "Miranda!"

Gage's gaze tracked along the empty hallway and darted back to the nurses behind the counter. Nobody else looked up.

Randi was still arguing with the nurse.

"She's my cousin and I demand to see her."

"Ma'am…"

"Miranda!"

The woman reached the nurses' station and grabbed Randi's arm and shook it. "Miranda."

Randi dropped the photo and spun around, her eyes wide. "You know who I am?"

The woman's brows knitted. "Of course I do. You're Jessica's best friend, Miranda Lewis."

I HAVE A NAME.

Randi braced herself against the counter for support as her knees buckled, but she didn't need it since Gage had placed a steadying hand on the small of her back to lend his support—just like always.

"What's wrong, Miranda?" The woman patted Randi's hand lying limply on the counter. "You look like you just saw a ghost."

Randi worked her jaw but she couldn't form any words.

Gage took over. "Ma'am, are you Jessica's mother?"

"Yes, I am, and who are you?"

"I'm Randi's friend, Gage Booker."

"From Colombia? I don't understand. How did you hear about Jessica's accident, Miranda?"

"I—I…" How could she tell Jessica's mother that she was the one responsible for her daughter's accident? How could she explain anything?

Gage slipped his arm through Randi's. "Let's talk in the waiting room. We have a few questions to ask you, Mrs. Lehman."

"It's Bloom. Carrie Bloom."

A few knots of people had staked out different corners of the waiting room, and Gage gestured to a vinyl love seat near the coffeemaker. "Please, sit down. Randi has quite a story to tell you."

She did? Did Gage expect her to tell Jessica's mother everything? She glanced at him and he quirked one eyebrow. Probably not.

Randi sat beside Mrs. Bloom and folded her hands in her lap. "This is going to sound crazy, Mrs. Bloom, but until you told me my full name, I didn't know who I was. I still don't know who I am. I have amnesia."

Mrs. Bloom gasped and covered Randi's hands with

one of her own. "My God, Miranda. What's happening to you two girls?"

"I had an accident, too. I fell from a balcony in Colombia." She touched her head where her hair covered the scab forming over her wound. "It's a long story, but I didn't know anyone there and nobody knew me. Gage, Mr. Booker, is in law enforcement. He's been helping me."

"You must be so frightened. I can't even imagine." Mrs. Bloom put her hand across her forehead. "But then how did you know about Jessica? How did you learn about her accident?"

"J-just some clues we followed, a note from Jessica. We were hoping to find more clues here, and you just gave me the biggest one—my full name."

Gage hunched forward, elbows on his knees. "We need your help, Mrs. Bloom. I know you have a lot on your plate right now."

"Nonsense." She waved a hand. "I'll help as much as I can. Jessica wouldn't have it any other way. What do you need to know?"

Randi closed her eyes and released a long breath. "What was I doing in Colombia?"

Mrs. Bloom put her fingers to her lips and her eyes filled with tears. "You don't even know that?"

Randi shook her head.

"You took your grandmother there, back to the village where she was born."

Mrs. Bloom's words felt like a punch to the gut. "My grandmother? Does she live near Barranquilla? What's her name? Does Jessica have her address?"

"I'm sorry, Miranda. Your grandmother is dead. I'm afraid I never knew her name. Jessica always called her

Abuelita. She was your mother's mother, so her last name isn't Lewis."

"She's dead?" Could you grieve for someone you didn't remember? "Do you know when she died?"

"At least a year ago, I think."

"If she died over a year ago, what was I still doing in Colombia?" Randi chewed on her lower lip and shot a glance at Gage.

"That I can't tell you." She patted Randi's knee. "Jessica only mentioned that you were staying on there. If she told me why, I don't remember. I'm sorry."

Randi slumped in her seat. She could've very well stayed on in Colombia because she'd met Zendaris while she'd lived with her grandmother. "My parents?"

"They're dead. You don't have any family in Houston, Miranda, at least none that I know of. I wish I could help you more. Once Jessica comes out of this coma, she can tell you everything."

By then it might be too late.

Randi took the older woman's hand. "I'm sorry I put you through this third degree when your daughter is lying in a hospital bed unconscious."

"Would you like to see her? Maybe seeing Jessica will jog your memory."

"I'd like that."

"Are you getting help?" Mrs. Bloom's gaze shifted to Gage and then back to Randi's face. "Professional help?"

"Yes. Yes, I am." Randi pushed up from the love seat. "And now that I know my full name, I can probably fill in some details of my life. That'll help a lot."

When Mrs. Bloom entered Jessica's hospital room, Randi tiptoed in behind her. Gage waited in the hallway.

The machines in the room hissed and beeped in stereo as another set of noises came from the other side of the curtain that divided the room. Clear tubes ran into the arms of the woman on the bed, her dark hair wrapped in a bun on top of her head.

Mrs. Bloom pulled up a chair and waved Randi to the chair on the other side of the bed. "Miranda's here, Jessica. Wouldn't it be nice to see her again? She's right here. Open your eyes."

Jessica's dark lashes lay against her cheeks, and her hospital gown rose and fell with her steady breathing.

Randi stared into her face, waiting for some sign, some jolt of recognition. She felt nothing but guilt for having brought this upon her friend.

"Jessica?" Randi ran her fingertips down the warm skin of Jessica's arm. "Please come out of this. I need you."

Mrs. Bloom pulled a book from her handbag and slipped her finger between the pages. "I've been reading to her. I have no idea if it helps or not, but I do what I can. I'll put your name on the list of approved visitors, so you can come back."

Randi heard dismissal in Mrs. Bloom's voice, and she didn't blame her. Randi had come to Jessica's bedside seeking answers instead of bringing comfort. And Mrs. Bloom didn't even know the worst of it—that Randi was the reason for Jessica's accident.

Gage punched the elevator button. "No recognition, huh?"

"No. Just a pretty, dark-haired woman in a coma."

"But we can do a search on Miranda Lewis, just like we did on Jessica Lehman. We should be able to discover something about you."

"Then I guess we'd better get back to that laptop."

As they walked past the nurses' station, one of the nurses looked up. "Are you Randi?"

"Yes. Mrs. Bloom is putting me on the list of visitors for Jessica Lehman."

"It's not that." The nurse held out a piece of paper pinched between two fingers. "Someone left this for you, a young man."

"Thank you." Randi took the paper from the nurse and unfolded it with trembling fingers.

"What is it?" Gage hovered over her shoulder and she held it up for him to read. "Randi, I can tell you all about yourself. Meet me in the cafeteria. Sergio."

Gage snatched the paper from her hands and spun back toward the nurse. "Who gave this to you?"

Her eyes widened and she scooted her chair back. "A-a young man. He'd been around before, but he's not on the list of approved visitors. Said he was Ms. Lehman's boyfriend."

"What did he look like?" Gage crumpled the paper in his fist.

"Are you a cop or something? He asked me to deliver a note to this young woman, and I did so. I didn't have to do it, you know."

Randi stepped between Gage's menacing stare and the defiant nurse. "He's asked me to meet him, and I don't know what he looks like. We just want to know who to look for in the cafeteria."

The nurse shuffled some papers and pursed her lips. "A young man with dark hair, curly. He was wearing a denim jacket."

"Okay, thanks. That's all we wanted." She grabbed Gage's hand and pulled him toward the elevator. "What's wrong with you? I thought you were going to bite her head off."

"I don't like it." He punched the button for the elevator twice, three times. "Who is this guy and how does
he know you have amnesia? Why didn't he step forward
when you were talking to Jessica's mother?"

"I guess we'll find out."

The doors slid open and Gage smacked his hand
against one side of the opening. "You're not seriously
considering meeting this guy?"

"Of course I am. He knows me. He can tell me everything, or at least everything he knows."

"We don't know that, Randi. How did he know you
have amnesia? Mrs. Bloom didn't know until you told
her."

"The nurses probably heard me. There were people
in the waiting room."

"We'll stick to plan A. We'll go back to the hotel
room and do a search on the internet."

"That's not going to tell me what I need to know.
Someone who knows who I am is waiting in the cafeteria right now, and you can't stop me from meeting
him. If you wanted me to be a prisoner, you would've
turned me over to Prospero, right?"

"It's foolish and dangerous to meet up with a stranger
under the circumstances."

"I don't have a choice right now, and besides, I'll be
in a public place with you by my side."

"Damn right."

His protectiveness made her feel safe, but maybe
she'd be ready to stand on her own soon. Maybe with
the information she gleaned today and the session with
the mysterious Dr. Elle tomorrow, she'd be on the road
to recovery and not be so dependent on Gage.

They made a right turn off the elevator, following the

signs to the cafeteria. Gage stepped through the doors first, his hand at his hip.

Did he plan to burst into the cafeteria, guns blazing?

Randi scanned the room, her stomach rumbling at the smell of some spicy chili. She pointed to the back of a man hunched over a table in the corner, curly, dark hair spilling over the collar of his denim jacket.

Gage's brows collided over his nose. "Why isn't he facing the doorway on the lookout for you?"

"Every little thing is suspicious to you." She shoved her hands against his back. "Let's see what he has to say. He's not going to attack me here in the hospital cafeteria—especially with you growling at him."

They approached him, their shoes making squeaking noises on the just-mopped floor.

Randi called out. "Sergio?"

He didn't turn around or lift his head, which was tilted forward.

Randi circled the table. "Are you Sergio?"

Her nostrils flared at the sour smell coming from the table. Vomit streamed down the front of Sergio's chest and puddled on the table in front of him.

Stepping back, Randi covered her nose and mouth and gave a muffled cry. "Gage."

He crouched beside Sergio, pressing his fingers against his neck and peering into his bulging eyes.

"Sergio's dead."

Chapter Thirteen

"Looks like a drug overdose." The doctor closed Sergio's eyes with a sweep of his hand.

Mrs. Bloom had collapsed at another table. "Maybe I should've allowed him to see her."

Randi had her arm around Mrs. Bloom, murmuring comforting words, even though the glassiness of Mrs. Bloom's eyes reflected her own shock at the turn of events.

At least Sergio had OD'd in the right place. Hospital orderlies were already loading up his body on a stretcher to take him to the morgue.

Gage would be interested in that autopsy report.

He pulled up a chair to Mrs. Bloom's table. "Sergio was Jessica's boyfriend?"

"Ex-boyfriend. They broke up a few months ago, and that's exactly why." She pointed to the stretcher being wheeled out of the cafeteria. "He had a drug problem. Jessica had had enough."

"He'd been here before to see her?" Randi clasped Mrs. Bloom's pale, veined hand.

"Every minute of every day since she had the accident. I wouldn't allow him to see her. I thought... I thought if Jessica could really hear us, she'd be upset if Sergio came."

"You probably did the right thing. What Sergio chose to do is not your fault."

Mrs. Bloom put a hand to her eyes. "How did you know who he was? How did you two find him?"

"He left a note for Randi. Told her he had information for her. How do you think he found out about Randi's memory loss?"

"He probably got it from the nurses, charmed it out of them. If there was one thing Sergio had, it was charm. Jessica found him irresistible." Mrs. Bloom massaged her temples. "I suppose I should've thought of that myself. If you were looking for information about yourself, Miranda, Sergio probably would've known more about your recent activities than I would. Jessica probably would've told him about you, maybe even what you'd been doing in Colombia after your grandmother died. Selfish of me not to think of that."

"Please, you have enough to think about. I'd like to visit Jessica tomorrow again if I could."

"She'd like that. Just don't tell her about Sergio."

"Of course not."

After they finished speaking to the police and had seen Mrs. Bloom to her car, Gage slumped in the driver's seat of the rental car. "They got to him."

Randi closed her eyes. "I was afraid you were going to say that."

"You knew it, too. I could see it in your face."

Her eyes flew open and she peered out the window into the dark. "They were at the hospital. They were watching Sergio, watching us. They knew he'd left that note for me. They don't want me to remember."

"Then they're out of luck." Gage set his jaw and threw the car into reverse. "It starts tonight and it will continue tomorrow with Elle. You're going to remember everything, and I'm going to keep you safe until you do."

And then what? Would the U.S. government detain her as an accomplice? He couldn't keep her from Prospero forever. Once she remembered her relationship with Zendaris, she'd have no protection from the law. Even Gage couldn't guarantee that.

Gage took a circuitous route back to the hotel, making sure nobody followed them. As soon as they hit the hotel room, he fired up the laptop.

He brought it to the bed and positioned it in his lap as he typed in "Miranda Lewis." He turned to Randi who'd curled up beside him. "Are you ready?"

She nodded and he clicked Search.

They filtered through a few social network sites and a singer before getting a hit at Rice University.

"Here we go." Gage tapped the screen. "Miranda Lewis, graduate student and teaching assistant in Latin-American literature."

"So that's the connection between me and Jessica. Is there any bio info on me?"

"Not much. Some publications, some poetry and your academic credentials. At least we know you're not a stripper."

She punched him in the arm. "Nothing about Colombia."

"Just that you're of Colombian heritage, but we already knew that. Your mother was Colombian, and you went down there with your grandmother. You must've been there about four years because that's when everything stops here at Rice."

"So my parents are dead. I have some useless degree in Latin-American literature, and I'm a published poet.

But why did I stay in Colombia after my grandmother died? What was I doing at Zendaris's compound?"

"Jessica Lehman and Sergio Cortez could've told us that."

"And one's in a coma and one's dead."

"Zendaris is a man of the arts. We know that. In addition to arms dealing, he's been known to deal in stolen art. He's probably a lover of poetry, as well. Maybe that's how you met."

"Why would an American graduate student and poetess take up with an arms dealer? And why would he take up with me?"

"Maybe you didn't know what he was until it was too late. And as far as Zendaris wanting you? That's easy." He closed the computer and shoved it off his lap. "You're the most desirable woman I've ever met."

He didn't tell her she was the only woman who didn't know about his money and family connections. Is that what made her so desirable?

She placed her hand flat on his stomach. "Tomorrow might be too late for us, Gage. Will you still want me if you discover I'm in league with Zendaris? His lover? His partner in every way? Will you still want me when I'm rotting in some federal prison or interrogation room?"

"I don't know, Randi." He rolled to his side. "I only know I want you right now."

"Then take me."

He traced the line of her jaw with the tip of his finger. "I'm wondering if this is all fate, meeting you."

"What do you mean?"

"For a man who's always had to wonder if a woman was more interested in his money and family pedigree than him, meeting a woman with no memory and no knowledge of his background is priceless. And then there's your name."

"Randi?"

"Miranda. The founder of Prospero, Jack Coburn, is a Shakespeare buff. In *The Tempest,* Miranda is the wizard Prospero's daughter."

Her hand inched beneath his shirt and her fingernails trailed across his bare skin. "Then it's meant to be. I'm the daughter of Prospero."

He couldn't stop now even if he wanted to. He shut out all the voices, that of Coburn, of Elle, of his own conscience and enveloped Randi in his arms.

If that's all it took to break through Gage's defenses, she wished she would've remembered her full name sooner.

She drank in his kiss, and yanked up his T-shirt to explore the hard ridges and grooves of his chest with her hands. He shivered as she skimmed his nipple with her palm.

He grabbed the edge of her sweater and tugged. She broke away from his lips only long enough for him to pull the sweater over her head.

He unclasped her bra without looking. There must've been a lot of women interested in his money and power for him to be that practiced. She didn't care.

When her bare chest met his, she could've sworn she heard a sizzle. She felt it, anyway, right down to her toes.

Between the two of them, they managed to shimmy out of their jeans.

Their hands and mouths became more frenzied. It was as if a giant clock ticked over her head. Did Gage hear it, too?

She'd come on to him before and had been smacked

down. This had to be all him. If he couldn't get over the notion tonight that she just *might* be Zendaris's girlfriend—ex-girlfriend—he never would. They may never have this opportunity again, but he had to realize it and want it.

She shifted onto her back, and his hands never lost connection with her body. He skimmed his fingers down her sides and over her hips, hooking the elastic band of her panties and pulling them off.

His eyes kindled with a blue flame, and he pressed a kiss against the base of her throat. She'd wanted to remain cool and detached, but he must feel the wild beat of her pulse.

"You're so beautiful, every inch of you."

She ran a hand across his shoulders despite herself. How could she resist all this gorgeous masculinity hovering over her, as if ready to devour her? "Thank you, but it's nothing you haven't seen before."

"That other time doesn't count." He cupped her breasts and planted another kiss between them. "I was rescuing you."

"When aren't you rescuing me?" She shivered as his kisses continued down to her belly.

He looked up, a grin spreading across his face. "When I'm making love to you."

Really? Because it felt as if he were rescuing her again. She had nothing and nobody except this man, and his need of her filled a void.

His trail of kisses headed farther south, and she gasped her pleasure. His hands opened her thighs, and his tongue plunged inside of her.

She raised her pelvis to escape the exquisite torture just for a moment, but her position only facilitated his tender assault.

His hands curved around her bottom to steady her undulating hips. As he drove her closer and closer to the edge, she dug her fingers into his thick hair, urging him on now. But he needed no urging, no instructions. He knew exactly what to do, exactly how to touch her, exactly how to love her.

Her toes tingled and a delicious warmth coursed through her body. She cried out as a wave of pleasure crashed over her, dragged her under and crashed again. And the name on her lips as her passion took control of her mind and body?

"Gage. Gage."

There was no other. He was her first and her only.

"At your service." He rose, kneeling between her legs, his briefs barely sufficient to contain his erection.

"No fair." She lifted her head, her arms stretching forward. "Why do you still have even one scrap of clothing on?"

"You didn't seem that interested in seeing—" he coughed "—the rest of me."

"I was distracted." She sat up and lunged for his underwear, yanking them down his hips where they twined around his muscled thighs.

She cupped him in her hands and blew out a breath. "Talk about beautiful."

He snorted. "It's not a museum piece."

"Patience." She stroked the length of him, and he uttered a guttural noise deep in his throat. She teased him with fluttering touches, skimming with her fingernails and dabbing with her tongue, until he began pumping his hips.

Then she took him in her mouth, his tight flesh smooth against her lips. His fingers tangled her hair as he hissed, "Yess."

Just when she thought he'd explode, he pulled away from her. "I want you, Randi, in every way."

He pulled his briefs off and tossed them onto the floor. He then leaned over the side of the bed and searched the pockets of his jeans. He raised his hand, a foil package between two fingers.

"I stole a condom from Jessica's apartment. Do you think I'm despicable?"

She swung off the bed and padded to her handbag hanging over the back of a chair. She dipped into the side pocket and withdrew an identical foil packet. "If you are, then I am."

When she returned to the bed, he wrapped his arms around her and then they fell onto the mattress together. Their kiss lasted longer than it should have with their naked bodies pressed against each other.

Randi didn't feel the same urgency that she'd felt when they'd started on this path tonight. She knew Gage wouldn't stop now, couldn't stop any more than she could, and it had nothing to do with his physical urges. For some reason, he needed her just as much as she needed him.

She didn't want to analyze it, and once he entered her, she couldn't. All rational thought had seeped away, had been sucked away by that last kiss.

Wrapping her legs around his hips as he drove into her, only one thought pierced through the fog of sensations that clouded her brain—they still had another condom.

A SHARP RAP on the door shot through Randi's chest, and the adrenaline started pumping. Could that be room service? Had Gage ordered breakfast?

She didn't have to roll over to see if Gage was up.

One heavy arm draped across her body and warm, bare skin pressed against her back.

"Gage. Someone's at the door."

She'd whispered the words, but he shot up as if she'd screamed them in his ear.

Another knock at the door had him bounding from the bed. He pressed his eye to the peephole and swore.

He swung back toward the room, clutching his hair, his gaze bouncing from the floor littered with clothing, to the disheveled bed, to Randi, gathering the covers to her chest.

"Who is it, Gage?"

Whoever it was knocked again and called out. "Gage, are you awake?"

A woman's voice. It must be the psychiatrist, Elle. Is that why Gage was so panicked?

He leaned both hands against the door as if barricading it. "I'm here. Just a minute."

Then he walked back toward the bed, plucking his clothes from the floor along the way. "Get dressed. It's Elle."

Randi clenched her teeth and stepped into her panties and jeans. She stuffed her arms into her sweater and popped her head through the neck.

Gage had pulled on his jeans and dragged his T-shirt over his head. He yanked the bedspread over the bed and smoothed out a few bulges.

"Go—" his head swiveled around the room "—look at the computer."

Smoothing his hands over his hair, he released the chain on the door and pulled it open. "Elle, great to see you here. Thanks for coming."

He wrapped his arms around a tall woman with

gleaming blond hair, and then pulled her into the room. "You're early. Room not ready yet?"

Her blue eyes tracked to Randi, standing foolishly next to the laptop trying to boot it up, then to the bed, and back to Gage.

"Oh, my God. You slept with her, didn't you?" She pushed away from Gage and stamped a booted foot.

Randi slammed down the laptop and wedged her hands on her hips. "Is this your wife, Gage? Is Elle your wife?"

Two pairs of identical bright blue eyes stared at her. "My wife?"

Elle pressed a hand to her forehead. "Oh, God, no. Gage is my twin brother."

Chapter Fourteen

Gage snapped his mouth shut. His wife? Is that what she'd been thinking all along? Surely he'd told Randi Elle was his sister? What other doctor would he trust with a mission this important?

But now his sister knew he'd bedded her patient. And he'd never live it down.

"Your twin sister?" Randi strode forward with her hand outstretched. "It's so nice to meet you, Elle. Or should I call you Dr. Booker?"

"Call me Elle, and it's Dr. Fonesca. I'm married, and if David ever found out that I helped you with your... subterfuge, Gage, he'd divorce me."

Relieved to have the spotlight off him and his misdeeds, Gage laughed. "If he hasn't divorced you yet, I doubt helping your twin in need would push him over the edge."

Still gripping Randi's hand, Elle had backed her up to the bed and nudged her to sit down. She brushed Randi's hair from her forehead and inspected the scabbed-over injury. "Yeah, except David knows when you have a problem, there's usually danger attached to it."

"There's obviously some risk involved, Elle, but I'll keep you safe."

"You always do." She pointed to the suitcase she'd

dropped by the door. "Dig in there and bring me my medical bag."

"I think Randi's physical wounds are healing nicely. It's her psychological wound we're hoping you can fix." He opened the black leather bag and placed it on the bed next to Randi.

"I can tell you're really concerned about Randi's psychological well-being." She clicked on a penlight and shined it in Randi's eyes. "Randi, why don't you take the bandage off your arm, shower and then I'll take a look at everything from top to bottom."

Randi raised her brows at him and he nodded. At least his sister planned to lay into him in private.

Randi grabbed some clean clothes from her bag and clutched them to her chest at the bathroom door. "Don't be too hard on him, Elle. I was a willing participant."

When the bathroom door shut, Elle rounded on him. "Are you out of your mind? How could you sleep with a woman in her condition? Not only does she have amnesia, she's an important witness in a huge international case, a witness you stole from the CIA."

"Whoa." Gage made a cross with his two index fingers and held them in front of him. "Where did you hear that?"

"Where do you think? Dad called me."

Gage crossed his arms and puffed out his chest. "What did he say?"

"He'd heard from some crony that you'd snatched an important witness away from a secure CIA compound in Central America. That you'd jeopardized national security and the relations between U.S. covert groups. And you did this, why? Because you wanted to play house with her in some hotel room in Houston?"

"Are you done?"

Elle took a turn around the room, clutching her blond hair into a ponytail. "What am I supposed to think, Gage? I know you're a ladies' man, but this is ridiculous."

Pain sliced through his temple, and he ground it out with the heel of his hand. The old man had been the only one who could ever drive a wedge between him and his sister. And he tried constantly.

"You know me better than that, Elle. That CIA compound in Central America planned to use Randi in the most vile way. Do you want to know what they were going to do to her?"

"No." She covered her ears like she used to do when they were kids. "You and Dad keep that stuff between yourselves. I don't want to hear the gory details."

"Are you eight years old or are you Dr. Elle Fonesca, kick-ass psychiatrist?"

She dropped her hands and stuffed them into the pockets of her coat. "What were they going to do to Randi?"

"They were going to forcibly impregnate her to lure out a bad guy."

"That's horrible, draconian." She hunched her shoulders. "Of course you had to rescue her from that, but what about Prospero? How come you haven't contacted your own agency?"

"Too risky. Too many connections to the CIA there, and I can't reach my own team members. Just tell me you can help."

"I'll try. Anything for my big brother." She gave him a quick hug. "But why did you sleep with her? She has amnesia, Gage. You took advantage of her almost as much as the CIA wanted to."

He closed his eyes, reliving last night when Randi's

hands and mouth were all over him, giving and taking so much pleasure. He hadn't taken advantage of her. She'd wanted him. She'd wanted him for himself, for the moment and nothing more.

"Hello?" Elle tapped him on the shoulder.

"You don't understand."

"I understand the male libido. What if she's in league with that arms dealer?"

If she was, last night was even more important, but Elle would never understand that, either. He had to get back on logical ground with her, had to put his indiscretion in terms she'd accept. "That's what we're hoping to find out. And if she is, don't you think sleeping with her is a sure way to cement her loyalty to me?"

"Oh." Elle tilted her head and wrinkled her nose. "I can't say I approve of your methods, but you're the spy. That still doesn't make it right."

A gust of lemon-scented steam rolled into the room, and Randi stood framed by the bathroom door. "Is it safe?"

"Absolutely." Gage shot a warning glance at his sister. "Why don't you let Elle see what a good job I did addressing your medical needs, and I'll take a shower. You two can order some room service, and then Dr. Fonesca can pick your brain."

"Sounds like you have it all figured out." Randi whipped the towel from her head and shook out her wet hair.

Gage left Randi in Elle's capable hands and stepped into the shower. Had he made a mess of things by giving in to his urges and making love with Randi last night? Holding her in his arms and melding his body to hers felt like anything but a mess.

No matter what happened today, he'd work things out

with Randi. She wouldn't possibly want to go back to Zendaris after everything that SOB had put her through. Zendaris wouldn't take her back, anyway...except to kill her.

Could he be with a woman who'd belonged to his enemy? Who'd slept in his enemy's bed? Who'd touched his enemy the way she'd touched him last night?

He pounded the tile with his fist. Not if he kept thinking about the two of them together. But how could he stop? Once Randi regained her memory, he couldn't keep separating the brave, fearless woman he knew from the woman who'd associated with a dangerous, lowlife criminal, sharing his life and his blood money and his bed.

When he rejoined the women, Randi sported a fresh bandage on her arm and a dubious look in her eyes.

Had Elle done a number on her? Maybe now that his twin believed he'd slept with Randi for the good of the country and U.S. intelligence, she'd leave it alone.

Elle snapped her bag closed. "You did a good job on Randi's injuries."

"You checked the bullet wound on her shoulder, too?"

"Barely a scuff now."

"The injury to her arm?"

"Healing nicely. If we can just get her mind in shape like her body, we'll be in business." Elle waved the room-service menu. "We ordered some eggs and bacon and pastries along with a pot of coffee."

"I brought Elle up to speed on everything we know so far, everything we discovered from Jessica's mother and the internet." Randi pulled the sleeve of her sweater over her new bandage.

Elle said, "You neglected to tell me about the additional body at the hospital last night."

"Jessica's ex-boyfriend? No time."

"It means they're here, doesn't it? Zendaris's men are in Houston."

"They didn't follow us to the hotel. I made sure of that."

"Look, Gage." Elle took his hand. "This isn't going to be some one-shot deal—I hypnotize Randi and she remembers everything down to Zendaris's favorite pair of socks."

"I know that."

"Good." She squeezed his hand and smiled at Randi. "I already explained to Randi that this might take some time. I also detailed the use of Sodium Pentothal in such situations."

He stepped back. "Truth serum? You sound like crazy Dr. Murdoch at the CIA compound."

"It can speed things up, and Randi's agreed."

He glanced at Randi and she shrugged. "The sooner you find out all about Zendaris, the better, right? I mean, that's why you saved me from his estate and that's why you snatched me from the CIA. Isn't it?"

"That's part of the reason, but…"

"Room service!" A knock accompanied the words.

"Then let's eat and get this show on the road." Randi took a step toward the door, but Gage stopped her. Something had cooled between them since Elle arrived, but that didn't mean he still didn't have her back.

"Let me." He tucked his gun into the back of his waistband and peeked through the peephole. A waiter hunched over a tray laden with silver-domed covers.

Gage cracked the door open. "I'll bring it in."

He signed off for the food and wheeled the cart into

the room. "Stand back, Elle. Randi and I haven't eaten since yesterday afternoon."

"So, I guess you didn't sate all your appetites."

Elle began lifting the covers from the plates while Gage rolled his eyes at Randi. She didn't even crack a smile. She must be as worried about what lay ahead as he was.

They polished off the breakfast down to the last crumb, he and Randi claiming the lion's share.

He shoved the tray into the hallway and returned to the room, rubbing his hands together. "How are we going to proceed? Should I leave the room?"

"That's up to Randi."

Gage held his breath. Last night he would've had no doubts at all that she'd want him here. But this morning they were playing a different game.

"Gage can stay."

"Okay, Randi. Get comfortable. You can lie on the bed or sit in the chair."

"I'll sit in the chair." Randi sat down in an upholstered chair by the window, stretching her long legs in front of her, folding her hands in her lap.

Elle pulled up a chair across from her and held up her penlight. "Watch this pen, Randi, Miranda Lewis, or watch the light if you like. Don't take your eyes from it. Clear your mind, relax your muscles, breathe in, breathe out."

Randi's hands opened in her lap and her shoulders slumped.

"Your eyelids are getting heavy, so heavy. I'm going to start counting backward, Miranda Lewis, and with each number you're going to get more and more sleepy."

Elle started counting, and Randi's chest rose and fell. Her eyelids drooped and her lips parted.

"When I get to the number one, you're going to be completely relaxed and rested."

Randi's chin dipped to her chest and her eyes closed even before Elle reached the number one, but his sister kept counting in a rhythmic, monotone voice until she reached the end.

"Can you hear me, Miranda Lewis?"

"Yes."

"What's your name?"

"Miranda Lewis. Everyone calls me Randi."

"Who's everyone?"

"Jessica, all my friends. Everyone except Abuelita."

"Is Abuelita your grandmother?"

"Yes."

"Where is Abuelita, Randi?"

"In Colombia."

"Is she still in Colombia?"

"Yes. No." Randi's lower lip quivered.

"Where is Abuelita, Randi?"

"She's dead."

"Were you with her in Colombia when she died?"

"Yes."

Elle took a deep breath. "Why did you stay in Colombia after Abuelita died, Randi?"

"The children." Randi's breathing grew more rapid, and her fingernails dug into the arms of the chair. "Save the children."

She jolted forward in the chair, and her arms flailed at her sides. Her mouth hung open in a silent scream.

"Your children, Randi? Are you trying to save your children?"

"Stop it, Elle. She's had enough. Can't you see she's had enough?"

Gage jumped from the bed, but Elle held up her hand. "Wait."

She stood up and took Randi by the arm. "It's okay, Randi. I'm bringing you out now."

She started counting from one and by the time she reached ten, Randi had dropped back into the chair, her breathing back to normal.

Several more seconds of counting and Randi was blinking her eyes and licking her lips.

"Will she remember any of that, Elle?"

"She should. I didn't give her a cue that she shouldn't remember what transpired during hypnosis."

Randi cleared her throat. "I remember. I had the same memory I had when Jose shot that man. Someone was pointing a gun at me, and the children were screaming."

Elle placed both hands on Randi's knees. "Were they your children, Randi? Your children with Zendaris?"

Gage's gut twisted in knots, and his hands formed into fists. How could he have any future with Randi if she shared children with Nico Zendaris?

"No." Randi shook her head. "I'd know if I had children. I'd remember that. I told you before. Those kids called me *mademoiselle*. Why would they call their own mother *mademoiselle?*"

"Maybe that's your way of protecting yourself against the loss of your children."

Randi crossed her arms, her chin forming a hard line. "Or maybe it's because I'm not their mother."

Gage stepped between the two women and placed his hands on Randi's shoulders. "Take a break and relax."

Randi shrugged him off and crowded past him to get out of the chair. "Why do I keep coming back to that one memory, the one where I'm shot?"

Elle tapped her penlight on the blank pad of paper in her lap. "Because that's the trauma. It's a good sign, actually. It means that your memory loss was caused by the psychological trauma of the shooting more than the head injury."

"Why is that a good thing?" Randi paced the room like a caged cat.

"A physical trauma usually takes longer to heal. I think you can break through that moment to regain the rest of your memory."

"Then let's do it."

"The Sodium Pentothal?"

"Yes."

"Wait a minute." Gage grabbed Elle's medical bag and hugged it to his chest as if it could stop either of these women. "Do you understand the consequences of being injected with truth serum, Randi?"

"Yeah, the truth." She narrowed her eyes looking even more like a cat. "What are you afraid of? Do you want me to remember or don't you?"

"Exactly." Elle extended her hand, wiggling her fingers for her bag. "What *are* you afraid of, Gage?"

He was afraid of never holding Randi in his arms again.

"Are you going to at least warn her about the possible side effects?"

"Dizziness, lightheadedness, nausea, respiratory distress, cardiac arrhythmias and in rare cases, death." Elle ticked off each side effect on her fingers.

"Sounds good to me." Randi dropped to the bed, lay down and crossed her ankles. "Let's get started."

Elle withdrew a syringe and three small vials from her medical bag. "I'm going to have to inject this in a vein in your arm. If you're squeamish, look away."

"My arm's been a pincushion the past few days. What's one more injection?" Randi rolled up the sleeve of her sweater. "Just as long as this one won't make me pregnant."

Elle held the needle up to the light. "Nope, no sperm swimming around in here."

They both laughed, and Gage's brows shot up. "You think this is funny? You're taking this lightly."

"What am I supposed to do, Gage, cry? I want to find out for sure what I was doing in Colombia in Zendaris's house. Don't you?"

"Absolutely."

Elle prepped the syringe and cleaned a spot on the inside of Randi's arm.

The alcohol felt cool on her flesh, and her nostrils twitched at the scent. The needle pricked her skin as it went in, but the pain was negligible after what she'd been through the past few days.

Especially the pain she'd felt when she overheard Gage telling his sister that he'd slept with her only to cement her loyalty. She'd never recover from that pain.

Elle's voice floated above her. "You'll be feeling really drowsy in a few minutes. I'm going to ask you some questions. Let your mind go."

Elle's questions came and went. Randi tried to form the answers, but moving her lips became a huge effort.

Why did you stay in Colombia after Abuelita died?

What were you doing at Zendaris's palatial home?

Who visited the house?

Did you know about Zendaris's illegal activities?

The children. Randi smiled. She was reading them a story, and the girl had a pink, spangled scarf wrapped around her shoulders. But then Randi flew out the window and left the children behind.

Randi's eyes opened to slits and she surveyed the room. Her gaze slid over Gage sprawled in a chair, watching TV. Randi coughed, and Gage's head jerked up.

"Are you awake? Are you feeling okay?" He strode to the bed and hovered over her. "Elle's in the next room, but she wanted me to get her as soon as you woke up."

"I'm okay. Just thirsty."

He grabbed a bottle of water from the table and knocked on the door that connected their room with another. As he handed Randi the bottle, Elle emerged from the other room.

"How are you feeling, Randi?"

"Okay. What happened?"

Elle sat on the edge of the bed and felt Randi's pulse. "You fell asleep. That's the way some people react to Sodium Pentothal, and I guess you're one of them."

"Oh." Randi rubbed her temples. "Big disappointment, huh?"

"Not completely. The hypnosis worked okay, and we can try that again later. It may just take time."

"Time we don't have. The sooner Randi regains her memory, the safer she'll be. There will be no reason for Zendaris to come after her once he realizes it's a done deal."

"I realize that, Gage." Elle peered into Randi's eyes. "Why don't you just spread the word that Randi told you everything there is to know about Zendaris?"

"We'd have to back up that knowledge with something solid or he'd see it for what it was—a scam."

"I did have a dream while I was under." Randi pushed Elle's hands away. She'd had enough of people fussing over her.

"What was the dream?" Gage sat on the other side of the bed.

"I dreamt about the children."

Gage and his sister exchanged a look.

"They're not mine. That pink scarf that you're using as proof that I'm the same woman in the airport with Zendaris? It belongs to the little girl. She was wearing the scarf in the dream."

"That wasn't a little girl's scarf."

Randi rolled her eyes. "And just what do you know about little girls? It was pink and it had sparkles on it. What else could a little girl possibly want in a scarf?"

"It was too big for her." Gage rubbed the dark stubble on his chin.

"Maybe it did belong to the woman in the airport, Zendaris's girlfriend, or…"

Gage snapped his fingers. "His wife, the girl's mother."

"That would explain why the girl kept it. It belonged to her mother…not me. I had the scarf. It doesn't mean it was mine."

"Did the dream give you any sense of what you were doing with the kids?"

"I was reading to them. I was their nanny." She scooted up to a sitting position, folding her legs beneath her, her heart pounding. "It makes sense, Gage. I'm a graduate student. I speak English, Spanish and French. The kids called me *mademoiselle*. I was there to teach the children."

"It does make sense, Randi, but I keep coming back to the picture in the airport—the brunette with the pink scarf."

"The picture is not that clear. You had the picture, you found me and the pink scarf and you made me fit what you wanted to find. If you'd never had that photo and discovered me injured at the compound, I could've been anyone—the cook, the housekeeper, the nanny."

"I hope you're right, Randi." He cupped the side of her face, his fingers entangling her hair. "God, I hope you're right."

She wanted to jerk away from him and scream at him that he didn't have to pretend anymore. She would've helped him, anyway. She would've helped her country.

"Nobody's asking, but it sounds plausible to me, too." Elle stood up and stretched. "You've come out of the sedation just fine, Randi. Do you want to do another hypnosis session tonight or tomorrow morning?"

"Yes. I feel like I'm on the edge of remembering everything."

"I'm going to call Dave and take a nap in my room, and then order some room service. Are you two going out?"

Gage checked the alarm clock on the bedside table. "We're going to the hospital to visit Randi's friend."

"It sure seems like anyone who can help Randi with her memory is being systematically taken out." Elle hugged herself and shivered. "I hope they don't find out about me."

"Not a chance." Gage gave her a quick hug. "If Randi feels up to it and you're awake when we get back, you can do another session."

Elle paused with her hand on the doorknob to the adjoining room, her gaze flicking between Gage and Randi. "I'm glad you're not an arms dealer's mistress, Randi."

"I never thought I was."

It didn't matter now, anyway. She had no future with Gage. She'd been a fool to even imagine that could be a possibility. He wanted to make sure she'd fall on the side of the good guys, and he'd been prepared to do anything to make that a reality.

Even if it broke her heart.

When Elle had closed the door between the two rooms, Gage turned to her. "Do you want to eat first or visit Jessica?"

"It's getting late. Let's go to the hospital first. You haven't heard anything from Mrs. Bloom, have you?"

"No, but tonight may be the night Jessica comes out of her coma. You never know."

Twenty minutes later, Gage pulled his rental car into the parking structure of the hospital. A smattering of people wandered the halls of the ICU and clusters of visitors dotted the waiting room. Orderlies whisked patients back and forth, and the nurses at the station scrambled to handle all of the details.

Randi approached the counter. "We're here to visit Jessica Lehman."

A different nurse from the one last night pulled up a computer screen. "Name?"

"Miranda Lewis."

The nurse pointed at Gage. "Him?"

"Oh, I don't think Jessica's mother put him on the list."

"Sir, you'll have to wait in the waiting room."

"Okay." Gage shoved his hands in his pockets and tilted his chin toward the hallway. "You go ahead. I'll be right out here. Don't leave the room until you see me in the hallway."

"Okay. Nurse, has Jessica come out of her coma yet?"

"Not yet, but the signs look encouraging."

Randi grimaced at Gage. "I probably won't be too long."

He nodded and she sailed down the hallway. Maybe with a few memories coming back, seeing Jessica would prompt a few more.

She tiptoed into the room, though she should've be stomping her feet to wake her friend. Jessica's mother must've been in for a visit, as she'd left a few grooming items on the table beside Jessica's bed.

Randi pulled up a chair, sat down and leaned toward Jessica. "What a pair we make." She took Jessica's hand, warm with life. "I'm so sorry I got you into this mess, Jessica. You must be a loyal friend to protect me. I saw the picture of the two of us in Cozumel. Maybe when this is all over, we can go back."

Randi drew her brows together at the rustling of paper from the other side of the curtain dividing the room. It hadn't occurred to her that the other patient might have a visitor.

She put her lips close to Jessica's ear. "Wake up, Jessica. Let's get out of this together."

A man coughed and murmured a few words on the other side of the hospital room. He was trying to get through to his loved one, too.

Randi returned her gaze to Jessica's serene face. "I need your help, Jessica. I need to remember everything. I need to know what I was doing in that household."

The metal hooks holding up the curtain tinkled and a soft footstep shuffled on the floor.

Randi looked up at a tall, bald man bunching the curtain in one hand.

He said, "Sorry to disturb you. This is hard, no?"

The man had an accent Randi couldn't place. She nodded. "Yes, it's very hard."

The man shuffled closer, and the scent of his cologne wafted across Jessica's bed, hitting Randi full force. Her nostrils flared. Prickles dashed across the back of her neck. She reached behind her and slid the metal nail file from the table into her back pocket.

"All we can do is talk to them. Share our memories and hope they respond." Taking another step forward, he shrugged a pair of huge shoulders in his orderly scrubs.

Randi licked her lips. Was he a visitor or did he work here? She scooted the chair back from the bed and glanced at the closed door and the blinds pulled down over the large window onto the hallway. "That's right."

"Remind them of the good times, no?" The man's next step brought him almost to Randi's side.

His overpowering cologne caused a shaft of pain to pierce her temple, and she pressed a palm against the side of her head.

The gunshot. She heard the gunshot and the children's cries.

The man loomed over her. "Only you can't do that, can you, *mademoiselle?*"

By the time she'd worked her mouth open for a scream, he clamped his hand over it. Then she felt the prick of a needle in the side of her neck.

Another damned needle.

Chapter Fifteen

Gage paced in front of the hallway that led to the ICU rooms and checked his watch for the hundredth time. She should be out soon. If Jessica had regained consciousness, Randi would've come out to tell the nurses.

Unless seeing Jessica again had prompted some memories to return. Elle had told him anything could prompt the memories—the sight of something, hearing a noise, tasting a special flavor and even smelling something familiar.

Randi's explanation of the scarf and her insistence that the children didn't belong to her and that she didn't belong to Zendaris had given him hope. Zendaris could've been married and had those children. What did they really know about him?

Not much. Not enough.

Another session with Elle, and Randi just might break through that barrier. She might break through the trauma of the shooting and fall to reach back and remember everything.

The hospital loudspeaker filled the ICU. The announcement mentioned a car on level three in the parking lot, and Gage paused and cocked his head.

A car had been hit in the parking lot and the alarm

wouldn't quit. The location and the description of the car matched his rental.

Digging his keys from his pocket, he strode to the nurses' station. "My friend, Randi, is visiting Ms. Lehman in room five twenty-eight. If she comes out while I'm gone, can you please tell her to wait right here for me?"

The nurse glanced up from her paperwork. "Sure."

"Right here." Gage pounded the counter.

The nurse raised one brow. "Sure."

Gage jogged to the elevator and smacked the button for the parking garage. When he got to his parking level, two security guards were standing near his blaring car.

He pointed his remote and clicked. The alarm stopped.

Approaching the security guards, he said, "What happened?"

"This happened." One of the men aimed a boot at the crumpled bumper of Gage's rental.

"Where's the person who hit it? I don't think I even got the extra insurance from the car company."

"Sorry, sir. It was a hit and run. We just heard the alarm and came over to investigate. I'm assuming this dent wasn't here when you left the car."

"Nope." Gage ran a hand through his hair, and his gut knotted. "Anyone see anything? Security cameras?"

"Nobody has come forward, and the cameras don't operate in this area of the garage."

"Not much good then, are they?" Gage kicked the bumper and turned back toward the elevator. The adrenaline pumping through his system had nothing to do with the accident. It was the coincidence of the accident occurring at the hospital that had the blood racing through his veins.

He marched to the nurses' station and flattened his palms on top of the counter, hunching forward. "Did my friend leave Ms. Lehman's room yet?"

The nurse eyed him as if he were a lunatic. "No. She's still in there."

He smacked his fist into his palm, and the nurse jumped. "It's been almost an hour. What's she doing in there?"

"Is that a rhetorical question, sir? Because I'm sure I don't know. Visiting hours are still going on and she has every right to be there."

But he didn't.

"Call her if you're in such a big hurry."

Randi hadn't gotten a phone when she got to the States. She didn't need one. Who would she call? He was the only person she knew, and he'd stuck by her side night and day.

Until now.

"Can you check the room for me? Tell her I'm waiting?"

"I'm not in the habit of interrupting patient visits, and I have work to do."

"Is there another exit from the ICU? Could she have walked out a different way?"

"This is the only way out, unless…"

Gage's heart slammed against his rib cage. "Unless what?"

The nurse cupped her hand around her mouth. "Unless you're dead. There's an elevator to the morgue at the other end of the hallway."

A chill snaked up Gage's back. He had to get into

that room if only to calm the insistent thrum of dread in his chest.

If he demanded the nurse let him in there and she refused, she'd only be looking out for him later.

He cleared his throat. "Well, she didn't go out that way. I guess all I can do is wait."

"You'd be surprised how long people spend with comatose patients. It's that desire to try anything." She tapped a file folder on her desk and swiveled her chair in the other direction.

Gage backed up toward the waiting room and made for the stairwell. On the floor below the ICU he sidled along the corridor, checking doors. On his fourth try, he found a white doctor's coat on a tree.

On his seventh try, he scooped up an orderly's badge.

He took the stairs back up to the ICU. He slouched by the restroom in the waiting room until a couple checked in with the nurses' station. When the couple started down the hallway, Gage joined them, dipping his head over his phone.

Only one nurse at the station glanced up when they walked by. He must've passed muster because she went back to her computer screen.

The couple peeled off to enter a room, and Gage continued two doors down. Pressing his ear against the door, he tapped.

When Randi didn't answer, he tapped louder. "Randi, it's Gage."

His mouth dry, he eased open the door. Jessica reposed on the hospital bed like Sleeping Beauty, Sleeping Beauty with no visitors.

Gage stepped into the room, his gaze darting to the four visible corners. "Randi?"

He yanked at the curtain dividing the room, and an

empty bed stretched in front of him. Hadn't there been a patient in there last night?

Two long steps took him to the window where he placed his hands against the tempered glass. Five stories up with a sealed window and no ledge.

He spun around, crashing into a cart and knocking its contents to the floor. If she hadn't gone past the nurses' station, she was in one of these rooms…or she'd gone down to the morgue.

He careened up and down the hallway, poking his head into rooms, startling visitors and patients alike. When he ran out of rooms, he faced the elevator at the end of the corridor. He jabbed the down arrow, but the car didn't budge.

He traced the slot beneath the button and then slipped the stolen badge from the plastic lanyard. He slid the badge into the slot and pressed the button. The elevator cranked into gear.

Gage held his breath. The car settled on the fifth floor and the doors shifted apart. With a backward glance, he entered the empty elevator and pressed the only available button—M for Morgue.

The car trundled past the rest of the floors without stopping and burrowed into the bowels of the hospital. When it came to a stop, Gage pulled out his weapon and aimed it at the door, the old metal throwing back his distorted reflection.

The doors creaked open onto an empty hallway. Gage eased out of the elevator, leading with his shoulder, clutching his gun.

The silence closed around him. The chill seeped into the marrow of his bones.

And it smelled like death.

SHE WAS IN A COFFIN.

She drove the heels of her hands into the lid of the coffin and the clanging sound rang in her ears.

She was in a metal coffin.

Yelling and screaming, she kicked her feet against the base of her prison. The sound reverberated all around her, suffocating her.

Her teeth chattered and her knees shook, but it was the cold and not the fear causing her reaction.

She heard a noise like a latch being lifted, and her coffin bed rolled into the light, a dim light in a white-on-white room. She bolted upright and squinted at a figure in the shadows.

"Who are you? What am I doing here?"

A looming shape stalked forward, his musky, spicy scent heralding his presence. The same cologne of the man in the hospital room. The same cologne of the man who'd locked her in the nursery and had ripped the children from her arms.

Costa.

She scrambled off the slab where he'd stashed her as if she were a dead body. But she wasn't dead yet.

"It's too late, Costa. I remembered everything. I told them everything."

A tsking sound came from a darkened corner of the room, and Randi spun around. She peered at the man lounging against the wall, but he was behind a bright light shining into her face and she could see nothing more than his outline.

"She's lying, boss. I heard her in that hospital room talking to her friend, asking for help, asking to remember. She remembers nothing."

The man in the corner sighed. "Apparently, she remembers your name, you fool."

"Maybe when she saw my face, but she doesn't have the rest of it."

"I believe you're right, Costa. My dear, if you'd told them everything, I'd be feeling the heat, and—" he shrugged "—I feel no heat."

Nico Zendaris. The room just got colder. "Th-they just want you to believe that."

"Hmm, now why would Prospero want me to believe you had no memory of me, of our life together? The sooner you regained your memory, the safer you'd be. Are you trying to tell me that the gallant agents of Prospero aren't concerned with your well-being?"

"We're talking about national security—and we had no life together."

He chuckled. "Are you sure about that, my dear?"

"I was your children's nanny."

"My children?" His cold tone sent more chills coursing down her back. "What are their names, nanny?"

"I—I don't remember their names, but I read to them and your daughter had a pink scarf, a pink scarf with silver thread."

"Did you try to tell that nanny story to the CIA? They obviously didn't believe you, since they planned to use your pregnancy to lure me out."

Randi gasped. "How did you know about that?"

"Do you think Gage Booker is the only one with friends in high places?"

Gage. Where was he? How had Costa gotten her out of Jessica's room without everyone seeing them?

"Those rogue CIA doctors may not believe me, but Ga—Prospero does."

"And that's why Booker is trying so hard to protect you, a nanny?" He snorted. "What would a nanny know about me? Ah, but a mistress, a beloved mistress privy to all of my intimate details…"

Nausea swept through Randi and she swayed against the body drawer.

"Mark my words. Prospero knows you're my woman, and that's why Booker is hell-bent on protecting you. And once you fully regain your memory, don't think Prospero isn't going to use you. Oh, they may not impregnate you, but they will systematically break you down. And when they get what they want?" He brushed his hands together. "They'll toss you out or lock you up."

"Boss." Costa stepped toward the door, cocking his head, which gleamed like a dome in the darkness. "I hear the elevator."

"It's either Booker or one dead coroner." Zendaris pressed back into the corner of the room and slipped something out of his pocket.

Randi made a dash for the door, but Costa lunged toward her and hooked her around the neck with one beefy arm, his gun pressed to her temple.

Randi held her breath, praying. *Don't come in here, Gage. Don't come in.*

The door inched open, and Costa released the safety on his gun. The click echoed in the room.

The barrel of a gun poked through the crack in the door, and Costa dragged Randi into the shaft of light that beamed in from the corridor.

"Drop your weapon, Booker, and kick it across the room. Come inside slowly, or your witness gets a bullet—in the head this time."

"Don't do it, Gage. Run!"

The gun dropped and then skittered across the floor

as Gage kicked it into the room. He emerged from the door, hands held high. "Are you okay, Randi?"

"I'm fine, Gage. Zendaris is here. In the corner."

Costa choked off her last words by tightening his arm around her throat. "Shut up!"

Gage said, "We meet again, Zendaris."

The voice came from the corner of the room, muffled now. "We never met that day five years ago. I slipped out of your grasp, just like I always do. Prospero doesn't call me the Phantom for nothing."

"You slipped from our clutches but we still disrupted your deal, set you back a few years."

"But now I'm back, and if you thought I was going to allow you to abscond with my treasured mistress, Miranda, you are not thinking straight."

Gage gave a sharp bark. "Randi's not your mistress. She's your children's nanny. Did you think you could hide the fact that you had children at your compound?"

"Not my children."

"Don't worry, Zendaris. Prospero doesn't operate like you. We'd never harm a child to get to you."

"Really? You'd never harm a woman, either?"

"We don't have any intention of harming Randi."

"I'm not talking about Randi." Zendaris paused before continuing. "Do you remember the burned-out munitions factory?"

"How could I ever forget it?"

"You remember the bodies, burnt beyond recognition?"

"Of course I do, but that's on you. You had those people working there, all of them criminals."

"Not all."

Randi's stomach churned and she shot a glance at Gage, whose face had whitened in the gloom.

"If they were working for you, they were all criminals."

"But they weren't all working for me." Zendaris slammed his fist against the wall.

"Boss, not a good idea." Costa adjusted his grip on Randi.

If she could slip away, knock the gun out of his hand or toward the ceiling… She didn't even know if Zendaris was armed.

"What are you talking about, Zendaris?" Gage shifted his body toward Costa.

"My wife. My wife was in that munitions factory. She'd foolishly dropped by to show me some bauble she'd bought. She was there, Booker. The noble agents of Prospero murdered my wife."

"Your fault, Zendaris. She shouldn't have been anywhere near that factory."

"But she was. Why do you think Randi's still alive? I used her to lure you here. I could've had Costa take care of her in that hospital room. Now you're going to pay. You're all going to pay. I missed my chance with Stark and Douglas—screw-ups."

"They sacrificed an opportunity to nail you for the ones they loved. Did you do the same? Instead of protecting your wife, instead of keeping her out of danger, you were careless. How did she even know about the munitions factory?"

"Shut up!"

"Let him go." Randi twisted in Costa's grasp. "I lied. I started remembering about us, but I lied to him. Told him I was your nanny. I didn't tell him anything about you, about our life together. I just want to go home with you now. I don't want them coming after you for the death of this agent."

Gage jerked his head toward her. Did he realize she was lying now? She'd do anything to save him.

"That's very touching, Miranda. Weren't you just insisting to me moments ago that you were my nanny?"

"I—I don't remember. I'm confused. I'll go with you now. Let's leave this place."

Her fingers had been clawing at Costa's arm, trying to keep it from closing off her throat. Now she dropped one hand to her back pocket where something was poking her.

She traced the outline of the metal file through her jeans. She had to act now or Zendaris would kill Gage. She slipped her fingers in her back pocket and pulled out the file.

She drew her arm back and swung it across her body to stab Costa in the arm that held his weapon.

He cursed and squeezed off a shot, the gunfire deafening in the cavernous room. Gage lunged at Costa, knocking him off his feet. Randi went down with them, pinned between the two men.

Zendaris launched from the corner, something gleaming in his own hand. He loomed above the bodies grappling on the floor. Raising the knife with both hands, he plunged toward the back of Gage's neck.

Randi screamed. At the final moment, Gage twisted to the side, dragging Randi from Costa's body. The gun exploded again as Zendaris sank his knife into Costa's chest.

Warm blood spattered the side of Randi's face and she choked out a cry. Gage rolled on top of her and grabbed for the gun in Costa's hand.

He swung it toward Zendaris, collapsed on top of Costa, his hands still wrapped around the knife's handle. Gage held the weapon to Zendaris's ear and scrabbled to his haunches.

"They're dead, Randi. They're both dead. It's over." He grabbed the black ski mask on Zendaris's head and peeled it off.

Randi rolled to her stomach and hitched up to her elbows. "It's not over, Gage."

"It will be. It'll be okay. You'll regain your memory, and I'll be with you every step of the way, Randi. I'm not giving up on you. I'm not leaving you."

"You don't understand. It's not over."

"What do you mean?"

She pointed a steady finger at the face of the man lying in a pool of his own blood. "That's not Zendaris."

Epilogue

Randi surveyed the sketch artist's finished product—a handsome man with a strong chin, aquiline nose and dark, brooding eyes.

She released a sigh. "That's him. That's Nico Zendaris, my former employer."

Gage leaned across the table and kissed her. "Great job."

The sketch artist packed up her supplies and smiled. "You've been a dream to work with, Randi. I'll leave this sketch to you two."

The artist nodded at Gage and J.D., Gage's fellow team member from Prospero.

Gage smoothed a corner of the drawing. "How's Jessica doing since she came out of the coma?"

"She's recovering. I'd like to go back to Houston to visit her and apologize."

"Collateral damage in a dangerous game." J.D. clenched his hands. "Zendaris doesn't care who he hurts."

"The kids will be okay, won't they?" Randi grabbed Gage's hands. "You won't use Nicky and Angelina to get to Zendaris, will you?"

"We don't do that, Randi." He threaded his fingers through hers. "I don't even know if the story that imposter told about Zendaris's wife dying at the munitions factory is true."

J.D. drummed his fingers on the table. "It makes sense. He's had a personal vendetta against the four of us in Prospero Team Three since we disrupted that deal. It goes way beyond business."

J.D. had come in from an extended vacation with his fiancée just to hear Randi's report on Zendaris and to see the sketch firsthand.

How did his fiancée feel about that? Is that what life would be like with Gage? Would she have an opportunity to find out?

"Do you think Zendaris gave the imposter authorization to reveal the story?" Gage picked up the sketch. He couldn't seem to leave it alone.

"Nothing happens in that organization without Zendaris's stamp of approval." J.D. flicked the sketch with his finger. "I think Zendaris's stand-in was in Colorado, too. I didn't come face-to-face with Zendaris. He wouldn't put himself in jeopardy like that—not even to kill us."

Randi shivered and squeezed Gage's hands tighter. "Do you think my information will help you find him?"

"Your information is the best we've had on this guy yet. Once you started remembering, your level of detail on the house, his associates, his habits—amazing. I always knew you were amazing." He brought her hands to his lips and kissed them.

"Even when you thought I was a stripper and Zendaris's mistress?"

J.D.'s brows shot up and he coughed. "You thought she was a stripper?"

"Sort of an inside joke."

"Okay. Count me out of the inside jokes." J.D. pushed

back from the table and circled an arm around Randi's shoulders. "You *are* amazing, darlin'. Thanks for helping us out, and I apologize for whatever this guy put you through."

"I plan to make up for all of it." Gage hopped up from his chair and clasped J.D.'s hand.

"Gage didn't put me through as much as Dr. Murdoch and Lawrence Jessup at that CIA house of horrors in Panama. Is anything being done about those people?"

J.D. slipped his jacket off the back of the chair. "The CIA director is launching an investigation, and the Agency is leaving the heavy lifting to us when it comes to Zendaris and those anti-drone plans."

Gage snapped his fingers. "I heard Deb has a line on those missing plans."

"I heard the same thing, but then she went off on some unexplained leave of absence a few days ago. Her lead probably fell through because if Deb had those plans in her sights, she wouldn't let up."

"Now you need to continue your leave of absence. Go back to your fiancée."

J.D. wiggled his eyebrows. "Gladly."

When the door slammed behind J.D., Randi dropped her gaze to the table, avoiding the eyes in the sketch, and traced the grain of wood with her fingertip. "You know, I overheard you tell your sister that you had to keep me close to form a bond of loyalty with you so that I'd tell you everything about Zendaris when the time came."

"You're kidding." Gage smacked his forehead with the heel of his hand. "I'm an idiot, Randi. I didn't mean a word of it. Elle had caught me out in an unprofessional situation, and I was just trying to save face."

"I wasn't sure. I was so dependent on you I didn't

know whether or not that dependency was the reason for the sparks between us."

"You're not dependent on me now." He pulled her into his arms and sealed his lips over hers. Then he cupped her face in his hands and rolled his eyes to the ceiling. "I think those sparks are still there."

"They are." She pressed her thumb to his lower lip. "But I wouldn't say I'm no longer dependent on you. Now that I have my memory back, I need you more than ever."

"And now that you've given us everything you know about Zendaris, I find that I still need you more than ever."

He kissed her again and she felt the truth of his words on his lips.

* * * * *

Don't miss the exciting conclusion of Carol Ericson's
BROTHERS IN ARMS: FULLY ENGAGED
miniseries next month.
Look for CATCH, RELEASE
wherever Harlequin Intrigue books are sold!

NAVY SEAL
SECURITY

CAST OF CHARACTERS

Amy Prescott—A San Diego County lifeguard, Amy gets embroiled in a drugs-for-arms deal that brings her past crashing down around her. Can the sexy navy SEAL who comes to her rescue keep her safe, or will falling for him torpedo her well-ordered world?

Riley Hammond—A former member of the covert ops team Prospero, Riley has a single-minded mission—locate missing Prospero member Jack Coburn. However, when his mission lands him on the beach of a lifeguard with plenty to hide, he's not sure whether to interrogate her or take her in his arms.

Carlos Castillo—The ex-boyfriend Amy dumps when she finds out he's married, but Amy soon discovers Carlos has a lot more to hide than a wife.

Ethan Prescott—Amy's half brother is the heir apparent to their father's criminal enterprise. Although Amy hasn't seen him in years, he knows all about her and is willing to jeopardize her safety for his own means.

Eli Prescott—Amy's father sits in prison a broken man, but do his connections and influence extend beyond the bars of his cell?

Farouk—Prospero's former nemesis has expanded his business model and taken his terror worldwide, and this time it's personal.

Colonel Scripps—Prospero's coordinator, the colonel knows he can summon all of the former team members with one call. He just hopes it's not too late to save Prospero's leader, Jack Coburn.

Jack Coburn—The former leader of Prospero and current hostage negotiator has run into a little trouble. Can he depend on his brothers in arms to save him, or is he going to have to save himself?

To K.F. and L.F., the best Los Angeles County junior lifeguards on the beach.

Prologue

Jack Coburn could think of about a thousand tastes more pleasant than his own blood—so he spit it out. The behemoth facing him sneered and readied his ham-hock fists for another round of punch-the-stupid-American. Lurch had to be the biggest Afghan Jack had ever seen in his life, and he'd seen plenty.

Jack hadn't escaped his captivity from a small, airless tent to be thwarted here. He dug his boots into the dirt outside the cave and tensed his muscles. If he could take care of Lurch and drag his body into the scrubby bushes that clung to the side of the mountain, he could get back to eavesdropping on the conversation in the cave.

And if he'd correctly heard the name they'd dropped in there just before Lurch materialized, he had to listen in on the rest of that discussion. His life depended on it, as did the lives of his brothers in arms—the whole gang from Prospero.

Lurch charged forward, and Jack met his assault with a kick to the substantial gut. Lurch staggered back, emitting a guttural cry from his throat. The howl unleashed several pairs of footsteps from the front of the cave, and Jack spun around to meet his adversaries.

The Afghans gathered in a semicircle around Jack

and, as he waited for the gunshots, a muscle ticking wildly in his jaw, he whispered, "Bring it on."

The men closed in on him and the stench of their sweat permeated his nostrils. Or was it his own sweat?

Still, not one of the fierce mujahideen raised a weapon. Licking his lips, Jack took two steps back to the edge of the cliff and glanced over his shoulder at the outcroppings that dotted the long way down to the village where he'd been staying. Would his young friend, Yasir, be looking for him?

The leader of the group brandished his sword. He growled in the Darwazi dialect, "Who are you? What are you doing here?"

Jack pretended not to understand the man's words. He spread his hands and smiled, nodding like a fool and taking another step toward the precipice.

Even if they believed him to be harmless, they'd never let him live. And once they compared notes with their brethren, the men who'd captured him two days ago, they'd torture him for information.

If he had to die sooner rather than later, he'd prefer to die swiftly and while in control of his own destiny.

So he stepped off the ledge and into the dark abyss. Before he hit the vicious rocks below, one thought pierced his brain.

Sorry I failed you, Lola. Whoever you are.

Chapter One

A dark shape bobbed on the water, outlined by a muted orange sunset, and then disappeared. A seal? Amy squinted at the horizon, spotting another object in the fog-shrouded distance. That one had to be a boat.

She leaned the flag in the corner of the lifeguard tower and grabbed a broom. After sweeping the sand out the door, she dumped the hot water from the bucket onto the beach. They kept the hot water available in the tower to treat stingray stings, but with the kids back in school and the summer crowds gone, they didn't really need it. She liked to follow the rules in case anyone challenged her. She didn't need trouble. She'd had enough.

She lifted the receiver of the red phone and called the main lifeguard station up the coast. Zeke Shepherd picked up on the first ring.

"This is Amy Prescott in tower twenty-eight. I'm out of here."

"Hey, Amy. Catch any excitement on your last day?"

"Not unless you count an older couple out for a walk with their metal detectors and a couple of joggers. This fog is starting to roll in pretty fast. It drove everyone away about a half hour ago."

Zeke snorted. "I hate tower twenty-eight once the

summer's over. No people, no action. Do you want me to pick you up in the truck and give you a ride back to your car?"

"No, thanks. I'm jogging back."

"You're in such good shape you should've kicked that guy's butt when you found out—"

Amy cut him off. "See you later, Zeke."

Had every lifeguard in San Diego County heard she'd been duped by a married man a couple months ago?

She slammed the receiver back in its cradle. She might as well have Gullible Sap tattooed on her forehead. For all the precautions she usually took with relationships, Carlos had really played her.

Reaching up to unlatch the cover of the lookout window to swing it down, she glanced at the ocean. The animal on the water had moved closer to shore and now looked bigger than a seal. Amy snagged the binoculars from the hook and turned them toward the object.

A breath hitched in her throat. Two scuba divers had broken the surface and seemed to be struggling toward the beach. Had one of them lost air? Embolized?

Amy shimmied out of her sweat pants, yanked the sweatshirt over her head and dropped them both on top of her open backpack. With her heart racing, she lifted the phone off the hook and left it dangling. Of course, she'd already told Zeke she was leaving, but protocol prevailed. If someone did call the tower, the busy signal would indicate a rescue.

Grabbing her orange rescue can, she sprinted down the ramp of the lifeguard tower and churned up dry sand on her way to the ocean.

The divers, still struggling, had moved closer to the shoreline. Amy high-stepped over the waves and plunged into the chilly water, dolphin-kicking her way to the two people.

One diver had his arm around the other diver's neck, the man flailing in his grasp. *That technique would kill him, not rescue him.*

Amy shouted as she neared the duo, and the stronger diver looked up. The person in his arms slumped and he released him into the water. Adrenaline pumped through Amy's system as she shot forward and caught the disabled diver before the next wave rolled in, dragging him back out to sea.

She hooked one arm around his chest while offering the rescue can to the other diver. He shook his head and plowed through the water toward the beach with a strong stroke.

He seemed to have a lot of strength left; why hadn't he helped his buddy? He might be disoriented or in shock. She'd call the station as soon as she got this one to shore and revived him.

Still clutching the unconscious diver, Amy rode the last wave onto the wet sand. The other diver had reached the beach ahead of her and now struggled out of his gear, dropping his tank to the ground.

Rolling the victim onto his back, Amy called out to the other man. "Are you okay?"

He ripped his mask from his face and tossed it onto the sand. "Don't bother. He's dead."

His cold words felt like another splash of ocean water on her face. Then she took in his heaving chest and a jagged rip along the side of his wet suit. He probably needed medical attention for shock.

She flipped up the mask from the injured man's face and tipped his head back, placing one hand on his chest. His companion spoke too soon. A feeble heart-beat struggled beneath the diver's wet suit.

A warm, sticky substance oozed through her stiff fingers and she gasped. The man's wet suit sported a huge gash down the front and blood seeped from the tear. *What the heck had gone on out there?*

Amy clamped both hands against the wound to staunch the loss of blood. The man's body shuddered and jerked. His arms flew up and he grabbed her around the neck, his strong fingers creating a vise and grind-ing her gold chain into her neck. Choking, she clawed at his arms with her bloody hands, her nails skimming off the thick neoprene of the wet suit.

The diver behind her charged toward them and drove his knee into the man's throat. Her attacker's hands dropped from her neck and he slumped, a gush of air escaping from his lungs, a gurgle of blood spouting from the tear in his wet suit.

Amy hacked and tumbled backward, her hands hit-ting the sand behind her. She scrambled like a crab across the wet surface, leaving bloody indentations in her wake.

"Sorry about that." The stranger pressed his fingers against the throat of the man who'd just tried to strangle her. "Thought I had him. He's dead now."

"W-what happened to him? Why did he attack me when I was trying to save him?" She raised her gaze to the other diver, now on his knees, peeling his wet suit from the top half of his body and toeing off his fins.

He cocked his head, squinting into the fog with a steely blue gaze. "I stabbed him."

Then she noticed a knife plunged into the sand next to him. Screaming, she rolled onto her stomach and launched to her knees. A hand encircled her ankle, yanking her leg back, and she landed on her belly again. She spun around, kicking wildly with her other leg.

The man fell on top of her, covering her mouth with his hand, grinding salty grains of sand against her lips. She struggled to knee him in the crotch, but his body felt like a lead weight against her, immobilizing her.

His face inches from hers, he brought a finger to his lips. "Shh."

A chill raced up her spine. Then she heard it—the low whine of a motorboat. *Salvation.* She bucked beneath her captor and worked her jaw to open her mouth and bite his hand.

His voice growled close to her ear, his briny scent invading her nostrils. "Stop fighting me. Those are some very dangerous men out there on that boat."

His words sucked the already-diminishing air out of her lungs, and she slumped beneath his rock-hard body. She moved her lips against his palm in a silent question, the saltwater on his hand working its way into her mouth.

The maniac flashed a smile, rows of white teeth in a tanned face. They gleamed in the fog that now surrounded them like damp cotton. He winked. "Don't worry. I'm one of the good guys."

Her eyes darted to the dead diver slumped in a heap at the water's edge.

"He's one of the bad guys." He shifted his muscular frame, giving her some breathing room. "I'm going to remove my hand from your mouth and let you up, but you need to stay close to me and we need to get off this beach. Nice job on that rescue, by the way."

Amy swallowed, not even minding the sand that scratched her throat. Two lunatics had invaded her beach and now one of them planned to kidnap her. *The perfect ending to a lousy couple of months.*

As soon as he removed his hand and his hold, she planned to scream bloody murder and run toward the sound of the boat. She could swim a long distance if she had to. Her gaze tracked over the muscled shoulders and corded arms of the man who held her, and her stomach fluttered. He could probably swim just as fast and far.

And he had a knife.

He slid his hand from her mouth, resting it on her throat. Amy dropped her gaze to the stranger's sinewy forearm and gulped. He could easily finish the job the dead guy started. As she gathered air in her lungs for a big scream, a motor whirred fast, loud and close.

In one movement her captor rolled off her body and grabbed her arm, yanking her to her feet. At the same time, a scream ripped from her throat. A loud pop followed her cry for help and the man beside her cursed.

"Thanks a lot, beach girl. You just gave them a target in this muck."

The people on the boat confirmed his words as they fired two more shots in the general direction of Amy's head.

"Let's move." The man shoved her in front of him and she stumbled as her feet hit dry sand. At least if any more bullets came their way, they'd have to go through his large frame first. And he made a great shield.

Was he protecting her?

Keeping his hand pressed against the small of her back, he said, "This fog should give us enough cover to make it to the lifeguard truck—as long as you keep your screaming to a minimum."

Either she followed the man with the knife or turned

toward the men with the guns. Since he hadn't used the knife on her—yet—and the guys on the boat insisted on shooting at vague shapes in the fog, even after she screamed, Amy put her money on the guy with the knife.

Her legs pumped in the sand. She veered toward the tower and grabbed her backpack with her sweats on top. She didn't hear any more gunshots and the occupants of the boat must've cut the motor because she couldn't hear the distinctive whine.

The thick fog almost obscured her companion. He didn't even seem to be breathing heavily, or maybe she couldn't hear him over the roaring in her ears and her own ragged breath.

He bumped her side, grabbing her upper arm. "Where's the lifeguard truck?"

"I don't have a truck on this beach. My car's parked in the lot." She tried to shake him off, but his fingers pinched harder.

"You'd better not be lying and leading me into some kind of trap. That could get us both killed." His icy blue eyes almost glowed in the fog.

"You're the one with the knife." She pried his fingers off her arm and kicked up sand behind her, hoping she got some in his face.

The beach remained eerily quiet behind them, but the dense fog could mute sounds. Amy kept up a steady pace, her feet leading her to the parking lot where her car waited. Once they got there, she'd dig her cell phone out of her backpack and call the police. The stranger couldn't object if he really was on the right side of the law.

A strip of dark asphalt appeared and Amy pointed. "It's right there."

When the soles of her feet slapped against the gritty asphalt, she swung her backpack from her shoulder and clawed for her keys in the front compartment. She clicked the remote and gasped when the man swept her in front of him, pushing her toward the car.

"Get in and drive."

Before she had a chance to figure out if she could take off without him, he scrambled into the passenger seat. He pounded the dashboard. "What are you waiting for? I said *drive*."

She curled her left fist around her keys and fumbled with a zipper on the backpack crushed between her lap and the bottom edge of the steering wheel. Her fingers skimmed the smooth metal of her cell phone and she pulled it out.

"I'm going to call 911 first."

His jaw hardened as he sluiced back his wet hair, beginning to curl at the ends. With a pair of broad shoulders and washboard abs that tapered to the wet suit peeled down to his slim hips, he looked like Triton or at least some sexy merman. Then he opened his mouth.

"No, you're not. We need to get out of here. Now."

Sounded like he knew his enemies well. Who was she to argue? She tossed her backpack in the backseat and started the car. "You're right. Those guys seemed determined."

A breath hitched in her throat. Maybe they were determined because they were cops or the Coast Guard, but would they start shooting into a bank of fog after she screamed without even shouting out a warning? Experience had taught her they just might. Her father had taught her to never trust the law.

Her gaze slid to the knife resting on the man's powerful thigh encased in black neoprene. She didn't have a choice right now, anyway, but his reaction to her call to 911 would tell her a lot.

As she accelerated out of the beach parking lot, she scooped her cell phone from her lap where she'd dropped it and flipped it open. She'd pressed 9 before the man beside her snatched the phone from her hand.

"You can't call the cops." He cradled the phone in his palm and snapped it shut.

Amy clung to the steering wheel, her knuckles turning white. "You're going to kill me, aren't you? F-for witnessing that murder...."

He tossed the phone into the backseat and let out a ragged breath. Squeezing her bare thigh with his long fingers, he said, "I'm not going to hurt you, beach girl. I'm sorry you're scared."

If he meant to soothe her with his gentle touch on her leg, it sent a ripple of fear across her skin instead. Did he plan to rape her before he murdered her?

Amy swallowed. He seemed like a fairly reasonable lunatic. Maybe she could use logic on him. "Why can't I call 911? The operator can alert the Coast Guard and go after the...the bad guys. You could be long gone by the time they picked them up, and I swear I won't tell them anything about you."

"You wouldn't be a very good lifeguard if you did that, would you?" He clicked his tongue as he rummaged through her glove compartment. He pulled out her registration and peered at it. "You can call the cops when you get home. By that time, I will be long gone and so will that dead body on the beach."

Her heart did a somersault in her chest. "When I get home?"

He flicked the paper registration with his finger.

"Yeah. Drive back to your place and I'll disappear in a puff of smoke or more likely a blanket of fog."

When she'd pulled out of the beach parking lot, she'd headed in the general direction of her house since he hadn't given her any orders about where to go. Would he really let her just go home and then call the authorities after he left without hurting her?

He was right about her responsibilities as a lifeguard. She'd have to report him and give the cops as good a description as she could. She gave him a sidelong glance—over six feet tall, muscular build, a wild, tawny mane of hair that brushed his shoulders, piercing blue eyes.

She'd have to scale back on the admiration of his masculine good looks when she gave her description to the cops or they'd think she'd fallen prey to that Stockholm syndrome where victims fell for their captors.

He glanced at the registration again before shoving it back into her glove compartment. "You live close, right?"

"Yeah, we're almost there." She gripped the steering wheel with clammy hands as another thought slammed against her like a sledgehammer. He'd retrieved her registration to see her address. She did not want this dangerous man in her house, but now he knew her address. "My husband, who's six foot five and very jealous, will be home, too."

He snorted. "I'll take my chances."

"Can't I just drop you off somewhere? Why do you have to come to my house with me?"

"Just want to see you home safely." He brushed some sand off the leg of his wet suit. "Is there a work schedule posted in the tower listing the shifts for the guards?"

"N-no."

"I suppose the main station wouldn't give out the guards' names if someone called making inquiries about which guards are working which beaches?"

Her clammy grasp on the wheel got tighter. "Of course not. What are you driving at? Do you think those people in the boat will try to find out who I am?"

He lifted a shoulder, which touched the ends of his wet hair. "If they can. But it doesn't sound like they're going to be successful."

"What if they come back to that beach, that tower, looking for me? Today was my last day for the summer, but I left everything wide open back there. I'm going to have to return to close up properly."

Was he playing her to make her fear the men in the boat more than she feared him? The dying man had choked her, and the guys in the boat had shot at her. This one hadn't lifted a finger against her. In fact, he'd protected her from the other attacks.

"I don't think they'd do that." But two lines formed a deep crevice between his eyebrows. "They'd have difficulty finding the beach again, and there are plenty of lifeguard towers up and down the coast."

She chewed her bottom lip. "I don't know about that. Imperial Beach is one of the southernmost beaches in San Diego County before you hit the Mexican border."

"Request a transfer. They're not going to find you."

"They're not going to find me, anyway." She rolled her tight shoulders. "I already told you. I'm done for the season since I only work summers. Today was my last shift."

He patted her leg again. "That's good to hear. And don't return. Let someone else lock up. What's your name, anyway?"

"Amy." She gasped and covered her mouth. How had

this man lured her into such a state of naive stupidity so quickly? Next she'd be giving him her social security number. She jerked her leg, dislodging his hand.

He had the nerve to laugh.

"Don't worry. I'm not going to use your first name against you, and I can just reach in the glove compartment to find out the rest if I want." He combed his fingers through tangled hair. "And just so we're even, I'm going to tell you my first name, too. It's Riley."

"Riley." The name rolled off her tongue. Riley didn't seem too concerned about the cops knowing his name. Did he think just because he had a friendly, non-threatening demeanor and a gorgeous body she wasn't going to report this?

Even though Amy had an innate distrust of authority, Riley had placed his confidence in the wrong woman. She'd had it in for all men since she'd discovered the guy she'd been dating for two months had a wife. *Scumbag.*

She rounded the corner of her block and pulled up to the curb in front of her rental house. She cut the engine and dropped her hands in her lap. "You can get out now. Although how you think you're going to be inconspicuous roaming around in a full-body wet suit is beyond me."

"Thanks for caring." A boyish grin claimed his face. "I have trunks on underneath—just another surfer."

"Just another surfer carrying a knife."

She shouldn't have reminded him.

His fingers curled around the handle and he said, "Let's go inside to make sure everything's okay."

Tension knotted her shoulders again as she climbed out of the car, groping for her backpack in the backseat.

She wouldn't be able to breathe easily until Riley left the premises and she had 911 on the line.

It took her three tries to insert her key into the dead bolt with Riley standing behind her, the heat from his body warming her bare back. And then she didn't even need to unlock the dead bolt—she must've left it unlocked when she took off this afternoon. She shoved the key into the handle, turning the knob and pushing open the door.

Riley stepped in front of her, tucking her behind his broad frame. "Everything look okay?"

"How can I tell? I'm staring at your back." Her nose practically touched the cool, smooth skin between his shoulder blades.

Riley stalked to the center of the small living room, dwarfing it with his take-control presence. Amy shifted her gaze around the objects of the room, her pulse quickening when she spotted a book on the floor by the coffee table. Her cat, Clarence, probably knocked that over before he took off for his pre-dinner prowl.

"I'm going to have a look in the back rooms." Riley pointed to the short hallway, gripping the knife in front of him.

Amy crept toward the book and crouched to retrieve it from the floor. She glanced toward the entry that led to the kitchen and then tilted her head back to peer at Riley disappearing into the bathroom, knife still drawn.

She could make a run for the portable phone in the kitchen and slip out the back, maybe bang on her neighbor's door for help. Riley would probably take off, and she'd be safe.

Launching to her feet, she hurtled toward the kitchen. Just inside the entryway, she tripped over a soft object splayed across the floor. Yelping, she thudded against the linoleum. She scrambled to her hands and knees and spun around.

A sour knot of fear lodged in her throat as her gaze skidded across the deathly still form of her ex-boyfriend.

Chapter Two

A shriek sliced through the small house, and Riley barreled out the bathroom door, stubbing his toe on the frame. He gripped the knife at his side, ready to do battle. Careening through the empty living room, he launched toward the entryway to what had to be the kitchen. He stopped short, almost falling into the room and over a body on the floor.

Amy huddled against the cabinets, her hands pressed against her mouth, her eyes forming huge, coffee-colored saucers. A man sprawled across the faded yellow linoleum on his back, one perfectly shined loafer hanging from his toes, and his legs in pressed slacks crossed one over the other. Looked like he could be taking a nap on the kitchen floor.

Riley squatted beside the man, noting a red blotch on his right cheek, and extended two fingers toward his neck to check his pulse.

Amy screamed, "Don't touch him."

God, he must've been a friend or relative of Amy's. Boyfriend? His gaze flew to her face, drained of all color beneath her mocha skin. "Who is he?"

"Carlos… My ex-boyfriend." She mumbled through her fingers, which seemed frozen in place.

Very-ex-boyfriend from the look of him. Riley

stepped over the body and kneeled beside Amy. "We need to get out of here."

"What happened to him?"

"I can't tell. I don't see any blood, just a contusion on his face. Maybe someone strangled him or hit him on the back of the head." He turned back toward the body. "I can turn him…"

"No." She sobbed, curling into a tight ball. "We need to call the police."

"You don't get it, Amy. Somehow those guys in the boat tracked you down to your house. Carlos must've surprised them. They probably came at him from behind and strangled him or hit him. Carlos's presence spooked them, but that doesn't mean they won't come back."

"That's why we call the police." She scooted to her left to avoid Carlos's outstretched hand.

Riley rubbed his chin with his knuckles. He was flying so far below the radar of the police right now he couldn't afford to have them question him at a murder scene. Hell, he was flying below the radar of the CIA.

"The police can't protect you." He left the rest of that statement hanging in the air between them. Only he could protect her now, and he didn't need the encumbrance.

Surprisingly, she didn't dispute his claim.

"Who are these people? Who are you?"

"The less you know, the better." Not that he knew much himself. When the call had come from Colonel Scripps, the former leader of the undercover-ops unit, Prospero, Riley had jumped into action. Jack Coburn, one of their own, had disappeared.

Riley would go through hell and back to find him.

He cupped his hand, wiggling his fingers. "Come on, beach girl. Let's go."

Amy's gaze traveled from his hand to his face. She must've seen something she liked because she sighed and pushed to her feet. He helped her over the body of her ex-boyfriend. Feeling a tremble roll through her athletic frame, Riley pulled her close and folded his arms around her.

She stiffened in his embrace and then buried her face against his bare chest as sobs wracked her body. He stroked her dark hair, clumped in wet tangles of saltwater.

Rubbing her nose, she stepped back from him and pinched her swimsuit between two fingers, yanking it forward. "Do I have time to change, or…or do you think we should get out now?"

"I don't think they'll be returning to the scene of the crime immediately." Riley crossed the room and lifted the curtains of the front window with the tip of his knife. He'd prefer a gun, but he couldn't have taken one of those with him. "They might be out there now, watching, waiting, wondering if we'll call the police."

She called from the bedroom. "I'm wondering the same thing. We can't just leave him there on the kitchen floor. H-he has a wife."

Riley swallowed. The beach girl liked married men? He cleared his throat. "We'll call the police as soon as we're out of here."

"Wait a minute." She stumbled from the bedroom in a pair of jeans, pulling a T-shirt over her head. He caught a glimpse of a lacy white bra. "Won't that look suspicious? There's a dead man in my house, and I'm not even here."

"I'll clear things up for you later. You're not safe in this house."

Her eyes narrowed as she hooked a finger along the gold chain around her neck, pulling a large locket out of her T-shirt. "*You're* not safe in this house. For whatever reason, you don't want the cops to find out about your activities. And why would you? You murdered a man on the beach and you kidnapped me."

Frustration gave an edge to his voice as he jerked his thumb toward the kitchen. "I didn't murder *him*. Don't you get it? They discovered your identity and came after you."

"They came after *you*." She hugged herself and rubbed her upper arms. "They probably figured you used me to escape. That's why they came to this house and killed Carlos. Once you get away from me, I'll be safe."

Too bad his wife hadn't figured that one out.

Pain sliced behind his eyes, and he ran a hand over his hair, clasping it in a ponytail at the nape of his neck. "You're in it, Amy, whether you want to be or not. These people don't leave loose ends."

"I'm not a loose end." She widened her stance and shoved her hands in the pockets of her jeans. "I didn't see those people. I don't know who they are. But I know who you are."

Damn. She didn't trust him. And why would she? He didn't trust himself to protect her, either.

He swiped the back of his hand across his mouth. Could he leave her here? He'd take off for his safe house, and she could stay here and call the cops. She'd tell her wild story of one scuba diver killing another and people shooting at them from a boat. But there would be no body. There would be no blood. No bullets. No evidence at all.

The Velasquez Drug Cartel didn't leave evidence. Or witnesses.

Even if the cops believed Amy's fantastic story, they couldn't do much to protect her. If the Velasquez gang decided to kill her, the cops couldn't stop them.

Or maybe he'd overreacted from the get-go. From the minute she'd valiantly pulled his enemy's body from the ocean, Riley had felt protective of her. She'd only been doing her job and had landed in the middle of an international intrigue.

If he distanced himself from her now, it just might save her life. He was dangerous company.

"Okay." Riley blew out a long breath. "I'll stay with you until the cops arrive, and then I'll head out the back door."

"Really?" Her voice squeaked and her eyebrows shot up.

"Really." He tugged at the wet suit around his waist and peeled it off his body, standing on one foot at a time to free his legs from the constricting neoprene. "What are you going to tell the police?"

Her gaze raked his body as her chest rose and fell. "The truth."

"The guys on the boat will have removed the body of their comrade and my scuba gear from the beach by now." He nudged the wet suit lying in a twisted heap on the carpet. "I can leave this here if you think it will bolster your story."

"Why would I need to bolster my story?" She dragged her gaze from his wet trunks, meeting his eyes, a pleasing shade of pink washing over her cheeks.

The beach girl had been checking him out. And he liked it.

Riley's fingers plowed through his long hair. "You plan to report a murder on the beach with no body. Your ex-boyfriend is dead on your kitchen floor with no signs of a struggle or break-in. Why is he your ex? Bad breakup?"

"No. Yes." She folded her arms across her stomach. "He lied to me about being married."

Riley whistled through his teeth. "Do you have a history of violence?"

"Not yet." Amy clenched her fists and took a step toward him.

"I'm just sayin'." A strange sense of relief flooded his veins. He knew a valiant woman like Amy wouldn't knowingly get mixed up with a married man.

"Do you think they'll suspect me of murdering Carlos? I'm pretty strong, but not strong enough to strangle a man. I broke it off as soon as I discovered his marital status. Why would I kill him and then call the cops? It would look much worse if I ran out now, wouldn't it?"

She covered her face with her hands, and guilt stabbed his belly. He didn't want her to feel worse. He wanted to smooth everything over and make sure she kept safe after he left.

He tripped over the wet suit as he rushed to her side and curled an arm around her shoulders. She leaned into him. Her T-shirt felt soft against his bare chest, brushing a tingle of desire along his skin.

Her salty hair tickled his lips as he spoke. "Just tell the truth. You'll be fine. There's no evidence that you killed Carlos even if the police find your story unbelievable."

"C-can't you stay and talk to the cops with me?" She clutched his arm, her nails digging into his skin.

"I wish I could help you out, beach girl, but I can't afford the time if they decide to arrest me." He couldn't afford the exposure, either. Having his picture splashed all over the newspapers in connection with two murders would torpedo any chance he'd have to follow his lead on the Velasquez Cartel and any of its customers.

And right now the Velasquez lead was the only thread they had in connection with Jack Coburn's disappearance.

Amy took a shaky breath and stepped back. "You're not going to tell me anything else, are you?"

"No."

"Then you'd better get ready to leave so I can call 911. I can't bear to be here with Carlos like that." Her bottom lip quivered, and her dark eyes brimmed with unshed tears.

Riley cupped her face with one hand, smoothing the pad of his thumb across her cheekbone. "I'm sorry about Carlos. What do you think he was doing here?"

At his touch, she'd closed her eyes, but now her eyelids flew open, droplets of tears trembling on the edges of her long lashes. "Huh?"

"Carlos. Why was he in your house and how did he get in? Did you give him a key?"

"I gave him a key once to feed my cat when I was gone for the weekend. But he gave it back to me."

"He made a copy."

Her eyes widened. "He wouldn't do that."

"Really? The man entered your home while you were at work. I thought you broke up with him a few months ago?"

"I did." She wiped her palms on the thighs of her jeans.

"Did he contact you after the breakup?"

"A few times but…" Her arms flailed at her sides.

"Face it, Amy. The guy never got over you. He probably came here hoping he could change your mind. Didn't work out too well for him."

She dug her fists in her hips. "The back door is in the kitchen. You can leave before the cops get here."

"If he made a copy of your key, it's probably still in his pocket. Do you want me to take it?"

"So you can have a key to my place? No, thanks. Why would I want you to take the key? I don't want to disturb a crime scene."

"Too late for that. You changed clothing and you didn't notify the police as soon as you discovered the body." He shrugged. "I'm just thinking it might look better for you if the dead ex-boyfriend didn't still have a key to your house."

"Okay. You know what?" She grabbed his arm and dragged him toward the kitchen. "There's the back door. Use it."

Instead he crouched next to the body and slid his hand into the front pocket of the man's expensive slacks. His nostrils flared at the sweet scent emanating from his clothing. Carlos liked his cologne strong.

Nothing in that pocket except a few bills. Riley reached for the other pocket, but he didn't have to go digging. Carlos's keychain was on the floor by the pocket. Riley's fingers closed around the silver ring and he dangled it from his index finger.

"Is this your key?" A removable ring was hanging from the main keychain, and he shook it in front of Amy's face.

"It could be. What difference does it make? Now you've corrupted the crime scene even more. Put it back and get out, and maybe you should leave some more of your fingerprints around here so the cops can identify you…Riley…if that's even your name."

"I didn't touch anything in here." He twirled the keychain around his finger. "Except you."

Amy's eyes glittered, shooting gold sparks, but a soft rose color swept across her cheeks. Stepping behind him to avoid the body on the floor, she grabbed the knob to the back door. She turned quickly, her hair whipping across his chest. "What will you do for clothes?"

Still clutching the keychain, Riley adjusted the waistband of his board shorts while her gaze tracked his movements feeling like a whisper of fingertips. "We're a mile from the beach—nothing unusual about someone walking around in swim trunks. If you give me a couple of bucks for the bus, that would make my life a lot easier."

"Gladly." She slipped past him and snagged her backpack from the coffee table where she'd dropped it. She groped inside a side compartment and gasped. "My wallet."

"It's gone?"

"It must've fallen out in the sand when I grabbed my pack from the tower."

"That explains how the bad guys found you."

"But how'd they get here so fast?" She hugged the backpack to her chest.

"The men who killed Carlos aren't the same men who shot at us on the beach. This is an organization, not a few petty crooks."

She swayed and he caught her. "Are you sure you don't want to get out of here with me?" Riley asked.

"No. I want to call the police. Th-they'll keep me safe."

Even she didn't sound like she believed that. If Amy expected the San Diego Sheriff's Department to put a twenty-four-hour guard on her, she didn't understand how police departments operated. That would happen only if they arrested her for the murder of her ex.

Riley could protect her. He knew the danger she faced, but he couldn't drag her out of her house if she didn't want to go. And she clearly didn't want to go.

He brushed her knotted hair from her face. "Okay, beach girl. You call the cops and stay safe."

"Hold on." She spun around and rummaged through a purse on the desk by the front window. She withdrew her hand, clutching several bills between her fingers. "Take this. And you stay safe, too."

His hand covered hers and he drew her close. She smelled like the sea, tangy and fresh. He had bent his head to brush her lips with his when a movement outside the window caught his attention.

With a grunt, Riley threw both of his arms around Amy. As they tumbled to the floor, she opened her mouth to scream. He clapped his hand across her lips for the second time that day.

Chapter Three

He'd fooled her. He planned to kill her and had just been stringing her along for his sadistic pleasure.

She was batting a thousand—a married man and now a killer.

Riley brushed her ear with a whisper. "They're outside."

His words sent a river of chills down her spine, and she reflexively dug her nails into his back.

"Stay low." Riley heaved to a crouching position and tugged at the waistband of her jeans. "Let's go out the back."

Amy slid across the floor on her belly, twisting her head toward the front window. Adrenaline charged through her body when she saw the outline of a gun.

She wriggled faster, like a snake shedding its skin. When she reached the kitchen, she gagged at the sight of Carlos on the floor.

Riley rose to his haunches. "Get the back door."

Turning the knob, she eased open the door, scooping in deep breaths of fresh air. Riley bumped her outside and told her to close the door behind them. He really didn't want to leave any fingerprints in her house.

She grabbed his hand, pulling him toward the small backyard. "This way."

They dashed across the lawn, the wet grass sticking to her feet in their flimsy flip-flops. Riley cinched her around the waist and hoisted her up the fence. She clambered over and fell into her neighbor's yard. Riley swooped over the fence after her.

"Let's keep running and hope we don't meet a dog."

She yanked on the hem of his board shorts. "Do you still have those keys you took out of Carlos's pocket?"

He patted his own pocket. "Yep."

"He used to park his car on the side street. We can get to it from here without going to the front of the house."

"You're brilliant, beach girl." He grabbed her head with both hands and kissed her forehead.

Not exactly the kiss she'd anticipated in the house, but it would do—for now.

They crouched at the side of the house behind hers, then charged through the gate, stumbling into her neighbor's front yard.

"This street." She pointed to the left and they hit the sidewalk running. Two kids playing basketball with a garage hoop looked up and snickered as they jogged by.

They reached the corner and Riley held her back. "Hang on."

He peered both ways down the street. "It's clear. Which car is his?"

She pointed to Carlos's black BMW parked at the curb. When they'd dated, she'd always wondered why he'd preferred to park his car on the street around the corner from her house. He'd told her there was less traffic on this street, and he'd wanted to protect his car. He'd really wanted to protect himself.

Guess that hadn't worked out for him today.

"On the count of three, sprint for the car." Riley held

up the keys. "I won't hit the remote until we get there… just in case they're closer than we think."

Amy kicked off her flip-flops and scooped them up from the sidewalk with one hand. Holding her breath, she waited for Riley's signal. At three, she shot off as if she was heading into the ocean for a rescue.

The car alarm beeped once, and she grabbed the handle and dropped onto the leather seat. Before she closed the door, the car lurched forward and Riley careened around the corner. Panting, Amy twisted in her seat. No headlights followed them.

She snapped on her seat belt and leaned against the headrest, closing her eyes. "Where to?"

"I can drop you off at the police station or at least down the block from the police station. Then you can report everything, and they'll come back to the house with you. Those men won't try anything with the cops there."

She stuffed her feet into her flip-flops. "What about when the cops leave?"

"Can you stay with someone for a few days until this blows over? Chances are once Carlos's killers realize you don't know anything, and you keep your distance from me, they'll leave you alone."

"Chances are?" She gripped the edge of the seat, her damp hands slipping off the leather.

"Those boys have bigger fish to fry to risk going after a witness who may or may not even be a witness."

"All right then. Take me to the police station." She knotted her fingers in her lap. "What should I tell them…about you, I mean?"

His boyish grin danced across his face. "Tell them the truth. I have a feeling nothing-but will do for you."

"I'll tell them you saved my life…twice."

He cocked his head. "Are you always so loyal?"

"I don't know about that. If you're telling me the truth, you don't need to be locked up in a jail cell while the cops try to figure out your involvement and degree of culpability. Sometimes the cops aren't too particular."

He squeezed her clenched hands with a firm grasp. "Don't worry about me, beach girl. The cops aren't going to find me."

She glanced at his large hand, brown from the sun, his calluses rough against her skin. "What are you, Riley?"

"I told you before, the less you know, the better. This way you don't have to lie to the cops."

She snorted. "I don't mind lying to the cops if there's a good reason. Where will you go after you drop me off? You're not finished with those men, are you?"

His mouth formed a thin line as he fumbled with Carlos's built-in GPS. Amy sighed. She'd never know anything more about him than his name—and how his body felt against hers, shielding her, protecting her.

"There's a police station pretty close. I'll drop you off down the block, watch you go inside, and then I'll be out of your life."

She swallowed. "What are you going to do with Carlos's car?"

"I'll leave it someplace where it can be recovered and returned to his…wife." He raised one eyebrow. "How'd that happen anyway?"

Hunching her shoulders, Amy clasped her hands between her knees. "I met him at the beach while I was working. We went out a few times from there. He came to my place a few times…"

She clenched her jaw. She didn't want to waste her last few minutes with Riley talking about her train wreck of a love life. "You know, I never thanked you for saving me on the beach. And if you hadn't come back with me to my house, that man outside with the gun could've killed me."

"It's the least I could do." He brushed his fingers along her arm. "I put you in danger by landing on your beach."

Every time Riley touched her, she felt a current of electricity run through her body. She'd better turn that off. This mysterious man would be disappearing from her life in a matter of minutes.

She rubbed her eyes. "Didn't look like you had much choice."

Drawing his brows together, he scratched his chin. "Yeah. I don't know why they decided to anchor off the coast at that particular spot. But I plan to find out."

Amy's heart galloped in her chest. Riley was a man who lived dangerously—and seemed to enjoy it. Just her type. She'd tried and tried to gravitate toward stable men with stable jobs, but it never seemed to work out. Carlos had his own import/export business, but he hadn't turned out to be dependable, either. Maybe her excitement radar had somehow picked up on that, too.

The car slowed and Riley pulled into the parking lot of a strip mall. "There's the police station. I'll watch from here until you're safely inside."

Amy rubbed her tingling nose. Once she got rid of Riley she'd be safe. Wouldn't she? She grabbed the door handle.

His hand dropped to her shoulder, and she twisted around. He slid his fingers up to her throat, his eyes now a dark blue, clouding over like a stormy sea. Her pulse ticked wildly beneath his touch.

"Be careful, beach girl." Then he cupped the back of her head and drew her close, sealing his lips over hers.

The quick kiss didn't feel like goodbye. It felt like a protective stamp that she'd carry with her forever.

She managed an inarticulate goodbye as she scrambled out of the car. Walking toward the police station, she didn't dare turn around, even though she could feel Riley's gaze searing her back.

God, she hoped the police could help her, even though she didn't trust them. She hoped for once they could reassure her and make her feel safe.

As safe as she'd felt with Riley.

RILEY EXHALED HIS pent-up breath as Amy swung open the glass door of the San Diego Sheriff's Station and disappeared inside.

Velasquez's people murdered Carlos because they expected Riley to show up there with Amy. Why didn't they just wait there? Why did they leave then return? Carlos must've upset their plans even though it didn't look like the guy put up much of a fight.

He rolled his shoulders and put the car in gear. Once Amy returned with the sheriff's deputies, Velasquez's men would realize Riley had taken flight. Then they'd leave Amy alone.

They'd better leave Amy alone.

He swung the sleek car back onto Imperial Beach Boulevard and accelerated toward the highway. He had to get back to that beach to find out why it had been such a strategic location for the Velasquez Cartel. The boat hadn't moored off that coast and sent a diver in by accident.

If the guy hadn't spotted him and attacked him un-derwater, Riley could have surprised a meeting or interrupted a drop. Maybe their fight had scared off the contact on the beach.

He smacked the leather steering wheel with the heels of his hands. He'd have to wait until morning, anyway. The cops would most likely follow Amy back to the scene of the crime and light up that beach like a Christmas tree.

Until they realized there was no evidence of a crime. No evidence. No crime.

They'd find plenty of evidence at Amy's house though. Really sucked for Carlos. Should be a warning to married men everywhere not to cheat.

Although, after spending a few hours with Amy, he could understand the temptation Carlos had faced.

A buzzing noise filled the car, and Riley almost swerved into the next lane. Tilting his head, he determined the sound was coming from the backseat. Cell phone?

He took the next exit and swung into an empty parking lot next to some train tracks. He unsnapped his seat belt, twisting in his seat. A small light glowed from the pocket of a jacket on the backseat. Riley reached over, slid his hand in the pocket and pulled out the cell phone, which flashed Missed Call.

The guy's wife? He flipped open the phone and checked the display, which read Restricted. The caller hadn't bothered to leave a voice mail or text message, either.

Riley glanced at the clock on the dashboard. He had to check in with the colonel. Might as well use Carlos's phone before dumping it. He wouldn't need it, and his wife probably wouldn't care to see all those calls to Amy.

The colonel picked up on the first ring.

"Colonel, it's Riley."

"Did you get anything from the lead on that boat?"

"A couple of dead bodies. The boat dropped anchor off the coast near Imperial Beach and sent in a diver. Let's just say we mixed it up a little before we reached the shore. He could've been meeting someone or scouting the location. I didn't stick around to find out because his buddies started shooting at us."

"Us?"

"There was a lifeguard on the beach."

The colonel swore. "Is he okay?"

"*She's* okay." And then Riley reported what had occurred, taking full responsibility for the screwup.

The colonel swore again. "You're going to have to go back to that beach and figure out why it's important to the Velasquez crew."

"Any more news about Jack?" Riley held his breath.

"The CIA is calling him a traitor. They're convinced he's working for the other side."

Riley choked on his bitter rage. "That's not possible. You know it and I know it."

"I know Jack Coburn's name came up in chatter between the Velasquez Drug Cartel and an arms dealer in Colorado. Find out the link between those two, Riley, and we might be on the first step to finding Jack and proving his innocence."

"I'm on it. I owe Jack."

"We all do. I have another name to give you— Castillo. My CIA contact slipped it to me. He's connected to the Velasquez boys. And one more thing, I'm giving you a new number for me."

As the colonel rattled off the number, Riley lunged for the glove compartment. He groped in the dark recess, and his fingers tripped across a pen and a scrap of paper as other papers floated to the floor of the car. He jotted down the colonel's new number and ended the call.

Glancing at the cell phone in his hand, he realized he couldn't leave the phone in Carlos's car for the police to find. Not that the colonel had an even remotely traceable phone number, but just like the fingerprints in Amy's house, he wanted to err on the side of caution. That included the fingerprints in this car. He'd wipe it clean before abandoning it.

Then he'd get back to his safe house, claim his own car and skulk outside Amy's house after the cops left just to make sure she got off to her friends' house okay.

He pressed his knuckle against the switch for the dome light and bent forward to retrieve the papers from the car mat. A few receipts. A scribbled address. Registration.

Pinching the corner of the registration between two fingers, Riley raised it to the light. He read the name aloud. "Carlos Castillo."

Castillo.

The name slammed against his brain, and bright spots danced in front of his eyes. Amy's ex hadn't been the victim of bad luck. Carlos had chosen Amy for a reason. The Velasquez cartel had chosen that beach for a reason. Someone killed Carlos Castillo for a reason.

And now they might have a reason to kill Amy.

AMY GULPED IN a lungful of the damp evening air as she squared off with the San Diego Sheriff's deputy. She pointed a shaky finger toward her house. "His body was on my kitchen floor. He was dead."

"Ms. Prescott, can you explain to us how not one, but

two dead bodies can disappear in one night?" Deputy Sampson crossed his arms over his chest.

He and another sheriff's deputy had accompanied her to the beach, and just as Riley had predicted, someone had collected the body of the diver and Riley's diving gear. In the meantime, the sheriff's department had sent another car to Amy's house to check on the dead body of Carlos Castillo. Amy hadn't expected that one to disappear, too.

Why? Why would this drug cartel remove Carlos's body?

She closed her eyes. Maybe she had dreamed the entire episode. She licked her lips, still salty from Riley's kiss, and knew she'd been wide awake.

"Call Carlos's wife. I'm sure she'll verify that he's missing."

Deputy Sampson slipped a phone out of his pocket. "What's the number?"

"I—I don't know his home number, just his cell."

"What's that, then?"

"I don't know that, either. I can't remember it, and I deleted it from my contacts."

The deputy rolled his eyes, and Amy clenched her jaw to keep from screaming. She ground out between clenched teeth, "Why would I lie about a couple of dead bodies and a mysterious spy?"

"Look, Ms. Prescott. I'm not saying you're lying, but there's not much we can do right now with no bodies to back up your story and your, uh, spy nowhere to be found." He jerked his thumb over his shoulder. "Maybe Mr. Castillo wasn't dead, and he got up and walked away."

"He was dead." She clenched her hands in front of

her, recalling that she wouldn't let Riley touch Carlos's body. "H-he looked dead."

"Maybe you did stumble on some kind of drug deal. God knows, this close to the Mexican border we've seen plenty of crap going down. We'll send someone out to the beach again tomorrow. The body just might wash up on shore. And obviously if we get a call from Mrs. Castillo reporting a missing husband, we'll be back."

Another deputy jogged down her front steps. "If someone did snatch the body, whoever it was did a great cleanup job."

"And what about the wet suit?" Amy shoved her hands in the back pockets of her jeans. Not that she wanted to put the cops on Riley's trail, but a little bit of evidence might show she hadn't been delusional.

"Did you find the wet suit on the living room floor?" Deputy Sampson jerked his chin toward the other deputy.

"No. There's some sand around, but isn't she a lifeguard who just got off work?"

Amy stamped her foot, feeling about two years old. "I'm not making this up. A man saved my life on the beach and came home with me. He's the one who dropped me off at the station."

"Did you have a bad breakup with this ex-boyfriend of yours, Ms. Prescott? You found out he was married, you went a little crazy?" He held up his hands. "Hey, I don't blame you. Maybe you changed your mind and you wanted him back. He'd rush to your rescue or something, leave his wife."

Amy's jaw dropped. "That is so not me, Deputy Sampson."

He lifted his shoulders as the other two deputies ambled toward their squad cars parked at the curb, their red lights still casting a glow over the few neighbors who'd remained outside during the excitement.

Amy rubbed her arms. This was it. They were leaving. They didn't believe her, or they strongly doubted her. Thought she was some love-obsessed loon.

"I'll tell you what." Deputy Sampson shoved his useless little notebook in his pocket. "Like I said, we'll send someone to check out the beach tomorrow. In the meantime, I'll look into the whereabouts of Carlos Castillo. If he's missing, we'll be back."

"I probably won't be here." She squared her shoulders. "I'm not going to stick around to see if they bring the body back. You don't plan to stick around—do you?"

"I'm sorry, Ms. Prescott. We're not in the bodyguard business, but I'll make sure a patrol car takes a couple of turns around your neighborhood tonight."

Yeah, that makes me feel warm and fuzzy. Amy gripped her upper arms. It didn't matter. These sheriff's deputies with their rolling eyes and tight-lipped suspicions didn't make her feel safe, anyway. Only one man could make her feel safe right now: Riley, her phantom spy.

She pointed to Deputy Sampson's notebook, now tucked away in his pocket. "You have my cell phone number. I'll probably be spending a few days with some friends."

"Good idea."

With their so-called investigation wrapped up, the cops scrambled for their squad cars and started their engines. Amy turned her back on her neighbors' curious stares and slammed the front door of her rental house. She couldn't bring herself to go into the kitchen to make a cup of tea.

How could there be no evidence of a dead body? *Professionals.* Riley had warned her about these drug dealers. But Carlos's wife would miss him and contact the police. Then they'd come running back here with the smirks wiped off their officious faces.

Right now she planned to get out of there. Riley had tried to reassure her that the murderous thugs were after him, not her, but those same murderous thugs had slipped into her house while she was gone and stolen the dead body of her ex-boyfriend. Not a good sign.

She'd spend a few days with Sarah and Cliff. She didn't figure she'd have much luck rounding up her cat, Clarence, tonight. Maybe she'd leave a note for the girl down the street to put out food for him in her absence.

Amy crept down the hallway toward her bedroom, flipping on all the lights. She perched at the end of her bed and reached for the phone. She called Sarah and Cliff and got the babysitter.

"Could you ask them to call me as soon as they get home? It doesn't matter how late."

Amy dragged a suitcase from her hall closet and heaved it on top of her bed. She scooped up an armful of shorts and jeans and shoved them into the bag. She threw open her closet door and swept T-shirts and sweaters from their hangers.

After cramming everything in the suitcase, including her damp lifeguard swimsuit, she headed for the bathroom. She dumped some toiletries into a small bag and spun around.

Right into the solid form of a naked man.

A scream gathered in Amy's lungs, but before she could let loose, she realized the naked man was only half-naked—and he was no stranger.

"Riley! What are you doing here? The cops just left,

and they didn't believe more than half of my story, especially since Carlos's body is gone."

He gripped her shoulders, his fingers pinching her flesh. "You need to get out, Amy."

She swung the toiletry bag from her arm. "That's what I'm doing."

"I mean you need to leave now, with me."

"W-what are you talking about?"

"Your ex-boyfriend, Carlos Castillo, wasn't who he said he was."

"I know that. He was married."

"It's worse than that, Amy. He was involved with the Velasquez Drug Cartel. And now so are you."

Chapter Four

A jolt speared Amy's chest and she sucked in a sharp breath. "I don't believe you. Why are you saying this?"

"My…associate gave me his name. Carlos Castillo, right?" Riley tightened his grip on her shoulders and gave her a shake.

Squeezing her eyes shut, she nodded. She hadn't told him Carlos's last name. As her heartbeat raced, her mind slowed to a sluggish crawl. Her tongue felt thick and numb in her mouth. She didn't want to move. She didn't want to face any of it. Hadn't she endured enough drama in her life already from her childhood?

"I'm sorry." Riley released his grip and rubbed her upper arms. "I'm worried about you. What was Carlos doing here? Why did he single you out?"

"I don't know." Amy dragged her hands through her tangled hair and blew out a breath, expelling all her self-pity with it.

She straightened her spine. "It must have something to do with the beach. That's where we met. He must've sought me out there for a reason."

"Hold that thought." Riley grabbed the toiletry bag from her hand and charged past her into the bedroom. He dropped the bag into the open suitcase and glanced over his shoulder. "You have everything you need? I'm getting you out of here."

It looked like she had everything she needed standing right beside the bed. Riley knew how to take control of a situation and obviously relished the challenge. "I was waiting for a call from my friends before heading over to their place."

"How about you head over to my place for now? With what you know and what I know, maybe we can figure out your level of involvement in this mess." He zipped up her suitcase and hauled it off the bed.

She tilted her head. "You're going to tell me what you know?"

Shrugging, he yanked up the handle on her bag and wheeled it out the door as she stepped aside. "You're in it up to your pretty chin, so you deserve to know what's going on. And I'm relieved to find out I'm not responsible for your involvement or Carlos's death."

He thought she had a pretty chin? She rubbed it and then clenched her teeth. "I'm glad the fact that Carlos targeted me for some kind of criminal enterprise is making you feel warm and fuzzy inside."

Riley grinned, and then she felt warm and sticky inside. If she had to take off into the wild unknown with drug dealers pursuing her, at least she had a hot guy along for the ride.

"You know what I mean." He pointed to the front door. "I still have Carlos's car. Let's use that instead of yours."

She held up her index finger. "Hang on. I need to leave a note for the neighbor girl to feed my cat."

As she scribbled the note, Riley flung open the front door and peered into the darkness. "It's all clear. Where does the girl live?"

"Two doors down." She waved the piece of paper stuck to her finger with tape.

She jogged down the sidewalk and slapped the note on the outside of the mailbox. Poor Clarence must've hightailed it out of there when Carlos came calling. Her cat never liked Carlos. She should've paid more attention to his feline instincts.

She joined Riley at the rear of the BMW. He popped the trunk and heaved the suitcase inside. "When we get to my house, we'll search the car. I haven't had time yet."

"Looks like you haven't had time for anything." Amy allowed her gaze to wander down his body to his swim trunks, now dry and hanging loosely from his slim hips. The muscles of his flat belly clenched as he slammed down the trunk.

He tugged at a stiff lock of her hair. "You, either. When we get to my place, we can take a shower."

Her cheeks warmed, and Riley lifted one brow. "One at a time."

How'd he see her blush in the dark? Unless the same naughty thought had popped into his head.

As she slid onto the passenger seat, Amy drew her eyebrows together. She must be overcoming her trust issues—by leaps and bounds—since she'd accepted Riley's story so readily. Something about the man instilled confidence—and a whole lot more.

Of course, she'd been willing to trust Carlos, too, and look where that had landed her. Or had she? She'd never let Carlos completely into her life. She'd never slept with him. He had accused her so many times of holding back. That's why she was surprised when she'd discovered his marital status. Usually men cheated on their wives so they could sleep around, not hold hands and walk on the beach.

Unless those men were sinister drug dealers with ulterior motives. Carlos probably didn't even have a wife.

Riley hit the highway and accelerated. "So the cops didn't believe you?"

"It's like you said." She slumped in the leather seat. "They didn't find anything at the beach, and then when we got to my place, someone had removed Carlos's body."

"Did they question you about me?" He slid a sidelong glance at her.

She snorted. "They thought I'd watched too many James Bond movies."

He smiled, but she heard him release a long breath. "I wonder why they took Carlos, and how. You'd think your neighbors would've noticed people dragging a dead body from your house."

"Lots of older folks in that neighborhood—not much activity at night. So how'd you find out about Carlos's connection to the drug dealers?"

"I saw his registration minutes after my contact gave me his name. It makes sense, but it doesn't explain what he was doing at your house at the time of the drop, or why his associates killed him. What can you tell me about Carlos?"

Amy curled a leg beneath her and gazed out the window. "I met him before summer started. He was charming and interesting and he kept coming back to my beach. We started dating and then I discovered he had a wife."

"How'd that happen?"

It sounded so petty now, but any information she could give Riley might help. Amy cleared her throat.

"I—I didn't trust Carlos. Some of his actions seemed suspicious—the parking around the corner, the excuses for never meeting at his place, the endless cell phone calls. So one day I answered his cell phone."

Riley reached over and tucked a stray lock of hair behind her ear. "Don't look so sheepish. You had good reason to suspect him and you followed your instincts. Who'd you find on the other end, the wife?"

"Yep." She clasped her hands between her knees. "Of course, now I'm not so sure. For a wife, she didn't seem very upset that another woman had just answered her husband's cell phone."

"Did you confront Carlos?"

"I did and he admitted it. I immediately ended the relationship."

Riley drummed his thumbs on the steering wheel and narrowed his eyes. "She could've been the real deal. Drug dealers get married, too."

"I guess." She lifted a shoulder. "So why do you think he hooked up with me in the first place?"

"He wanted access to that beach." His lips quirked in a quick grin. "Not that you aren't without your charms."

Amy rolled her eyes. "Don't worry. No offense taken."

"He probably wanted to find out about lifeguard schedules and procedures and pass the information on to the guys in the boat."

"He did ask a lot of questions, which seemed natural at the time. But what was he doing back at my place tonight? Why'd his associates kill him and why'd they come back for me...or you?"

"And now you're asking a lot of questions, none of which I can answer."

"How about I start asking some you can answer?"

Amy shifted in her seat and studied Riley's profile. This man with his ready grin and sarcastic quips could turn lethal in a matter of seconds. His dark blue eyes could shine with humor and cloud over with secrets just as fast. She wanted to dig deeper to solve the enigma of Riley... Riley. She didn't even know his last name.

"I'll answer anything you like once I've had a shower and something to eat." He jerked his thumb toward the window. "We're here."

Riley wheeled the car into the parking lot of a non-descript apartment complex. Amy didn't know what she expected for a safe house, but a sprawling apartment building in the middle of San Diego didn't exactly fit the bill for a secret agent.

Riley pulled into a numbered parking slot. "Good thing I stole Carlos's car since I left mine down by the harbor."

"It won't be such a good thing if Carlos's wife reports the car stolen."

Riley grabbed the door handle and raised his brows. "If Carlos had a wife."

Amy scrambled from the car while Riley unlocked the trunk. She joined him at the rear of the car as he yanked her suitcase from the back and set it on its wheels. Then he ducked back inside the trunk, sweeping his hands across its surface.

"Doesn't look like Carlos kept anything in here, but he left his jacket in the backseat along with his cell phone. We can take a closer look at the phone once we're inside." He slammed the trunk closed and locked up again.

Amy liked the sound of that. Riley really did plan to include her. Must be because the drug cartel had put her directly in their line of fire.

Every crisis had a silver lining.

She followed Riley to the elevator as he dragged her bag behind him. He had a small place tucked away in the corner on the third floor of the building.

He threw open the door for her, and she stepped into the apartment that had the look and feel of a standard motel. Serviceable furniture populated the living room and small dining area. The blank walls stared back at her.

"Homey place." She tossed her purse onto one of two matching gray chairs.

"The agency isn't known for its decorating skills."

"So you're working for the CIA?" Amy swallowed against her dry throat. Not great news, but she'd rather be on the run with a CIA agent than an FBI agent. Any day.

"Not exactly." He dumped Carlos's keychain in a basket on the kitchen counter. "They're financing this operation, but they don't know it."

"That's kind of them. So what are you, an undercover agent?" She liked the sound of that even better. Maybe she *had* watched too many Bond movies.

"Me?" That sexy grin spread across his face again, made sexier by the stubble on his chin. "I run a dive boat in Mexico. Cabo San Lucas, to be exact."

Tilting her head, Amy put her hands on her hips. "You're just messing with me now."

"God's honest truth." He held up his fingers, Boy Scout–style, but Amy doubted his Boy Scout credentials, especially when that dangerous glint lit up his blue eyes.

Riley yanked up the handle of her suitcase and dragged it toward the back of the apartment. "Take a shower, and I'll whip up something to eat. It's almost midnight. You must be as hungry as I am."

Amy's stomach growled to punctuate his comment. Maybe she could blame hunger for making her weak in the knees instead of Riley's devil-may-care grin. "I'm starving, but then we talk."

"Deal."

He disappeared through a door, and Amy followed him into a small bedroom. The neatly made bed dominated the room and for one crazy moment, she wanted to pull those covers over her head and sleep for about a week.

Riley wheeled her bag into a corner and then grabbed a T-shirt from a hanger in the closet. He pointed to another door across the hall. "The bathroom's in there and the towels are in the cupboard. Leave some hot water for me."

He clicked the door behind him and Amy fell across the bed. *Safety.*

RILEY DROPPED FOUR pieces of bacon onto the paper towel and blotted the grease from the strips as his belly rumbled. Inhaling the salty aroma of the bacon, he broke off an edge and popped it into his watering mouth.

He whistled while he whisked the eggs, halting in midrambling tune when he heard the shower finally stop. Amy must've thought he was kidding about that hot water.

But then she needed a warm shower more than he did. She'd held up well under the stress of the situation—no crying, screaming or gnashing of teeth—but the pallor beneath her sun-kissed skin and her wide dark eyes hinted at her fear. Or anger. The woman definitely had an edge—and he liked it.

Several minutes later, as he crumbled the bacon on top of the bubbling eggs, the bedroom door swung open and Amy tiptoed into the living room.

"Everything still okay?"

Riley concentrated on flipping the omelet. "Did you think the Velasquez Drug Cartel was in here cooking eggs and bacon?"

"You never know." She huffed out a breath and sauntered to the kitchen counter. "They could've surprised you mid-egg and then enjoyed the fruits of your labor over your dead body."

He laughed and slid the omelet onto the waiting plate. "You have a twisted way of thinking, Amy Prescott."

"How'd you know my last name?" She clutched the edge of the counter, her knuckles turning white.

Guess that warm shower didn't do much to relax her. His gaze raked her from head to toe, taking in the warm mahogany hair falling over one shoulder and those long legs encased in the same faded denim she'd worn earlier.

"Relax, beach girl. It didn't take a trained observer to see the tag on your backpack. I thought you trusted me now. I made omelets."

"Omelets are the new olive branch or something?" She sniffed the air. "They smell good. I guess I'll have to suspend suspicion to eat."

"That's a start. And to make things even, my name's Riley Hammond." He snagged two forks from a drawer and slid a plate toward her. "I'm going to hit the shower. I've been wearing these board shorts longer than a man should wear anything."

Except a long lean woman like Amy.

Riley compressed his lips as if he'd spoken his thought aloud. Amy, gazing longingly at the plate, hadn't noticed his shift from protector to wolf.

"Do you want me to wait until you're out of the shower?" She pointed the tines of the fork at the omelet.

"Nah. This ain't the Ritz. Dig in."

He grabbed a clean towel from the closet and crossed the hall to the bathroom.

As he pulled the door behind him, Amy called out, "Don't close it."

He twisted around, raising his brows.

Two spots of color brightened her cheeks. "I—I'd just feel better with the door open. I promise I won't peek."

Too bad.

"You'd better not." He shook his finger at her. "Because I'm really modest."

Amy cackled and stabbed her omelet.

Riley cranked on the shower and bent forward as he flattened his palms against the tile. The warm water cascaded down his back, and he rolled his shoulders. As he lathered his hair and body, thoughts of Amy poked and prodded him.

He didn't need a companion to do his job, especially not one as distracting as Amy. Even though Carlos had dragged her into this situation, Riley wanted to keep her well away from it. And well away from him.

If his wife, April, had steered clear of him, she'd be alive. But Amy was made of stronger stuff than April. Riley lifted his face to the spray of suddenly cold water to punish himself for his disloyal thoughts about April.

She was dead and had taken their unborn baby with her. Their deaths had compelled him to banish all the resentment he'd felt toward her for tricking him into a marriage he didn't want. And he had to keep that resentment at bay or fall into a black hole of never-ending guilt.

"Your cell phone is buzzing."

Riley shut off the water and cracked open the shower door. Amy's hand, clutching his phone, wiggled in the bathroom doorway.

"Can you bring it over before I miss the call?" He sluiced back his hair.

Holding the vibrating phone in front of her, she stumbled into the bathroom with eyes squeezed shut. She tripped over the toilet, banging her knee on the lid.

"Don't let your embarrassment be the death of you." He crossed one arm in front of his body and held out his other hand for the phone.

Amy peeled her eyes open and pinned her gaze to his face as she handed him the phone. Once he had it in hand, she whipped around and scurried out of the bathroom.

Swallowing hard, he slid the phone open with his wet hand. "Hello?"

"Hope I didn't wake you." The colonel's gruff voice doused any desire Riley had felt over Amy's intrusion.

"I'm in the shower. It's been a long day."

"Hate to make it longer, but I thought you were going to check out that beach."

"I'll be on it tomorrow, Colonel. You know I'm accustomed to Jack's hands-off leadership." Riley pulled a towel from the rack and slung it over his shoulder, his eyes darting to the door Amy had left wide open.

"Yeah, I know. The ends justify the means and all that. Maybe that's how Jack got into trouble. Did you go back to the beach?"

Riley's jaw clenched at the colonel's criticism of Jack. Colonel Scripps hadn't been on the front line with them. Although the colonel had served his time, he filled the role of paper pusher now. He didn't understand that

Jack's leadership fit their missions. They all would've been dead a long time ago if it hadn't.

Riley blew out a breath. "We—I—plan to do that tomorrow." The colonel didn't need to know about Amy's involvement. "I figured the cops would be all over that beach tonight once the lifeguard reported the incident."

"Did she bring up your name?"

"She didn't have it," Riley lied smoothly. The colonel also didn't need to know he'd blabbed his name to Amy. If he bristled at the way Jack conducted himself, he'd pull out the little hair he had left over Riley's business model. "I'll get right on it and report back—when I have something to report."

As usual, Colonel Scripps ended the call. Even though the team didn't report to the colonel in an official capacity anymore, the man was still in charge.

Riley ran the towel over his goose-pimpled flesh and hitched it around his waist. He rubbed his fist along the mirror to clear it. Then he plowed his fingers through his long hair, sluicing it back.

Wiping his hand against the towel snugly covering his backside, he poked his head into the living room. "You okay in here? How was the omelet?"

Perched on the stool at the counter, Amy tapped her empty plate. "Yummy, but I feel guilty. Come and eat your food before it gets any colder."

"Pop it in the microwave for a few seconds. I'm going to get dressed. A guy can only go commando for so long." He tugged at the towel.

"Go commando?"

"You know. No underwear." He grinned as Amy blushed. He knew he was playing with fire, but the heat felt so good.

He strolled into his bedroom and dressed quickly in

shorts and a T-shirt. September in Southern California usually went out on a hot wave of summer heat—and the woman in his kitchen only made it hotter.

He sat down at the counter, and Amy placed a plate in front of him, steam curling from the yellow concoction. "Let me know if you want me to heat it up some more."

He wanted her to heat it up a lot more, but he didn't have food in mind. He sliced through the corner of his omelet with a fork and devoured it. "Mmm. That's fine."

She balanced on the edge of the stool next to him. "Can we talk now? Who was on the phone?"

"That was Colonel Frank Scripps. He pulled us all back together to find Jack and has all the right connections for this assignment."

She nodded encouragingly. "And what is this assignment?"

"I'm looking for my buddy, Jack Coburn." Riley sawed off another piece of egg.

"He's involved with this drug cartel or something?"

Riley slammed his fist on the counter. "No."

Amy's brows shot up. "Sorry. Touchy subject, huh?"

"I'd better start at the beginning." He ran his hands across his face. Where had it all begun? "I was a Navy SEAL serving in the Middle East. Colonel Scripps and a few other officers assembled a couple of special-ops divisions to gather intelligence and generally work under the radar of military protocol."

"So you were a kind of spy?" The gold lights in Amy's dark eyes sparkled.

This woman likes living on the edge. "Don't look so excited. Our lives didn't exactly mimic a Robert Ludlum novel. This team of officers recruited me, Ian Dempsey from the U.S. Army Mountain Division, Buzz

Richardson from the Air Force Special Ops Command, and the leader of Prospero, Jack Coburn, from the Office of Naval Intelligence."

"Prospero? Were you sorcerers like the character in Shakespeare's play?"

"Yeah, we pulled off a lot of magic." Riley shoved his plate away and planted his elbows on the counter. "Jack came up with the name. Usually he'd take a break from reading only long enough to round up terrorists."

A smile flitted across Amy's face. "He sounds…interesting. So you all retired from Prospero, except Jack, and now he's missing?"

"Even Jack retired from the military and Prospero, but instead of taking his hard-earned cash like the rest of us and kicking back, he took a job as a hostage negotiator. He disappeared while on a job in Afghanistan."

Amy shivered and clutched her arms. "That's a dangerous place. What does he have to do with the Velasquez Drug Cartel?"

"We don't know yet." Riley hunched his shoulders. "The Velasquez bunch was supposed to be getting a shipment of heroin from some terrorist organization with ties to Afghanistan. Jack's name came up in some chatter the CIA picked up. It's our first clue."

"A terrorist organization in Afghanistan? I can't believe Carlos Castillo was involved in all this." Shaking her head, she scooped up Riley's empty plate and stalked toward the sink.

Riley grabbed a glass of water and downed half of it. "I'm glad you brought up Carlos. It's my turn now. You met him on the beach and you two started dating?"

"That's pretty much it. You know as much as I do now." She cranked on the faucet and scrubbed the plate so hard Riley figured he might need a new plate before she finished.

He ran his knuckles across his stubble. "Carlos obviously targeted you for access to that beach, but why? Did he ever approach you about bringing a boat up on shore? Maybe he thought he could sweet-talk you into looking the other way while his buddies picked up their shipment."

"That would take a ton of sugar, unless..." The plate cracked against the side of the sink. She held up the two pieces. "Sorry."

Riley hopped off the stool. "That's okay. Just be careful you don't cut yourself."

He took the plate from her and dropped the pieces into the trash. "What were you going to say about Carlos?"

She slid the shiny forks into the dish drainer and turned, leaning her hips against the sink. "I forgot. Carlos probably just wanted info from me. He did ask a lot of questions about my job. He knew the beach would be deserted this time of year. He knew what time I got off work, and he probably knew it was my last shift today."

"But that still doesn't tell us what he was doing at your house." Riley crossed his arms over his chest.

"Maybe he wanted to warn me or make sure I was okay." She must have noticed the scowl twisting his face. "He wasn't a bad person, Riley."

"He was a drug dealer, Amy."

She reached over and toyed with the keys in the basket, making them jingle like wind chimes. "I know that. Sometimes criminals...people...do bad things, but they're still people. They have their good sides."

Riley cocked his head. He hadn't figured Amy for

the bleeding-heart type, but she must've liked Carlos since she'd dated him.

Did she sleep with him, too? He dug his fingers into his biceps until it hurt. He didn't want to know the answer to that question.

"We need to check out the beach tomorrow. I want to get a good look at it during daylight. Will there be anyone there?"

"It's a weekday. No lifeguards on that beach anymore, and I think it's supposed to be overcast again." She cupped a set of keys in her palm. "Are these Carlos's keys?"

"Yeah. We should remove your house key from the ring since I'm going to be leaving his car somewhere along with his keys."

Amy fiddled with the key chain, a crease forming between her brows. Then she gasped.

Riley's heart jumped. "What is it?"

Amy pinched a small gold key between her fingers, holding it aloft while the rest of the keys dangled below it. "I know what Carlos wanted on that beach."

Chapter Five

Riley lifted one brow and his gaze shifted from the key clutched between Amy's fingers to her eyes, bright and round above flushed cheeks.

"You do?"

"Yep." She jangled the keys that caught the recessed lighting and reflected in her eyes, giving them an added sparkle. "This is a distinctive key and it belongs to the storage unit on my beach."

"Storage unit?"

"We have a storage unit on that beach for buoys, extra equipment and supplies for the junior lifeguard program, which ended in the middle of the summer." She tossed the key chain to Riley, and he caught it with one hand.

He plucked out the gold key, with its squared-off end and dip in the middle. He hadn't wanted to involve Amy in any of this, but she'd jumped in with both feet and seemed to thrive on the thrill. Who was he to deny her?

"Would anyone else be in and out of this storage bin?"

"It's pretty much reserved for the junior lifeguards. When the program ends, nobody uses the storage until the following summer."

"A perfect drop location." Riley traced the edges of

the unusual key with the tip of his finger. "Carlos got close to you to get access to the storage unit. He probably arranged for his contacts to leave the drugs in the storage unit, and the Velasquez Cartel was on its way to pick them up or scope out the location when we interrupted them."

Amy folded her arms on the counter and hunched over. "We interrupted them? I was in the lifeguard tower doing my job."

Riley grimaced. Just showed how much she'd become a part of the equation in his mind. "The diver was the scout to give the all clear for the boat to come up on the beach."

"Do you think they picked up the drugs?" She jerked upright and slapped the counter with her palms. "Maybe Carlos never left the drugs. Maybe that's why they killed him."

"I like the way you think, Amy. You ever consider a career in law enforcement?"

His teasing comment elicited bright red cheeks and a nervous laugh from her. "They wouldn't have me."

"I suppose it wouldn't do any good to suggest you stay here tomorrow while I search the beach?"

She shook her head and her ponytail whipped from side to side. "No. That's my beach. Besides—" she glanced over her shoulder at the kitchen window "—I don't want to be by myself."

Riley didn't want to leave her by herself, either. "That's what I figured. Let's get some sleep. You can have the bedroom. I'll bunk out here on the couch."

"Are you sure?" Amy wrinkled her nose as she peered around his shoulder at the small couch. "I think I'd fit more comfortably on the couch than you."

He shrugged. "I've slept on worse."

Riley dragged a blanket from the hall closet and tossed it onto his new bed while Amy slipped into the bedroom and shut the door. He brushed his teeth, and she stepped into the hallway clutching a pillow to her chest.

"Here's an extra pillow from the bed."

"Thanks."

He held out his arms, and she smashed the pillow against his chest and scurried into the bathroom. He caught a glimpse of her baggy nightshirt before she slammed the door. His brow furrowed. Why the modesty? She wasn't wearing anything from the pages of one of those sexy lingerie catalogs. Not that she needed to. Amy's natural beauty and feisty personality pushed all his buttons—including some he didn't even know he had.

He didn't figure he'd ever want to involve a woman in his business again, especially not after what had happened to April. But Amy wanted in, and not for the same reasons as April. Carlos Castillo had dragged Amy into his business, and she had a burning desire to finish it.

Riley dropped his shorts by the edge of the couch and peeled off his T-shirt. He punched the pillow a few times and dragged the blanket over his shoulders.

The bathroom door clicked open, a shaft of light slicing across the hall.

Amy poked her head into the living room. "Are you okay? There's still time to switch."

"I'm good." He waved his arm, the blanket slipping from his shoulder. "Go ahead and make yourself comfortable in my bed."

Without me.

Amy hesitated, a soft sigh escaping from her lips.

Riley held his breath. Was she about to issue an invitation?

"Th-thanks, Riley. Good night."

Riley eased back against the cushion. Of course she wouldn't ask him to join her. They'd just met. Today. On the beach. Under fire. They barely knew each other.

AMY PEELED OPEN one eyelid and focused on the sunlight sifting through the blinds. After thrashing around and twisting the bedcovers into a hopeless knot, she welcomed the morning after the sleepless night she'd spent in Riley's bed.

Replaying the previous day's events in her mind had kept her wide-awake, wide-eyed and fearful. Once she'd talked herself back away from the ledge, her thoughts scrambled down another just-as-torturous path—Riley Hammond half-naked in the other room.

For one crazy moment last night, she'd almost suggested he join her in bed. The lust factor did play a role in her almost-invitation, but she also craved a warm body for comfort. Those old familiar feelings of loneliness had washed over her when she'd slipped between the cool sheets of Riley's bed alone.

She snorted and buried her face in the pillow. As if Riley would've been interested in cuddling away her fears all night. That wouldn't have even been enough for her. Once she got her hands on his rock-hard bod...

The rap on the bedroom door had her yanking the covers to her chin. She cleared her throat. "Yes?"

The door cracked open a sliver.

"You're awake? I didn't want to disturb you before, but we should get going."

She gasped and shot upright. "Is it late?"

"About ten o'clock." He pushed open the door and

wedged a shoulder against the doorjamb, his long hair wet and slicked back from his face. "We had a late night, and you needed your sleep."

She rubbed her eyes. She still needed her sleep. It figured. She'd dozed off at the break of dawn and slept in.

Scrambling from the bed, she said, "Looks like you already showered. You probably need to get in here and get dressed."

Pulling her oversize T-shirt past her thighs, Amy's gaze tracked across Riley's bare chest. She worked on the beach and all the male lifeguards she knew spent half their time shirtless, but the sight of Riley's flat planes of muscle and ridged abs left her breathless.

His blue eyes darkened as he crossed his arms over those amazing pecs. Had she unsettled him with her unabashed appreciation of his male assets?

He cocked one brow and a lazy smile played across his lips as his muscles seemed to bunch up even more.

Unsettled? Hardly.

Amy turned and dipped her head into her suitcase. "I'll grab some clothes and hit the shower."

She pawed through a jumble of shorts and T-shirts. What did one wear on a spying mission? Wrapping her arms around a bundle of clothes, she headed for the door where Riley's solid frame loomed in the opening.

He stepped aside and she brushed past him, her arm skimming his.

"How'd you sleep?"

His voice so close to her ear made her jump. "Huh?"

"How'd you sleep? No bumps in the night?"

"Plenty, but they were all in my head." She stumbled into the bathroom, still misty from Riley's shower. She inhaled the steam and savored the scent of masculinity that whispered on the air.

She shook her head. Maybe she should adjust the water temperature to freezing to quell these fantasies about Riley. After her lukewarm shower, she toweled off and pulled on a pair of shorts and a T-shirt. Then she padded to the living room.

Riley, dressed in jeans and a black T-shirt, sat hunched over the counter, nursing a cup of coffee and scanning a newspaper.

He glanced up when she walked into the room. "Do you want some bran flakes or instant oatmeal?"

"I'll take the cold cereal." She plopped down on the stool across from him and reached for the box of bran flakes. "Anything in that paper about last night's activities?"

"Nope. I guess you weren't that convincing." He collected a bowl and a spoon from the dish drainer on the sink and shoved them across to her.

"I wouldn't trust those cops to find a lollipop in a candy store anyway."

Riley blinked and studied her face.

Tone down the vehemence about the police, girl. Amy ignored his puzzled gaze and dumped some cereal in her bowl. Riley got the hint and retreated to his bedroom where he proceeded to bang closet doors and drawers. She hoped he'd emerge with some tools of his trade—guns, knives, grenades.

Riley joined her in the kitchen with a promising black bag slung over one shoulder. He scooped up Carlos's keychain and swung it around his finger. "Are you ready to investigate?"

Amy dropped her dishes in the sink. "I'm as ready as I'll ever be, but what happens if we don't find anything? What next?"

"I search for new leads, and you watch your back."

Amy shivered and clenched her teeth. She didn't like the sound of that proposition at all.

A half hour later, Riley pulled Carlos's car into the almost deserted beach parking lot. With summer over and school back in session, only a few die-hard runners and walkers occupied the barren sands. Surfers found better waves up the coast and fishermen had the pier farther north for their activities.

As he rolled past the empty spaces, Riley asked, "Where's the storage container?"

"South end of the beach, just over that rise. You can't see it from the parking lot."

Perfect place to stash some illegal contraband. Riley nabbed the last space on the south side of the lot and grabbed his black bag out of the trunk.

Amy pointed to the bag as Riley hitched it over his shoulder. "What's in there?"

"A few necessities of life."

"Bet your necessities are a lot different from mine."

"If you hang out with me long enough, you'll come to appreciate mine more."

She wouldn't mind giving it a try. Amy clumped across the dry sand next to Riley. But back at his place he'd made it pretty clear that if they hit a dead end on the beach, she'd be on her own, Looking over her shoulder.

Not that she was any stranger to looking over her shoulder. Or being on her own.

They traipsed up a small dune and the storage unit rose from the sand, an ominous dark gray shape. Amy shoved her hands in her pockets to hide their slight trembling. She'd never considered the junior-lifeguard shed scary before.

"Do you want to do the honors?" Riley dragged the

keys from his front pocket and dangled them from one finger.

Amy held out her hand, and Riley dropped them into her palm. She selected the unusual key from the ring and lifted the lock securing the door. With shaky fingers, she tried to insert the key into the lock, finding success on her third try.

Riley helped her pull open the heavy door, which creaked on rusty hinges. Amy sniffed at the briny scent that lived in every corner of the storage unit.

As her gaze tracked across the cleared-out space in the center of the unit, her breath hitched, and she grabbed the edge of the door.

"What's wrong?" Riley hovered over her left shoulder.

"This." She swept one arm in front of her. "We didn't leave it like this."

"You mean this clearing?" Riley stepped around her and parked in the middle of the circle ringed with buoys, life vests, surfboards and paddleboards.

"We stacked all this equipment at the end of the junior-guard session. Someone's pushed it out of the way to make room for…" Amy hugged herself, suddenly cold in the stuffy unit.

Riley crouched beside her, running his hands over the cement flooring just beyond the shaft of light from the open door. He turned his hands over and studied his palms, as if trying to read his future.

"Do you see anything?" Amy leaned over his shoulder and peered at the sand and grit stuck to his palms.

"No." He brushed his hands together. "But then I didn't expect them to leave any heroin behind."

"W-what would it look like?" Her gaze darted around the storage facility.

"Probably a brown powder or a black tar form. The couriers from Afghanistan might have already packaged it in balloons for Velasquez to sell on the street." Riley braced his hands on his knees. "But I think it's clear Carlos made this space available to the dealers from Afghanistan to leave their delivery for the Velasquez Cartel."

Amy squatted next to him, wrapping her arms around her knees. "And Velasquez's boys picked it up last night. That's why they didn't come after us after those initial shots. They found what they came for. That could've been the end of it."

"Except for Carlos." Riley brushed a wisp of hair from her cheek. "They came after Carlos because they didn't trust him or because he didn't deliver the money for the shipment."

"That still doesn't get us beyond square one. Why did Carlos return to my house? I just don't—"

"Shh." Riley sliced a hand across his throat.

Amy covered her mouth with her hand as a shadow passed by the open door to the unit, momentarily blocking the sun that had given them their only light.

Jumping to his feet, Riley pulled the gun from his waistband. Amy toppled sideways into the paddleboards. *How'd he whip that out so fast?* She hadn't even realized he'd been packing anything other than the stash in the black bag.

Clutching the weapon in his right hand, Riley crept toward the door and poked his head outside. He called over his shoulder, "You saw that, right?"

"I saw a darkening at the door, but it could've been a cloud moving over the sun, or a bird."

"That's one helluva bird to blot out the sun."

"Do you see anything?"

"Just a couple walking in the distance, but these dunes make it hard to see for any distance." He spun around, tucking the gun back into his waistband. "Let's get out of here and take a look at the lifeguard tower."

Amy scrambled to her knees and gripped the thick edges of the paddleboard, shoving it back against the others. A sliver of silver glinted behind the board. Amy's fingers inched along the gritty floor and she slid the hard, smooth object toward her.

She pinched her find between two fingers and shifted into the light, holding it up for inspection. Her heart slammed against her rib cage.

"What's that?" Riley knelt beside her.

Amy opened her mouth, emitted tiny gasps of air. Squeezing her eyes shut, she shook her head and scooped in a deep breath.

Don't be ridiculous, Amy. Dad's in prison.

"It's a cigarette holder." She held the slim tube flattened on one end under Riley's nose, her fingers covering the initials engraved on the end.

"You don't see many of those around anymore." He plucked the holder from her fingers and pushed to his feet. In two steps he reached the square of sunlight and examined the holder. "I suppose none of the lifeguards smoke or happen to use a cigarette holder?"

Feeling like she had just aged twenty years, Amy staggered to her feet and stretched. "None of the lifeguards smoke, and I've never seen any of them use a cigarette holder."

"What about Carlos?"

"Not a smoker."

"And his initials aren't E.P." Riley rubbed the pad of his thumb along the edge of the cigarette holder.

"Initials?" Amy clenched her jaw and swallowed hard.

"Engraved on the side." Riley tossed the object into the air and caught it, closing his fist around it. "Looks like we have a piece of evidence."

"I don't see what good some anonymous cigarette holder is going to do us." Amy pushed the hair out of her face and stalked past Riley. Once outside, she gulped in the fresh sea air.

The hinges of the storage unit protested as Riley swung the door shut with a bang. "You never know. Any evidence is better than none. Are you okay?"

"Yeah." She spun around and heaved against the heavy door with her shoulder as Riley secured the lock.

He snapped the lock into place and cocked his head. "You look pale. I mean, beneath your suntan, which is even weirder."

"I was getting creeped out in there." She wiped the back of her hand across her mouth, relieved the trembling had stopped. "I'm half-Mexican, you know. I tan easily."

Riley wedged a finger beneath her chin and tilted. "Is that where the pretty, dark eyes come from and the dark hair with the auburn sheen to it? Your mother must be Mexican. Is Prescott English?"

Amy slipped from his inspection, a swath of that dark hair with the auburn sheen hiding her hot face. Had he really noticed that much about her?

"I guess. Just a mishmash of American mutt." *With an emphasis on mutt.* "Hey, can we check out the rest of the beach now?"

He paused for a few seconds and then pocketed the key and the cigarette holder. "Let's go."

Amy shuffled behind Riley, twisting her hands in front of her. She really didn't want to go into her family lineage with him. After discovering her background, he just might suspect her entire involvement in this mess.

They searched the area near the water where Velasquez's man died. Then they poked around the lifeguard tower, which Amy had locked up last night when she'd returned with the sheriff's deputies.

Riley grabbed the base of the tower and leaned forward, the muscles in his back and shoulders a rippled outline beneath his T-shirt. "Did you ever find your wallet?"

"Right here where I dropped it." Amy pointed her toe at the sand beneath the tower. "So if the guys from the boat did use it to get my address, they left it behind."

Dropping his lashes over his blue eyes, Riley mumbled, "I don't think they needed your wallet, Amy."

"You think they already had my address?" She licked her lips, tasting the salt from the moist air. "Carlos must've told them about me. But how did they know to find Carlos at my place?"

"They either followed him or staked out your house."

"Riley." Amy burrowed the toes of her tennis shoes into the dry sand. "If the Velasquez goons or their customers already killed Carlos and picked up their drugs from the storage unit, what did they want from me last night? Why'd they return?"

Riley spread his hands, sand clinging to his palms and fingers, and lifted his shoulders. Strong shoulders. Capable hands. A man you could trust. Maybe.

"Let's put a positive spin on this." He shifted his gaze to the ocean, his eyes reflecting the grayish-blue water.

"I'm ready for positive."

"Carlos double-crossed both parties, so they were both after him. Someone got lucky and nailed him first. The other party was still after him last night, and maybe now they know he's dead. If so, your involvement ends there."

"I like the sound of that. I'll stay with my friends for a few days to be on the safe side, and then I'm going to try to put this behind me."

His eyes widened. "You can do that?"

Riley had no idea how much she'd already put behind her. What was one murdered, drug-dealing ex-boyfriend? As she watched the sea breeze toss the ends of Riley's sun-washed hair, Amy swallowed. Putting Riley behind her was a whole other matter.

"I had already forgotten about Carlos. Now it'll just be easier."

Riley whistled. "Ooh, that's cold. Okay, I'm just going to have to be satisfied with my cigarette holder. Maybe it will lead me to someone or something."

Amy opened her mouth and then snapped it shut. The fact that her father used a cigarette holder would be of no interest to Riley. Her father had nothing to do with the events of the past twenty-four hours.

"Are you ready?" Riley grabbed her hand, the grit from his fingers grating across her skin.

She left her hand in his, wondering if the buzz she felt at their connection would dull to a hum. She had to steel herself to walk away from this man. She was probably mistaking the adrenaline rush for attraction.

He opened the car door for her and she slid onto the warm leather seat and closed her eyes. She didn't need the excitement. She didn't want the excitement. She could have a typical relationship with a normal, boring guy. Women did it every day.

Riley dropped onto the driver's seat and blew out a breath. "I'd call this a productive outing."

"You would? Finding a random cigarette holder is productive?"

He pulled it out of his pocket and held it up to the windshield. "It's unusual. It has the owner's initials. I have a few contacts with the Velasquez Cartel. It should be easy to track down the owner."

Amy tucked her hands beneath her thighs. She just hoped the owner had nothing to do with her father. "I'll leave the spy work to you. I'll grab my stuff from your place and drop in on my friends. They left me a text message on my cell."

Cranking on the engine, Riley slanted a cool gaze her way. "Are you sure you're going to be okay?"

"I have to go back to my normal life at some point." Amy clicked her seat belt and powered down the window. She needed air.

Riley wheeled out of the parking lot, the sand crunching beneath the tires. He pulled onto the street and idled at the first red light, glancing into his rearview mirror.

His gaze wandered back to the mirror and then he checked his side mirror. His hands tensed on the steering wheel.

Amy's pulse ratcheted up several notches as an engine roared behind them. She checked the mirror on the passenger side and gripped the armrest. A black SUV was barreling toward them. She braced her feet against the floor of the car, waiting for the impact. "What the…?"

Riley cursed and punched the accelerator. "The guy's coming right for us. And he's not going to stop."

Chapter Six

Riley gripped the steering wheel, held his breath and flew through the intersection, narrowly avoiding a mini-van. Amy squealed beside him, jerking forward against her suddenly taut seat belt.

The BMW hugged the road while Riley eased off the gas pedal. He checked his mirror again. The black SUV careened through the intersection against the light and lunged toward them.

"Hold on," Riley shouted. He grasped the leather-wrapped wheel and turned sharply, taking the corner at high speed and giving silent thanks to Carlos for his high-performance car.

The SUV lumbered after them, squealing around the corner with purpose. A sick feeling lodged in Riley's belly as the yellow school-crossing signs flashed ahead.

Thank God the streets remained empty. School must still be in session. He sped through the crosswalk just slow enough to see the crossing guard's mouth drop open. The SUV followed in his path, knocking over the sign with the yellow flashing lights.

From his mirror, Riley saw the crossing guard shake her fist and reach inside her vest. *That's right, sweetheart. Call the cops.*

He couldn't afford to be pulled over in a car that

belonged to a dead man, but the inhabitants of that black SUV would have a lot of explaining to do, too. He wouldn't be surprised if the cops found a few outstanding warrants in that car.

Velasquez always employed punks to do his dirty work.

Riley took the next turn, and Amy fell against his shoulder. "How you doing, beach girl?"

She hunched over to look in the passenger mirror. "That's them isn't it? That's Velasquez."

"I don't know who else would be chasing us around town." Riley planned to avoid the freeway—too much visibility. He could lose them faster in the side streets, and he knew just the area.

Imperial Beach was always a little more working class than its glittery neighbors, Coronado and La Jolla. And it had the warehouses to prove it.

Riley let the Beemer do its thing as he peeled out, reaching almost a hundred down a straight shot toward a collection of silver-and-dun-colored warehouse buildings. Trucks trundled in and around the buildings, delivering goods from the harbor.

"Where are you heading? We're going to get cornered."

"Do you think those thugs are going to try anything with a bunch of truckers around? Besides, I have a plan. I always have a plan."

The car hummed as Riley maneuvered it through two parking lots. He'd left the SUV in the dust a half mile ago. Would the driver have the *cojones* to follow him into this maze of buildings?

A warehouse door gaped open in front of Riley, and he zoomed into the building, pulling the car to the side.

Amy swiveled her head around. "Are you going to hide in here?"

"Why not?"

"That's why." She jerked her thumb toward the back window where a couple of the warehouse workers started to amble their way.

"They're not going to bother a couple looking for a little privacy." He reached across the console, wrapped one hand behind her neck and pulled her close.

Amy's eyelids fluttered shut as she braced a hand against his chest. His heart thundered beneath her light touch. He weaved his fingers through the hair at the nape of her neck and brushed her lips with his.

They panted against each other's mouths. The adrenaline continued to rush through Riley's veins at warp speed. He couldn't distinguish between the thrill of the chase and the passion that pounded in his blood.

Ah, hell. Sometimes they were one and the same.

He possessed Amy's sweet lips in a kiss so pure it made his teeth ache. Chaste. Make-believe. At least that's what he wanted her to think.

She turned her head so that his lips ended up somewhere on her jaw. She sighed. He cupped her face for a repeat performance. She laughed.

"It worked."

"Huh?"

"Not only did our nosy, blue-collar workers back off, but we outmaneuvered the SUV. They won't find us here."

Disappointment speared his gut. "They could still be lurking around."

"I don't think so." She twisted in her seat. "I guess that positive scenario you dreamed up is just that. A dream. They want me for something."

"Or they want *me* for something."

She clasped her hands between her knees. "Then maybe we'd better split up and find out who they prefer."

Riley's breathing slowed down and he regained partial use of his brain. He wanted to keep Amy with him to protect her, but maybe the threat of danger hung over his head and not hers. In which case, her proximity to him would endanger her, not protect her.

It all had a familiar ring.

He had to cut her loose and allow her to get back to her life. There didn't appear to be any logical reason why the Velasquez Cartel would be interested in Amy. She couldn't identify even one of them. She'd demonstrated that in her report to the police. The police who didn't believe a word of her story. They had to know that by now, had to know she didn't pose any threat to them at all.

"You're probably right. I don't want to endanger you any more than I already have." Riley buzzed down the window and gulped diesel-scented air.

"You didn't endanger me, Riley. That was Carlos."

"I'm not making your life any easier." He turned over the engine and rolled out the other side of the warehouse, poking the nose of the car into the parking lot. He scanned the area, ignoring the grins of the warehouse workers. No sign of the black SUV.

"I'll take you back to my place and you can grab your stuff and I'll drop you off at your car. I still think you should hang out with your friends for a day or two."

"I will." She tapped her purse. "My friend left me that text message. I'll let her know I'm on my way over."

Blowing out a breath, Riley sped toward the highway. He had to get rid of this car now that Velasquez's guys had it on their radar.

Twenty minutes later he pulled into the parking garage of his apartment building. His hands tightened briefly on the steering wheel as Amy exited the car. Every nerve fiber in his body protested at letting her go, but she had a life to live. She couldn't spend it running around with him chasing bad guys.

He made a habit out of pursuing bad guys. For Amy, this incident would be a blip in her calm life. Something to tell the grandkids about.

His feet felt like lead as he tromped down the hallway toward the elevator behind her. They rode in silence, staring at the lighted numbers like a couple of strangers.

She leaned against the outside wall while he fumbled for his keys. He asked, "Do you want something to eat before you head over to your friends' place?"

"I don't want to be a bother to you anymore."

Riley shrugged, trying hard to mimic a nonchalance that he didn't feel. *Let her go. Keep her safe.*

They entered the apartment and Amy propped a hip against the counter, texting on her phone, the little beeps as she entered each letter reverberating in his head like a death knell.

He really did have control issues. He passed a hand across his face and grabbed a glass from the cupboard. "Water?"

She looked up from her phone and hit one final button. "Sure. High-speed car chases really make me thirsty."

"I'm sorry."

"Stop—" she sliced her hand through the air "—apologizing. It's not your fault, Riley. You saved my life on more than one occasion. I trusted the right guy last night."

And now he had to honor that trust and get her clear of this madness. "I'll get your bag."

She trailed after him, the sweet smell of her hair giving him all sorts of crazy ideas. She made a detour into the bathroom and collected her things while he wheeled her suitcase into the living room next to the door.

"I guess that's everything." She stuffed her toiletry bag into the side compartment of the suitcase.

"Did you hear back from your friends yet?" He gestured toward the cell phone clutched in her right hand.

"Not yet, but they'll come through. They always do. I just sent a text that I was on my way."

"Let's get you back to your car."

Amy ambled down the corridor, moving at half-speed. Could she be feeling the same reluctance as he felt?

Riley kept conversation to a minimum on the ride back to Amy's place. What more could he say? He pulled up behind her car and grabbed her bag from Carlos's Beemer.

She popped her trunk, and he hoisted the suitcase inside and slammed it shut for her. He rested his hand on the driver's door handle. "I know you told me to stop apologizing, but I need to go there once more."

Amy shook her head and a swath of dark hair swept over her shoulder. "I think you already hit your apology quota."

"The kiss." He blurted it out like a pimply faced teen. What had happened to his smooth lines? He swung open her door. "One of the many tricks of the trade."

He gritted his teeth behind his stupid grin. Now he sounded like a seventies disco dude.

Amy raised her brows. "Okay, whatever. It wasn't a big deal."

Now his grin was hurting his face. *Not a big deal?* "Right. I just wanted to make it look good for the guys in the warehouse. No big deal."

She stuck out her hand. "Thanks for sticking with me. I'm pretty sure I would've fallen apart without your support."

Riley narrowed his eyes. He seriously doubted that. Taking her hand, he swirled his thumb along her inner wrist. "Be careful, beach girl. You have my cell phone number in there. Use it if you need help."

"Will do." She slipped her hand from his and ducked into the car.

As she pulled away from the curb, he smacked the trunk of the car and waved. He'd cursed his bad luck when Amy came running into the ocean to save him.

Now as he watched her take the turn and disappear, he felt as if a vital organ had just been ripped from his chest.

AMY BLINKED AWAY TEARS as she watched Riley's blurry form in her rearview mirror. She dashed a hand across her eyes. *Buck up, girl. You operate better on your own anyway. Always have.*

She planned to put this little bump on the road to a normal, sedate life firmly behind her. No more married men. No more drug dealers. No more secret agents. She giggled at her list. Most women wouldn't even dream of making a list like that.

Most women didn't have Elijah Prescott for a father.

Amy's cell phone buzzed and she groped for it in her purse. She checked the display and let out a noisy sigh. "Hi, Sarah."

"Amy? Are you okay? Your message was weird."

Weird? Amy had a few other choice words about her predicament. "You don't know the half of it, and I don't have the energy to explain it. Can I crash at your place for a few days? I'll even babysit for free."

"Of course you can stay here, but we're leaving tonight for Florida. Cliff's mom had another fall. She's not doing well, so we're taking the kids back for a visit. It might be their last."

"Sorry to hear that. I can house-sit for you."

"Is it Carlos?"

Amy caught her breath. "What?"

"Is Carlos calling you again? Don't go back to him, Amy. That's a dead end."

Oh, boy. Sarah had never spoken truer words. "Going back to Carlos is an impossibility at this point."

"I'm glad to hear you say that, even though I never suspected for a minute you'd take him back. There's a new attorney at Cliff's firm. Maybe we can all get together for dinner some night."

Amy drew in a quick breath. If he didn't have deep blue eyes, a boyish grin, a fondness for knives and a penchant for engaging in high-speed chases, she'd have to pass.

"Maybe. I'm on my way to your place right now. Is that okay, or are you too busy packing for Florida?"

"We're done packing. You can join us for dinner and then save us taxi fare to the airport by giving us a ride."

"Sounds like a deal."

Amy ended the call and dropped her cell phone into the cup holder. She could always count on Sarah. Sarah had been like a big sister to her when she'd volunteered at Amy's middle school to tutor at-risk kids. Sarah was the one who had gotten Amy involved in the San Diego County Junior Lifeguard program.

Sarah had saved her life.

When Amy arrived at the house, she busied herself playing with the kids and avoided Sarah's worried, questioning glances. Her face must have had Major Stress written all over it.

When Cliff took the kids with him to pick up their dinner from the neighborhood Chinese restaurant, Sarah planted herself in front of Amy and placed her hands on Amy's shoulders.

"What happened to you? You're jumpier than one of the girls' Mexican jumping beans."

Amy's shoulders sagged beneath Sarah's light touch. She never could keep anything from her. Didn't want to.

As Amy recounted the previous day's adventures and today's car chase, Sarah's soft doe eyes grew rounder and bigger.

"How do you know you can trust this Riley character?"

"Sarah, he saved my life more than once in the past twenty-four hours. I can trust him." Amy dropped her lashes. "Besides, he's moved on anyway. I doubt I'll ever see him again."

"That's a good thing, Amy. You need to extricate yourself from this situation pronto." She rubbed Amy's shoulder. "Stay here while we're gone. Are you done with lifeguarding right now?"

"Yeah, yesterday was my last shift. That tower closes until next summer."

"When does EMT school start?"

"In two weeks, and then I might start applying to fire departments."

"You can do whatever you set out to do. I've seen

it." Sarah jerked her head toward the front door as Cliff staggered into the room carrying a daughter in one arm and bags of take-out food in the other.

Amy put her finger to her lips, and Sarah rolled her eyes. Amy knew Sarah would tell her husband everything, but probably not until they reached thirty thousand feet. That's how far away Amy needed Cliff to be to avoid his interference. He'd taken on the role of big brother, always eager to pick up any cause of Sarah's.

Amy stashed her worries in the corner as she helped Sarah's daughters navigate their food with chopsticks. Their squeals and giggles washed over her like a soothing balm.

This glimpse into Sarah's family life always created a small ache in the pit of her belly. But it made her more determined to find that for herself—if she could only banish one blue-eyed adventurer from her mind.

While the girls brushed their teeth, Amy grabbed the dinner plates and stacked them in the sink. She waved off Sarah. "Go help the girls get ready. I'll clean up when I come back from dropping you off at the airport."

The family bustled out of the house, and Amy took their minivan to drop them off. When she arrived back at the house, she double-checked the locks on the doors and windows. Couldn't be too safe when you had drug dealers on your trail.

Maybe now those drug dealers had just one trail to follow—Riley's. A sprinkling of goose bumps raced up her arms, even though if anyone knew how to take care of himself, Riley did. He knew how to take care of her, too.

Enough. She smacked her hands together, the sound echoing through the silent house. And enough of this hand-wringing over her fate or, worse, leaving it to

Riley to sort out. When did she ever wait for someone else to take action?

She dumped out the contents of her purse and snatched her cell phone. She scrolled through her contacts and selected the one she dreaded the most. Placing the call, she paced the length of the family room, avoiding dollhouses and a railroad track.

She held her breath as the man on the other end answered the phone. "San Miguel Federal Penitentiary."

Chapter Seven

Amy Prescott was a liar.

Riley ran his finger along the smooth cigarette holder and then tapped it against his palm. Amy knew something about this holder and for some reason had decided to keep that information to herself.

He should've figured this seemingly innocent bystander had secrets. Maybe Carlos hadn't been an exboyfriend but a current one, and Amy was not only his lover but his partner in crime.

Which made the kiss in the car even dumber. The thought left a sour taste in his mouth, and he took another gulp of coffee to wash it away. Amy should've realized you never lie to a liar.

His cell phone vibrated and he slid it open. "Do you have something for me, Chet?"

Chet whistled. "You have yourself a doozy. I sure hope this is professional and not personal because you need to stay far, far away from this girl."

Riley clenched his gut as if expecting a blow to the midsection. So Amy had played him all along. "Professional. Go ahead."

"Do you remember Eli Prescott?"

Riley dug his fingers into the arm of his chair. This was gonna be bad. "No."

Chet snorted. "Yeah, I guess you're a young 'un. Before your time."

"Well?" Riley gritted his teeth. Chet Bennett, the seasoned CIA agent always had to lord his knowledge over the younger guys. Riley hated owing the man favors, but Chet could conjure up information with the snap of his fingers.

"Elijah Benjamin Prescott was a militia-style survivalist in Idaho. When things got too hot in the States, he high-tailed it to Mexico and set up shop there. The Mexican government didn't mind too much until old Eli started making deals with some of the drug lords. Then the Mexican government decided to cooperate with the FBI, and the two agencies raided the compound."

"Amy Prescott is related to this man?" Riley hoped the words came out casually despite his dry throat.

"Amy Prescott is his daughter."

Riley grunted, his fingers almost drilling holes in the fabric of the chair. So Amy and Carlos had had a deal with the Velazquez Cartel, and the situation had gotten a little too hot to handle. She had used him to get away.

"It gets better."

At the sound of Chet's smug voice, Riley wanted to punch him. He wanted to punch someone or something.

"Your Amy was at the compound when the fibbies raided it. Eli had no intention of going down without a fight. Amy's Mexican-born mother was killed during the raid, and her father was arrested."

Riley's anger shifted from Amy to the clods who had raided the compound. Amy must have been a child when this happened. "When did this all go down?"

"Let's see." Chet clicked a few keys. "The raid occurred over fifteen years ago."

"What happened to Amy?"

"Relatives took in the kids if they wanted them, but Amy's relatives didn't want anything to do with crazy Eli's spawn. She went into the system."

No surprise Amy didn't trust law enforcement. "Kids? Amy has siblings?"

"I guess. But it would take a geneticist to figure out the familial relationships at the compound. Eli had multiple wives. Amy's mother was just one of three or four."

Riley satisfied himself by punching the cushion next to him. What Amy went through didn't justify illegal activity, but she'd had a helluva time growing up.

"If you like, I have a picture I can send you of Eli with his very extended family."

"Sure." Riley rattled off his email address. "Is Eli still alive?"

"He's at the San Miguel FCI. He'll never get out, though."

Riley thanked Chet for the information and ended the call. He sprang from the chair and buried his fingers in his hair as he wandered toward the window.

Just because Amy had a criminal, drug-dealing father didn't necessarily mean she'd cooperated with a criminal, drug-dealing boyfriend. Could all be just some weird cosmic coincidence.

He powered up his laptop on the coffee table and accessed his email. Chet's message scrolled by, and Riley opened it and clicked on the attachment.

The picture filled his screen—a tall man, holding a long cigarette, with his hair pulled back in a ponytail standing among a group of women and children. Riley counted four women and nine children.

He peered closely at the screen, running his finger along the faces of the children. It hovered over the smiling face of a young girl with long brown hair, long legs and dirty bare feet. Had to be Amy.

He skimmed over the remaining children. Amy looked about ten years old in this picture. Some of the other children were younger, and some looked to be in their teens.

Riley shifted his attention back to Eli Prescott and squinted at the long cigarette he held in his hand. Why was it so long? Looked like the ones FDR used to smoke.

His pulse ticked in his jaw while he reached for the cigarette holder. He saved the picture to his computer and opened it with a photo editor. Then he zoomed in on the object Prescott held carelessly in his right hand while his left rested on top of a child's head.

Eli Prescott had a cigarette holder—one exactly like the one Riley cradled in the palm of his hand. A weird cosmic coincidence?

THE FOLLOWING MORNING, Amy raced up the 805 freeway with the cool air-conditioning blowing on her face. She'd made this journey before and had never found what she was looking for. She didn't know what to expect this time. Maybe some answers.

She pulled up to the gate of the San Miguel Federal Penitentiary and handed over her driver's license. The guard at the gate held it pinched between two fingers, as if he feared contamination, and tipped his dark sunglasses down on his nose.

He muttered, "Prescott."

Amy met his gaze with an unflinching one of her own. If he wanted to tar her with the same brush as her infamous father, it wouldn't be the first time. Wouldn't be the last.

She narrowed her eyes. "You done checking out the freak?"

He shrugged and handed back the license. She snatched it from his fingers and tossed it onto the passenger seat as she accelerated through the gate toward the gray buildings.

A red balloon sailed over the barbwire gates, incongruous against the drab backdrop of the prison. Amy tracked it until she lost it over the line of trees. Had one of the inmates had a birthday party?

The pen had an administrative building outside the main prison gates, but Amy had never been inside. Her visits took place in the bowels of the prison. No balloons there.

After running the security gauntlet, Amy perched on the edge of a plastic chair in the visiting room. She jumped each time the door behind the glass panel buzzed.

On the fourth buzz, a tall, lean man with close-cropped gray hair shuffled into the room behind the barrier. As his blue gaze alighted on Amy, a wide smile split his craggy face.

Amy scooted her chair closer to the glass as the guard led her father to an opposing chair. With a hammering heart, she picked up the red receiver first and waited while Dad settled into his seat, his movements stiff and jerky.

"Hello, Amy. It's been a while."

"Hey, Dad."

"You look good, healthy. Tall like me and pretty like your mother."

He remembered which child belonged with which mother? Oh, yeah. Her mother was special. She's the one the Feds murdered. She pursed her lips. She never talked back to her father. The man scared her—always had.

"You look...different."

His hacking laugh turned into a cough, and the guard brought him a cup of water.

"You mean old."

Amy didn't refute him. The tall, vigorous man who had controlled his cult with an iron fist now walked with a shuffle and stoop. His hair, once pulled back into his trademark ponytail, now lay like a gray cap close to his skull.

She lifted a shoulder. "Different."

"What brings you here? Of all my children, I believe you resent me the most. Of course, you were Loretta's only child, and she babied you a bit. I know her death hit you hard. You shouldn't blame me, Amy. Put the blame on those hot-headed FBI agents."

For once she didn't come here to relive the past, to get answers as to why he seriously messed up her childhood. The present concerned her now. The present and that silver cigarette holder in the storage bin.

She waved her hand at the glass as if to dispel the image there. "Are you involved in any illegal activity on the outside?"

His tired blue eyes brightened as he shifted his gaze toward the guard. "Why do you ask? I'm in here paying my debt to society—no more, no less."

"Do you still use those silver cigarette holders with your initials?"

"In here?" He shook his head. "I still smoke, but they wouldn't allow me to have a cigarette holder inside. You remember those, huh?"

"I just saw one yesterday, and it had an *E* and a *P* engraved on it."

His gaze narrowed and he hunched forward. Amy automatically shifted away from the glass. She could feel his presence emanating from behind the glass like a snake preparing to strike.

He whispered into the phone. "You saw a silver cigarette holder with my initials?"

Amy nodded and swallowed hard as her childhood fears assailed her once again. Maybe this wasn't such a great idea.

"Where?" The word came out like a breath of chilly air. She almost expected the glass to ice over and crack.

"Let's just say it was at the scene of a crime."

"Someone probably copying my style. Why do you care?" He shifted back in his chair, crossing an ankle over his knee.

"I care because that someone got me involved in a dangerous situation, and I want to know who and why."

"You didn't really think I'd made an escape from my current digs, did you? Even I can't manage that."

"Of course not, but maybe you know someone who might have a cigarette holder with your initials, someone who would want to copy your style."

"Maybe you should've kept in touch with your half siblings over the years, Amy."

"What does that mean?"

"Leave it alone, girl." He settled the receiver in its cradle and pushed back from the table.

Amy dug the phone against her ear as her father held out his wrists for the cuffs and slipped through the door, escaping her questions once again.

She banged the receiver into the cradle a couple of times, and then slumped forward, resting her forehead against the glass. Did she really believe she'd get anything out of the man? Apparently, the FBI hadn't gotten much out of him after his arrest. What chance did she have?

Sighing, she stumbled to her feet and pressed the call button next to the door. After a loud click, the guard in the hallway swung open the door, and she followed his ramrod back in his pressed khaki shirt down the long corridor.

She shoved her hands into the pockets of her billowing skirt and filled her lungs with fresh air, blinking in the radiant sunlight. The squeals of the children in the picnic area near the administration building conjured images of just another day in the park, but the barbed wire and armed guards told a different story.

Would these children return here as adults seeking answers to unfathomable questions? Would they walk away empty?

The gravel crunched beneath her flats as she walked toward the parking lot. Engrossed in her own pathetic musings, she nearly collided with a tall man in black slacks and a snowy-white shirt.

"Making your escape?"

She jerked up her head and choked. "Riley!"

"Quick, I'll drive the getaway car."

"What are you doing here?" Amy rubbed her eyes as if she couldn't believe the vision shimmering before her in the desert heat—Riley, all six-foot-something of him, decked out in sharp black slacks and a white dress shirt tucked neatly into the pants, emphasizing the trim waist flaring into a set of broad shoulders.

He cleaned up nicely—damned nicely.

She wedged her hands on her hips and dug her heels into the gravel. "Have you been following me?"

"Didn't need to. I had a tip you were headed out here

today." He grabbed her arm. "Let's sit down at that picnic table under the tree. The guards won't mind."

"H-how did you know? You know about my father,
Eli Prescott, don't you?"

He brushed off a spot on the bench and waved her
to sit. "I'm in the information business, beach girl."

"When did you find out?"

"After I left you yesterday. Could've bowled me over
with a grain of sand."

Riley straddled the bench and Amy swung her legs
over and leaned on the attached table. Riley still main-
tained his easy manner, but a new wariness had crept
into his blue eyes. Heck, that always happened when
people found out her identity, but she couldn't suppress
the stab of disappointment that Riley followed suit.

He placed his hands on his knees, lifting his shoulders. "Why didn't you tell me your father was involved
in dealing drugs?"

Amy's jaw dropped. He suspected her of...some-
thing, something more than just being the daughter of
an imprisoned militia leader. "Wait a minute."

He quirked one brow, but his jaw hardened. "I have
all the time in the world."

"Do you think I had something to do with Carlos's
plans with the Velasquez Cartel?" The words spoken
aloud sounded wild, crazy, but this stranger in the expensive getup didn't even crack a smile.

"You have to admit, it's a coincidence. Daughter of a
former drug dealer involved with another drug dealer,
dead bodies in her house, drugs on her beach."

"I wouldn't call my father a drug dealer."

"Defending him?"

"Never." She slammed her palms against the picnic table. "That's not what I meant. Dear old Dad was

involved in all kinds of illegal activities. He used the militia front to make his endeavors sound more noble or worthy, but really he just led a cult and engaged in criminal behavior to get money to keep it going."

"And one of those illegal activities was dealing drugs." Riley rubbed a hand across his face and closed his eyes. "What do you expect me to think?"

"I don't expect you to think the worst of me. I gave you the benefit of the doubt when I stumbled across you on the beach after you'd just killed a man."

He clenched his eyes briefly before opening them. "I'll give you the benefit of the doubt if you start coming clean."

"I am clean." She spread her hands in front of her as the lie tumbled from her mouth.

"Why didn't you say anything about that cigarette holder we found in the storage unit with your father's initials inscribed on it? You recognized it immediately, didn't you?"

Amy pinched the bridge of her nose. "You're good."

"My contacts are good. Did you rush out here to San Miguel to find out if your father had snuck out to facilitate another drug deal and happened to drop his holder?"

She snorted. "Obviously not. I wanted to find out if anyone had those cigarette holders."

"Did he tell you?"

"He told me to leave it alone."

"Maybe he's looking out for your welfare."

Amy laughed, tipping her head back to the sky. "That would be a first."

"Someone needs to."

Her head snapped forward, and she huffed out a breath. "I think I'm capable of looking out for myself."

"In normal circumstances. But these aren't normal circumstances."

"My life has never consisted of normal circumstances. I'm accustomed to drama."

"I know." Riley brushed a lock of hair from her face, tucking it behind her ear. "Foster care must've been tough."

Amy squared her shoulders, her lips twisting into a halfhearted smile. "It was no picnic, but I got through it—with the help of my friend Sarah."

"Good. And now you're going to get through this with my help." He chucked her under the chin. "For the first time in your life, maybe you should listen to your father. Stay out of this."

"If he's telling me to butt out, it's for his own good, not mine. I think I have a right to know who nominated me to be Carlos's cohort."

A crease formed between Riley's eyebrows. "So you *do* think your father is mixed up in this?"

"I'm not sure if he's involved directly, but he may know something."

"What makes you think that?"

"He told me not to get involved, didn't he? Why would he care otherwise?"

"Do you think he knows where the cigarette holder came from?"

Amy caught her breath and grabbed the material of Riley's dress shirt. "He said something about my siblings."

Riley reached into his shirt pocket and pulled out a folded piece of paper. He flattened it out on the picnic table, running his finger along the creases. "Is this your family?"

Amy peered at the picture printed in muddy colors

from a laser printer. Her gaze scanned the women and children in the photo and tears pooled in her eyes as she pressed her locket against her chest. Those other women had been like second mothers to her, but the U.S. government had ripped her away from them.

One fat tear rolled over her lower lid and splashed on the page. "Th-that's my family. My father's other wives and their children. I was my mother's only child. Those are my half siblings."

"Are you in touch with any of them?" Riley blotted the circle of moisture with his thumb.

"No. Social Services took me away from the others because I had a different mother. When I was a child, I had no opportunity to reach them. When I became an adult, I had no desire."

Riley's finger traced along the back row of children in the picture, along the taller kids, the teens. "You must remember them."

She flicked at the faces with her finger. "Maisie got the hell out, Ethan was an SOB, Rosalinda married a Mexican national..."

"Ethan?" Riley swept the photo from the table and held it close to his face.

She wrinkled her nose. She hadn't thought about Ethan in years. "Ethan was the oldest and a bully. He idolized Dad."

"Did he smoke?"

"Smoke?" Her heart skipped a beat. Could it really be that easy?

Riley smacked the photo with his hand. "If he smokes and admired his father, he just might have a cigarette holder with his initials—*E.P.* Just like Dad."

Chapter Eight

Amy caught her bottom lip between her teeth, and her dark eyes widened. She choked out, "Do you think my half brother is working with Carlos?"

She had to be one heck of an actress if she was really involved in all this. Riley didn't give a damn about Eli Prescott or Ethan Prescott, for that matter. A rush of warm relief had flooded his senses once he'd determined that Amy was as unaware and baffled by Carlos's nefarious connections as she appeared to be that first night on the beach.

As they peeled back every layer of the onion skin, Amy's danger from the Velasquez Cartel grew stronger. Had her own half brother set her up? Did they want something from her now?

"What do you know about your brother, Ethan?"

"I know I didn't like him. He bullied the rest of us and worshipped Dad. He almost wanted a confrontation with the Federales. I guess he hadn't counted on the Mexican government cooperating with the FBI."

Amy's father had to have been involved in some bigtime crime for the Feds to step into a foreign country. "Where is he today?"

Amy shook her head, her long ponytail shimmering in the summer sun.

Riley folded the printed picture and ran his thumb along the crease. "Did Ethan ever try to contact you?"

"No. Not that he would've gotten very far. I didn't like him when I was a child. I can't imagine the raid on the compound and the circumstances of Dad's arrest would've turned him into someone I wanted to know."

"In fact, it could've turned him into a criminal."

"That wouldn't have been a huge leap for Ethan."

"Maybe Ethan was aware of your job and your location and set up the exchange thinking you'd help, given your history with law enforcement."

"I guess." Amy snatched the picture from the picnic table and smoothed it out. "I can't believe he tracked me down and actually thought I'd meekly agree to stash drugs on the beach."

Riley lifted a shoulder. "You guys had the same upbringing. You're not exactly a big fan of law enforcement, are you?"

"Distrusting the long arm of the law and engaging in criminal behavior are two different things."

"Not to Ethan." He pointed to the crinkled picture. "Do you want to keep that?"

"No, thanks." She shoved it back at him and swung her legs over the bench. "I'm going to get back to my friends' place."

"Maybe that's a good idea. Are you finished sleuthing around?" He hoped so. The more she dug into Carlos's motives, the more she exposed herself to danger.

"I just wanted to find out why Carlos used me, and what my father's cigarette holder was doing in the storage bin. I have answers to both of those questions. I'm done."

Riley expelled a breath and crumpled the picture of her family in his fist. He shoved it into his pants' pocket. *Out of sight, out of mind.* "Yeah, get back to your friends' place. That's the safest place for you. At this point, your involvement is over."

Nodding, she blinked rapidly. "I agree. I'm no threat to my brother or his business associates, and I'm certainly no threat to Carlos."

A muscle twitched in Riley's jaw. Was it all just wishful thinking? He couldn't shake the unanswered questions that threatened Amy's safety, but he couldn't shake the dread he felt keeping her with him. Those around him usually ended up burned—or worse.

"Is something wrong?" Her eyebrows shot up over a pair of wide eyes.

What happened to his poker face? Riley ran his palm across his smoothly shaven chin. "Why was Carlos at your place after the drop?"

She jerked her shoulders. "We've been through this a million times. Maybe he was on the run and went to the closest place he knew. The guys he ripped off followed him and killed him."

"Who'd he rip off—his own associates or their clients? I wonder if the men who killed him ever found what they were looking for."

"Well, I can't help them there." Amy brushed her hands together and placed them on her hips.

Did she want him to offer his protection? With his record, she'd be safer on her own. "I'll walk you to your car."

Her shoulders rolled forward before she stalked toward the parking lot. Looked like she didn't even want this level of protection from him.

When she reached her car, she spun around and thrust out her hand. "Okay, well, good luck sorting this all out. If you run across my brother, tell him thanks a lot."

Definitely didn't want his protection.

He took her hand and clasped it between both of his. "I'm sorry I went digging around in your past. I just wanted to make sure—"

She twisted out of his grip. "You wanted to make sure I wasn't in cahoots with Carlos. I get it. I'm not the most trustworthy person in the world, and you figured that out pretty quickly."

"That's not true, Amy." He reached for her hand again and lightly twined his fingers with hers. "I knew you were hiding something about that cigarette holder. I never suspected your complicity before that, and I don't now."

"You don't have to explain anything, Riley. I know you want to help your friend. I understand that."

He brought her hand to his lips and kissed her damp palm. He wanted to do so much more, but her narrowed eyes and stiff spine screamed *back off.*

He reached around her and opened the car door. She slid inside, and he held the door. "You have my cell number. If anything happens—if you need any help—give me a call."

"I think you're the one who needs to be careful now." She snatched the door from his hand and slammed it.

Riley had no intention of allowing her to peel out of the prison parking lot without him. He could at least make sure no one followed her. He rushed to his car and beat her to the exit. Then he followed her down the highway.

His gut twisted when she put on her signal to take the next exit. He wanted to keep her with him and protect her.

Except the last woman who came to him for protection wound up dead.

Amy beeped her horn as she swerved onto the off-ramp and Riley flashed his lights. She might be done digging for answers, but he'd just begun. And he planned to start with Ethan Prescott.

When Riley arrived back at his house, he opened his laptop and got on the phone. He may be a dive-boat operator in Cabo, but he still had his law enforcement connections. He started with the San Diego Sheriff's Department and a former member of Riley's first SEAL unit, Walt Moreau.

"What would you spooks do without us regular cops?"

Riley snorted. "We'd be lost without you, but we spare you the ugly stuff."

"Yeah, right. You guys cause us more trouble than you're worth. I thought you were retired from spying, too."

"I did retire. I'm back for an encore. Long story."

"I don't wanna know. What do you need this time?"

"Ethan Prescott. Does he live here? Does he have a rap sheet? Is he a known drug dealer?"

Walt swore. "That SOB." He clicked some keys on his computer. "He's been in for a few petty crimes, but we can't nail him on the big stuff. He's a facilitator. Takes his cut for brokering deals."

"Do you have an address on him?"

"You paying him a social call?"

"Something like that. I'm real social when I want to be."

Walt gave him an address for Prescott in San Diego with his usual admonition. "You didn't get this from me."

Riley punched the address in on his GPS and followed the directions to Amy's brother's place in La Jolla, a well-heeled area of San Diego. The house was located near where Amy was staying. *Lifestyles of the rich and criminal.*

Riley pulled up across the street from a big, well-lit property. Cars lined the street in front of the house. Dinner party? That would work, and he still had on his slacks and dress shirt from the visit to the penitentiary. Hell, he was feeling social.

He marched up the walkway and pressed the door-bell. A member of the catering staff answered the door. First class all the way.

Riley pasted on his smoothest smile. "Good evening."

"Do you have an invitation, sir?" The party guests murmured behind him, clinking glasses. Sounded like a blast.

"Yes." Riley squared his shoulders and shook out his cuffs.

The man coughed. "Do you have it with you?"

Riley patted his pockets. "Looks like I forgot it."

"I'm sorry, sir. You have to have an invitation." The man's lips pursed as he folded his arms.

Riley rolled his eyes. Like this dude with his black apron and bow tie was going to keep him away from Ethan Prescott. "I'm sure if you tell Mr. Prescott his sister's friend is here, he'll make an exception."

"His sister?"

"Amy."

The waiter held up his hand. "Wait here, please."

When he walked away, Riley stepped into the foyer and clicked the door behind him. The caterers had gone all out for this party. The smell of sizzling steak made his mouth water, and he closed his eyes as his stomach rumbled in protest. He could've at least bought Amy some dinner.

"You know Amy?"

The sharp words jerked Riley out of his food fantasies, and his eyelids flew open. The tall, angular man in front of him clutched a wineglass in one hand and a fork in the other.

Riley's gaze darted between the hovering caterer and Ethan Prescott's lean, hard face. "I do."

Prescott jerked his thumb at the waiter. "Get lost."

He turned back to Riley, his blue eyes glittering. "What do you want?"

"What do *you* want? Why are you following me? If you want to kill me for killing one of your guys, here I am." Riley spread his arms wide and grinned.

Prescott took a swig of wine and gestured to his left. A tall, beefy guy with a neck like a tree trunk emerged from the shadows. He shoved Riley against the wall and patted him down.

He grunted, "He's clean."

Riley had more sense than to bring a weapon—or wear a wire—to a dinner party.

Prescott handed the fork to his henchman and adjusted his collar. "Who are you? CIA? Private investigator? I know you're not law enforcement. They're too polite to barge in unannounced like this."

"Yeah, I'm not polite at all." Riley smoothed his shirt. "I'm investigating another case and the Velazquez deal crossed into my radar, and then you crossed into my radar."

"I'm not following you, and that wasn't one of my guys. I'm just the broker. I don't give a rat's ass what happens to the two parties."

"Why did you involve your sister?"

Prescott swirled his wine. "You want a glass?"

"No." Riley shoved a clenched fist in his pocket. "Your sister?"

"I needed to find a drop location. That storage bin looked perfect, and I needed access. Pretty simple. I thought I could get her to work with me. I know she has no love for law enforcement, but Dad figured she wouldn't give me the time of day. So I used my charming friend, Carlos."

Riley scooped in a deep breath. Amy was just a means to an end. Nothing more. "What do you think happened to Carlos?"

"He disappeared."

"He's dead."

Prescott clicked his tongue. "This is a high-risk business. That's why I have bodyguards."

"If Carlos double-crossed someone, doesn't that put you at risk? He *was* your guy."

Prescott lifted one eyebrow. "Not really. Velasquez had used him before. I did my part. They can try to come after me, but Carlos is the one who took the clients' money."

Riley whistled. "Is that what happened? The Velasquez Cartel entrusted Carlos with the money to give to the terrorists in exchange for the drugs, and he stole it instead?"

Prescott whistled back. "You're good. I didn't even know the identity of the clients."

"Did the so-called clients get their money back when they murdered Carlos?"

A smile spread across Prescott's face, and Riley flinched at the pure evil emanating from the man. How could he and Amy be related? They didn't even seem like the same species.

"No, I don't believe they did get their money back."

"Is that why they're still on my tail? They think I have it or something?" Riley clenched his jaw. He'd have to disabuse them of that notion—fast.

Prescott chuckled and shook his head. "They're not after you. They're after Amy."

WHEN RILEY FLASHED HIS LIGHTS as Amy had careened onto the off ramp, she had to blink back tears to focus on the road. She knew Riley would've stayed with her if she'd begged, but she had too much pride for that. Her desire for his company had nothing to do with fear and everything to do with her attraction to him.

But he seemed determined to keep his distance. It was almost as if he considered himself toxic, but he was torn between that and his protective instincts, which ran strong and deep.

She probably could've played on that aspect of Riley's character, but that was stooping pretty low. She didn't play games with men. Maybe that's why she didn't have one in her life.

Her stomach growled and she rubbed it. She should've suggested dinner. He would've gone for that, figuring they could at least eat together without putting her life in danger.

Before making the turn to Sarah's house, Amy pulled into the parking lot of a shopping center with a bookstore, a coffee place, a bank and several restaurants. She stopped in at the bookstore first. Had to have something to read at dinner so she wouldn't look like a total loser eating by herself.

She tucked the glossy magazines under her arm as she pulled open the door to a small Japanese restaurant. She turned down the saki in favor of a large iced tea and ordered some sushi and tempura. As if she didn't get enough fish.

When she finished her meal, she left one of the magazines on the table for the next loner to enjoy and stepped into the breezy evening.

Several turns and several miles later, she pulled into the long drive of Sarah's house and threw her car into park. Closing her eyes, she leaned her head back and sighed.

The events of the day had drained her emotionally. She hadn't visited her father in a few years. He had nothing she wanted anymore. Still didn't.

She slipped into the house, flicked on the light and locked the door behind her. She kicked off her flats and padded across the cool tile of the kitchen floor. She needed more caffeine to stay awake and figure out the rest of her life. Grabbing a soda from the fridge, she cocked her head at a tinkling sound from upstairs.

She snapped the lid of her can and trudged up the curved staircase, straightening a picture on the wall on her way up. She paused on the landing while slurping a sip of soda. The tinkle of the wind chimes floated through the door of the master bedroom. She poked her head around the corner, frowning at the curtains billowing into the room. A gust of wind sent the wind chimes into overdrive.

Sarah had mentioned her maid would be coming in today. Had she opened the window? The wind was kicking up from the ocean now strong enough to blow over those pretty little glass figures littering Sarah's dresser. Amy put her soda can on top of the dresser, and then paused to admire the view before sliding the window closed and clicking it into place.

She brushed some sand from the windowsill into

her palm and dusted off her hands into the toilet in the master bathroom. A rustling noise from outside the bedroom caused her to freeze. A tingle raced up her spine.

The Lynches had boarded their dog before they left for vacation, but the girls had a hamster. It was probably Chester the hamster making all that racket. *Please be Chester the hamster.*

Amy tiptoed back into the master bedroom and peeked around the corner into the hallway, holding her breath. The rustling stopped. She'd better check on Chester in the kids' playroom.

She glanced into the guest bedroom and stumbled to a stop. Her suitcase, which she hadn't unpacked yet, gaped open on the bed. Its contents spilled over the sides and lay scattered across the floor.

Amy gripped the doorjamb for support, her gaze darting around the room. Someone had tossed the room—no other word for it.

The open window.

Her heart slammed against her rib cage and a cold chill ran through her body. Clenching her chattering teeth, she twisted to see over her shoulder. A shadow passed across the playroom door.

She had to get out of the house. Now.

Chapter Nine

Amy spun around and dashed for the stairs. As she reached the top step, she heard a footfall behind her. Clutching the banister, she took the steps two at a time, her feet barely skimming the tile.

When she reached the bottom and took the corner, her shoulder glanced off the wall. She gasped in pain. She scrambled for the front door, bracing her back for an attack and sucking in air to let loose with a scream when it happened.

She may not be ready with a weapon if someone grabbed her from behind, but she'd be ready with a scream loud enough to pierce his eardrums.

She shoved open the door and stumbled down the steps. She had no purse, no keys, no phone. The long driveway stretched in front of her, and she sprinted toward the street.

Tires squealed and a car flew up the drive. Amy dived to the side, landing in a clump of bushes. She screamed and thrashed until she tore herself away from the clinging twigs of the shrubbery.

"Amy!"

That voice. The small blue compact car. Help. Safety. *Riley*.

Sobbing, she stumbled toward him. He reached for

her, and she threw herself against his chest. He held her. He soothed her. He didn't seem at all surprised.

"What happened, Amy?"

With her head still buried in his shoulder, she pointed toward the house. "There's someone in the house."

His frame hardened and coiled beneath her. "Right now?"

"I don't know. I think so. Someone searched my bag. I heard footsteps and took off."

With one arm curled around her waist, Riley ducked into his car and withdrew a gun. He started for the house, clinching her to his side. "I'm not leaving you. Not this time."

In her haste to flee the house, she'd left the door wide open. Brandishing his weapon, Riley crept into the foyer. "Did you actually see anyone?"

"N-no." Her gaze darted around the family room. "I saw an open window and my disheveled suitcase. Then I heard some noises and saw a shadow, which sent me flying down the staircase. I thought someone was coming after me."

Riley marched across the family room toward the dining room. He leveled a finger at the sliding door, open to the back patio and the beach beyond. "Did you leave that open?"

"No. He must've slipped out the back while I was running helter-skelter out the front."

"Or he was coming after you until he heard my car in the drive."

Amy folded her arms across her belly as a chill snaked up her spine. "Why?"

"We'll get to that." He smoothed his hands down her back. "Let's secure this door first and check upstairs."

She followed Riley up the staircase, and they visited

each room, searching the closets and under the beds. Chester the hamster was spinning on his wheel, his little feet responding to all the excitement.

They ended up in Amy's room, her rifled suitcase a stark testament to the danger that stalked her.

She sank onto the bed, slouching forward. "What do they want from me, Riley?"

"They want their money."

She jerked her shoulders back. "What?"

"The men who delivered the drugs from Afghanistan want their money. They have big plans for that cash."

She sprang from the bed and grabbed his forearm. "Terrorists are after me?"

"They think you have their money. They believe that's what Carlos was doing at your house."

"Stashing money from a drug deal? But where? I'm assuming they're looking for a lot of cash. It would have to be in a bag or a suitcase." She flipped down the lid of her own bag. "And not one filled with women's clothing."

Riley shook his head and raked back his long hair from his forehead. "They think you have something. And they want it."

Amy paced toward the window and then spun around. "Wait a minute. How do you know all of this? Two hours ago at the penitentiary you were convincing both of us that the bad guys wanted you."

"Your brother told me."

She dropped to the bed again, like a boxer taking one to the gut. "You spoke to Ethan?"

"I met him." He settled next to her on the bed and draped his arm across her shoulder. "After I left you, I went on a mission to find your brother."

"Did he confirm that he set me up with Carlos?"

"He did."

Riley rubbed a circle on her back as if that could assuage the misery of your own half brother setting you up with criminals and terrorists. Amy closed her eyes and breathed deeply through her nose. The pressure of Riley's hand did help a little. Okay, it helped a lot.

"Ethan told you these men from some terrorist cell—" butterflies whirred in her belly at the words "—think I have their money?"

"That's the word on the street."

"My name is on the street?" She launched from the bed and away from Riley's comfort. Couldn't get too accustomed to his protection. "That can't be good."

"None of it's good, Amy. I don't want to scare you, but…" He grabbed a couple of fistfuls of bedspread and clenched his jaw.

"Don't stop now." She leaned against the wall, pressing her clammy palms against the smooth surface. She'd take whatever he had to throw at her standing up, not crouched on the floor like a quivering mass of jelly.

"Whoever searched this house didn't follow you here. I made sure of that."

She swallowed and squeezed her eyes shut briefly. "And that means…?"

"They know about you. They know your friends and your habits."

"But I don't have their money. Once they figure that out, they'll leave me alone."

"Don't you?" He pushed up from the bed and strode toward her, sweeping his gun from the dresser on his way.

Amy's gaze shifted from the weapon in his hand to the dark blue eyes beneath disheveled hair. Was he back to that again? "You think I worked this out with Carlos?"

"No." He tucked the weapon in the back of his waistband. "Maybe you have the money and you just don't know you have the money."

"Uh, I'm pretty sure I'd know if I had—what?—several hundred thousand dollars on my person or in the trunk of my car."

"If Carlos had cash on him." Riley rubbed the dark gold stubble on his chin.

Amy dragged her gaze away from his sexy scruff and blinked. "What do you mean? You lost me."

"Carlos didn't stash a load of money at your house, but what if he left the means to get that money?"

She snorted. "Like a treasure map?"

Riley snapped his fingers in front of her face. "Think, Amy."

She ran her hands over her face and twirled her ponytail around her hand. She could think more clearly if she couldn't smell Riley's musky scent every time he touched her. And a lot more clearly if he didn't touch her at all.

Studying his blue eyes, all lit up with excitement, Amy nodded. "You mean like the number to a Swiss bank account or something?"

He clapped his hands. "That's the idea. He planned to steal that money. He coordinated the drug drop at the storage bin and then hightailed it to your place to claim his ticket for the money. Only the Velasquez Cartel was one step ahead of him. When the money didn't turn up at the conclusion of the deal, they came after him."

Amy marched to the bed and dug through her tousled clothing. "What could it be? Where could it be? I need to somehow convince the men after me that I don't have what they want."

"You must have it." He did a double take and then raised his brows. "You don't propose working with the terrorists to find their money, do you?"

"Of course not." Her cheeks heated. He still didn't completely trust her.

He shrugged his shoulders. "Then it doesn't matter what they think. They won't believe you anyway."

"When am I ever going to feel safe again?" She gripped her upper arms, allowing a rare bout of self-pity to wash over her in a wave so strong, her knees buckled.

Riley caught her in his arms, and she burrowed into his shoulder, ashamed of her pitiful weakness.

He whispered against her hair. "I'll protect you, Amy."

He sounded so sure and strong, she almost believed him. She straightened her spine jerking out of the embrace. "How? I can't help these people even if I wanted to." She held up her hands. "And I don't want to."

"You're coming with me." He squeezed her shoulder. "We'll figure this out together. Once that money is in the hands of the proper authorities, you'll be safe."

"I won't be safe until then?"

His mouth tightened and storm clouds rolled across his blue eyes. "Nothing's a sure thing."

She pushed away from him and began stuffing her clothes back into the suitcase. "Well, that's a resounding endorsement of your capabilities."

"Just don't say I didn't warn you."

She spun around at the harshness of his tone. The pain etched across his face caused a lump to form in her throat. What happened to the easygoing surfer dude?

"I—I'm sure I'll be better off with you than on my own."

He stuffed his hands into his black slacks and lifted his shoulders. "Let's lock up here and get back to my place. Maybe we should swing by your house first and do a thorough search. You didn't spend much time there after we found Carlos's body. You don't know what he might have left as a parting gift."

"You're sure my brother doesn't have any idea?"

"He didn't seem too concerned. He got paid up-front for facilitating the deal."

"He wouldn't be above turning on Carlos. Look what he did to me, and we're related."

"Stuff in the bathroom?" He jerked his thumb over his shoulder, and she nodded.

Amy left a note for Sarah and Cliff. Then they locked up the house and headed for the driveway, deciding to take both cars.

"What did you do with Carlos's car?"

"I dumped it. Not my style." He gestured to the little blue compact. "I'll follow you, and I'll look out for anyone following me."

"Funny how you're the secret agent and it was me they were after all along."

"Don't flatter yourself too much. I'm sure they'd be happy to see me out of the way."

"Guess we were just born under a couple of lucky stars, huh?"

He cocked his head. "I never considered myself very lucky…up until now."

He ducked into his car and slammed the door before she had a chance to ask him to clarify that. A warm thrill had coursed through her body at his words and the look in his eyes. If she had to choose anyone in the world to hide out with, it would be Riley Hammond.

She started her car and followed him down the driveway. He hadn't wanted her with him because he doubted his own ability to keep her safe, but why? He seemed to have supreme confidence in everything else he did.

It took nerves of steel to march up to her brother and demand answers. He could've been walking right into a nest of snakes. In fact, snake was an apt word for Ethan.

She flipped on her turn signal and watched in her rearview mirror as Riley's car followed her onto the highway. They had to find this money. What would a bunch of terrorists want with her after that?

What would Riley want with her after that?

Good news—find the money. Bad news—never see Riley again.

She let out a long breath. Just her luck to meet a hot new guy at the same time a terrorist cell was hot on her heels.

Who was she kidding? She'd lived with that kind of luck all her life. She gripped the steering wheel. *Get serious, Amy.* She searched her mind for anything Carlos might have said or done regarding money or bank accounts. She drew a blank. They never talked about stuff like that. He'd been too busy impressing her with his vast knowledge of art and literature, and she'd fallen for it like a ton of bricks.

Glancing in her mirror, she hit her signal for the off-ramp. The comforting glow of Riley's headlights shined into her back window. Her car crawled onto her dark street. She'd forgotten to leave a porch light on when she left and she had nothing on a timer.

She just hoped the neighbor girl was taking pity on Clarence.

She swung into her driveway and Riley pulled up to the curb. He landed on the sidewalk before she even opened her car door.

"Nobody followed us?"

"Would I be standing here calmly if they had?"

She wagged her finger at him. "No need to get testy."

"Is it dark enough out here?"

"I did leave in a hurry, remember? You're the one who hustled me out of here."

He dug the heels of his hands into his eyes. "I'm on edge."

"You and me both."

She stumbled over the porch step and Riley grabbed her waist from behind. His large hand rested on her hip and she gulped. The terrorists weren't the only ones keeping her on edge.

With a shaky hand, Amy inserted her key into the dead bolt. At least this time the dead bolt was locked. The unlocked dead bolt should've warned her last time. She eased open the door and flicked on the lamp nearest the entryway.

Her gaze tracked across the small living room and she took a step back to feel Riley's solid form behind her.

Yeah, these people were good.

Chapter Ten

Riley shifted to high alert as a little gasp escaped from Amy's lips and she fell against him. He tensed and wrapped one arm around her while reaching back for his weapon.

He whispered into her ear. "What is it?"

"They're back."

Riley tucked her behind him and crept into the room. At least this house was a lot easier to search than the Lynches' sprawling beach house. And he should know—this was his second go-around.

Amy clung to the back of his shirt as he moved through each room. He kept telling himself he didn't mind, but her growing dependence on him for protection filled him with cold dread. The circumstances of the past few days had thrust him into the role of protector, even though he'd vowed to forgo that particular pastime. Easier said than done—especially with a plucky woman in danger tripping over his feet at every turn.

Once he'd satisfied himself the house didn't contain any bogeymen, Riley collapsed on the couch. "You're sure they were here?"

Amy nodded. "Things are out of place, although I don't have a clue why they're being so careful now after ransacking my suitcase at Sarah's house."

"They don't know that you're onto them. They could've searched this house yesterday." He checked the safety on his gun and placed it on the coffee table. "They obviously didn't find what they were looking for since they were at your friends' house today."

"I almost wish they'd just find their money and leave me alone." She folded her hands in her lap and slid a glance his way. "I know you think that's selfish, that I should be actively trying to keep the money out of their filthy hands."

He covered her clasped hands with one of his own. "I don't think that's selfish, Amy. I don't expect you to want to bring down a terrorist cell. That's completely out of your job description."

She turned her head, searching his face with an anxious look. "It's not because I'm on their side or I want to punish law enforcement, despite my crazy background and infamous family members."

"I know that, too." His gaze wandered around the room. "Of course, if we do find the money first and turn it over to the CIA, it will have the same effect. They'll leave you alone."

"I don't have any idea what Carlos could've hidden in my place or where."

Tilting his head back, he closed his eyes. "Let's think. He obviously didn't hide the money itself—too big, too noticeable."

"Did my brother indicate when the Velasquez people gave him the money to give to the clients?"

"In advance."

"So he had time to stash the money before the drop, and he didn't hide it at my house. So where would you put that kind of cash for safekeeping? A bank?"

Riley opened one eye. "Never. It would leave a paper

trail a mile long and Carlos wouldn't have wanted that. If he deposited it in an account, it would have to be some kind of offshore, untraceable one."

Amy sighed and hunched forward. "I just don't know. Why would Carlos leave anything with me? Did he hate me that much?"

Riley's fingers tingled to feel Amy's dark mahogany hair slip through his fingers as it slid across her back. He doubted Carlos hated Amy—probably felt damned lucky the Velazquez Cartel had chosen her as his dupe. Hiding his mode of access to the drug money with Amy had more to do with covering his own hide than endangering Amy. But that's exactly what Carlos had done.

Riley pushed up from the couch and extended his hand. "Let's get out of here. If the people who searched this house didn't find what they wanted, we won't either. Maybe they're wrong anyway."

She put her hand in his, and he pulled her up and toward him, so close he could see the gold flecks in her puzzled eyes.

He tried to reassure her. "Maybe Carlos headed back here after the drop because it was familiar territory. Maybe he never did leave anything in your possession."

Pressing her lips together, she shook her head. "That's even worse. As long as the terrorists think I have the money, it doesn't much matter whether I do or not. They're going to try to get it back."

Riley wrapped his arms around her, pulling her against his chest where he felt her heart galloping at a rapid pace. Then he said the dumbest thing he'd said in five years. "They'll have to come through me first."

BACK AT RILEY'S SAFE HOUSE Amy felt…safe, but it had nothing to do with the boxy, nondescript apartment and everything to do with the man at her side.

As Riley hauled her suitcase into the bedroom once again, Amy twisted the gold locket at her neck with nervous fingers.

"Do you always wear that necklace?" He walked into the kitchen and yanked on the fridge door.

She held the chain out with one finger and the large heart-shaped locket dangled from it. "It was the only thing I had left from my mother. That's why I wear it, even though it's too big and not stylish at all."

"Water?" He held up an empty glass. Amy nodded. "How'd your mother end up with a man like Eli Prescott?"

"The usual way, I guess. She fell in love with him."

"But he already had his harem going by the time she came to live with him, didn't he?"

"Yes." She dropped the locket where it thunked against her chest. "My father was a very persuasive man. We weren't the only family living at the compound. He'd convinced others to join us. He could convince anyone of just about anything."

"Too bad he used those talents in the wrong way." Riley handed her a glass of water.

She traced the rim of the glass with her fingertip. "The FBI charged onto that property and killed my mother."

Riley placed his hand on her lower back and guided her to the sofa. "I'm sorry, Amy."

"It should've been him." She gulped the water and slammed the glass on the coffee table. "They wanted him."

"And now your family has dragged you back into the

muck with them." He massaged between her shoulder blades, and she leaned her elbows on her knees.

"I tried to make peace with my feelings for my father, but in the end decided to put it all behind me. I guess you can only run so fast before the bad stuff catches up to you."

"You don't deserve this. Any of it."

The pressure of his hands grew harder, and she leaned into his strength, closing her eyes. She usually deflected others' sympathy and pity, but now she allowed herself to wallow in it. She'd been wallowing a lot these past few days—even crying. She hadn't permitted herself many tears over the years—too dangerous to show weakness.

He squeezed the back of her neck with one hand. "Did you get something to eat tonight?"

"Yeah, did you?" She rolled her head back, not wanting Riley's magic hands to stop.

"No. Your brother was having a swanky dinner party, but I had other plans."

She twisted around, cupping her chin in her palm. "Thanks again for coming to the rescue. You have a knack for that sort of thing, don't you?"

"As a Navy SEAL it's second nature, but…" He stopped and shrugged.

"I know. You're a dive-boat operator from Cabo now."

"And what about you, Amy?" He stroked her hair and she almost purred like her abandoned cat, Clarence. "What do you do when you're not rescuing people from the ocean?"

"Well, before you killed a guy on my beach, I was planning to start EMT school in a few weeks and try to get on with a fire department in the next year or two."

He lifted one eyebrow. "Talk about being born to rescue. Why do you gravitate toward those professions?"

"I never thought of it as a gravitational pull." She avoided his piercing blue gaze. "I can pretty much do what I like anyway. I'm independently wealthy."

He started to snort and then ended on a choke. "You're serious, aren't you?"

"The FBI killed my mother. I got a fat settlement for that, which didn't start paying out until I was eighteen. My friend's husband, Cliff, is my attorney, and he's managed my money very well."

Riley whistled. "Maybe Carlos was after your money, too."

"I doubt it. He didn't know anything about my money."

"Played it kind of close to the vest with Carlos, didn't you?"

"We dated only a few months. I'm not going to spill my guts after two months of dinners and movies."

"You told me after two days of car chases and break-ins."

"That's different."

He cocked his head. "How so?"

Amy twirled a lock of hair around her finger. If she had to explain the connection she felt with him, the electricity that zapped her senses every time he touched her, then maybe her attraction was all one-sided. Maybe she'd better quit while she was ahead and not make a fool out of herself.

"Uh, you know. The excitement and adrenaline rush gives everything an urgency."

"Like this?" He pulled her into the crook of his arm, tilted her head back and kissed her mouth.

Guess he feels it, too.

Her mouth tingled as his gentle caress grew more demanding. A pulse throbbed in her bottom lip and she reached up and twined her fingers around his hair.

He shifted, pulling her across his lap and linking his hands behind her back. "I've wanted you in my arms like this for a long time."

She murmured against his mouth, "You've known me for less than three days."

"Must be that urgency thing you were talking about." He pinched her chin and ran his thumb across her mouth.

"Speaking of urgency—" she sat up "—I thought we were coming back to your safe house to figure out why these guys think I have the money from the drug deal gone bad."

"First things first. I brought you back to my safe house to keep you safe."

The way her brain fogged over every time Riley kissed her felt anything but safe, but it did feel...right.

"I'm glad we're putting off thinking about our problems, because I can't think straight when you're kissing me like...that." She sighed as his lips trailed across her throat.

"How about if I kiss you like this."

He planted a line of kisses along her jaw and ended with a kiss at the corner of her mouth. She couldn't figure out how such a hard man could have such soft lips. Then she was done figuring when he slipped his tongue between her lips and tickled the roof of her mouth.

A gasp escaped from her throat, half laugh, half moan. She dug her nails into his shoulders, searching for something steady to hold on to as he deepened his kiss and slid his hands beneath her T-shirt. His palms, calloused and rough, brushed her skin and she squirmed beneath his touch.

"Is this doing anything to help you think straight?"

She nipped his ear. "You know it's not. I don't get how you can engage in...a flirtation...when terrorists are hunting you down."

Technically, they were hunting her down, but Riley had taken her cause on as his own. And that was even sexier than his hands rubbing those little circles on her back. Almost.

His brows shot up to the shaggy hair falling across his forehead. "You call this a flirtation? I must be slipping."

He curled his hands around her waist, pulling her against his chest. Then he dipped his head and possessed her lips as if he didn't have one thought in his brain except pleasure. Her pleasure.

Without losing their connection, Amy fumbled with the buttons of Riley's shirt until it hung open on his chest. Then she yanked at the white T-shirt tucked into his slacks, scraping his flat belly with her fingernails. "You are way overdressed."

His gaze swept over her skirt and top, lingering on her bare legs hanging over his lap. "So are you."

He staggered from the couch, clutching her to his chest. "Are we going to fumble around on the couch like a couple of teenagers?"

Shaking her head, she entwined her arms around his neck. "Take me anywhere, sailor."

In a few quick strides he shoved open his bedroom door with his shoulder and kissed her again before dropping her on the bed. Without losing eye contact, they both scrambled out of their clothes. Only then did Amy allow herself to savor Riley's naked body.

He had the perfect swimmer's form with his wide shoulders, broad chest, narrow hips and flaring thighs. Amy's lashes fluttered as desire coursed through her veins. Riley was no accountant or banker or plumber—probably didn't have one stable, boring bone in his body. But God she wanted him.

"Done with the inventory?" He grinned, his blue eyes shooting sparks.

She shrugged and faked a yawn. "Nothing I haven't seen a million times before."

Riley scrambled onto the bed and hitched her around the waist with one arm, dragging her against his hard planes. "How about I rock your world with something you haven't felt a million times before?"

Before she could answer in the affirmative, he landed a hard kiss on her mouth—punishment for her sarcastic tongue. Then he laid her out on the bed and used his tongue, which wasn't sarcastic at all, to bring her to dizzying heights of ecstasy.

Digging her nails into his muscled buttocks, she panted against his shoulder. "You made your point, sailor. Now finish the job."

"Don't forget." He cupped her breast in his hand and massaged her nipple with his thumb. "I live in Mexico now. We take things slow and easy down there."

She squirmed from beneath the weight of his body and rolled on top of him. "I'll give you slow and easy."

She kissed his eyelids and the bridge of his prominent nose. Although the heat of her passion thumped with urgency, she closed her eyes and pressed her lips against the stubble along his jaw and twirled her tongue in the hollow of his throat.

He hissed and grabbed her hips, grinding his erection into her belly.

She nipped his earlobe. "Slow and easy, remember?"

He growled. "We're in *Los Estados Unidos* now, baby."

He flipped her onto her back and drove into her with such force she bumped her head on the headboard—and she didn't mind one bit. She thrust back against him, enjoying the ride, enjoying the thrill of having this dangerous, exciting man in her bed and in her life. She'd deal with the consequences later.

Like they'd known each other all their lives, they reached their climaxes together in perfect sync, noisily, heartily and completely. A matched pair.

Riley rolled to her side, but pulled her close to maintain their connection. He brushed a strand of hair from her lips, which parted with each short gasp of breath she took. "Too much for you?"

Narrowing her eyes, she slapped his backside with her palm. "I'm ready for another round."

He kissed the tip of her nose. "You're fearless in every situation, Amy, not like—"

Riley's cell phone rang from the pocket of his slacks, crumpled on the bedroom floor. He blew her a noisy kiss. "Keep the bed warm."

He launched off the bed and clawed through his pants to find the phone. "Hello?" His head shot up as three sharp knocks cracked on the front door.

A tingle of fear raced across Amy's flesh, chasing away desire. "Who is it?"

Riley tossed aside the phone and pulled on his slacks. "One of my brothers in arms."

Amy had dragged the sheet up to her chin and her long, dark hair tumbled around her face with its wide, glossy brown eyes and trembling lips, plump from his kisses. His need for this woman, still unabated, coiled hot and firm in his belly.

But duty called.

Ian Dempsey stood outside his front door, and he might have news of Jack.

Riley pulled his T-shirt over his head and pointed to the phone. "That was my buddy on the phone letting me know he's outside. Unfortunately, I have to let him in."

The strain on Amy's face smoothed out and she sighed. "Oh, of course. I'll get dressed."

"That's a good idea because that dude out there is a wolf." He winked and snapped the bedroom door behind him.

Riley shoved his eye against the peephole and scanned the tall man parked at his doorway. At least he'd called first instead of showing up unannounced— just might have saved himself from a bullet between the eyes.

Riley yanked open the door. "You do know this is a safe house, don't you? You sure you weren't followed?"

Ian laughed and pushed his way into the apartment. "Good to see you, too, Riley. Besides, we always had you pegged as the careless one."

Riley slammed the door and locked it. Then he thrust out his hand. "How the hell are you, man?"

Ian shrugged. "I've been better. They're calling Jack a traitor."

"I know." Riley balled his fists. "It's a lie."

"You don't have to convince me." Ian held up his hands. "This is a big-time operation. You don't think our old friends have anything to do with it, do you?"

"Why would they be out here now? They used to be strictly local." A bitter bile rose from Riley's gut when he thought about the team of terrorists operating in the Middle East that Prospero had repeatedly come up against. Prospero had almost taken down their leader, Farouk, on their last mission together.

"Those drugs came from Farouk's territory." Ian shrugged. "Whoever they are, they sold a lot of heroin to the Velasquez Cartel for a lot of money, and I don't think they plan to use the money to open flower shops."

"They've been linked to an arms dealer here in the States. We just need a name." Ian paced the room, absently picked up Riley's jacket, then dropped it.

"How is that going to get us closer to Jack?"

Ian spread his hands. "It's the whole setup. The entire deal is linked to some doctor who was kidnapped in Afghanistan. Jack was hired to negotiate for his release, and he disappeared."

"You know more than I do then. Do we have a name on the doc?"

"No name. It's hush-hush. We know his sister hired Jack, but we can't track her down."

"Did the colonel tell you I ran into a hitch here?" Riley ran his hands through his tangled hair; they had recently wound around Amy's fingers as he coaxed her to her climax. He swallowed.

"You tried to disrupt the deal, and now either the Velasquez Cartel or the client is after you."

"Actually, they're after me."

Amy strode into the room, looking a helluva lot more put together than he did in his dress slacks, un-tucked T-shirt and bare feet.

Ian's brows shot up and his gaze darted between Amy and Riley. "And you are...?"

Riley stepped between them as if to shield Amy from Ian's scrutiny. "This is Amy Prescott, the lifeguard from the beach. Amy, this is Ian Dempsey, another former member of Prospero. He was in the Army Mountain Division and leads climbing expeditions now."

Amy maneuvered around him and thrust her hand out toward Ian. "Nice to meet you."

As he clasped her hand, Ian slid a glance toward Riley. "Good to meet you, too, but Colonel Scripps gave me the distinct impression the lifeguard was male."

Riley cocked his head. "Can't imagine why."

"I can." Ian gave Riley a hard stare.

Riley turned his back on Ian's accusing green eyes. "Do you want something to drink while we fill you in?"

"Soda or juice, whatever you have. I'll skip the beer."

Riley returned from the kitchen with a can of soda and thrust it into Ian's hand. "Have a seat."

Ian popped the lid and then aimed a finger, glistening with drops of soda, at Riley's hair hanging to his shoulders. "You look like the scruffy owner of a dive boat."

Riley pointed to Ian's dark hair—close-cropped and creating a cap around his head. "And you look like you never left the military."

Ian ran a hand over his short hair. "Habit."

Amy had gotten herself a glass of water and scrunched into the corner of the sofa, curling her long legs beneath her. "Are we going to tell him everything?" Riley asked her.

He studied Amy's face. He'd leave it up to her whether or not she wanted to reveal her personal connection to the events of the past few days. It was her life. Everyone had a right to a few secrets.

Her dark lashes swept her cheeks and she gave a brief nod.

"If we're going to help Jack, I think I need to hear everything." Ian perched on the stool at the kitchen counter, wrapping his hands around his soda.

Riley settled on the other end of the couch from Amy and drew a deep breath. He'd tell Ian everything from the beginning, everything except for his feelings for Amy, the way she made his head spin, the way her silky skin felt against his body, his intense desire to protect her. He'd keep all that to himself.

For the next hour, Riley told Ian about his tussle on the beach and the car chase and the discovery of Amy's identity and the realization that members of the terrorist cell were after Amy because they thought she had their money.

Ian asked the hard questions nobody could answer and seemed to dodge around the relationship between Riley and Amy, accepting that Riley could keep Amy safe in his apartment while they worked through the puzzle of where Carlos hid the money.

Ian had drained his soda long ago and sat fiddling with the silver tab. "There is one option you haven't explored yet."

"I'm sure there are plenty of those." Riley pushed up from the couch and stretched. "More water, Amy?"

"No, thanks."

Riley swept up his own glass and ambled toward the kitchen. "What option are you talking about, Ian?"

Ian had worked the tab loose and dropped it into the can. "We want the name of their arms dealer and they want their money."

"So?" Riley dropped his glass in the sink harder than he intended and a crack zipped up the side.

Ian looked up from playing with his soda can and hardened his jaw. Riley knew that look. He didn't like it.

"Maybe we can offer an exchange."

"What?" Riley dropped the glass in the trash where it smashed against an empty jar. "We don't have anything to exchange, Ian. Weren't you listening? Amy doesn't have the money."

"The clients don't know that."

Riley laughed through gritted teeth. "Yeah, right. They'll find out soon enough. They're not going to give up the name of their arms dealer anyway. It would defeat the purpose of the whole operation. Dude, you've been spending too much time at high altitudes. It's turning your brain to mush."

Ian stood up and crushed the soda can. "It's just a start, Riley. If your enemies think you have something they want, it can be a bargaining chip. You know that, or at least you used to. Maybe all that sun and surf are turning *your* brain to mush."

"I see what he means." Amy uncurled her legs and rose from the couch. "If they think I have their money, they might be willing to give you some information to get it back."

Riley's jaw dropped. "You two seem to be forgetting one important fact. We don't have their money."

"Think outside the box for a minute, Riley. You used to be so good at that." Ian slid a glance toward Amy.

Riley clenched his hands and stalked back into the living room. "Are you questioning my handling of this operation or my commitment to finding Jack?"

"Just wondering why you haven't come up with any options other than hiding in your safe house."

His blood boiling, Riley took another step toward Ian.

"Okay, you know what?" Amy stepped between them. "I'm really tired right now and I have a headache. I'm in no mood to watch a couple of grown men duke it out."

Riley let out a long breath. "Nobody's going to duke it out. We just have a difference of opinion. I have some ibuprofen in the bathroom."

When Amy left the room and closed the door of the bathroom, Riley turned on Ian. "I haven't been hiding in the safe house. I had to kill one of Velasquez's men when he threatened Amy on the beach. I had to track down her slimy half brother to gauge his involvement. I had to rescue her when some scumbag tracked her down to her friends' house and searched the place."

Ian grunted. "Yeah, I'm seeing a common theme here. Are you interested in getting information about this deal or in protecting Amy?"

Riley dug his bare feet into the carpet to keep from launching across the few feet separating him from Ian and grabbing his throat. "Both. I'm doing both."

"Because it sounds to me like you're letting your feelings for Amy get in the way of your mission."

"You'd never do that, would you, Ian?" Riley crossed his arms over his chest. "That's why Meg left you. You'd never let your wife come before your duty."

Ian squared his shoulders, his green eyes glittering like chunks of glass. "Meg understood."

"Yeah, she understood. But she probably didn't understand completely until she lost the baby and you turned away from her."

"Damn you. I was on assignment."

"I understand, but she still left you."

Ian had lost his cool—a rare event. He slammed his fist on the counter, his voice exploding. "You're talking to me about *my* wife? What about your wife?"

"You have a wife?" Amy had left the bathroom and

was leaning against the wall, her arms wrapped around her stomach.

And the look in her eyes twisted a knife in Riley's gut.

Chapter Eleven

Amy drove her shoulder into the wall, seeking support. Did her past make her some kind of magnet for married men looking for an escape? Oh, right, she didn't know if Carlos really had a wife. He may have been a completely single drug dealer.

She hadn't meant to eavesdrop on Riley's conversation with Ian, but when their voices crescendoed in anger she'd worried about the two men coming to blows. Now the big, strong men, full of fury, looked like guilty little boys.

All the bluster had seeped out of Ian. He dropped his gaze from hers, running a hand across his short, dark hair.

Her eyes flicked to Riley. He seemed to have forgotten Ian's existence. A thousand different emotions charged across his handsome face until it settled into lines of concern.

At least she didn't discern any pity. She didn't like pity—from anyone.

She shoved off the wall and straightened her spine. "What were you saying about Riley's wife, Ian?"

Ian hunched his shoulders and rolled them back as if loosening the last grip of his anger. "I'm sorry, Riley. I never should've thrown April in your face like that.

Amy, it's not what it looks like. I'm sure Riley will explain everything."

Amy smirked because that seemed to stop the trembling of her lips. "Yeah, like how he gets it on with damsels in distress while his wifey is safely at home?"

Ian spread his hands in front of him, a helpless gesture from an anything-but-helpless man. In fact, Amy had a hard time believing these two men, with their athletic bodies and take-charge attitudes, couldn't bring down the terrorists and the Velasquez drug cartel by themselves. That Jack Coburn was one lucky SOB to have these two on his side.

"Tell her, Riley."

Riley seemed to wake up from his trance. He shook his head and rubbed his chin with its golden stubble. Reaching over, he clapped Ian on the shoulder. "I'm sorry, man. I know Meg never blamed you for the end of the marriage."

Amy folded her hands behind her back. She didn't want to hear about Ian's marriage, but at least the former colleagues weren't at each other's throats anymore. She cleared her own throat.

"She didn't, but I did. You had it dead right." Ian shrugged off Riley's hand and walked toward Amy. "I know you're doing your best to help Jack, but you don't have anything to prove. What happened to April wasn't your fault, but you owe Amy the truth. Give her a chance to help you, Riley. She's not April."

Amy's mouth went dry, and she dropped her chin to her chest. What had happened to Riley's wife?

Ian took her hand. "You're an amazing woman, Amy. Riley's met his match."

Riley scooped in a big breath. "I will tell her as soon as you give us a little privacy. I've spilled my guts in front of you enough already. And you'd better savor that apology because it'll be another millennium before you hear another one out of me."

"I know that." Ian squeezed Amy's hand. He whispered, "Give him a chance to explain, Amy. Give him a chance."

When Ian shut the front door behind him, Riley stood with his back to her. His shoulders heaved before he turned around.

"I'm sorry." He smacked his forehead with the heel of his hand. "That's twice in one night."

Despite his easy words, Riley crossed his arms, digging his fingers into his bunched biceps.

Amy clutched her hands in front of her just as hard. "What happened to April?"

"I killed her."

Tilting her head, Amy raised one eyebrow. She didn't realize Riley had the capacity for so much melodrama. He had a lethal side, but she knew he'd never hurt a woman. Her next words almost stalled in her throat. "She's dead?"

He nodded. "April was my wife and she's dead."

Amy uprooted her feet from the carpet and almost tiptoed to Riley's side. Now she felt like a fool, a monster, really, for being jealous of a dead woman.

"How'd it happen?" She caressed his forearm—as hard as steel to match the blue steel of his eyes.

He blinked, the knuckles on his hand turning white and the veins popping on his corded arm. "She came to me for protection and I failed her."

Grabbing his hand, she pulled him away from the door and led him to the couch. She leveled her palms on his chest and pressed firmly. "Sit."

He sank to the couch, his knees bumping the coffee

table. "I didn't want to tell you about April. I wanted to keep you safe, not scare you away."

"You have kept me safe. I would've been toast without you." She rubbed a circle on his back, her hand skimming across hard slabs of muscle and tension. "Tell me what happened to April."

Riley dug the heels of his hands into his eyes and let out a shuddering breath. "April was from a wealthy family, the daughter of a politician. She'd had an easy life filled with easy opportunities and luxuries. She worked as a reporter and went along with her father to Iraq on a junket. That's where we met."

"You saw her in that dangerous setting and you wanted to protect her forever."

"I'm that transparent, huh?" He turned his head, plowing fingers through his hair.

Brushing the hair from his forehead, she whispered, "That honorable."

"I figured out quickly we'd made a mistake. She not only feared the atmosphere in Iraq but everywhere else—Italy, where we went on our honeymoon, and even San Francisco, where we'd settled between my assignments."

"She'd become accustomed to being well guarded all her life?"

"Something like that—secret service, boarding schools, the works. When I'd leave her for missions, she'd call constantly, distracting me, making me feel guilty and miserable. She saw me not so much as a husband, but her own personal bodyguard."

"I know the feeling." She rubbed her hand along his thigh. "You do inspire that kind of confidence in a girl."

"It didn't quite work out that way. April imagined carjackers on every corner and peeping toms at every window. She didn't want to stay alone anymore and became convinced that she'd be safe only with me…even if that meant in Iraq."

Amy widened her eyes and covered her mouth with her hand. "She went back to Iraq?"

"Yes. And it was even less safe than before. She wasn't part of a large delegation of U.S. politicians this time."

"D-did you invite her to come out?"

"No." Riley smacked his palms on the coffee table. "She surprised me, used her connections to come out and faked an assignment. I was too busy at the time to send her right back home. I left her at what I thought was a safe hotel, but I should've known. Nothing is safe in Iraq."

"She felt safe with you, wherever that led her." She covered one of his large, rough hands with her own. "I can understand that."

"It's the opposite." Riley raked a hand through his hair. "Terrorists drove a car bomb into that hotel and fifteen people died, including April."

Amy sucked in a breath. April had been irrational following Riley to Iraq. Did she really believe she'd be safer in some hotel in Iraq than her upper-middle-class neighborhood in San Francisco?

She studied Riley's hard profile. She could understand April's compulsion to follow this man to the ends of the earth. April may have told Riley she felt safer with him, but maybe she just couldn't let her husband out of her sight.

Amy wouldn't be able to, if he belonged to her.

With a tight throat, she murmured, "It's not your fault, Riley. You didn't ask her to join you."

"But she did, and I didn't act quickly enough to send

her back. Her closeness to me killed her. I'm a walking, living, breathing disaster area. Look at you."

"What?" She jerked her head, and her hair swept across their clasped hands. "I am not in danger because of you."

He slipped his hand from hers and massaged his temple. "I can't help thinking I'm bringing this all down on you. If I'd never landed on your beach, you'd be packing up for EMT school right now."

"That's just dumb. You didn't land on my beach. You followed a drug dealer to my beach, which had been chosen specifically because I worked there. My own crazy background catapulted me into this mess, and if you hadn't come along when you did, I'd be dead." She cupped his lean jaw with one hand. "So stop blaming yourself for my situation and maybe you'll eventually stop blaming yourself for your wife's death."

He closed his eyes. "April wasn't the only one who died. She was pregnant."

Amy's nose stung with tears as she trailed her thumb across Riley's lips. "I'm sorry."

Riley continued in a low voice, his eyes still closed. "I accused Ian of putting his job before his wife, but I did the same. April and I had discussed having kids, but I told her I wasn't ready. In fact, I'd started doubting the relationship would last much longer. She got pregnant anyway, but I never had to get used to the idea of becoming a father. I didn't have the chance."

He carried the guilt of his wife's death along with that of his unborn baby, as if his doubts about the marriage and his unwillingness to have children had contributed to the tragedy.

"Riley." She ran the pad of her thumb along his cheekbone. "Let go of the guilt."

His eyelids flew open and he grabbed her hands. "I'm not putting my job ahead of you, Amy. I'm not using you as some kind of bargaining chip with a bunch of thugs. Ian and his options can go to hell."

"We'll find the money. Once we do, maybe we can make our own deal with the arms merchant, a deal that could lead to information about Jack. We'll start fresh tomorrow."

Riley groaned. "God, what time is it? After everything you've endured today, I'm keeping you awake with my self-pitying story."

"There you go again." She kissed his rough cheek. "You don't need to look after me twenty-four hours a day. I can stand on my own two feet. I wouldn't be here right now if I couldn't."

He cupped the back of her head, entwining his fingers in her hair. "You're nothing like April, Amy, and God help me, I feel guilty about that, too."

"April made her choices. We all do." She tugged at his hand. "Let's get some sleep so we can brainstorm tomorrow. I think if Carlos did leave the money with me, he left it at my rental house. That makes the most sense since he returned there after dropping the drugs at the beach. Otherwise, why come back to my place?"

Riley followed her to the bedroom, resting a hand on her hip. "That occurred to me, but someone made a thorough search of your place and came up empty. They wouldn't have tracked you down to the beach house if they'd found anything."

"Who knows if they searched the house completely? They don't even know what they're looking for."

"Neither do we."

Amy spun around and put two fingers to his lips. "Don't be so sure about that."

Riley captured her hand and placed a kiss on the center of her palm, his eyes alight with desire. She didn't know what Riley wanted, but she may have already found what she was looking for in the arms of this protective man.

Could she hold on to him when the danger dissipated? Would she want to?

THE FOLLOWING MORNING, Amy sat cross-legged on the floor of Riley's small apartment, balancing a notebook on her knees and tapping the end of her nose with a pencil. "We searched the entire house for a big bag of money, right? If Carlos didn't leave the money itself, he must've left a means to access it."

Riley hunched over his coffee, peering into the steaming, dark liquid. Coming clean about April had scattered the fog that had swirled around his relationship with Amy from the beginning, but he hadn't minded the murkiness.

He'd rather be tarred and feathered than peel back his armor to reveal his weaknesses and fears to anyone, especially a woman he'd vowed to protect. But Ian had forced him into it with his surprise visit. Riley didn't know what he'd expected after his confession, but it hadn't made Amy distrust him with her safety.

Opening up hadn't lessened his guilt any, either. He'd carry that with him always.

"Don't you think?"

"Huh?" Riley glanced up from his mug.

Jabbing the air with her pencil, Amy said, "Access to the money. Where did Carlos leave the money and what did he leave in my house that would give him access to it? That's where I'm going with all this."

Riley sipped the strong brew and nodded. "I think

you're right. Carlos wasn't going to haul around bags of cash with him. He stashed it."

"Do you think my brother could've been in on it? Maybe he and Carlos decided to double-cross the clients together, and then Ethan double-double-crossed Carlos." She swirled the pencil with a flourish.

Riley raised one eyebrow. When Amy attacked something, she went all out. He'd have to remember that. "That could be a possibility, but Carlos came back to your place, not your brother's."

"You have a point, but I gather you didn't question Ethan very closely."

"Uh, no. Once he told me the terrorist cell had its sights set on you, I left the party."

"I'm glad you did." One corner of her mouth tilted up and Riley had a strong inclination to kiss it where it dimpled. She continued, oblivious to his desires. "But maybe we should pay another visit to Ethan to find out what he knows."

Riley choked and sprayed the countertop with coffee. "You want to see your half brother after all these years?"

"I think the situation warrants an impromptu family reunion. I visited my father in the federal pen. What's one more disgraced family member?"

"I don't know, Amy." Riley grabbed a paper towel and blotted the drops of coffee. "You go to your family looking for answers and they turn against you. Why should Ethan tell you anything?"

"Couldn't you threaten him with something? Tell him you'll bring the FBI down on his head if he doesn't cooperate with us." She jabbed her chest with her thumb. "Ethan loves the FBI as much as I do."

Riley swept the soggy paper towel from the counter and tossed it into the trash. "I don't have anything on Ethan. I didn't have a recording device on me when he confessed to working with Carlos and the Velasquez Cartel. And, believe me, the FBI already has your brother on its radar, and he knows it."

Amy uncurled her long limbs and jumped to her feet. "Then I'll just use the old blood-is-thicker-than-water plan. What does he have to lose by telling me what he knows?"

"His life."

Amy's big eyes got bigger. "Do you think so?"

"If Velasquez's client believed your brother knew the location of that money, he'd be a dead man. Ethan wants to keep as far away as possible from you in case someone is watching him. He warned me not to return and definitely not to return with you in tow."

"Then we need to find a way to get to Ethan. You don't happen to have his cell phone number, do you?" Amy dug her teeth into her lower lip.

"No, we didn't make it to the let's-be-friends-and-exchange-numbers stage. But if you're serious, I can pay him a visit without anyone the wiser."

"*You* can pay him a visit? No, no, no." She waved her hands, the line of her jaw hardening.

Riley had hoped she hadn't noticed his use of the singular pronoun, but Amy had her own agenda now. And she was hell-bent on putting it into action. "It's safer if I go alone."

She cut him off, slicing her hand through the air. "I don't believe I'm safer away from you than with you, Riley. You're not some walking jinx. And I'm not April."

He flinched. The woman played hardball, but her

stripping away of his private thoughts felt like a bracing blast of fresh, clean air. He filled his lungs.

"So let's pay Ethan that visit." She tossed her head, her dark hair whipping over her shoulder and her gold locket winking in the morning sun.

Riley nodded and held out his arms. She came to him, wordlessly and without hesitation. They held on to each other like a drowning couple clutching their last lifeline.

Then he kissed her temple and stared out the window over her head.

Riley Hammond, you just met your match.

AMY HUNCHED FORWARD, the black knit cap scratchy against her cheek. She tucked a finger inside the edge and ran it along the curve of her face. Riley hadn't been kidding about paying a covert visit to her half brother.

She twisted her head toward the dark street and swallowed. Did he really think some terrorist might be watching Ethan?

The white columns of Ethan's house gleamed in the moonlight, and a few windows from the upper story glowed with a faint yellow light. They'd been lucky Ethan hadn't been in full entertainment mode tonight. They still didn't know whether or not he was home, but if not, they'd wait for him.

She'd wait a long time to get answers from her half brother.

Riley whispered, his words tickling her ear. "The street looks clear from here. When I ran a perimeter around the house, I spotted the box for the security system. Wait here while I disable it."

She twisted her hands together as Riley crouched

and traveled swiftly across the lawn, barely disturbing a blade of grass.

She didn't want to stay ensconced in the bushes ringing Ethan's palatial house, every rustling leaf, every chirp from a cricket making the hair on the back of her neck quiver with fear. But hadn't she disassociated herself from April earlier?

Clamping her chattering teeth, she felt a strong kinship with Riley's fearful wife. Bravado caused you to do stupid things. She wasn't even sure if her plan was an effort to confront Ethan or just a ruse to gain Riley's admiration and undying respect.

She'd focus on undying for now.

A twig snapped beside her and she almost jumped out of her skin until Riley's face hovered in front of her. The man moved as stealthily as a panther. She hadn't even tracked his return to the foliage.

"Shh." He held up one hand. "It's done. We're going around to that back door I pointed out to you earlier."

Riley hadn't known if Ethan lived alone, had a wife or children or had twenty-four-hour bodyguard protection. Guess they'd find out soon enough.

Doubling over, Riley emerged from the bushes again, and this time Amy followed him. He hadn't trusted her with a weapon since she'd never fired a gun before, but he had his weapon. A big one.

She held her breath as Riley tinkered with the sliding door, slicing out a portion of the glass with a glass cutter. When the door slid open without a clanging alarm bell sounding, Amy released her breath in a gush of air.

They stepped into the kitchen where circles of lights from the various gadgets and kitchen appliances winked at them from the darkness. The ice maker cranked, and Amy clutched Riley's arm.

He looked at her over his shoulder, raising his eyebrows to the folded edge of his knit cap.

She released her death grip and shrugged as if ice makers terrified her every day.

They tiptoed from the kitchen into the great room where a shaft of light from the entryway beamed across the carpet. An empty chair stood sentry in the foyer and Riley's brow furrowed as he pointed toward it.

Amy gulped. Looked like a good place for a bodyguard to stand watch but, if the bodyguard wasn't occupying the chair, where was he?

Riley placed one gloved hand on the banister of the curving staircase while his other hovered over the gun in his waistband. He tested the first step with his running shoe, and meeting no resistance or creaking, he began his ascent.

Amy trailed after him, keeping watch behind them. She didn't want some thug to come barreling out of the shadows. On the one hand, she wanted to find Ethan home and tucked into his bed so they could question him and get the heck out of there. On the other, she dreaded the encounter and wanted more time to shore up her nerves while they waited for him to come home.

Several rooms lined the hallway upstairs, most with their doors gaping open. The lights they'd seen from outside spilled from two rooms next to each other, their doors ajar.

Would they find Ethan reading quietly in bed? It seemed so out of character for him, and the eerie silence of the house indicated emptiness. Surely they'd hear a cough, the rustle of a page, the clinking of a glass if Ethan occupied one of those rooms.

Riley held a hand out behind him as he crept down

the hallway, gripping his weapon in front of him. Her muscles stiff with tension, Amy followed behind him.

Grabbing the doorjamb of the first room, Riley poked his head through the doorway. His shoulders stiffened and the muscles of his back beneath his black T-shirt rippled.

He cranked his head over his shoulder and mouthed, "Wait here."

Amy's blood thundered in her ears. Ethan must be in there, but he obviously hadn't spotted Riley yet. He had to be sleeping.

Riley disappeared into the room and panic washed over Amy's flesh. She tripped toward the door and grasped the doorjamb. The king-sized bed looked like a raft afloat in the ocean in the cavernous bedroom decorated in dark blues and greens.

Riley's body blocked her view of Ethan, but a pair of bare feet pointed inward at the foot of the bed. Tilting her head, Amy drew her brows together. Ethan lay on top of the covers, not beneath, so maybe he had fallen asleep reading.

Ethan hadn't yet made a noise. He'd have a nice surprise waking up with a big gun in his face. *Served him right.*

Riley leaned forward, his weapon dangling at his side. Amy scratched her head beneath the cap and sighed as she drew closer to the bed.

Riley spun around with his arms splayed at his sides. "Stay where you are, Amy."

Did he think Ethan might wake up with guns blazing or something? She took a few more steps. Suddenly, her nose twitched, and then her nostrils flared. A sickening odor wafted from the bed, engulfing her, invading her nostrils and triggering her gag reflex. Her gut rolled as she clapped a hand over her mouth.

She staggered back and hissed. "What is that?"

Riley stepped to the side, revealing Ethan's prone form on the bed. Amy's gaze traveled the length of Ethan's body, clothed in a blue silk dressing gown splashed with red and black. Her examination ended with his white feet, toes oddly pointing inward.

Something nudged her brain and her eyes shifted direction, gaining focus as she scanned Ethan's robe with its strange color pattern. She studied his face, his eyes closed and his head resting against a pillow, a pillow soaked in blood.

Chapter Twelve

Amy screamed, the sound ripping through the room and banishing the silence in the house. The scream died in her throat and she gathered breath for another one, her gaze pinned to the deep slash across Ethan's throat.

Riley lunged forward and pulled her into his arms. He cupped the back of her head with his hand and crushed her face against his T-shirt, now damp with sweat. She inhaled his masculine scent, anything to get the rancid smell of blood and death out of her nose.

He shushed her. "Quiet, Amy. They might still be here."

His words sent a spike of fear to her heart, and she bucked in his arms.

He clasped one arm around her waist and half dragged her toward the door while thrusting his gun before him. He stalked to the other lighted room, peered inside and cursed.

Amy peeled her head from his shoulder, but he clamped it back down. "You don't need to see that."

She licked her lips, her tongue meeting his rough T-shirt. She didn't need to see whatever lurked in that room, but she prayed to God Ethan didn't have a family.

"We need to get out of here." He squeezed her shoulder. "Are you okay to walk?"

She jerked her head up. Did Riley think he needed to carry her away from the carnage? She realized she hadn't stood on her own two feet since she saw Ethan's body. She steadied her rubbery legs and drew a deep breath. "I'm okay."

Still holding his gun, Riley grabbed her hand and charged downstairs. They flew across the great room, burst through the sliding door of the kitchen and stumbled into the backyard. Their soft shoes squished against the damp grass as they made a beeline toward the foliage ringing the yard.

They scrambled through the bushes and hopped over the fence of the next-door neighbors. Amy had been so worried on the way over about meeting a pit bull in this yard; now she'd take on five pit bulls just to get away from that grisly scene in the house.

When they made it to Riley's car, they both sat panting in the front seat. Amy's heart pounded in her chest like she'd just made an ocean rescue. Except this time she hadn't rescued anybody.

She gripped her bouncing knees with gloved hands. "Riley, what was in that other room? N-not his family?"

He slipped off his cap and bunched it in his fist. "No, thank God. His bodyguards—two of them."

Amy choked and covered her face. "Why?"

"His attackers must've figured he knew something." His fingers inched inside her cap and massaged her scalp. "I'm sorry you had to see that."

She peeked through her fingers, the streetlights blurring through her tears. "Do you think Ethan told them anything? Maybe he did know where Carlos stashed the money. If so…"

"If so, then they'll have what they want and leave you alone."

"And if Ethan didn't know anything, they killed him anyway. I don't know anything." Amy pulled off her gloves and hugged herself against the cold fear that touched the base of her spine.

"They won't get to you, Amy. I won't let them."

She met his eyes and, even in the darkness of the car, she could see the fierce protective light gleaming from their depths. Dropping her eyelids, she rolled her shoulders. She had faith in Riley.

He picked up her hand and traced the lines of her palm with his fingertip. "I think it's time for you to leave."

She curled her hand around his finger. "Okay. Let's go back to your place. Should we call the police or something?"

"I have someone I can call at the sheriff's department. I know Ethan's your brother, Amy, but the police aren't going to be choked up over his death." He slipped his hand from hers and cranked on the car's engine.

"He wasn't a good person, even as a teenager. I suppose the authorities will notify Dad. I'm not going to be the one to tell him his favored son is dead."

"I'm sure your father will be notified. It'll be reported as just another murder due to drug trafficking."

"Now I'll never get any information from Ethan. I hope his killers had better luck and they have what they want now. Otherwise, we're back to square one trying to figure out where Carlos hid that money."

"Didn't you hear me?" Riley cocked his head as he took the next turn.

"You think Ethan gave it up?"

"No, not that. I said you need to leave."

Her nostrils flared as she studied his profile, the ends

of his long, sandy blond hair highlighted by the head-lights from the oncoming cars. "You mean *leave* leave?"

"Yeah. Leave the area. Where's that EMT school you were going to attend?"

"Right here in San Diego." She sat up and yanked off the itchy cap. "Where do you propose I go and for how long? If the client never gets his money back, they'll never leave me alone. What am I supposed to do, join the Witness Protection Program?" She slammed her hands against the dashboard. "I already went through a similar experience when I was ten years old— uprooted, taken away from everything I'd ever known and loved, thrust into an alien environment. I'm not doing that again."

He brushed her cheek with the back of his hand. "It won't be like that, Amy. I can send you to stay with a friend, Ian's ex-wife, in Colorado. They wouldn't be able to track you there. When all this blows over…"

"How's that going to happen?" She ducked out of his reach. "Carlos left the means to that money with me, somehow, somewhere. How are you going to find it without my help? And if you never find it, they'll never stop looking for me. I don't want to permanently settle in Colorado. I don't like the snow."

Tears pricked her eyes, and she turned her head to rest her forehead against the cool glass of the window. She'd been an idiot to expect Riley to whisk her away to his dive boat in Cabo. The excitement and the thrill of the chase had fueled his attraction for her. Nothing more. Maybe he wanted to prove to himself that he could protect someone and do it right this time.

And what did she want to prove?

She'd been fooling herself all these years thinking she could settle down with a stable man—no excitement, no drama. Then this situation had fallen into her lap like a ripe fruit, and she'd grabbed it with both hands and sunk her teeth into it.

Riley swung into his parking slot and cut the engine. "I have to call my friend at the San Diego Sheriff's Department to report that carnage."

"Will you tell him the truth?"

"As much as I can. Ethan Prescott was involved in a drug deal that took a wrong turn, and he paid with his life."

After they'd locked the doors behind them in Riley's apartment, Amy watched Riley end his call to the sheriff's department. "No questions asked?"

He shook his head as he pocketed his phone. "That was my contact, Walt. He's a former Navy SEAL and he doesn't ask questions."

"Why'd they do it, Riley?" Amy twisted her fingers in front of her. "Why would a bunch of terrorists kill Ethan?"

"He was involved in the drug trade. He had bodyguards living in his house. He knew the risks."

"But the day before he was throwing a dinner party. It doesn't seem as if he was in fear for his life."

"Then he was a fool."

Amy pressed the heels of her hands against her temples. "Do you think they killed him because of me?"

"What do you mean?" Riley shifted his gaze away from her to study the newspaper on the counter.

For a covert-ops guy, his lying skills needed work. "Come on. Don't pretend with me. Do you think the terrorists went after Ethan to find me?"

He folded the newspaper, running his thumb along the crease. "They probably don't even know about the relationship between the two of you. But they probably do know about his connection to Carlos. When he couldn't tell them anything about the money, they killed him."

"If Ethan had known where Carlos had hidden the money, he would've told them. My half brother had a keen sense of self-preservation."

Riley snorted. "Most criminals do." He took two steps toward her and grabbed her hands. "Put it behind you, Amy. Get some sleep. You've had a shock today."

"That's three dead bodies in as many days." A half smile trembled on her lips. "That's gotta be some kind of record."

He cradled her face in his large, comforting hands. "That's too much for anyone to bear. You need to get out of this, and I'm going to help you."

"Before you do that, can you help me with one more thing?" She turned her head to kiss his palm, fluttering her lashes against his fingers. She wasn't above using her feminine wiles to get her way.

"Anything." He dropped a kiss on top of her head.

"Get me in to see my father tomorrow."

He gasped against the top of her head, a gush of warm air hitting her scalp. "Why do you want to see your father? The police will notify him of Ethan's death."

"Now that I know Ethan was responsible for involving me in a crime, I want to find out what else my father knows about it. Maybe Ethan confided in him about Carlos. Maybe my father has some ideas about the money."

"I thought you'd given up on finding the money." Riley gripped Amy's shoulders and pushed her away, intently studying her upturned face.

"*You* gave up on finding the money. I never agreed

to that, Riley. I want to find it, turn it over to the proper authorities and get my life back."

"What if it doesn't work?" His fingers pinched into her flesh through the black sweatshirt. He continued, his tone harsh, his words brutal. "What if you find their money, turn it over and they kill you as a reward for your efforts?"

She hunched her shoulders, twisting out of his grasp. "That was supposed to make me feel better? That's your way of protecting me?"

"That's my way of talking sense into you. Don't play this game with terrorists, Amy. You'll lose."

"Even with the all-powerful Navy SEAL, Riley Hammond, at my side? You said you'd protect me from anything." Amy ground her teeth together after the childish words tumbled from her mouth. Riley had hurt her by not offering to take her back to Cabo with him, and now she wanted to hurt him in return.

"I will, Amy." He dragged her back against his chest, wrapping his arms around her body like a protective shield. The stubble on his chin caught the strands of her hair. "God knows, I will protect you from anything and anyone. That's why I want you out of here."

She sagged against him. "Do this one thing for me, Riley. It's not a regular visiting day tomorrow, but you can get me in. Do it and I'll leave San Diego. I'll go anywhere you want."

Especially Cabo.

He hugged her tighter. "I'll get you in to see your father tomorrow and when he doesn't come through for you, we'll get you the hell out of Dodge."

She turned in his embrace, wrapped her arms around his neck and pressed her cheek against the steady, sure

Carol Ericson 391

beating of his heart. She'd made a promise and she'd stick to it, but if her father gave her information—the game changed.

RILEY HADN'T SURPRISED the warden at the San Miguel Federal Penitentiary with his request to visit Eli Prescott. They'd already gotten word of Ethan's murder. The warden figured Riley's visit might be part of the ongoing investigation. Riley felt no inclination to correct the warden's impression.

He glanced at Amy in the seat next to him, humming and tapping her sandaled feet together to the beat of the music on the radio. The sight of Ethan with his throat slit had done her in last night, but she'd made a miraculous recovery. Nothing fazed this woman for long. She had the resiliency of a rubber band.

He pitied her for it.

She must've endured a lot as a kid to have built up that hardened shell. She needed his protection less than he cared to admit to himself. But she did need his contacts, and he'd been happy to accommodate her—especially since she'd agreed to leave town.

"So what's on the agenda?"

"What?" She turned her large, liquid brown eyes on him and he wondered how old Eli Prescott could refuse her anything. He sure as hell couldn't.

"What do you plan to ask your father?"

Her brows shot up. "The obvious. Did he know Carlos? Does he know about the money?"

"And even if he does, why should he tell you?"

She blinked her eyes rapidly. "To save my life."

He opened his mouth and then snapped it shut. He didn't need to explain her father's character to Amy. He couldn't help her if she refused to open her eyes.

She laughed, a hard, bitter sound. "I know what you're thinking. Why should he care about me now? Granted, if it came down to choosing between his life and mine, his choice would be a slam dunk. But if he could help me without hurting himself, he just might sign up for that."

"And you're okay with that?"

"I have to be." She lifted a shoulder and her long hair slid forward. "It's all I've got."

He made the turn onto the property of the prison and pointed to the right. "We have to park over there today since they're holding some kind of event in the administration building and the prison is closed to visitors."

He pulled his car into a slot near the front and cupped Amy's elbow as they strode toward the gate that led to the prison.

The guard checked their IDs. "Good thing you came early. That lot's going to fill up, and we're not letting anyone past the gates later today."

"What's going on?" Riley glanced back at a news van trundling up the drive.

"Warden's having a press conference."

Riley thanked the guard and threaded his fingers through Amy's as they walked toward the imposing gray penitentiary. "Are you nervous?"

"No more nervous than usual when I visit him. He always wants to talk about the good old days, and I'm always asking questions." She squeezed his hand. "Thanks for getting me in here today."

He squeezed back. "No problemo, but a promise is a promise."

"Colorado? I may need to buy a warm jacket."

Since Riley had made the visit request, he had to accompany Amy into the visiting room. The warden had told him that Eli Prescott didn't rate visits beyond the glass partition, but Amy seemed accustomed to the routine.

She settled into the plastic chair opposite the bullet-proof glass and rested her hand on the red receiver. Riley took the seat to her right, his knees bumping hers.

The door beyond the glass swung open, and the guard ushered in a tall, lean man with cropped gray hair. Amy got her coloring from her mother but her body type from this man, this criminal.

Prescott dropped into the chair across from Amy and leveled a finger at Riley as he picked up the receiver. "Who's he?"

"He's just a friend."

Just a friend? God, he wanted to be so much more.

The blue eyes flickered across Riley's face, and Riley felt scanned and categorized in that split second.

"And they let him just waltz in here? Don't play games with me, girl." He coughed and covered his face with one bony hand. "You know I lost a son."

"Do you want to lose a daughter, too?"

Prescott jerked up his head. "What do you mean by that?"

"The same men who killed Ethan are after me." She gripped the edge of the counter in front of her. "Or don't you care about that?"

"It's that Carlos. If he had delivered the money to the clients as expected, Ethan would be alive and you'd be on the beach somewhere."

"What do you know about Carlos? What do you know about the money?" Amy had slid her hand to the glass where she splayed her fingers almost in supplication to her father.

His hand met hers through the glass. "I don't know anything, Amy."

Riley blew a slow stream of air through his teeth, unaware he'd been holding his breath.

"Ethan mentioned his deals to me occasionally but never the details. Why would he? How could I help him from here? How can I help you?"

Amy slumped in her seat, but kept her hand in place on the glass. "I—I don't know. These people think I have their money, and I don't have a clue where it is. They're not going to stop until they find out one way or the other if I have it."

"Then get out." Prescott's gaze shifted to Riley again. "I'm sure your capable friend here can find you a way out. People disappear all the time."

"I don't want to disappear. I'm always disappearing." Amy's voice never quavered for a second.

Her father tapped his nails on the glass. "I see you're still wearing your mother's locket. When did she give that to you?"

"Do you really want to know?" Amy's fingers curled against the glass. "She gave it to me as she lay dying in the dirt of the compound under the hot Mexican sun. As the blood and life seeped from her body, she clasped it in her hand and told me to take it. To honor her last wish, I had to lift her heavy hair and slip the chain over her head…. I had to take it off her dead body."

Prescott dropped his piercing blue gaze. "I loved Loretta and she loved me. I didn't keep her on the compound against her will, Amy, no matter how much you want to believe that."

Riley ached to take this brave woman into his arms and give her license to break down. But she'd never allow it, especially not in front of Eli Prescott.

Amy sighed, the only sound of her pent-up emotion. "Then you have nothing for me? You can't tell me anything about Carlos or the money he stole?"

"I wish I could. I really wish I could." His gaze brightened. "You've searched for keys? Numbers to bank accounts? Computer files?"

"We've searched."

Prescott put his hand back against the glass. "Stay safe, girl. You've got more gumption than all my other children put together. You always did."

Amy uncurled her fingers and pressed the glass. Then she dropped the receiver in its cradle and turned to Riley. "Let's go."

As they left the room, Riley glanced over his shoulder at the beaten man shuffling toward lockup on the other side of the glass. If Eli Prescott could've, he would've given Amy what she wanted—this time.

Amy's low-heeled sandals clicked on the tiled floor as they walked down the hallway toward the reception area. The guards in the front were watching the event in the administration building on closed-circuit TVs.

"Is there a ladies' room in the administration building?"

"Yes." The guard at the desk nodded. "You'll probably have it all to yourself once this press conference gets under way."

Good. Amy needed a few minutes to herself.

"Are there any vending machines over there?" Riley slid his visitor's badge across the desk and Amy added hers.

"To the left once you enter the double doors."

Riley turned to Amy as they filed out of the prison into the bright sun. He skimmed his hand down her back, which she held stiff and straight. He figured she had to, or she might collapse into a puddle.

"Are you okay?"

Amy brushed the hair from her face and smiled a phony smile, too cheery for their surroundings. "I'm good."

"Do you want something to drink for the ride back?"

"Anything cold and wet." She fanned her legs with her skirt. "It's hot out here."

Riley pushed open the door of the stucco building, holding it for Amy. They waded through the crowd gathering before the podium at the end of the room. Riley vaguely remembered some news about a possible shutdown of the facility in the next few years. Maybe if they moved her father far, far away, Amy would have a good excuse not to visit him anymore. Nothing but disappointment and heartache lurked behind those prison bars for her.

Amy pointed to the sign on the wall for the restrooms. "I'll meet you out front. It's a zoo in here."

Riley watched her as she turned the corner, her head held high and her silky hair rippling down her back. He spun around and collided with a reporter. The man's press badge fell to the floor, and Riley bent down to pick it up.

"Sorry." He glanced at the badge from KASD Radio before holding it out to the dark-haired man in the ill-fitting suit.

Sweat beaded the reporter's brow as he snatched at his badge. Without a word of thanks, the man turned toward the empty podium.

With irritation pricking the back of his neck, Riley muttered, "You're welcome," to the man's back and then made a beeline for the hallway to the left of the entrance.

He sauntered toward the bank of vending machines against the wall, jingling the change in his pocket. He clutched the coins and pulled them out, frowning as he added up the change in his palm. The red light on the soda machine indicated exact change only.

A woman in a pantsuit, her badge swaying from her neck, jogged toward the machine. She pointed to it. "Are you getting something?"

"I need exact change." He bounced the coins in his hand. "Do you have change for a couple of dollar bills?"

"I might. Hang on." She pinched open the coin purse on her wallet and stirred the change with her index finger.

"Sorry, I don't." She plucked out a few coins and fed them into the machine as her badge hung forward.

His brows drawing together, Riley studied her badge. KASD Radio, just like the other guy. They sure had a lot of press here for a little station and a little event.

Her soda chugged through the machine and clanged into the dispenser. "Ah-ha." She tapped the light on the machine. "It's your lucky day. I guess my change was enough to break the spell."

Riley dragged his gaze away from her badge—red, white and blue, instead of just red and white like the other reporter's—to stare stupidly at the machine where the red light had gone out.

"Are you okay? I think you can stuff your bills in there now."

Her wide eyes met his over the top of her soda can after she popped it open.

"Yeah, thanks." He scratched his jaw and stopped

her as she turned away. "You're a reporter with KASD Radio?"

"Yep." She ran her thumb along the ribbon around her neck and held out her badge.

"I just ran into your colleague, literally. You're sure covering the warden's speech thoroughly. Is it that important?" He crumpled the bills in his fist, knowing the machine would never accept them now, but unable to curb the tension seizing his muscles.

She laughed. "I think you're mistaken. Our station doesn't have the budget to send two reporters to a news conference, even if the President himself showed up."

The blood roared in Riley's ears. "There's only you here from KASD?"

She nodded, taking a step back, the lines of her face creasing at the tone of his intense questioning.

"And this is the official badge for the event—red, white and blue?" He grabbed her badge and tapped the hard plastic. The other badge had just been in a plastic sleeve.

She grabbed the ribbon and yanked the badge out of his hand. "What's your problem?"

The blood thrummed through his veins, and his sluggish senses began firing on all cylinders. He had a problem, all right. Amy was alone in the ladies' room and a rude reporter with suspicious credentials had free reign amidst a crowded building.

The big story here today had nothing to do with the warden. Amy was in trouble.

Chapter Thirteen

Amy stumbled as soon as she rounded the corner to the bathroom, and threw out her arm to steady herself against the wall.

The conversation with her father had leeched the strength from her bones—not because he couldn't tell her anything about the money, but because he hadn't remembered her mother had never removed the gold locket he'd given to his wife. Hadn't he realized Amy had taken the locket from her mother's dead body?

She clutched her stomach and staggered the rest of the way down the empty hallway to the bathroom. She shoved open the door and peered beneath the stalls. Good, she had the place to herself.

Gripping the sink for support, she peered into the mirror. Despite the turmoil of her emotions, her face stared back at her, placid and serene. She'd gotten so good at hiding her feelings, no wonder Riley hadn't invited her to Cabo. He probably had no idea how much she wanted to stay with him.

She cranked on the faucet and splashed cold water on her face. It didn't help. Nausea swept over her, and she swung around and stumbled into one of the stalls. She slid the lock and leaned against the door, laying her hands flat against it.

She scooped in a deep breath and shuddered as she released it. Fresh air would do her more good than the stale, artificially perfumed air of the bathroom. The sooner they hit the road, the better. She closed her eyes and breathed deeply through her nose until the nausea passed.

The outer door to the bathroom whisked open as Amy yanked a length of toilet tissue from the roll and pressed it against her lips. The person who had opened that door gave her further incentive to buck up and fight off the sickness. She didn't want anyone to hear her retching in the bathroom.

She blew her nose into the tissue and tossed it into the toilet. After flushing, she slid back the lock and took two steps toward the sink. The woman in the other stall hadn't made a peep yet. Who knows? Maybe she was suppressing her nausea, too. The federal pen could make anyone ill.

The stall door banged open and Amy jumped. Her gaze darted to the reflection in the mirror—the reflection of a knife blade glinting in the fluorescent light.

Her blood turned to ice water in her veins as the face behind the knife came into focus. A stranger, a man who wanted to kill her.

"W-what do you want? I don't have the money. I don't know what Carlos did with the money."

The man wiped his brow with his other hand, and his eye twitched. "You're coming with me."

A pounding dread beat against her temples. If they believed she knew something, what would they do to her to get answers? She clutched her purse against her side. How would he manage to abduct her in the midst of the crowd, even if he did poke that knife in her side?

If she made a run for it, would he stab her in front of all those people?

Riley would never allow him to just walk away with her. But if he had her at knifepoint, would Riley make a move?

"I have nothing to give you. No money, no information."

The man glanced over his shoulder at the door and ran the tip of his tongue along his lips. "Who is the man who travels with you and protects you? CIA?"

She swallowed. Maybe she did have information to give them. The image of Ethan's slashed throat and blood-soaked pillow flashed in front of her eyes. What information had he given them? Whatever it was, it hadn't been enough, and she knew a lot less than Ethan.

He gestured with his knife. "Let's get moving."

"You don't really believe you can march me off the grounds of a federal prison during a press conference with a knife in my side, do you?"

"I have to do what I have to do." A bead of sweat rolled down his face and hung off the edge of his jaw.

He didn't like this any better than she did.

She shuffled back a few steps, but he lunged at her, grabbing the back of her neck with his free hand.

He pressed the blade against her side and growled. "Walk next to me. If you make a move or cry out, I'm going to slide this blade right into your flesh."

Her teeth chattered and goose bumps raced across her skin. Her hip glanced off the door as he pushed it open and looked both ways down the hallway.

Instead of turning left toward the murmuring crowd, the man veered to the right, his fist pressed against the small of her back and the blade pinching her side.

Her breath came out in short gasps. He had no intention of walking her through the crowd and possibly past Riley. There must be a back door to this place, and the guards didn't have to be as alert since the main gates to the prison remained locked.

A woman's voice called down the hallway to them. "Is this the way to the ladies' room?"

Amy craned her head over her shoulder and felt the blade poke her skin through her blouse. "Yes, that's it, on the right. We're leaving now. Enjoy the event."

"Shut up." The man drove his balled-up hand into her back.

Amy's too-familiar response didn't make the woman stop or ask if they knew each other. When they reached the end of the hallway, her captor pushed her toward an exit door at the bottom of a short staircase.

She had to make some kind of move. She coiled her muscles and jumped over the three steps, crashing into the metal door. She shoved against the bar on the door and tripped outside. But her assailant tackled her to the ground and held the knife to her throat.

"Don't be foolish again. I don't have orders to kill you, but I can cause you severe pain."

She swallowed against the blade and nodded as he dragged her to her feet. The exit door had deposited them at the side of the building with the open-air parking lot stretching to their left.

Amy cast a wild glance around for Riley or some prison guards, but spotted only a few reporters smoking cigarettes at the corner of the building. They weren't even looking her way.

The man hustled her toward the parking lot, gaining confidence with each step away from the prison. They weaved through the parked cars, the knife a constant reminder of the threat that faced her.

She wouldn't get in the car with him. She'd fight him off with every ounce of strength she had. He'd already confessed that he didn't have permission to kill her.

But he could do a lot worse with that wicked silver blade.

He reached into his pocket and clicked his remote. The lights of a nondescript gray sedan flashed from its parking space at the end of a row.

He yanked open the driver's door and pushed her ahead of him, the knife at her back. "Crawl over to the passenger seat. And don't think about exiting that way. It's impossible."

She looked across the interior of the car, zeroing in on the stripped panel of the passenger door. No door handle, no way to open the door.

Tensing her muscles, she gulped. She'd have to make her move now. He'd cut her now, or he'd cut her later, after she gave them unsatisfactory answers to their questions. Might as well make his life as miserable as possible.

She settled one knee on the car seat, bracing her other leg on the ground, ready to kick back. A scrambling noise behind them caused them both to freeze, and then her attacker grunted and tumbled to the side.

Amy twisted around, landing on the driver's seat, her legs splayed before her. Both fear and relief spiraled through her body as she saw Riley bend over the man and punch him in the gut.

The man groped for his knife, which he'd dropped at Riley's initial onslaught.

She screamed, "Look out. He has a knife."

Riley dropped onto the man's body, pinning his wrist with his knee. "Run, Amy. Get out of here."

She had no intention of leaving Riley in this parking

lot with a madman. Turning toward the steering wheel, she laid on the horn with both hands.

The stranger, knife in hand, swiped across Riley's midsection, ripping his shirt. With his other hand, he grabbed Amy's ankle and yanked her from the car. She gripped the steering wheel, hanging on, her palms sweaty.

Riley scrambled to his hands and knees, and the stranger kicked him in the throat. As Riley grunted and tumbled to the side, Amy's attacker launched forward, landing on top of her and waving his knife in her face.

Riley swayed to his feet. "I'm not going to let you take her."

With Amy crushed beneath his weight, the man brought the knife to her throat. Riley cursed and froze. He wouldn't make a move if he feared the man would cut her.

Amy took a deep breath and twisted her head away from the knife, ducking beneath the steering column. He yanked her hair and nicked her shoulder with the knife as he tried to pull her head back onto the seat.

Blood dripped onto the console. Amy gasped, but she worked an arm free and cinched the man's wrist, digging her nails into his flesh until he hissed in pain.

Riley threw open the passenger door and hooked one arm around her, dragging her from the car as he elbowed her attacker in the temple. With his knife still clutched in his hand, the man lunged toward them.

Amy jerked her head up at the sound of boots on the pavement. Two guards from the prison shouted as they jogged toward them.

Their assailant shoved them the rest of the way out of the car and gunned the engine. The car lurched forward, the passenger door slamming shut from the force of the forward motion. Exhaust filled Amy's nostrils as Riley yanked her out of the way of the tires grappling for purchase on the asphalt. He covered her body and rolled to the side.

The car squealed out of the parking lot and flew over the speed bumps, and Amy looked up to see it careen onto the road leading off the prison grounds.

With hands hovering over their weapons, the guards approached Amy and Riley. Amy slumped against Riley, panting against his chest. Riley hugged her close, murmuring in her ear. Her blood soaked through his shirt, and he must've felt the moisture because he glanced down and sucked in a breath.

"You're hurt."

"I'm all right. It's not deep."

He was already ripping off his shirt when the guards arrived, looming above them. "What the hell happened here?"

Riley staunched the bleeding of her arm with his shirt, and then squinted up at the prison guards. "It's a long story."

"Do you think anyone believed that terrorists infiltrated the press corps at the prison and tried to kidnap me?"

Riley lifted a shoulder. "It doesn't matter one way or the other. It's not as if a bunch of federal prison guards are going to track down terrorist operatives."

"At least they didn't arrest us for fighting in the parking lot."

She carried a glass of water to the couch and sank against the cushions. Riley had explained to her about the suspicious reporter and his badge, and how he had rushed to the ladies' room to find her. That woman in the hallway had saved Amy and didn't even know it.

When Riley had stopped her coming out of the bathroom, she'd pointed down the corridor and told him about the chatty woman and the surly man.

Smacking his fist into his palm, Riley said, "I should've stopped at my car first and retrieved my weapon."

"If you had done that, it might've been too late."

"Maybe. I just didn't want the guy to see me in the parking lot. I crouched down between the cars the whole time I was tracking you. I didn't want to take my eyes off of you for a second."

"I'm glad you didn't."

Riley was turning into her guardian angel, and did she ever need one. "How's your shoulder?" He swept his beer from the counter and twisted off the cap.

"It's fine." Amy picked at the snowy-white bandage peeping from the collar of her shirt. "They've moved on to the next step, haven't they? That man tried to kidnap me today. They're going to find out what I know, whether I know it or not."

Riley sauntered into the living room and slumped on the couch next to her, holding up his bottle. "Sure you don't want one? If ever someone needed a drink, it's you."

"I need my wits about me." Her knee bounced, and she hunched forward on her elbows to stop it.

"Those aren't wits. Those are nerves." He ran his hand between her shoulder blades. "Besides, you don't need wits anymore. You're getting out of town, remember?"

"You don't have to persuade me." She shivered, and Riley massaged her neck.

The attempted kidnapping today had convinced her to leave. Maybe fate dictated that she pull up her roots every ten years or so and move on. Her future didn't include hearth and home or stable and serene. She shot Riley a sideways glance.

And it didn't look like her future would include him, either.

"Good, because I'm just about done persuading you." He sipped his beer. "My next plan included throwing you over my shoulder."

Closing her eyes, Amy leaned against him, soaking up his strength. She wouldn't mind that at all. If she could trust this man with her life, she could trust him with her heart.

He slipped an arm around her. "Does Colorado sound good? There's no snow there—yet."

She dropped her head on his shoulder, allowing her hair to fan across her face. "Cabo sounds better, and there's no snow there—ever."

His body stiffened, and she held her breath. Had she gone too far? After today's rescue, she'd decided to tell him exactly how she felt. She'd weathered many calamities in her life. She could handle a broken heart.

"Cabo?"

"That's where you live, isn't it?" She flattened her hand against his belly. "Unless you've been lying to me all this time. Do you really own a dive boat in Mexico?"

"Yes, but…"

"But what?" Her confidence and resolve evaporated. She pushed away from him and jumped up from the couch. "This is just a job? It's in your nature to protect a damsel in distress? You only slept with me to make me feel better?"

She clenched her teeth, curling her hands into fists, bracing for the rejection, feeling foolish that she'd set herself up.

"But I'm not done with this job yet."

Amy blinked. "What does that mean?"

"I was called out of retirement to find my friend, Jack Coburn. The trail started with the Velasquez Drug Cartel and its deal with a terrorist cell from Afghanistan. I have to find out how they plan to use that money. It might lead to Jack and it might not, but right now it's all we have. When the job is done, when Jack is safe, then I can think about the future."

Looking down, her hair creating a veil around her face, Amy asked, "What's in your future, Riley?"

The couch squeaked as he rose. His body heat warmed her skin as he stood inches away from her. His scent of fresh soap and a hint of the sea—always a hint of the sea—flooded her senses.

He cupped his hand at the ends of her hair, her dark strands pooling in his palm. Then he scooped her hair away from her face into a ponytail behind her, tugging on it so her head tilted back, her face exposed to his scrutiny.

"Don't you know what's in my future, Amy?"

A gleam of blue shone from under his half-lidded eyes and his lips quirked at one side. She trailed her fingers along the reddish-gold stubble of his chin and whispered, "Me?"

He kissed her fingertips. He kissed the bandage on her shoulder. He kissed her mouth.

"It took you only one guess. I thought I'd have a tougher time convincing you of my intentions than getting you to leave San Diego."

"What exactly are your intentions?" She tugged on his earlobe and tucked his long hair behind his ear.

He rolled his eyes. "You still have doubts?"

"I'll always have doubts, Riley. Is that going to drive you crazy?"

He nuzzled her neck. "You already drive me crazy."

"I'm serious." She cradled his head with her arms. "Will my insecurities wear you down?"

"You're not going to have any insecurities with me. I'm not going anywhere, Amy. I won't abandon you."

She murmured against his hair, soft and damp from his shower. "What if I abandon you?"

"I'll come after you. It'll give me a good excuse to throw you over my shoulder." He kissed her hands and pulled her back toward the couch. "You do have to abandon me for a while, though. Let's get Ian's ex-wife, Meg, on the phone and see if she can take you in."

After two unsuccessful calls to Meg's house and her work, Riley tapped his phone against his palm. "Rocky Mountain Adventures, the place where Meg works, told me Meg's on vacation."

Amy's pulse ticked faster. Once she'd decided to leave town, she couldn't wait to get out, even if that meant leaving Riley behind. He'd come for her when this ended, when he found his friend.

"That's okay. I can find someplace to stay. I still have a lot of money at my disposal."

He shook his head. "I don't want you staying alone. I can send you to my sister and her husband in Hawaii. You'd get along great with them. They own a surf shop and spend most of the day surfing and hanging out at the beach."

"Do you come from a laid-back family? Surf shops in Hawaii. Dive boats in Cabo. What prompted you to enlist in the navy?"

"My dad was not laid-back—anything but. He was an admiral in the navy and ran our household like a tight ship. My sister, Leah, rebelled against all of that. I followed in Dad's footsteps, and then decided my sister had the right idea."

"Except when it comes to rescuing friends."

"Except that."

"Where are your parents now?"

"My mother remarried after my father died. She lives in Florida. My dad died of a heart attack at sixty-two. That's what being a type A personality gets you."

She folded her legs beneath her. Riley had two sides pulling at him. Maybe that's why they'd hit it off so quickly. They'd each recognized a kindred spirit. "A type A personality also allows you to control your destiny. I don't think you would've been satisfied kicking back in Cabo all your life. Your father wouldn't have been, either."

"You're right." He tugged her hair. "When the call came from Colonel Scripps about Jack, I jumped at the chance. I told myself I was responding to a friend in need, but I was also responding to my own need—my need for excitement, thrills and chills."

"I think it's also your need to feel useful, Riley, to have a hand in carving fate. Even your marriage to April was a challenge."

His nostrils flared briefly. *Have I gone too far?* She treaded on hallowed ground whenever she mentioned his marriage.

He blew out a breath and slid open his cell phone. "Sister in Hawaii? Does that work for you?"

"Will it work for her?"

"I told you she takes things in stride. She won't even raise an eyebrow."

After a conversation during which Riley seemed to do all the talking with very little explaining, he tossed his phone onto the coffee table. "Done. We'll put you on a flight tomorrow, and you can give Leah a call when you get there."

"You didn't tell her much."

"She knows not to ask too many questions." He clicked his beer on the table. "Are you ready to turn in?"

She set her water glass on the table next to his half-empty bottle. "It's our last night together. How...? When...?"

"We'll be together again when my job is done." He pinched her chin, and she closed her eyes.

She'd be safe in Hawaii, and he'd still be chasing terrorists and drug dealers, facing danger every day. But he wouldn't have it any other way, and she'd have to stand by that. She'd have to respect his commitment to finding his friend.

After all, that's what she loved about him. Why she loved him.

She covered his hand with hers. She'd never been in love before—never had the courage—and now, she didn't have the courage to tell him. Not even knowing she had to leave him.

His warm breath caressed her cheek and he kissed her eyelids. "I'm not going to waste this night worrying. I can finally relax knowing you're with my sister and her husband and away from this threat."

She opened one eye. "My involvement has complicated everything, hasn't it?"

"Only in a good way." Standing up, he extended his hand toward her. "Let's turn in, together. One last night with you, and I'll be highly motivated to wrap up this job."

Giggling, she placed her hand in his. She could forget her troubles for a while—as long as they made love. As long as he held her in his arms.

Her phone played its ringtone from her purse, and she squeezed Riley's hand. "Hold that thought. I hope this isn't Sarah. I'll have to tell her I abandoned her house."

She groped for the cell phone inside her purse and studied the unfamiliar number on the display. Her heart skipped a beat, and she caught her breath.

"Who is it?"

"Don't know. Could be the EMT school, but probably not at this time of night."

She punched the button to answer. "Hello?"

"*Mi amor.* I've missed you."

The blood rushed to Amy's head, and she flung out a hand to grab the arm of the chair. "Who is this?"

"It's Carlos. I'm coming for you."

Chapter Fourteen

Her face drained of its usual bronze glow, Amy dropped the phone and collapsed onto the chair. A man's voice squawked from the phone and Riley pinched it between his fingers and mouthed to Amy. "Who is it?"

She opened her mouth and emitted a croak. Then she cleared her throat and tried again. "Carlos."

Riley nearly dropped the phone a second time. Her dead ex-boyfriend? His mind raced. Who said he was dead? The so-called body vanished, and Amy had never given him a chance to check the man's pulse. They hadn't seen any blood, and Riley had seen no visible wounds.

He put his finger to his lips and pressed the speaker button on Amy's phone. Cradling the phone in his palm, he held out his hand to her.

A golden opportunity just dropped into their laps. Could she do this? Did he have a right to ask her?

Slowly she nodded and took the phone from him. She scooped in a shaky breath. "C-Carlos?"

He laughed. "That's right, *mi amor.* Did you think I was dead?"

"I saw you on my kitchen floor, Carlos. What happened?"

"I took a pill, a drug. Something that slowed my

heart rate, paralyzed me. Unless a doctor examined me, I appeared as good as dead."

Covert-ops guys carried those kinds of drugs in their arsenal. Carlos had been prepared for anything. The shock of discovering her ex-boyfriend alive and well and on the telephone hadn't worn off for Amy yet.

Riley tapped her shoulder and mouthed, *Why?*

She blinked her eyes. "Why, Carlos? Why would you take something like that?"

"It has its dangers, Amy, but nothing compared to the threats of terrorist scum. When I knew they had followed me to your house, I swallowed a little yellow pill and faked my death. I didn't know if they'd figure it out and kill me anyway, but I had to take the chance."

Riley twirled his finger in the air. She had to get as much out of Carlos as possible while he was still alive.

"I thought they'd come to my house and removed your body."

"No. I came to and walked out of your house. I knew you'd been there because I saw a wet suit on the floor, unless that belonged to the clients or Velazquez's men. I'm pretty sure both were after me when I didn't deliver the money."

Amy closed her eyes, the color gradually returning to her cheeks. "Why'd you do it, Carlos? Why did you double-cross them all?"

"Surely you know, *mi amor*."

"I don't know, and please don't…"

She trailed off as Riley drew his finger across his throat. No sense in angering Carlos at this point. They needed him.

"Please don't tell me I know. I haven't seen you in a few months. Do you even have a wife?"

Carlos chuckled. "Of course not. How could there be

anyone for me but you? When you accused me of being married, I figured it was a good way to draw back until I pulled off this deal."

"Why, Carlos?"

"I wanted the money for us, Amy. We can go away now, be together."

Amy's eyes widened and she swallowed. "B-be together?"

Riley bunched his fists, but he nodded. Carlos had the money, and Riley needed to get his hands on it.

"You and me, *mi amor.* You need someone to take care of you."

Her gaze slid to Riley, and he rubbed her thigh. *She has someone to take care of her.*

She blew out a long, silent breath. "Why did you come back to my place after the deal went bad?"

"To get the money and to get you."

"Where's the money, Carlos?"

Riley held his breath.

"The money is in a self-storage facility. I got the idea from that storage shed on the beach."

"So why come to my place to get the money?"

"I left the key with you." He coughed. "I didn't think it would put you in danger. I couldn't keep it myself in case I was captured."

"You didn't think it would put me in danger?" Amy ran her hands through her hair, clutching it at her scalp. "They figured you were at my house for a reason. They're after me now."

"I know that, *mi amor. Lo siento.* I had no idea they'd put things together so quickly."

Amy massaged her left temple with her fingertips. "Where did you leave the key?"

Carlos drew in a sharp breath, and Riley held Amy's dark gaze, still glassy with shock.

"Come to me. Come to me and we'll get the money together and then sail away."

Riley rolled his eyes. Was this guy for real? Carlos didn't know Amy if he thought that kind of amour talk would work with her.

From his crouching position, Riley pushed up and paced toward the window. It had just ended. Carlos wouldn't tell Amy where he'd hidden the key to the storage container unless he got Amy in the bargain. Of course, Carlos wouldn't get the money, either.

"Where do you want me to meet you?"

Riley spun around and stalked to Amy's side. He held up his hands and shook his head.

She ignored him. "I'll come to you anywhere, Carlos."

Carlos sighed a noisy, wet sigh, and Riley grunted. Was he crying now?

"I knew it wasn't the end. I knew you wouldn't give up on us. Meet me at the marina tomorrow at seven in the evening, slip eight-fifteen."

The guy wasn't kidding about sailing away.

"Do I need to bring anything? How will you know I have the key with me?"

"Let me worry about that. I know what to do. Just pack a bag." Carlos paused. "You'll come alone, won't you? This isn't some kind of trick? You won't show up with the police?"

Amy finally made eye contact with Riley. "No trick. I'll be there alone."

"Until tomorrow, *mi amor*."

"Until tomorrow."

Amy slid her phone shut and Riley snatched it to

view the number. "Probably a prepaid phone." He fired her cell phone at the couch and it hit the cushion and bounced to the floor. "What do you think you're doing?"

"I'm meeting Carlos tomorrow, and we're going to get that money." She stood up and stretched, tousling her hair. "Once you get the money, you can halt the terrorists' plans and maybe get some information about Jack."

He surveyed her through narrowed eyes. "How do you plan to get the money from Lover Boy?"

"You just said it. Lover Boy. I'll get Carlos to do what I want one way or another."

"You're crazy. He's a criminal. He had the nerve to double-cross a terrorist cell and the Velasquez boys. He's not going to kowtow to you for the sake of love."

"You never know."

"You're not going alone."

"If he sees you, he'll run."

"He won't see me." He pulled her into his arms. "If you're going through with this insane plan, I'm going to be by your side...*mi amor.*"

Amy placed her hands on either side of his face and drew him down for a hard kiss on the mouth. "Don't call me that—ever."

THE FOLLOWING DAY after hours of planning, Amy sipped her coffee as Riley outlined plans and escape routes on a legal pad for the hundredth time. "I don't want you getting into a boat, plane or automobile with Carlos."

Amy tipped more milk into her cup. "I'm kinda gonna have to if we want to find the money. You'll be following us anyway, right? And maybe we'll get lucky, and Carlos and I will use my car."

He tapped a small metal disk on the counter for the

umpteenth time. "I think we should use the bug. Even if Carlos suspects you, he won't be able to detect this if we tuck it in your waistband."

"Are you trying to convince me or yourself? I already told you—I'm game."

"If Carlos discovers it…"

"He's not going to discover it. How else am I supposed to let you know where we're going? If you're going to be watching us from some concealed location or from far away, what am I supposed to do, send up smoke signals?"

"I can always follow you at a discreet distance. He won't detect me, and we'll have the GPS on your car just in case." He cupped his hand and bounced the little listening device up and down in his palm.

Riley had more jitters than a Thoroughbred at the starting gates of the Kentucky Derby. She laid her hand flat against his, trapping the disc. "If he won't discover you following us, he's not going to find this little microphone on my body or in my clothes. Hook that baby up."

The deep lines between his eyebrows didn't budge, but he nodded. "I may be out of sight, but I'll be close. You say the word, and I'll be at your side."

"I know." Just like he'd been at her side all night long. They'd made love again, but slowly this time, drinking each other in, filling each other up. Neither of them wanted to admit it, but they'd made love as if they might never make love again.

An hour later, Riley wheeled her suitcase from his bedroom and parked it by the front door. Once again they'd sifted through all her items, this time looking for a key to a padlock. Carlos had seemed confident that Amy would have the key when she went to meet him, but how could he be so sure?

Amy jerked her chin toward her bag. "Do you think we should check one more time? He told me to pack a bag, so I'm assuming he hid it somewhere in my suitcase."

"We don't even know that for sure. What if he plans to take a crowbar to the lock or melt it off with a blowtorch? Maybe he ditched the key a long time ago or isn't worried that you'll bring it with you. He wants you, not the key."

"You're probably right." Amy passed her hands across her face. "Even if we found the key, there are plenty of self-storage places in San Diego with hundreds of containers. How would we ever find the right one?"

"We won't. That's why we need Carlos to lead us to the money. Once we get it and turn it over to the CIA, the cell will have no reason to go after you, and they'll have to go back to the drawing board for funding whatever it was they were planning to fund with that money."

"But that won't get you any closer to finding Jack."

"Maybe, maybe not. But I have a gut feeling Jack will be safer if we disrupt the terrorists' plans."

"We all will."

After Riley loaded her suitcase into the trunk of her car, he attached a GPS device behind her back wheel. He straightened up and brushed his hands together. "I don't think Carlos will agree to take your car, but just in case."

"You're good, Riley Hammond. You should come out of retirement."

"I'm good at taking tourists out on my dive boat, too, and it's a lot safer."

She snorted. "You don't seem like a man interested in safe."

"Will that be a problem?" He cocked his head. "Maybe *you're* not interested in safe."

The heat raced to her cheeks and she dipped her head. She'd had the same thought a hundred times, but maybe she'd finally met a man who understood the pull. She brushed her hair out of her face and smiled. "After this adventure, I'm longing for it."

"Then let's get this adventure over with." He held out his hand and she grabbed it.

He understood.

Amy jumped into her car alone, but that didn't fully describe her situation. She had the tracking device on her car and the listening device on her person. With Riley on her side, she'd never be alone.

She drove a few miles and shouted, "Can you hear me?"

Her cell phone played its ringtone immediately and she answered Riley's call.

"You don't have to shout. It's sensitive. Put the phone down and speak in a normal tone of voice, not like you're directing an ocean rescue."

Amy tossed the phone onto the seat next to her. "Is this better?"

She picked up the phone again and put it to her ear.

Riley said, "That's perfect. Now whisper sweet nothings so I can test the sound level."

Amy put the phone away from her again and whispered what she wanted to do to him once they were safely at home.

"I'd better not be hearing any of that while you're talking to Carlos."

"Hopefully, all you'll hear from me is the location of this self-storage place."

They ended the call and with it the banter, and then

the enormity of her mission sucked the air from her lungs. She gripped the steering wheel, her knuckles turning white.

She'd reach the harbor soon and face Carlos, a man she once cared about. She'd have to convince him she still cared, at least long enough for Riley to track them down at the self-storage lockers and whisk her away— along with the money.

Always the money. Two sources drove Riley's motivation to steal this money out from under the terrorists' noses—to end her involvement and to disrupt any plans involving Jack. Which had the stronger pull for him?

Did it really matter? A little, persistent voice in her head argued that it did, but she ignored it. Now wasn't the time to be questioning Riley's motives.

She took the off-ramp toward the harbor and buzzed down her window to drink in the salty air. Wheeling into the parking lot, she leaned forward to study the slip numbers looking for number 815. She drove past the tourist boats, empty on this September evening in the middle of the week.

She spoke quietly as if to herself. "I'm at the harbor now. Eight-fifteen must be toward the end of the slips on the right of the parking lot entrance."

She wanted to hear Riley's confident voice in response, but she didn't dare pick up her cell phone now. Carlos could be watching her. Giving herself a brisk shake, she swung into a parking slot opposite the slips.

Would Carlos be waiting for her out in the open? She slid from the car and swung open a gate leading to the docks, the boats outlined against the sinking sun. She trudged up the ramp, spotting slip 815 with a midsize sailboat bobbing in the water.

"Carlos?" She drew back her shoulders and strode toward the boat.

A dark head popped up from the deck of the boat. His face broke out in a smile. "*Mi amor*. You made it."

"Of course."

He rose to his feet, his head jerking back and forth. "You're alone?"

"Who would I bring with me?" She spread her arms wide. "I was so happy when you called. When I thought you were dead—" She broke off and covered her face with her hands.

"*Lo siento*. There was no other way. Velasquez or the terrorists would've killed me or worse." He stretched his arms out to her. "I hoped I would regain consciousness before you came home, but when I woke up you were gone—along with my car. You know there's no wife, don't you?"

"Yes, I do. I know you pretended to be married to keep me safe until you could come for me." Amy reached the boat and grabbed his cool hand. "Those men came after me, Carlos. I had to get away quickly and I remembered you always parked your car in the back."

He kissed her hand. "The car is nothing. We can have everything and more."

"Where is the money?"

Carlos narrowed his almost-black eyes, and Amy's pulse ticked faster. She'd have to show a little more interest in Carlos and a little less interest in his cash.

"You've come here for me and not the money, haven't you?"

Amy brushed a dark curl from his forehead. "The money is a nice surprise, but it wouldn't mean anything without you."

He nodded, his gaze shifting past her shoulder at

the water. A muscle ticked in his jaw, and Amy's heart hammered. Had he seen something?

Glancing her way, he smiled, but furrows remained across his brow. "I knew I could trust you, Amy. I knew a little subterfuge wouldn't scare you off. Your brother told me a lot about you. I don't think he ever imagined I'd fall in love with you, though. For him you were a means to an end—storing the drugs on the beach—but for me you became much more."

She moved her lips beneath his kiss, fighting her revulsion. Running her hand through his hair, she pulled away. "Were you planning to take the money from the deal before you met me?"

"Yes."

His eyes darted toward the water again, but Amy kept her gaze pinned to his face. She didn't want to turn around. She didn't want to give away Riley with any deed or word.

He shook his head and kissed her again. "I decided to keep that money as soon as Ethan laid out the deal to me, but once I met you my resolve deepened. I could get into my storage facility without the key, but the money would be worthless without sharing it with someone. I always wanted you and the money, Amy."

It seems as if the money and I are a package deal for everyone.

"I'm glad." She pasted a smile on her face. Her jaw ached with the effort.

She'd had enough of this reunion. Where had Carlos stashed the money? If he told her now, Riley would have a chance to get there before them. He might even have a chance to break off the lock and get the money before they even arrived.

She ground her teeth together. She didn't want to

ask Carlos about the money again. She had to let him play this out his way.

"Of course now that you're here, I can use the padlock key to get into the storage locker." His sly smile spread across his face. "Do you want to know where I hid the key?"

A seagull shrieked overhead and an outboard motor hummed in the harbor while Amy held her breath. As Riley mentioned before, finding the key didn't mean a thing without the location of the self-storage facility. What if Carlos didn't tell her the location and just took her there? That would make the situation more difficult for Riley.

But Riley had a contingency plan. He had a plan for everything.

She smiled sweetly. "Where did you hide the key?"

He drew her close again, and she almost gagged on his cologne. How had she ever found that scent sexy? She preferred Riley's clean masculine smell.

Carlos ran a finger along the chain of her necklace and hooked it around his fingertip, dangling the gold heart-shaped locket at the end. "I put it in something that I knew you'd keep with you always."

Gasping, Amy closed her fingers around the keepsake from her mother. Carlos tapped her hand and she released her hold on the necklace. She glanced down as he flicked the catch with his thumbnail. A small key nestled inside the locket.

Amy choked back her fury. He'd hidden the means to his vile money in her most sacred possession? He could call her his love all he wanted. He knew nothing of love. He knew nothing of her.

She coughed and dumped the key into her hand.

"Very clever. I would've never looked for it in my locket."

Riley must be smacking his forehead about now.

Carlos shrugged. "I didn't want the key on me, and I didn't want anyone to discover it on you."

"So where is this self-storage facility?" Amy flicked back her hair and slipped the key into her pocket, not meeting Carlos's steady gaze.

"Now that I have the key and you, we'll go together, and then our options are wide open. We can go to any beach in the world."

"Is it nearby? Do you want to take my car?" If Carlos didn't plan to tell her the location of the self-storage place, at least Riley could track them on the GPS.

"It's close, but we don't need to take your car."

Amy waved an arm toward the parking lot while her knees trembled. "But my suitcase is in the trunk. It would be easy to take my car and leave it at the airport."

"You don't need your suitcase. Did you bring your passport like I asked?"

She'd brought it for show, but she had no intention of getting on a plane with Carlos and flying off to a foreign country, beach or no beach. "Yes, I have it, but I'm not going anywhere without my clothes."

His jaw tightened. "Don't be difficult now, Amy. We can get your bag from the car if you like."

She wrapped her arms around his waist and hoped Riley wasn't watching. "I can't wait to start our journey together. When I thought you were dead…"

Burying her head against his shoulder, she forced a sob from her throat.

"Shh." He smoothed her hair down her back. "It's almost over. We're almost there."

She sniffled. "I hope the facility is nearby. I can't take any more drama. Is it? Is it close?"

"It's just a few miles from here on Yale Street. I rented a unit in the very back row. It's a small place, no security guards, no security cameras."

Did you get that, Riley? She blew out a tiny, measured breath against Carlos's shirt.

"We'll be there soon, *mi amor.*"

The roaring engine of a powerboat drowned out the rest of his words. Carlos tightened his grip on her and she instinctively pulled away. As she did so, she felt the small metal disc slip from her waistband. She glanced down in time to see it bounce into the water.

Carlos shouted, and it took her several seconds to realize he was yelling at the boat charging in their direction and not the listening device sinking to the bottom of the harbor.

Her eyes focused on the figures in the boat, and she screamed and staggered back. The powerboat drew up next to the slip with two men on deck pointing guns at them.

One of the men shouted, "Get down on the ground."

Amy shivered as she recognized her attacker from the federal pen. Her knees locked and she froze.

Carlos reached under his jacket, and a zipping sound pierced the air. Carlos crumpled to his knees and fell over sideways as Amy clapped a hand over her mouth.

The men hopped off the boat, brandishing their weapons. The shooter, the man from the prison, hovered over Carlos while the other trained his weapon on Amy. "I hope you didn't kill him, Farzad. We still need information from him."

The man she'd recognized from before, Farzad, nudged Carlos's body with his foot. Carlos's blood seeped onto the gangplank, mixing with the saltwater. "He was reaching for a gun."

Farzad groped inside Carlos's jacket and pulled out the weapon tucked inside. Amy's gut rolled. What would Carlos have done to her if she hadn't willingly gotten on a plane with him?

The man aiming his gun at Amy cursed. "At least make sure he's dead this time, because it doesn't look like we're going to get anything out of him."

Farzad felt for a pulse and then shoved Carlos's body into the water with a heavy kick to his midsection. "I'll make sure this time."

Amy's tongue cleaved to the roof of her dry mouth as she watched Carlos slip into the gently lapping water, his white face a ghastly mask before it disappeared.

Her gaze skimmed along the empty harbor, a few sailboats bobbed on the water in the distance, oblivious to the violence in their midst. Riley would be on his way to the storage facility, unaware that Carlos would never make it there alive.

Would *she?*

The man holding her at gunpoint strode toward her and jabbed his gun in her side. "Where's that man from the prison? Where's your protector?"

Good question. She lifted her shoulders. "I left him when Carlos called. I always knew Carlos wasn't dead. I just used that man for protection against you."

Farzad's eyes narrowed. "Who was he?"

Amy sneered and spat out, "CIA."

A stream of Arabic flowed from the man holding her at gunpoint. He punctuated every exclamation by poking her in the back with a long silencer attached to his weapon.

Farzad smiled. "But that's not a problem because she knows where the money is, don't you, Amy?"

Yeah, she knew where Carlos had stashed the money, and that information had to keep her alive until she reached Riley.

She pressed her hand against the pocket where she'd slipped the key and nodded slowly, holding Farzad's dark gaze. "I know where the money is, but you need me to get it."

Chapter Fifteen

Riley parked his car around the corner from the U-Store storage facility and slipped in the front gate. Carlos had chosen a completely low-tech facility—no gate requiring a code to get in, no security guard on duty, no cameras. Perfect.

Back row. Carlos hadn't given Amy the number of the unit, but he'd told her he'd rented one in the back row.

Riley had broken out in a cold sweat when he'd lost contact with Amy, but at least Carlos had given her the location of the money before the mic went dead. No way Carlos could've discovered the small listening device tucked in Amy's clothing. It must've fallen out.

He ducked behind a large unit and scanned the ten battered units lined up along the back row. He'd wait until Carlos and Amy arrived, and then he'd plan his attack. He'd take down Carlos, rescue Amy and secure the money, interrupting the terrorists' scheme and whatever plans they had for Jack.

His muscles taut, he crouched against the storage unit, the cold from the metal seeping into his shoulders. He'd promised Amy some kind of life together after this mission. Could he deliver? April had begged him to give up his life of danger. He knew Amy never would. They suited each other. He'd felt it from the moment she'd swum up next to him to rescue two divers from the rough sea.

She'd been with him every step of the way on this perilous journey. She'd led him to the client's money, and they'd come to the end of the line together. If she could do all that for him, he could deliver on his promise of a happily-ever-after.

He glanced at his watch with a furrowed brow and flare of fear in his belly. Before the mic went out, it sounded as if Carlos had been on the verge of leaving. Why the delay? They must have retrieved Amy's suitcase from her car.

He massaged the back of his neck, his fingers digging into his flesh at the sound of a car engine. He pushed up to his feet and flattened his body against the corrugated metal of the unit.

The car stopped out of his line of vision, and he heard the doors open and then slam shut. More than two car doors? He yanked his gun out of its holster and gripped it with two hands.

He caught his breath and then ground his teeth together. Two men bracketed Amy, one holding a gun to her back—and neither one of them was Carlos.

He recognized the one with the gun as the so-called reporter at the federal prison. He studied the other man and cursed under his breath. Ian's instincts had been correct. Farouk, the man they'd played cat and mouse with in the Middle East, was here in the flesh.

Someone must have ratted out Carlos. Maybe the Velasquez gang did it to save their own hides. Maybe Ethan had given him up before they slit his throat.

The trio started at the far end of the row, and Riley strained to hear them. Amy drew her hand out of her pocket and held up an object to the two men—the key Carlos had hidden in her locket.

Riley's throat closed and his nostrils flared. They'd kill Amy as soon as they got the money. He took aim at the head of Farouk, and then lowered his weapon once he realized Amy still had a gun shoved into her back. As much as he wanted to take down Farouk, if he shot now they'd kill her sooner rather than later.

He held his breath as Amy inserted the key into the lock of the first unit. The little group turned and shuffled toward the next unit, and Riley exhaled. Carlos had never told her which unit housed the money. They'd have to try every unit, and they wouldn't kill Amy until they had the money in their hands—just in case she was playing them.

He whispered to himself, "Keep coming this way. Keep coming this way."

They tried the second lock with no luck and then skipped the next unit as it had a combination lock on it. A bead of sweat rolled down Riley's face as he watched them approach the fourth unit.

They had come within earshot, but the three of them didn't have much to say to each other. In the quiet atmosphere, Riley's rasping breath sounded like a jet engine to his ears. They moved on to the next unit and Amy repeated the procedure. Only this time, she yelped and jumped back.

The padlock on the storage unit hung open, and Farouk and his cohort exchanged a quick glance. Riley's grip on his gun tightened as Farouk shoved Amy away from the entrance. He lifted the lock and swung open the door.

Raising his gun, Riley aimed at the man holding Amy. If he could just get her to step away from the target or drop to the ground Riley had the shot. Riley had to act quickly while Farouk was focused on the money and before he pulled out his weapon.

Farouk ducked his head into the storage unit, and adrenaline pumped through Riley's veins. He shouted, "Amy, get down."

Amy dropped to the ground as if she'd been expecting the command, and Riley squeezed the trigger. The bullet hit the man in the shoulder and he spun around with the force, dropping his weapon.

Riley charged forward while Amy kicked the gun out of the way and flung out her arms to grab the edge of the door and swing it shut. As she struggled to her knees, Farouk grabbed her around the neck, pulling her up and dragging her against his chest.

Riley loomed over the bleeding man losing consciousness on the ground and swung his weapon toward Amy's captor. The blood in his veins turned to ice when he saw the knife at her throat.

"Looks like we have a stand-off, Hammond." Farouk grinned. "I wondered if one of the Prospero team was involved. I can't say it's a pleasure to see you again, but my money's here, so if you let me leave peacefully, I'll let you have Amy."

Amy's eyes widened at the use of Riley's name.

"What if I told you reinforcements were on the way, Farouk?"

The man shrugged, skepticism etched on his face. "Then I'd kill Amy, and nobody would be happy."

Riley's hand clenched and he slid his gaze to Amy's white face. If Farouk killed Amy, it would be the last act of violence in his sorry life. "What are you going to buy with that money?"

Farouk stepped in front of the duffel bags on the

floor of the unit as if to protect them. "What's your interest? I thought you just wanted to rescue the girl. You always want to rescue the girl."

He did want to rescue Amy and he wanted to rescue Jack. Could he do both? Stepping back, he massaged his temple.

"Don't let him get away with the money, Riley." The knife gleamed at Amy's neck, and her jaw tightened with resolve. Did she really believe he'd sacrifice her to stop a terrorist's plans, even if those plans involved Jack?

Riley released a measured breath. "What do you know about Jack Coburn?"

Farouk's eyes flickered but he shrugged a shoulder. "Only that he got the better of me too many times."

The blood roared in Riley's ears. *He knew something.* "He's a hostage negotiator now. He went to Afghanistan to secure the release of a captive. We don't know much more than that."

"And I know even less. I thought you were retired. What are you doing back on the job?" When his question met a stony silence from Riley, Farouk continued. "You should understand I know only a part of the plan. My job is to secure this money from the drug deal."

Riley had nothing to use as a bargaining chip but the gun in his hand. He'd get nothing from Farouk. With his muscles taut, he stepped around the unconscious man on the ground and gestured with his gun. "Take the money and leave Amy."

"No." Amy's word sliced through the air. "Don't let him take the money, Riley."

Farouk clicked his tongue. "Brave words from the daughter and the sister of criminals. I'll leave her to you once you load up the bags in the car, Hammond. Sorry I can't help you. I'm otherwise engaged."

He brought the knife closer to Amy's throat as he stepped out of the storage unit. She stumbled over the edge, and he cinched his arm around her waist. He backed up to his car and popped the trunk. "Drop your gun and get the money."

Riley's hand steadied and he narrowed his eyes.

"You make one more move with that weapon, and I'll slide this knife right across her throat. You can trust me, Hammond."

Amy gasped as Riley chucked his gun near the other man's weapon on the ground. He clambered into the unit. The warm, dry air closed around him as he hoisted the two duffel bags. Emerging into the dim light of dusk, he swallowed hard as he glanced at Farouk, his arm wrapped around Amy's body, and his knife still poised at her throat.

"Put the bags in the trunk."

Riley heaved the bags into the trunk and slammed the lid. "Now what?"

"Now Amy accompanies me in the car just for a short distance, and then I'll release her. She doesn't have to worry about us ever again. You, however… Well, I'm sure we'll meet at some point in the future."

A muscle ticked wildly in Riley's jaw. His gaze darted toward the two guns lying uselessly on the ground.

Amy gave a strangled cry as Farouk shoved her into the driver's side of the car, the knife at her back. Riley shuffled closer to his gun as he watched Amy climb over to the passenger seat. Farouk started his engine and the car lurched forward.

Riley hunched over and ran toward his gun and

grabbed both weapons. He looked up in time to see the passenger door fly open and Amy tumble from the car, which never stopped. Riley scrambled for his weapon, rolled onto his stomach and took a shot at the speeding car. He got off another shot as the car careened around a corner, leaving nothing but dust in its wake.

Riley turned his attention to Amy, struggling to her knees and sobbing. He jumped to his feet and ran toward her, his heart thumping with every step.

He caught her in his arms, pulling her up and crushing her to his chest. "Are you okay? Did he hurt you?"

She dug her nails into his shoulders as she held on. "I'm fine. I just scraped my arm when I jumped from the moving car."

He ran his hand along her arm, brushing bits of dirt and gravel from her soft skin, marred with several red scratches. Now she had two injured arms. "Thank God you're okay. I would have done anything he asked while he had that knife to your throat."

"You shouldn't have let him take off with the money, Riley." She grabbed his hands and brought them to her lips. "Taking their money would have forced them to start over and given you more time to track down leads on Jack."

"I still have one lead on Jack." Riley turned his head and jerked his chin toward the wounded man on the ground.

"He's not dead?" When Farzad had crumpled to the ground, his shoulder spouting blood, Amy assumed Riley had killed him. But one dead man had already come back to life. Why not another?

Riley tugged her hand, and she reluctantly followed him back to the gaping storage unit and the man sprawled on the ground next to it. Riley crouched beside

Farzad and ripped off the bottom of the man's shirt. He bunched it up and pressed it against the wound. Were his last-ditch medical efforts too little too late?

He lightly slapped the pale face and propped up his head. "Get some water from my bag, which is around the corner from that unit."

Riley jerked his thumb over his shoulder and Amy jumped to her feet and ran toward the unit. She scooped up the black bag from the ground and plunged her hand inside for the water.

She squatted beside Riley and handed him the bottle. He twisted off the cap and splashed a few drops on Farzad's face. Farzad blinked his eyes and moaned. Riley held the bottle to his lips.

"His name is Farzad."

"You're going to be okay, Farzad. I'll call for an ambulance."

Amy cringed at the lie which brought false hope to a dying man, even though this dying man had held her at gunpoint less than fifteen minutes ago.

Farzad puckered his lips and drew the water into his mouth. Most of it ran down his chin, and he closed his eyes again. Riley dragged him to the storage unit and propped him up against the side.

"Tell me what you know about Jack Coburn."

The man squeezed his eyes and the corner of his mouth ticked up. He gasped and clutched his shoulder where fresh blood seeped from Riley's bandage.

Riley shook him and slapped his face. "Tell me what you know about Coburn."

Farzad sucked air into his mouth, and his eyes flew open. "Jack Coburn."

"That's right. Jack Coburn. What do you know about him?"

Farzad's breath rattled in his chest, and Amy knew nothing could save him now. Riley leaned in, his ear close to Farzad's moving lips.

With a last rasping breath, Farzad slumped, his head falling to the side. Riley checked his pulse and swept his palm over the dead man's eyes.

Amy dropped her head in her hands. "I'm sorry, Riley."

"Sorry? The man was a brutal killer, perhaps even involved in a plot for mass murder. There's nothing to be sorry about."

She looked up, drawing her brows over her nose. "Not that. I meant I'm sorry you didn't get anything out of him before he died."

Riley quirked an eyebrow. "Who said I didn't?"

"H-he whispered something to you at the end?"

"Yep." He pushed to his feet and pulled out his cell phone.

Amy fell back on her hands, staring up at him while a light breeze lifted his hair from his shoulders. "Well?"

Riley grinned. "He said Jack escaped."

AMY KICKED HER LEGS onto the coffee table and wrapped her hands around her sweating can of soda. She swiveled her head back and forth between Riley and his friend Ian as they discussed the implications of Farzad's dying words.

The two men didn't resemble each other in appearance. Riley's longish blond mane contrasted with Ian's dark, short-cropped hair. Riley's quick grin lit up his blue eyes, while Ian's slow smile sent a glow to his dark green eyes.

But energy emanated from both men's finely tuned and trained bodies. Their jobs since retiring from Prospero—Riley's running a dive boat and Ian's leading mountain climbing expeditions—both contained an element of adventure and danger. But the very air around them crackled with intensity as they exchanged ideas about Jack's situation.

Ian stretched and rubbed his knuckles across his head. "I had a feeling Farouk and his gang were involved, but the question remains. What exactly did Jack escape from?"

"And if he escaped—" Riley snapped his fingers "—he's not some kind of traitor."

"Then where is he? If your guy was telling the truth about Jack, why hasn't he contacted anyone?"

Riley shook his head. "I don't know. Follow the money. It's out of our hands now, but it will soon be in somebody else's. We need to pick up chatter and see where we're at."

Sipping her soda, Amy drew her brows together. "Where do you guys get this chatter anyway?"

"Should we tell her?" Riley raised his brows up and down.

Ian winked. "I don't know. It's top secret."

"After what I've been through? I should be an honorary member of Prospero."

Riley dropped on the couch next to her and squeezed her knee. "It's no mystery. We get chatter through tapped phones, hacked email accounts, undercover agents on the ground and imprisoned terrorists looking to make deals. We use any and all sources."

"We'll hear something soon about this money." Ian rose from his chair and crushed his empty beer can. "Something will give. Information about a deal this big will slip through somewhere. And I'll be ready."

"*You'll* be ready? What about me? What about Buzz?"

"Buzz, maybe, but you've done your part."

Riley threaded his fingers through Amy's and pulled her up with him. "Unless the hunt takes us back to the ocean. Then I'm your man."

Amy slipped her arm around his waist. "You're *my* man."

Ian laughed. "And with those well-chosen words, I'm off. Take a break, Riley. We'll keep you posted."

"If Jack's in any danger, any danger at all, come and get me."

Ian pulled Amy from Riley's arms and kissed her on the cheek. "Keep this guy out of trouble." Then he flashed a thumbs-up sign to Riley and left.

Riley tipped Ian's crushed beer can, which he'd left on the countertop, and sent it rocking back and forth. "If he calls, I have to go, Amy."

"I know that." She wound her arms around his neck. He kissed her mouth and she melted against him.

"And when the danger ends? When we find Jack?" He studied her face, but she had nothing to hide.

"Even if you never go on another mission for as long as you live, you're all I need, Riley."

Running his hands through her hair, he deepened the kiss. "I need you, too, Amy. But as long as one of my brothers in arms is in trouble, I'll go through hell and back to help him."

"I wouldn't have it any other way, Riley Hammond. In fact, I'm counting on it."

Epilogue

He rolled to his side and jerked back, inches from a twenty-five foot drop. He worked his jaw, grit and sand grinding between his teeth. Dragging himself up to a sitting position, he leaned against the rough surface of a flat rock. His lungs demanded air as he surveyed the mountainous terrain through squinted eyes. A village, or at least a collection of ramshackle buildings, lay in a valley gorge between two peaks.

His breathing eased and with each deep breath, all the pains in his body came roaring to life. Gasping, he gingerly probed his rib cage. A bruised or broken rib howled in protest at the intrusion.

He wiped a hand across his face and studied the streaks of blood and dirt on his palm. He ran his tongue around his lips, wincing at the pain in one tender spot, but tasting no blood. One side of his face felt scorched, and he dabbed his fingers along his right cheekbone, following the paths of several scratches across his face.

He wove his fingers through tangled hair, matted with a sticky substance—must be more blood. His fingertips traced around a huge knot on the back of his head. The blood had come from another cut. There was no broken skin across the solid lump.

Stretching out one arm and then the other, he wiggled

his fingers. Everything seemed to be in working—if painful—order. He hoisted to his haunches. His bones ached but they moved and supported his body.

A bird screeched overhead and he twisted around, catching a glimpse of the ledge above him. He could climb to the precipice, or he could scramble down the mountainside to the little village.

What kind of reception awaited him there?

He cleared his throat and shaded his eyes against the rising sun, a yellow egg yolk spreading in the morning sky. He crawled to the edge of his own private ledge, the ledge that probably saved his life.

Leaning forward, he spotted a rough trail meandering down the side of the mountain. If he could clamber down the boulders that tumbled toward that pathway, he could follow it into the village.

Surely, someone would offer help—food, some simple first aid for his injuries. Surely, someone could tell him where he was.

Maybe someone could even tell him who he was.

* * * * *

COMING NEXT MONTH FROM

HARLEQUIN

INTRIGUE

Available October 22, 2013

#1455 CHRISTMAS AT CARDWELL RANCH
by B.J. Daniels

Cardwell Ranch is a wonderland of winter beauty—until a body turns up in the snow. To find the killer, Tag Cardwell must work with Lily McCabe, a woman with a broken heart and a need for a cowboy just like Tag.

#1456 WOULD-BE CHRISTMAS WEDDING
Colby Agency: The Specialists • by Debra Webb

CIA agent Cecilia Manning has always chosen danger over playing it safe...in life *and* in love. And now Emmett Holt is her target.

#1457 RENEGADE GUARDIAN
The Marshals of Maverick County • by Delores Fossen

To save her child from a kidnapper, Maya Ellison must trust renegade marshal Slade Becker, even though he could cost her what she loves most—her son.

#1458 CATCH, RELEASE
Brothers in Arms: Fully Engaged • by Carol Ericson

When Deb Sinclair succumbed to the charms of a fellow spy for one night of passion, she never realized he would be both her nemesis and her salvation.

#1459 SPY IN THE SADDLE
HQ: Texas • by Dana Marton

FBI agent Lilly Tanner was once a thorn in his side. But Shep Lewis begins to rethink his stance when they're kidnapped together.

#1460 SCENE OF THE CRIME: RETURN TO BACHELOR MOON by Carla Cassidy

When FBI agent Gabriel Blakenship is dispatched to investigate a family's disappearance, the last thing he expects to find is a woman in danger and a desire he can't resist.

HICNM1013